# PROLOGUE

SOUTHERN CALIFORNIA, 12,000 YEARS AGO

It was early afternoon, and the tops of the tall snow-covered conifers were swaying gently in the soft breeze. Far below them, the sabretooth tiger left deep paw prints in the powdery snow as it ambled along the trail created by the other denizens of the forest. Sniffing the ground, it was able to make out the scent of the young pronghorn antelope that had passed through the woods just a few minutes earlier. The sun was shining from a clear blue sky and the wind had died down after the blizzard. The snow was no longer drifting, and this allowed for the scent of the pronghorn to remain on its surface long enough for the tiger to pick it up.

Weighing over three hundred kilos and measuring more than two metres in length, the tiger was a fearsome predator. Its long and sharp incisors protruded down past its jaw, giving it a permanent and intimidating snarl. Its spotted fur allowed it to blend into the forest, and its excellent sense of smell and keen hearing meant that it was able to stalk its prey for hours without losing track of it.

Several hundred kilometres to the north, a giant wall of ice more than a kilometre high rose up from the plains. The ice age was slowly coming to an end, and as the colossal glaciers melted and retreated ever further northward, they revealed more land for plants and animals to begin to recolonise after thousands of years of being buried under billions of tons of ice. This far south, the ice wall was not visible, and the forests here had now taken hold over the past several decades, providing new hunting grounds for the local population of predators.

Heading down the side of one of the mountains that would eventually be named the San Bernadino Mountain Range, the sabretooth tiger had been stalking the pronghorn for several hours. The small light-footed antelope was moving swiftly through the undergrowth of the forest, but the tiger was not about to give up. It had not eaten for several days, and at this time of year, food was becoming increasingly difficult to find. Over the past few days, the tiger had made its way west towards the coast, and coming off the slopes of the mountain and following what was later to be named the Santa Anna River, it was now less than thirty kilometres from the Pacific Ocean.

Creeping slowly and quietly up a rocky outcropping, placing its powerful paws silently and deliberately on the ground as it went, the tiger emerged on the crest and stopped. It turned its head slowly from side to side while sniffing the air. The pronghorn was close.

Just below the tiger's vantage point, a small twig snapped. The tiger moved silently to the very edge of the rocks overlooking another narrow forest trail between the hillside behind it and the river below. The pronghorn was moving cautiously along the trail, gingerly placing its hooves on the muddy snow-covered ground as it went.

Up above, the tiger silently shadowed the pronghorn along the trail until it swerved away from the rocky outcropping the tiger had been using to stalk its prey. If the tiger was going to eat today, it would have to do something. It was now or never.

Starting with a slow run, it quickly accelerated into a full sprint, and as it reached the ledge it leapt off and landed heavily on the defenceless pronghorn. The small antelope did not stand a chance as the tiger brought it down onto the ground and sank its fangs into its neck. For a few moments, the pronghorn's legs were flailing around as if it was still upright and attempting to run away, but the tiger held it tight with its powerful paws. Then it bit down hard on the pronghorn's neck. There was a sharp crunching noise as the tiger crushed its vertebrae, and then the pronghorn stopped moving.

The giant predator breathed heavily through its nose as it continued to grip the pronghorn in its vice-like jaws. It had barely exerted itself in bringing down the antelope, but the blood lust was making it pant hard. It finally let go of the pronghorn and then scanned its surroundings for possible competition. Finding none, it began to eat the pronghorn, starting with its nutritious innards.

About an hour later, with blood smeared all over its face and paws, and most of the pronghorn devoured, the sabretooth tiger rose and lumbered away along the trail next to the river. It had left a sizeable cadaver behind which would soon be picked clean by carrion birds and other animals. Soon after, the predator found a small cave where it lay down to digest its food. As darkness closed in, it fell asleep, well-fed and curled up at the back of the cave where it was safe and out of the wind.

The next morning at first light, the tiger made its way through the valley further west towards the coast. At one point it came to a clearing in the forest. The ground was almost completely flat and covered with leaves, so the sabretooth tiger started running slowly towards the other side of the clearing in order to get back into cover as soon as possible. It was a mistake it would not survive.

Within seconds, it had plunged through the thin layer of leaves and into the natural tar pit that had merely looked like a clearing. The heavy black and sticky substance had seeped out of the ground and collected in the pit over many decades, and the oily liquid clung to the tiger's feet. The more it tried to get out, the more it sank into the pit. It tried desperately to swim for the edge, but the tar was thick and clingy, and soon the tiger was covered in it and sinking further.

After less than a minute it was all over. The tar pit had swallowed up the sabretooth tiger, leaving only a faint trail on the surface where the leaves had been disturbed by its final death throes. Soon that trail had been covered by fresh leaves, and the tar pit was back to looking like an innocuous clearing in the forest.

*         *         *

AIGAI, MACEDONIA - OCTOBER 21ST, 336 BCE

Picking up the ornate golden diadem and holding it in his strong veined hands, king Philip II bowed his head slightly, closed his eyes, and took a deep breath. The near-constant warfare of the previous two decades since his ascension to the throne of the centuries-old Argead dynasty had taken its toll on his ageing body.

His bearded face was weathered and leathery, and he had the hard look of a soldier who had seen plenty of death up close. Almost every limb of his body bore the scars of battle, most notably the disfigurement where his right eye had once been. He had been hit by an arrow during the siege of the port city of Methone eighteen years earlier, after which the eye had to be surgically removed. The socket had healed over, but it had left him with a somewhat menacing look. Something he used to his advantage when required.

Always leading from the front, he had suffered many other serious injuries including an almost crippled left leg after having it skewered by an enemy spear. This gave him a distinctive limp, which meant that everyone in the royal palace could hear the sound of his characteristic gait when he was approaching.

When he had been a young boy, his father King Amyntas III, had told him stories of the great city-states of Athens, Thebes and Sparta to the south.

More than a century earlier, Athens had risen as a centre of philosophy, democracy, art and above all, naval power. Sparta on the other hand, had evolved into an austere militaristic society based on a strict code involving the induction of young boys into a life of more or less permanent warfare.

Around 480 BCE, the Achaemenid Empire, also known as the First Persian Empire, had crossed the Hellespont between Greece and Asia Minor and swept first west and then south through all of Greece. At that time, the Persian Empire stretched from Asia Minor in the north-west and Egypt in the south, to the Indus Valley in the south-east and the Aral Sea in the north-east.

The Achaemenid invasion of Greece had forced the great city-states of Athens and Sparta to join forces in the face of the overwhelming military might of the Persian Empire under Xerxes I. In what would become one of the most famous battles of all time, a small Greek force led by the legendary Spartan 300 held out for three days against the enormous Persian army in the pass of Thermopylae, before finally being surrounded and killed.

Then, in the straits of Salamis, near the largest island in the Saronic Gulf, the Greek fleet defeated the Persian Navy. The following year, in 479 BCE, the Greeks won a decisive land battle at Plataea, which finally forced the Persians to abandon their invasion of Greece, but not before the invaders had burned the sacred temple of the Acropolis in Athens to the ground. However, the Greeks eventually triumphed, which over the following many decades allowed the Greek city-states to re-establish themselves as prosperous and powerful entities once more.

Philip's father had also told him of how Athens, Sparta, and later Thebes had then warred with each other for generations, and how, through the attrition of the ten-year-long Third Sacred War, they had eventually decayed badly, both militarily and economically. Their decadence and self-centeredness had contributed to both them and all of Greece now being weak and arrogant. A fatal combination that Philip would eventually exploit.

As he had grown up to take over his father's reign, in what was then a small and weak kingdom under constant threat from all sides, the new king had quickly asserted himself both politically and militarily. Through shrewd alliances, both political and marital, he had subdued domestic dissent in Macedonia, eliminated threats of invasion from Thrace in present-day southern Bulgaria and eastern Turkey, and suppressed insurgencies in Illyria in present-day Albania and Montenegro.

In consolidating his kingdom and neutralising most of his nearest neighbours, Philip was also able to secure a plentiful and reliable supply of materials for his war machine. This supply took the form of cornel wood for spears, iron for spear tips and other weapons, and copper for bronze shields and armour.

It was also under him that a revolutionary military reform had taken place, centred around the introduction of the new and nearly invincible warfare unit, the Macedonian Phalanx. Previous armies had consisted mainly of individual foot soldiers carrying swords or short spears and a shield. The phalanx, however, was an entirely new and deadly weapon that no one in Greece had been able to counter.

It appeared deceptively simple, with several long rows of soldiers, each armed with a very long spear called a sarissa and a small but strong shield. Arranged in a tight formation sixteen men deep and eight men across, and with spears sticking out as much as four metres from the front of the unit, the phalanx was able to move forward behind a wall of shields. As soon as the phalanx was attacked by an enemy unit, its soldiers would thrust their long spears forward and into their opponents long before they were able to reach them.

Each phalanx unit typically contained one hundred and twenty-eight men, and with as many as forty spears stabbing out from the safety of the phalanx all at the same time, they could kill or incapacitate almost any opponent quickly, and then continue moving forward while taking limited casualties. With many phalanx units arranged side by side across a wide battlefield, the effect was devastating to enemy infantry.

The only downsides to the phalanx were its relatively slow pace and the fact that it was vulnerable to attacks from the side or from the rear. It was therefore typically protected on both sides by highly mobile cavalry units, which were often led by experienced generals or even the king himself.

A large army based around phalanx units arranged in this way had revolutionised warfare in Greece and proven unbeatable time and time again. Soon, most of King Philip II's opponents had been defeated or forced into accepting the primacy of Macedonia over their territories. As Philip's power grew, the great city-states to the south had become increasingly hostile toward what they saw as northern barbarians. Eventually, this had spilt over into open warfare.

The deciding battle had taken place at Chaeronea just over two years earlier in October 338 BCE. There, he had defeated an alliance between Thebes and Athens, after which he had razed Thebes to the ground and sold off its citizens as slaves. However, he had left Athens to continue to govern itself. This had been a shrewd move that had secured his complete control over all of Greece. It also meant that he avoided the administrative headache of having to govern such a large and complex city-state. In addition, this arrangement would give him effective control over the considerable maritime power of Athens. He was planning to employ this during future invasions of Asia Minor, which was still controlled by the Persian Achaemenid Empire under Artaxerxes III.

Philip also set up the League of Corinth, which was established to unite all Greek military power under him and was to be used to liberate the coastal city-states in Asia Minor that had fallen under Persian rule.

Philip now effectively ruled over an enormous kingdom stretching from the black sea in the north to Athens in the south. Over the next several months he was planning to prepare the ground, both politically and militarily, for the upcoming invasion of Asia Minor.

Today, however, was a day of celebration. Philip had secured a peace treaty with the restive region of Epirus on the western coast through the marriage of one of his daughters to the king of those lands. The night before, Philip had feasted with the new members of his extended family, and earlier in the day there had been parades of statues of all the major Greek gods. In the procession had also been a statue of Philip himself.

Now, the games were about to begin. It was to be an elaborate affair with many military disciplines included in the entertainment, and Philip was keen to take up his role as host and present himself as the undisputed ruler of all of Greece. Someone for the other great houses to rally around, but also someone to be venerated and feared.

Wearing a crisp white tunic with intricate golden embroidery, he was ready to greet his guests and welcome them to the amphitheatre where they had just taken their seats. Entertainment and plenty of wine were a guaranteed way of making sure that his guests would leave his capital more inclined to accept his continued rule.

The king placed his diadem on his head. It was a simple yet ornate golden headband and a symbol of his omnipotence. He looked up at his reflection in the polished copper mirror which hung near the corridor leading through the columned building to the main stage of the open-air theatre. Once this step in his consolidation of power was complete, he would then be able to turn his attention to Persia. He studied his reflection for a few moments. The man looking back at him might one day become ruler of the entire known world.

He straightened up, turned, and began to walk along the corridor towards the sunlit exit to the stage where his countrymen were waiting. His gait was uneven, and anyone familiar with his exploits on the battlefield would instantly have recognised the regent by that alone.

'Macedonians!' shouted a soldier already on the stage at the end of the corridor. 'Your king, his Royal Highness Philip the Second of Macedonia!'

The soldier stepped aside to allow the king to enter the amphitheatre and present himself to his subjects. Philip had specifically ordered that there be none of his personal bodyguards present on this occasion. He wanted to put his confidence and power on full display to his subjects, and being surrounded by bodyguards would convey the impression of a weak and paranoid king.

As he stepped out into the bright sunlight, he was squinting slightly and had to raise his right hand to block the sun in order to be able to see his audience. The amphitheatre was located on a small hill overlooking the Vergina Valley, and the semi-circular seating arrangement around the stage was tiered and made of stone. Arrayed across the theatre were most of the nobles, generals and religious leaders of the realm, with the most important visiting dignitaries placed in the front rows.

At the centre, directly opposite the entrance and the corridor from which he had just emerged, Philip's wives were seated. Most notable among them was Queen Olympias with her twenty-year-old son Alexander III. The queen was wearing a long flowing white dress and an elegant golden diadem on her head. She was playing absentmindedly with a gold bracelet in the shape of a serpent coiled around her left wrist. Olympias was a beautiful woman from the region of Epirus in north-western Greece, where she had been born the daughter of a local king. She was known to be highly ambitious for her son Alexander, as well as influential and ruthless in her efforts to position him as successor to Philip's throne. Some rumours even had it that she was practising witchcraft and performing rituals involving blood and venomous snakes in an attempt to mobilise mystical forces for her ends.

The twenty-year-old Alexander was fresh-faced and good-looking, his blond hair making him stand out in the crowd. Alexander had already proven himself on the battlefield, not least in the battle at Chaeronea where at only seventeen years of age his cavalry charge into the middle of the enemy's formations had caused such disarray as to allow Philip and his main force to secure the victory. The king was now only too aware that many of the soldiers believed Alexander to be a superior battlefield tactician to his father.

Philip smirked. Alexander was talented, that was true, but he still lacked a cool head and the experience that dozens of battles had given the old king. For the past several years Alexander had been tutored by the great philosopher Aristotle, which had helped him mature. It had also helped him tame his most impulsive behaviour. Perhaps one day his son would become king, and perhaps then he would be able to hold on to the kingdom that Philip had created.

As he entered the theatre and raised his arms to acknowledge the adulation of the crowd, the soldier in front of him halted and turned to face him.

'Pausanias?' said Philip, looking at his guard in surprise, a small sliver of irritation in his voice. 'I asked that no bodyguards be present today.'

Pausanias, who had been a part of Philip's close personal protection squad for several years, took a step toward his king and looked him in the eyes.

'My king,' said Pausanias, and placed his left hand on the king's shoulder. 'Today, justice is served.'

Pausanias then quickly reached with his right hand for the dagger that hung on his left side, swiftly unsheathed it and drove it with all his strength into the chest of the king. He gripped the king's shoulder tightly and thrust in the dagger all the way to the hilt. There was a collective gasp from the crowd and a few seconds later screaming and shouting began.

In shock and barely able to comprehend what had happened to him, King Philip staggered backwards half a step, but his assailant held on firmly to his shoulder. Pausanias then forcefully pulled out the blade, let go of his victim, turned, and started running through the corridor and out of the amphitheatre.

The king's legs gave way and he slumped down onto his knees, his eyes staring straight ahead, blood trickling out of his mouth. He blinked twice and looked down at his chest where crimson blood was already soaking his white tunic and pouring onto the marble stage. Within moments he was surrounded by the rest of his personal guard, and as he looked up at them with his one good eye, he was half expecting them to unsheathe their swords and finish him off.

Then the throng of people parted and his young son Alexander appeared, looking both shocked and angry. Arms gripped him and brought him gently to a sitting position. His personal physician was there attempting to bandage up the wound, but the blood kept coming.

He slumped down on his side as Alexander knelt next to him, cradling his father's head in his hands. Philip could feel his life draining away. As he looked up into Alexander's face one last time, he felt for a moment that he saw the dawning realisation in the young man's eyes. He was to be king. Today. Everything that Philip had conquered would now be his.

Then darkness closed in around him. The last thing he saw was Alexander's eyes watching him. The young man said nothing. He just watched as his father slipped away.

'The king is dead,' shouted a voice. 'The king is dead. Long live the king.'

★          ★          ★

COPHEN RIVER, BACTRIA – MAY 12TH, 327 BCE

Alexander rode back towards the camp with his personal guard close behind him. The battle had been won, but he had been wounded in the shoulder. Being wounded was an occupational hazard for kings who led from the front, as Alexander always did.

It had been six years since he had left Macedonia with his armies, and since then he had fought many battles and had never lost a single one. Immediately after King Philip II's brutal assassination, Alexander had received the support of his father's most important general, Antipater. Soon after, the senior general, Parmenion, who at the time was fighting in Asia Minor, had also been sufficiently incentivised to join with Antipater in his support of the new king. His support had effectively secured Alexander's position as heir to Macedonia and thereby effectively also the ruler of the rest of Greece.

This did not mean that everything had gone without problems. As soon as news of Philip's death had reached Thebes and Athens, those two city-states had attempted rebellion, but Alexander quickly rode south to assert his authority.

Having now subdued all of Greece as his father had done before him, Alexander set his sights on the invasion of the Persian empire. Crossing into Asia Minor, he had swept south through present-day Turkey defeating Persian armies several times on his way. He then continued through the Levant where he defeated all opposition, and eventually proceeded into Egypt where he was soon crowned pharaoh. Then he returned to present-day Syria where he defeated the last King of Persia, Darius III, thus effectively ending the Persian empire. After establishing himself in the city of Babylon south of what is today Baghdad in Iraq, he eventually struck east into present-day Iran and then further into present-day Afghanistan.

Now in the middle of a siege of the city of Massaga, in the land called Bactria which today is known as eastern Afghanistan, Alexander rode quickly to his tent and dismounted his horse with visible difficulty and in obvious pain. Assisted by one of his generals, Ptolemy, who was also in charge of Alexander's bodyguard, he then walked gingerly inside his tent where he sat down on his bed. One of his physicians was already waiting with all his tools of the trade, and as Alexander reclined on the bed, he winced at the pain in his shoulder.

An improvised bandage had been wrapped tightly around his shoulder, and the arrow had been left in the wound, lest pulling it out should cause more serious bleeding. He took a swig from a jug of wine and looked at the physician.

'Well?' he grimaced. 'Are we going to look at it, or are we going to get it out?'

The physician who was from the area around the newly founded city of Alexandria Ariana, had offered his services to Alexander's army and joined the campaign. He had quickly gained the confidence of the commander and his generals due to his skill and experience. He looked at the great commander nervously and then gently began to unwrap the temporary bandage. The arrow had lodged itself deep in Alexander's shoulder, and blood was trickling out of the wound.

'The tip does not appear to be serrated,' said the physician, studying the wound carefully. 'If I pull it out, it should do no more damage than what has already been caused. But it will hurt.'

Alexander laughed. 'Hephaestion,' he shouted to the man standing near the tent's exit. 'Did you hear that? It might hurt!'

His childhood friend smiled knowingly.

'Just get it over with,' said Alexander with a defiant grin, and looked at the physician. 'I don't have all day.'

General Ptolemy took a step closer, making it clear to the physician that he had better not make a mess of this. The physician gently grasped the arrow as Alexander took another swig of wine. Then he slowly but firmly pulled the arrow from his king's shoulder. It came out easily, and Alexander groaned, but then he smiled approvingly at the physician.

'Well done,' he said. 'Now sew me up so I can be on my way. The men will think I have gone to sleep if I don't get back to them quickly.'

Blood was now running down Alexander's arm since the arrow was no longer there to plug the wound. The physician grabbed a clean white cotton cloth and placed it over the open wound. Alexander barely reacted.

'I need to stop the bleeding and then I can sew up the wound,' he said nervously.

Alexander nodded. 'Just do what you have to do. This siege is not over yet.'

Pressing the cloth firmly against the wound for a few minutes reduced the flow of blood to a slow trickle, and so the physician was able to put the blood-soaked cloth down and start sewing up the wound. Once he had finished, he put on a new bandage, gathered his equipment and placed the cloth inside a small silver chest he had brought with him and closed its lid. Then he rose, bowed to the great king and left the tent.

As he was walking out, Ptolemy noticed that the small silver chest had three blue gemstones embedded in its lid in the shape of a triangle. The gemstones had been polished to a smooth rounded shape, and Ptolemy guessed that they were from one of the sapphire mines in the nearby mountains. Mines that would become Alexander's, once he had conquered this valley.

At the time, the physician was not quite sure why he did what he did. It was not so much that he wanted to keep the blood-soaked cloth. It was more that he simply could not bring himself to throw it away. It was soaked in the blood of the greatest king and the greatest conqueror the world had ever known. In fact, according to the oracles of Egypt and to the king himself, Alexander was a god. This blood was royal blood. Divine blood. Discarding it seemed sacrilegious, so the doctor had placed the cloth in the small silver chest which he intended to one day bring back with him to Alexandria Ariana. There it would be a memento which he would be able to show to his children and grandchildren one day, telling them of how, long ago, he tended to the wounded king, and perhaps even saved the life of a god.

★     ★     ★

BABYLON, PERSIA – JUNE 11TH, 323 BCE

A glorious life. This was Alexander's destiny. It was always meant to be that way. From the Battle of Chaeronea fighting alongside his father and proving himself fearless and resourceful, to his campaign through Asia Minor, the Levant, Egypt, Babylonia, Bactria and the easternmost parts of India. Over the course of ten years, Alexander had never lost a battle.

Now, however, the great king was at death's door. Lying on his grand bed in the royal palace in Babylon and surrounded by his generals and doctors, his life was ebbing away.

Two weeks earlier, Alexander had ordered a feast for his fleet admiral Nearchus and his friend Medius of Larissa, which in typical fashion had descended into heavy drinking, after which he fell into a mysterious fever. Gradually over the subsequent days, his health deteriorated and he became bedbound and increasingly weak.

As he lay there on his deathbed, his skin had become pale, and it had a strange almost translucent quality to it. His eyes looked dark and sunken, and his lips were an unnatural almost purple colour. Small beads of sweat were slowly making their way down his forehead, yet he occasionally shivered with cold.

Huddled around him were his generals, all of them sensing that the moment the great commander would depart this world was fast approaching. This left one inescapable question that was on all of their minds, even if none of them dared speak it. Who was going to be Alexander's successor? Who would he choose to take the reins of the largest empire ever controlled by a single individual? Would anyone be able to carry the burden of taking over from the God-King? It was a monumental decision that would impact millions of people across Alexander's new empire.

It was not at all obvious who his successor should be. Should it be his cerebral childhood friend Ptolemy? Should it be the politically shrewd battalion commander Perdiccas, or perhaps Antipater who had been maintaining control back home in Macedonia? Or should it instead be Craterus who was in charge of the largest part of Alexander's army?

'Who will you choose?' said one.

Alexander's lips moved wordlessly, and as one, his generals silently leaned in towards him, straining to hear the words of their king. He then took a shallow breath and whispered, *Kratisto*, meaning "To the strongest." Or did he say *Krater'oi*, which means "To Craterus"?

The room was as if frozen in time for several moments as each man in the gathering tried to make sense of that single ambiguous word uttered by Alexander. None of them dared to move or breathe.

The king then closed his eyes and took another laboured breath, and finally, he exhaled for the last time. Alexander the Great was dead.

★      ★      ★

MEMPHIS, EGYPT – MARCH, 320 BCE

Perdiccas lay dead in his tent, a pool of blood slowly spreading out from his lifeless body and seeping into the pale grey soil of the Egyptian Nile Delta. He had gambled it all and lost. Having been one of Alexander the Great's generals, he had put Alexander's signet ring on his finger after the great commander's death in Babylon three years earlier. He had then taken it upon himself to maintain the cohesion of Alexander's empire. But he had failed. From the moment Alexander had uttered that final and auspicious word, the enormous empire had begun to fracture.

Two years after Alexander's death, Perdiccas had attempted to return his body to his place of birth in

Aigai in Macedonia. But it had been seized by one of Alexander's other generals, Ptolemy, who was now the ruler of Egypt. Ptolemy claimed that Alexander had expressed a wish to be buried in Egypt, having been pronounced pharaoh and the son of Amun there, and so Ptolemy had captured the body of the great conqueror somewhere in the Levant as it was being transported in a huge funeral procession from Babylon back towards Greece.

Perdiccas and his army had then left Babylon and pursued Ptolemy, finally arriving at the Nile in Egypt. Here, Perdiccas had ordered several attempts to cross the great river and attack Ptolemy's forces in an effort to recapture Alexander's body. But all of them had failed, resulting in hundreds of soldiers drowning and his army being humiliated.

Upon the return to their camp on the eastern bank of the Nile, his three most senior officers, Peithon, Antigenes, and Seleucus, who themselves had been generals under Alexander the Great, turned on Perdiccas and murdered him in his tent. So disheartened were they by the catastrophic attempt to cross the Nile and by the prospect of fighting their fellow general Ptolemy, with whom they had fought side by side under Alexander for more than a decade, that together they decided to assassinate Perdiccas. Instead, they planned to join forces with Ptolemy, who had now declared himself pharaoh of Egypt and established the seat of his new kingdom in Alexandria on the Egyptian coast of the Mediterranean.

The tent where Perdiccas' body lay splayed on the ground was now empty. His assailants had left and gathered outside to decide how to announce the death of their commander to the troops without causing a mutiny. However, it was unlikely to be too problematic, as discontent with Perdiccas was widespread among the men, many of who were veterans of Alexander's campaign.

Carefully creeping closer to the back of the tent, a man crouched down next to it and pulled out a short knife. He placed the tip of the blade on the soft red linen and silently forced it through. Then he carefully pulled it downward, cutting an opening just big enough for him to slip through.

Inside the tent, the flames from the elevated fire baskets and torches flickered in the gentle breeze that was sweeping over the Nile Delta making the shadows jump around inside the tent. Perdiccas was lying in a dark red pool of his own blood next to his desk, his face contorted in pain and shock. He lay on his front with his face on the ground, dirt smeared across it with his mouth and eyes still open.

The intruder crept closer. He knew he did not have much time before the general's assailants would return. He knelt beside the body and grabbed the general's left hand, lifting it carefully towards himself. It was still warm to the touch, and the man could not help but glance at Perdiccas' face again, half expecting him to suddenly come back to life.

He pulled back the sleeve of Perdiccas' gown and immediately saw the prize he had come for. Alexander's signet ring, which Perdiccas had worn for three years, was there on his finger. It was made of silver with a hexagonal disk on top, showing the sixteen-pointed star of Macedon, the co-called Vergina Sun, which was the emblem of the House of

Argos. This symbol had adorned the shields of Alexander's phalanxes throughout his decade-long campaign, and it had struck fear into their enemies on the battlefield.

Hearing voices outside the tent, the man quickly grabbed the ring and pulled it off the general's hand. He wrapped it in a cloth and shoved it into a vest pocket. Then he hurried back to the slit at the back of the tent and slipped outside. Alexander's ring was his. Now to find the highest bidder. He knew just where to go.

★      ★      ★

ATHENS, GREECE – OCTOBER 24TH, 1978

It was unseasonably cold in the Greek capital. Grey clouds hung low over the cemetery, and the gloom amongst the attendees of the funeral was palpable. Like a heavy burden bearing down on everyone assembled there. Like too little oxygen in a dark room.

Everything about today was wrong. No parent should have to bury their child. No child should have to witness the coffin of their younger sibling being lowered into the ground. No child should have to stand next to an open grave waiting for her brother to be lowered into it. But that was what the young girl was made to endure.

She was ten years old and dressed in a black cardigan, a black skirt and shiny black shoes. Shivering in the cold and the wet, her pretty face looked distraught yet detached, as if she was not quite able to comprehend what was happening. Her jet-black hair was arranged in a ponytail, and in her hand, she held a small copper figurine of a soldier. It was her younger brother's favourite toy. Or rather, it *had* been. Nikos always kept it next to his bed when he slept. Even in the hospital, he would not let it out of his sight.

The young boy had died five days ago aged eight, just two weeks short of his ninth birthday. He had been diagnosed with leukaemia only seven months earlier, and despite their best efforts, the doctors had been powerless to stop the onslaught of the dreadful illness.

During those months, the girl had struggled to fathom what was happening to her brother. Their parents had done their best to try to make sense of it for her, but the truth was that none of it made sense. This was simply not supposed to happen. No one in her family had died in her short life so far, and now her brother was gone. She had taken care of him for as long as she could remember. Ever since he was a baby, she had insisted on helping her parents care for him, and despite her young age, she knew that one day she would want a child of her own.

The illness had shocked everyone with its speed and ferocity, and soon her brother had been reduced to an emaciated shell of the once gregarious and fun-loving boy she knew. It was a gradual, tormented extinguishing of a young life before it had even begun. He had spent the final weeks in a hospital bed, his hair falling out, his eyes dark and sunken, his skin turning ashen and paper-thin, tubes coming out of his arms and nose. He had tried to be brave, asking his older sister not to be too sad lest it should upset their parents. He had been courageous until the end.

During those final days, the girl had screamed at the heavens for help. Pleaded with both God and the Devil. Anyone that might be able to save him. She had begged for his life. Offered her own for his. But no help had come. In the end, the little boy had slipped away, and when it finally happened, she had felt as if half of her own soul had withered and died.

Now, here she was, watching her brother's final journey into the ground, the light rain mixing with tears slowly running down her cheeks. She could smell the soil that had been dug up earlier in the day to make the grave. Sweet and rich and fertile. It was a memory that would stay with her for the rest of her life.

With her head down, she gripped the toy soldier in her hand so tightly that her little knuckles turned white. Then she lifted her gaze to see the coffin slip beneath the edge of the freshly dug grave. As it disappeared from view, the sound of adults sobbing enveloped her, and her dark brown eyes gazed up at the sky.

As she looked up at the ominous clouds rolling overhead, tears were streaming down her cheeks. Her mouth quivered as she whispered weakly.

'I will find a way.'

# ONE

Pierre Dubois rose from his folding chair and exited the beige circular linen tent. It had been erected by his assistant Michel the day before next to a couple of olive trees that were clinging on to life in the dry and arid valley. Eons ago, the valley had been carved through the low mountains by a now long dried-up river. Boulders once pushed along and made smooth and round by the water, now dotted the valley and the rocky riverbed. There was a light breeze, but the air was so hot that it made little difference. Being outside in direct sunlight was like sitting in front of an oven. The air was dry and dusty, and overhead several large vultures were circling, hoping for misfortune to befall a creature down below.

Dubois winced in the bright sunlight and peered up towards the excavation site on the plateau above. A slim man in his early fifties, he was wearing light khaki trousers, a white shirt, a tan hat and dark brown hiking boots. He put on his designer sunglasses, opened a plastic bottle of fresh cold water and took a swig. Then he started walking towards the path that led up to the site where the day before they had finally uncovered the tomb they had been seeking for over a week. His research had been proven correct, as he knew it would, and his men were now busy excavating the site.

He was the only one on the team who could be said to be an academic, having spent most of his career as an archaeologist at the prestigious Université Paris Sorbonne in Paris. He had been quite content with his life, or at least that was how he thought of it at the time. It was only after a chance encounter in a bar in the Moroccan city of Marrakesh, that he had discovered the full potential of his research experience, scholarly credentials and natural ability for archaeological fieldwork.

At the time, he had been a part of a small team excavating a long-forgotten monastery in the Atlas Mountains in Morocco. There was nothing of monetary value at the site, but it had revealed an interesting story about a small community of Christian Berbers in what was then the Roman province of Mauretania Tingitana.

During a night out in Marrakesh, he and a colleague had gone for dinner with a local archaeologist called Mahmoud who, after a couple of bottles of red wine, had begun intimating how he had developed a small side-business as a black-market fence for antiquities. Without overtly offering his services, he had provided enough of a nod and a wink to let Pierre know that if he were ever to have in his possession an ancient artefact that had not yet been officially accounted for, Mahmoud would be both willing and able to funnel it towards private collectors, who in turn would be happy to pay him extremely well for such an item.

At first, Dubois had been genuinely horrified. It had never even occurred to him to do anything other than follow the correct procedure and ensure that any archaeological finds were handed over to the proper authorities in whatever country he was conducting excavations. But when Mahmoud had told him just how many ancient artefacts disappear from collections anyway, and how many items were never even recorded properly but instead sold on before they could make their way to a museum for cataloguing and display, Dubois had started to have second thoughts about his research orthodoxy. When Mahmoud had provided examples of some of the sums he had paid out in the past to other 'archaeologists', Pierre had started to question his entire life. The amounts of money supposedly on offer were potentially life-changing.

By the time Dubois had been on his way back to Paris, he had already decided to take the plunge. He was going to be returning to the dig site in Morocco two weeks later, and during his second outing at the monastery, he had surreptitiously spirited away several silver goblets that he had personally taken custody of after a couple of junior team members had unearthed them. The day before he was about to return to Paris, he had contacted Mahmoud who had immediately arranged for a meeting where the trade could be completed.

They had met in the same bar where Mahmoud had initially hinted at his side business, and within an hour or so Dubois had walked out of there with an envelope packed full of untraceable cash.

The transition from upstanding and responsible researcher to black-market artefact trader had been surprisingly swift and almost disturbingly easy. He had always thought of himself as a decent person, but objectively he knew that what he was doing was wrong. So why did he not feel guilty about it? Was it that he had managed to convince himself that if he did not deliver artefacts to the Mahmouds of this world, then someone else would? Was it because he felt that somehow it was his time to shine? His time to live an exciting life unbound by convention? Or was it that deep down he cared a lot less about the common good and notions of collective ownership of historical artefacts than he had been conditioned to think he did? Perhaps it was a little bit of everything.

Either way, the overriding feeling as he had left the bar and the handover meeting with Mahmoud, had been one of exhilaration. As if a new chapter in his life was beginning. A chapter where he was in control. Where he was no longer beholden to his superiors. No longer locked into being an underpaid and under-appreciated cog in a large inflexible bureaucratic machine that left him no choice over where to go, what to do and how to do it.

On top of that, of course, was the money. Within a year he had gone from being comfortable to being wealthy by almost any standard. Wealthy enough to mount entirely self-funded expeditions complete with budgets sufficient to cover all expenditure, including the necessary lubrication of the local officialdom to allow him to spend the time he needed at archaeological sites without the inconvenient administrative headache of proper permissions and documentation.

As Dubois walked the final paces up the trail to the plateau above the valley with the dried-up riverbed, he took off his hat and wiped his forehead with a handkerchief.

*Merde*, he thought to himself as he stopped to catch his breath. *I picked the wrong time of year for this.*

'Monsieur Dubois,' waved one of the local men that he had hired on a need-to-know basis as he came over to meet the Frenchman. 'Come and see, sir. We have found it.'

'Excellent,' smiled Dubois. 'Glad to see my intuition was correct. This was the only location that made any sense given the layout of the valley. Show me.'

The two men walked over to a deep pit that had been dug into the ground next to a sheer cliff. The pit was several metres wide, and steps led down to its bottom, where what appeared to be a sealed doorway had revealed itself.

Dubois descended the steps, approached the doorway and leaned in to study the intricate carvings that decorated it.

'Lovely,' he said. 'Lots of detail. Definitely the tomb we are looking for. Mohammad, you know what to do.'

The gangly local grabbed a mallet and walked up to the doorway. Here he placed his feet apart, brought the mallet out behind himself and then swung it with all his might. As it connected with the sealed doorway, splinters of stone and clouds of ancient mortar exploded outward, and the force of the mallet was enough for it to go through the marble.

'Perfect,' laughed Dubois, intoxicated by the complete disregard for protocol. 'Again!'

Mohammad swung the mallet again, and soon there was a hole large enough for them to squeeze through. Dubois led the way with a powerful LED torch. Inside, he was met by the sight of a modest sarcophagus with a granite lid. He ordered the men to push it off and onto the floor, and as they did so it shattered with a loud crash.

Dubois leaned in over the sarcophagus and shone his torch down into it. A broad smile spread across his face. There, in the light of the torch, lay a completely decomposed body. All that was left was a skeleton adorned with shiny gold jewellery. There was a headband, several bracelets and rings, a necklace, and a small pouch that seemed to have been placed gingerly in the dead woman's left hand.

Dubois reached down, grabbed the wrist and shook it violently, trying to shake the bracelets off. When that did not work, he instead pulled the skeleton's arm out over the edge of the sarcophagus and placed the weight of his body on it until it snapped. After that, he pulled the bracelets off the bony stump.

He held them up in front of his face with a grin. 'Superb,' he said to no one in particular. 'These will fetch a good price.'

'Alright men,' he shouted as he stepped back. 'Clear it out. I want this place picked clean in half an hour.'

Then he exited the tomb without looking back. As far as he was concerned, the excavation had ended successfully. No point in hanging around. The sooner he could get back to town the better.

Over the years since his first meeting with Mahmoud he had cultivated a network of black-market fences who would be able to shift almost anything he managed to get his hands on. The appetite of rich private collectors for ancient artefacts seemed insatiable, and one of them was bound to be willing to pay top dollar for today's gold relics. All he had to do now was spin an interesting story around its provenance, and then arrange for a few custom hardwood boxes to be made.

When he arrived back at his tent, his assistant was waiting for him with an impatient look on his face.

'Monsieur,' said Michel. 'An urgent call for you.'

Dubois frowned. 'Who?' he asked.

'He would not give me his name,' replied Michel.

'So how did he get my private number?'

Michel shrugged with a nervous look on his face and handed the phone to Dubois.

'Hello?' said Pierre sternly, and started walking away from the tent. 'Who is this?'

Michel watched him walk away towards where the river had once flowed, the small pebbles under his boots making a soft grinding noise. After a minute or so when he was out of earshot, he watched Dubois stop, do a half turn to his right, glance back towards him and then nod. Dubois then appeared to be asking several questions. Then more nodding. Michel could not hear what was being said, but he could make out his boss' tone of voice, and it seemed unusually acquiescing for a man he knew only as an impatient and unforgiving paymaster.

He then watched as the call ended, and Dubois stood for a moment holding the phone in his hand, staring at it as if it would provide him with more information than he had already received. Then he began to walk back briskly toward Michel.

'Pack up now,' ordered Dubois. 'And arrange for a flight for me to Saint Tropez this evening. I am going alone.'

★      ★      ★

Peter Lambert was by himself in the laboratory. It was late at night and everyone else had gone home, so the automatic motion-detecting lights had switched off in the entire building, except for the foyer where two security guards were watching the game, and also in the lab section on the third floor where he was still working. On the wall at the far end of the open-plan office near the elevators were large glass signs with the Greek letters Zeta, Omega and Eta, which together made the word $Z\Omega H$ or $ZOE$. They were about two metres tall and took up most of the wall emitting a faint blue glow. The Greek word for *Life* was very much at the centre of everything that happened at ZOE Technologies, and the logo was everywhere.

A tall lean man in his late forties, Lambert had dark hair and a short, neatly trimmed beard. He wore spectacles, and, as usual, was wearing a white short-sleeved shirt and tie with a pen placed in his shirt pocket. This had become his unofficial office uniform at the lab, and he only owned a handful of different ties that he cycled between. He had joined ZOE Technologies four years earlier, having been head-hunted from his research position at the Massachusetts Institute of Technology, where he had pioneered a new approach to genetic engineering.

Building on the foundations provided by the revolutionary CRISPER/Cas9 technique, he had been able to precisely edit hamster genomes, giving them traits that had never developed naturally, such as infrared vision, which allowed them to see perfectly in the dark. There was, of course, no obvious benefit to hamsters having perfect night vision, but as a proof of concept it was a powerful tool to persuade the higher-ups at MIT to continue to increase funding for his research.

He had often pondered the possible future implications for mankind of this type of technology, both in terms of how it would affect humanity's perception of what it means to be human, as well as the profound questions about whether it should be legal to manipulate the genomes of human embryos in order to make them resistant to various diseases or perhaps even extend the expected life span of a human being from the current average of around 80 to perhaps twice that, or maybe even indefinitely.

For now, though, ZOE Technologies was pushing ahead with research into targeted and limited changes to the genomes of different animals. The CEO of the company was about to make a major announcement about that in a few weeks, but Lambert was driving forward with another much more ambitious program that was being kept secret from the public. Its ethical implications were potentially far-reaching, and the last thing ZOE Technologies needed right now was to be dragged into a politicised debate about issues that were fundamental to its future earnings.

The program Lambert had been working on was called Project Anastasis, Greek for *resurrection*, and it was intended mainly as a technology demonstrator. But its other purpose was to push the envelope of what CRISPR technology would potentially be able to achieve in the future. There was no doubt that genetic engineering would soon revolutionize the medical industry, and whichever company managed to progress the furthest and the fastest, would be able to generate enormous profits. The industry would potentially be a trillion-dollar industry in just a few short years, and Lambert was determined to be on the leading edge of the research underpinning this great leap forward. His boss and research director, Doctor Fabian Ackerman had not yet told him the full scope of the program. But from what he had been able to glean at this stage, it was already obvious that it had the potential to make him a Nobel Prize winner.

The reason Lambert was in the lab this late was that he needed to prepare for the arrival of the specimen from Siberia that had been uncovered just a few days ago. The field team of freelancers hired by ZOE Technologies for this specific purpose had found an almost perfectly preserved woolly mammoth that had been buried in the permafrost for close to thirteen thousand years. After having been extracted from its icy tomb, it had been sealed inside a container, which was now in the process of being transported to the lab.

Upon arrival, a small section of it would be taken away for analysis, and then the team would start using high throughput analysis of hundreds of tiny sub-samples in order to completely map out the genome of the prehistoric animal using genetic sequencing. Once that was done, the real work could start. After being frozen for thousands of years deep beneath the Russian tundra, much of the DNA had degraded. However, with enough samples, the millions of base pairs in the DNA strands could be pieced together to form a complete and intact genome. This could then serve as the basis for future specimens, as long as the breeding process was successful. And the completed genome then had the potential for targeted trait-engineering if needed.

Lambert punched in a couple of commands on his console, and the automated system for high throughput sample retrieval began its self-testing and diagnostics procedure. If all went well, the system should then be ready to extract the frozen tissue samples and begin running them through a complex process using a range of ultra-pure chemicals and small centrifuges. This process would dissolve the organic materials and separate out the most likely candidates for DNA retrieval.

Most of the samples would be worthless, their DNA base pairs too degraded to be useful, but one in every few hundred sub-samples would yield quite long semi-intact base pair sequences, which could then be analysed and compared with other similar samples.

The entire batch of sequences could then be stitched together later to artificially create a complete and intact genome for the animal in question. Yet more samples would then be analysed to verify the sequence of the base pairs in the reconstructed DNA.

The entire process would have taken years just a few decades ago, but with the new enhanced CRISPR/Cas12 approach that Lambert and his team had developed, they could run through the entire genome of an animal in just a few days. Millions of base pairs were analysed, mapped and verified, and the end result was a beautiful 3D map of the double helix of the animal's DNA.

This was the second such specimen Lambert and his team had sequenced and processed, and the results of their first effort had been well beyond their most optimistic expectations. He decided to go over the structure of the main genome database again, just to make sure that everything was organised properly for the arrival of reams of new data for processing and analysis.

He logged into the central computer system and noticed that someone else had accessed the server that evening. It was research director Fabian Ackerman. Lambert involuntarily frowned and tilted his head slightly to one side. He had never seen the research director accessing the database this late at night. Having been given full administrative privileges on the server, Lambert could not resist the temptation to see what Doctor Ackerman had been accessing.

He quickly found and opened the log file that contained a complete set of information on all server activity. It revealed that Ackerman had accessed a separate portion of the database which Lambert had been unaware of until now. When he tried to access it himself, his request was denied.

Now Lambert was confused and irritated. He was supposed to have access to the entire network. Nothing was supposed to be off-limits to him. He sat back in his chair and stared at the cursor blinking mockingly in the 'password' box on the screen. Then he suddenly had an idea. Could it be that simple? And should he really do this? On the one hand, he was simply trying to access data that he was supposed to be able to access. On the other hand, this special partition of the database had clearly been set up to allow only Fabian Ackerman to access it.

In the end, Lambert's ego got the better of him. As far as he was concerned, this was *his* research project. Without him, there would be no research project. Ackerman was only the figurehead. Lambert leaned forward and typed in the name of Ackerman's dog, Demosthenes. The server instantly allowed him access to the secret partition, and Lambert started scrolling through the files and analysis results.

At first, nothing seemed unusual. It was just more results of genome analysis for different species, all of which Lambert had been personally involved in acquiring. But then he spotted something odd. Several of the genomes that had been mapped out did not look like anything he had seen before. They were much more complicated, and the sequences were far too long to belong to any of the animals he and the rest of the lab had been analysing. They certainly did not belong to the dataset from Project Anastasis.

When he looked into the provenance of the data, he realised that none of it had even come from his own lab, but had been supplied by a different lab in upstate New York that he had never heard of. This was extremely odd. As far as he knew, his lab was the only lab at ZOE Technologies involved in this type of work, and he had never heard of any of the other researchers listed on the internal scientific papers presenting the analysis results. The only name he recognised was that of Fabian Ackerman who seemed to have been personally involved in almost all of this alternate research. Not once had Ackerman mentioned any of this to him.

Confused and with an unpleasant sinking feeling in his stomach, he began to read some of the synopses of the research being carried out inside this to him entirely unknown research facility in New York.

Lambert was beginning to realise that he had been out of the loop on a huge portion of ZOE Technologies' research. It did not take him long to realise that what he was looking at was nothing like the research he was conducting. In fact, it was highly unusual research. It was also somewhat disturbing, and almost certainly illegal. This secret program was apparently called Project AnaGenesis, Greek for *rebirth*, and it was on a whole different level from what Lambert and his team had been working on.

Feeling restless and deeply disturbed, Lambert stood up behind the desk in his office and looked out over the lab as if expecting to be watched. The lab was still completely empty and dark, and his office was the only one with the lights still on. He looked at his watch, hesitated for a moment but then picked up his personal mobile phone and sent two encrypted messages to his two colleagues Samuel Hicks and Tim Dawson via their private messaging app. Both Hicks and Dawson had worked with him every step of the way since he joined ZOE Technologies, and he trusted them implicitly. A few minutes later, they had arranged to meet up in a bar a short drive from the lab. There was no way he could keep this to himself, and he knew that he would be unable to sleep if he went home. He had to tell them what he had found. This was urgent.

★          ★          ★

The next morning, Lambert and his two colleagues showed up early at the lab, intending to confront Fabian Ackerman about what Lambert had uncovered the night before. When they arrived, their entry was blocked by uniformed corporate security. The head of security quickly emerged and announced that their access privileges had been revoked and that their network accounts had been terminated. He also told them that their company-sponsored home computers and devices had been remotely wiped and disabled. Then he handed them each a letter from the legal department, reminding them of the terms of their employment, specifically the extensive non-disclosure agreements they had signed, which barred them from discussing any and all activities they had undertaken at ZOE Technologies now or in the future under penalty of ruinous legal fees.

They were then physically escorted off the premises, and left outside the gate of the large wooded estate the research facility was located on. As far as anyone working at ZOE Technologies was concerned, it was as if they had never existed.

In his office on the tenth floor, Fabian Ackerman was standing at the floor-to-ceiling windows overlooking the lush grounds of the sprawling ZOE Technologies compound. He watched calmly as the three now ex-employees were escorted out by corporate security. He then pulled out his phone from the inside pocket of his suit jacket and sent a short message. A couple of minutes later a large man in a dark suit appeared next to him.

'Sir?' he said and stood to attention. Some habits are impossible to shake.

'Mr Stone,' said Ackerman. 'Thank you for coming.'

'Not a problem, sir,' said the burly English ex-soldier in his calm baritone voice.

'I am going to need your assistance for a delicate job,' said Ackerman. 'Very sadly we have had to let three employees go today. There were various issues at play in this matter, not least the unauthorised access and dissemination of sensitive company data. They have of course signed multiple non-disclosure agreements relating to their work, but I am concerned that they may attempt to circumvent those agreements.'

'Right, sir,' said Stone.

'Our CEO is going to give a presentation in London in a couple of days,' continued Ackerman, 'and we can't have any bad news coming out before that. We need to make sure ZOE Technologies isn't compromised in any way. There is a lot at stake here. Do we understand each other?'

'Perfectly sir,' replied Stone. 'Leave it to me. I will take care of it.'

★     ★     ★

On the other side of the continent, in the rolling forest-covered hills of upstate New York, a black car pulled off Route 9G near the sleepy town of Rhinebeck, not far from the Hudson River about a hundred kilometres north of New York City. It continued through a small town and into a large wooded area to the east, where the road wound its way through the forest. After a few minutes, it turned off the main road and down an unmarked private road through the woods, at the end of which was a gated property with a small non-descript house in a clearing in the forest.

As the car approached the house, the doors to the adjacent parking garage opened and a small light came on inside it, revealing a light grey interior that seemed completely empty except for a panel on one of the walls.

The car drove slowly into the garage and came to a stop. The driver got out his phone, opened an app and entered his passcode. After a few seconds, the garage doors closed behind him. Then the car began to descend into the shaft as the giant elevator sprang into action. Just over one minute and around fifty metres later, the elevator stopped, allowing the car to drive out into a cavernous underground parking area. Three other cars were already parked there.

The driver stepped out and headed for the only door. Here he was met by a security guard who waved him through. There was no need for him to present his badge since his arrival here was a daily occurrence and the guards all knew him by sight.

'Phil,' said the driver and nodded.

'Mr Frost,' replied the guard and pressed the button to open the double doors to the interior of the research facility. 'Have a nice day, sir.'

'You too, Phil.'

As he entered the lab, George Frost greeted the secretary at the front desk. Then he proceeded into the lab section and sat down at his desk next to his three colleagues.

'How did the sample transfer go?' he asked his assistant, Emily Scott.

'All nominal,' replied Emily. 'No issues with refrigeration. Our guys at the prison managed to work around the usual import procedures. It is amazing what an envelope full of hard currency can do.'

'Mmhmm,' nodded Frost logging on to his PC. 'And the samples?'

'Already taken,' replied Emily. 'Ready for analysis.'

'Alright,' said Frost. 'Let's get going.'

# TWO

Racing through the streets of west London, Andrew Sterling fed the engine of the emerald green Aston Martin DB9 plenty of petrol. The V12 engine could produce 450 horsepower and it both felt and sounded like it. When idling, the engine seemed to be purring expectantly, but when he put the car into first gear and opened the throttle it positively roared to life and leapt ahead, pushing him back into the driver's seat.

He enjoyed driving his car, but he particularly liked accelerating away after having been stationary at a traffic light. The sensation of being pushed back into his seat as the powerful engine thrust the vehicle forward along the road was thrilling, no matter how many times he did it.

These days he had to get his thrills where he could find them. It used to be that he got his dopamine hits from rappelling down from a helicopter into hostile territory, or from storming a room in a hostage rescue exercise at the SAS training ground at Hereford, or throwing himself out of an aircraft during a HALO insertion behind enemy lines. High Altitude – Low Opening operations were few and far between, but when they had been required of him and his squad, he had relished the opportunity to take part in them. Plummeting towards the earth at terminal velocity evoked powerful basic instincts and floods of neurochemical effects that could not be achieved during what most people might call a normal day.

However, the days of active front line service were now behind him. In his late thirties, he was still relatively young and fit, but the higher-ups had decided that he was more efficiently employed as part of the anti-terror unit specialising in nuclear, chemical and biological threats, whether they came from lone wolves, rag-tag fundamentalist outfits in some third world backwater, or whether they originated with ideological extremists in rogue states or even within the United Kingdom itself.

He checked the time on his wristwatch as he turned the corner onto Great Russell Street. Right on time. As he slowed down to park the car outside the British Museum, he had his eyes peeled for Fiona. His girlfriend was still going by the surname Keane, and it was likely to stay that way. None of them had any inclination towards marriage, and children were also not on the cards. They were both at their best when they weren't tied down by commitments such as joint ownership of a house or a child.

Andrew parked the DB9, stepped out and adjusted his tie and his hand grenade cufflinks. He was rarely in a suit like this, but he enjoyed it, and he liked picking a set from his extensive cufflink collection. Many of them had rather unconventional themes, but most people would never notice unless their attention was pointed to them. It was Andrew's way of being slightly rebellious within the confines of civilised society.

As agreed, Fiona was already there waiting for him as he strode into the lobby. She was wearing black stilettos and dressed in a dark purple crushed velvet dress that hugged her figure snugly, and Andrew couldn't suppress a admitting smile as he spotted her and waved. She walked towards him, her heels clanging onto the marble floor and drawing attention from the people around her. She flicked her dark shoulder-length hair to one side and flashed him a smile. As she did so, she looked like she was walking down a runway at a Paris fashion show.

*Damn, she's gorgeous*, thought Andrew. And not for the first time.

'Hi Andy,' she beamed. 'You're on time.'

'Wouldn't miss it for the world,' he replied and gave her a gentlemanly kiss on the cheek while reaching around her waist with one hand and drawing her closer to himself.

'Really?' she smiled. 'Please remind me. What are we doing here?'

'Erh…' said Andrew, hesitating for a moment, but then decided to come clean. 'I honestly can't remember exactly. Something about Alexander the Great. That's all I've got. I don't really care as long as you're here.'

Fiona tilted her head back slightly and laughed that laugh he had come to love.

'I knew you'd forget,' she said with a smile. 'But thanks for the compliment.'

'Remind me again?' said Andrew.

'Alright,' replied Fiona. 'A global biotechnology company has rented the venue for an evening for some big corporate announcement. And I was asked to attend, just to pad out the crowd. Not that it is really needed. There's a whole gaggle of journalists over there at the bar loading up on free drinks and getting ready to ask difficult questions of the CEO.'

'And I am here to stop you from dying of boredom, is that correct?' smiled Andrew.

'Something like that,' she replied. 'Just smile nicely and be civilised. My boss will be upset if my plus-one causes a scene somehow.'

'You mean like starting a fight?' he said.

'Oh yes,' Fiona replied, feigning a rueful expression. 'Fighting would be bad.'

'Alright. I'll be good,' said Andrew and saluted. 'Scout's honour. Which pharmaceutical company is it?'

'ZOE Technologies,' replied Fiona.

'Never heard of it,' said Andrew.

'I am not surprised,' replied Fiona and shook her head slightly. 'Most people haven't. They are involved in bio-engineering, whatever that really means. Their CEO, Alistair Balfour, is the tall handsome one over there.'

Andrew looked over to his left where a tall man in a sharp pinstriped suit was talking to a group of people. He had a calm demeanour and an easy smile, and his body language suggested that he was used to being the centre of attention. Andrew could tell from the facial expressions of his small audience that they were enthralled by what the neatly trimmed salt-and-pepper haired and well-groomed CEO was saying. Or perhaps they were only pretending to be enthralled and simply excited to bask in the reflected glory of one of the most enigmatic corporate leaders in the world.

Very little was known about the privately held ZOE Technologies, except that they were pushing the technological boundaries in the rapidly developing field of genomics. There had been rumours that the company was about to be taken public, but a stock market listing had been rumoured several times in the past yet had never happened. Somehow the company had always been able to secure private funding either from its reclusive founder or from a small select group of anonymous private equity investors.

'Let's get some drinks,' said Andrew. 'Might as well entertain ourselves while the rest of them hobnob.'

He gently took Fiona's arm and led her towards the bar where a couple of journalists were already looking like they had met their daily quota of alcohol. They were huddled together and talking whilst observing the CEO.

'I'm not sure,' said one of them, just as Andrew and Fiona approached the bar. 'I have been trying to find out, but he seems to be the very definition of a recluse. There isn't a single picture of him to be found anywhere online. Trust me, I have looked.'

'Why all the secrecy?' said the other. 'If they are eventually going to list the company here in London or in New York, they are going to have to do a roadshow with the CEO, the board and all the other big-wigs. And that would have to include the founder, right?'

'Yes, I would agree. I just don't see large institutional investors allocating money to an initial public offering if they have never met the company's owner. You just can't do an IPO with that much secrecy.'

The second journalist downed the rest of his free drink.

'Is it true that the founder is obsessed with Alexander the Great? That's pretty much all I have been able to dig up. That and the fact that his name is Alex Galanis.'

'That's what I heard as well,' said the other. 'There is speculation that he is Greek and that Alexander the Great is a hero of his. But that could just be gossip. No one has ever managed to get an interview.'

'How are we supposed to do our jobs if we can't even access the founder and sole owner of this corporation?'

The other journalist shrugged. 'I guess we'll have to settle for the CEO.'

Andrew raised his eyebrows conspiratorially and leaned in close to Fiona.

'Seems like not all of them have drunk the Kool-Aid yet,' he whispered, and smiled.

Fiona brought an index finger up to her lips. 'No shenanigans Mr Sterling, please. You promised to be good.'

Andrew held up both hands in surrender. 'Alright. What would you like to drink?'

'Pina Colada please,' she replied.

Andrew turned and waved the barman over.

'One Pina Colada and one Mai Tai, please.'

The barman nodded and started mixing the cocktails.

A couple of minutes later, Andrew and Fiona meandered through the crowd of invited guests, which was now becoming larger. It appeared to consist of a mix of representatives from various media outlets as well as men and women in suits, most likely financial analysts and prospective investors.

'Interesting venue for a presentation like this,' said Andrew. 'Has this sort of thing ever happened before?'

'The British Museum does rent out its premises for corporate events from time to time,' replied Fiona. 'But I have never seen it this big, and I am frankly not sure why they would pick this particular venue.'

'I guess we're about to find out,' said Andrew and nodded towards the small stage in the middle of the room.

Alistair Balfour was just taking the stage, and as he checked his ear-mounted microphone and found his pre-marked spot to stand on, a hush came over the crowd as they gathered around him.

'Ladies and gentlemen,' he said in a powerful and authoritative voice. He took a moment to survey the assembled audience and then produced a winning smile.

'Welcome to the British Museum, and thank you all very much for coming today. Today is a big day for ZOE Technologies. I am going to be announcing several new and revolutionary initiatives that we have been working on for several years. They are now about to come to fruition and will be launched as commercial products before the end of this year. I will also have some news about our upcoming listing on the New York Stock Exchange.'

At the mention of the IPO, a murmur went through the crowd.

'I know this is something a lot of people have been wanting for a long time, and we are now almost ready.'

Balfour began walking calmly towards one side of the stage, giving the impression of strolling casually along in front of a group of friends, whilst skilfully using his body, facial expressions and hand movements to conjure the appearance of an intimate yet open forum where knowledge was about to be revealed and shared, and where no question was a dumb question.

'This is a special venue,' he said, gesturing to the large interior of the museum's lobby. 'A place of history. A place of discovery and achievement. At ZOE Technologies we strive for those very things every day, and now we aim to *make* history.'

Balfour stopped, paused, and then turned to stroll slowly towards the other side of the stage.

'Since the dawn of humanity, we have attempted to bend nature to our will. We have developed tools for hunting and foraging. We have built machines to do our labour. We have domesticated and bred animals that suit our needs, and we have done the same with plants like grain, fruits and vegetables. Through thousands of generations, we have kept selecting the best plants to continue to cultivate, thereby helping along the so-called natural selection that Darwin was the first person to formalise, but far from the first person to understand.'

Balfour reached for a glass of water sitting on a podium at the centre of the stage and took a sip.

'Cultivation of grain is an excellent example of something humans have spent millennia developing, using nothing more than their minds and empirical evidence. Starting out with simple grasses, somewhere in the so-called Fertile Crescent in the Middle East the first people to settle down and leave the hunter-gatherer life behind would cultivate the best and most bountiful grasses season after season. A kind of enhanced natural selection, you might call it. Eventually, they ended up with grains that had very large seeds, which could be ground into flour and made into bread. Many other plants and trees were cultivated in a similar way. Taking this a step further, humans began helping evolution along with husbandry and breeding of new varieties of domesticated animals. From wild oxen came cows. From boars came pigs. From various species of birds came what we today recognise as chicken, geese and turkeys. And each of these species was then bred for many more generations, in order to further enhance the traits that humans find desirable and to suppress the ones we do not. All of this was essentially just evolution, except it was guided by the human hand. It was in effect the first stage of primitive genetic engineering by human beings of their environment and their food resources.'

Another sip of water.

'For many years now, we as a species have been able to genetically alter crops to produce higher yields. An example is the legume plant which not very long ago was approved for commercialisation in Nigeria. It is a protein-rich type of cowpea that has been genetically modified to produce yields up to ten times higher than that of the standard variety found in nature. The implications of such developments are self-evident. In recent years, genetically modified crops have become increasingly commonplace in many nations across the globe. We at ZOE Technologies expect this trend to continue, not least because of the need to reduce the environmental impact of food production. As most of you will know, meat production is an extremely $CO_2$-heavy industry, and so replacing meat-based protein with plant-based protein for human consumption could have a large beneficial impact on our planet's climate.'

Balfour allowed for the quiet murmur of approval to ripple through the crowd.

'Allow me now to stray into a slightly more technical area for a moment. I would like to talk briefly about CRISPR, which many of you will have heard about already.'

Balfour took a couple of steps towards the middle of the stage.

'The acronym CRISPR is short for Clustered Regularly Interspaced Short Palindromic Repeats. It's quite a mouthful, I know,' he smiled.

'Without getting too deep into the details, CRISPR is a technique that allows precise editing of specific elements of the genetic code in the DNA of plants and animals, including humans. Over the past several decades our tools for mapping the entire genomes of living beings have made enormous progress, to the point where we can now describe the complete DNA of many species of plants and animals. The next logical step has of course been to come up with ways to edit those genomes, and this is where ZOE Technologies has made many important breakthroughs, several of which have already been patented. Others are still in development but about to further push the boundaries of our understanding of genomics and our ability to edit DNA.'

Balfour paused, seemingly taking a moment to collect his thoughts and considering his words carefully before resuming.

'To some people, this may sound disconcerting, but genetic engineering has already had a huge impact on many different global markets primarily in the food sector, and we believe this is only the beginning of what will become what I like to call a revolution of evolution.'

Balfour paused and smiled, allowing his wordplay to sink in and be remembered by the gathering, not least the journalists who were almost guaranteed to use it verbatim in their articles for tomorrow's papers.

'Ladies and gentlemen. I am here today to tell you that the future is already here. What we at ZOE Technologies have now developed goes well beyond what has been achieved before, whether in a research setting or as part of a commercial venture. What we are aiming to do, is to completely transform the global pet market.'

Another murmur went through the crowd as Balfour calmly sipped more water. He had clearly rehearsed his presentation and was taking his time, controlling the pace and tightly managing peoples' experience.

'Today the global pet market is valued at more than 300 billion dollars per year. That is the equivalent of the economic output of entire nations such as South Africa, Finland, Singapore or Denmark. It is already a giant market that is well developed, but we aim to take it to the next level, expanding it manyfold and capturing the majority of the profit that it will generate in the future.'

Balfour took a few steps towards the crowd to stand near the edge of the gathering in front of him. He pressed his palms together close to his chest and bowed his head so that his chin touched his fingertips, looking for a moment as if he was in prayer.

'Imagine for a moment,' he continued solemnly and looked up, 'if you could order a pet specified precisely to your personal requirements and preferences. And then imagine if we could offer a guarantee to you that your new pet would never be afflicted with any congenital diseases, and that it would never develop any hereditary illnesses that previous generations of pets had suffered from. Imagine if you knew at the point of purchase that your pet would have a zero percent chance of ever becoming ill with things like degenerative myelopathy, whereby dogs eventually develop degeneration of nerves in the spinal cord. Or imagine if you knew for certain that your dog would never develop cardiomyopathy, which results in weakening of the heart muscles and resultant premature death. There are dozens of such hereditary diseases that result in misery for hundreds of millions of pets and heartache for even more pet owners and families. Small children.'

There was another long pause where the audience was gripped by the performance and by the message Balfour was delivering.

'Imagine if you could reach into the DNA of your future pet, and entirely strip away those genetic predispositions.'

'A bit of a showman, isn't he?' whispered Andrew as he leaned towards Fiona.

She nodded, without taking her eyes off Balfour, who now spread his arms out to his sides.

'Yes,' Fiona replied in a hushed voice. 'Quite the public speaker.'

'This is what we offer at ZOE Technologies,' continued Balfour emphatically. 'Our new product line of enhanced pets under the brand name *PERITAS*, named after Alexander the Great's favourite dog, will supply pets that are genetically engineered to never develop any of those or a whole host of other illnesses. In addition, we aim to supply pets that meet any and all requirements in terms of appearance, such as size, the colour of fur and eyes, and even temperament, depending on the purpose of the pet. It might be intended as a guard dog, or it might be intended as a companion for a child. By editing specific base pairs in the genome of the DNA at the pre-embryonic stage, we can tailor the pet to your precise needs and ensure that they live a long and happy life free of affliction from almost all common hereditary diseases. Initially, we will only be marketing enhanced dogs, but there is no reason why we should not expand to most other pets at some stage in the future.'

Balfour brought up his right hand close to his head and extended his index finger.

'One trait that we have given particular attention is longevity,' he said, looking pensive. 'At the moment, most families will consider themselves lucky if their dog lives for ten years. Imagine if by tweaking the genes related to metabolism and other biochemical functions, we could increase the expected life span by just twenty percent. How do you put a price on that? We believe most consumers would be prepared to pay a premium for this. And what if that number was fifty percent?'

Balfour once again paused for dramatic effect.

'On a final note,' he continued. 'I would like to say a few words about the medium to long term future of our company. I obviously cannot divulge specific details about future initiatives, but as a teaser, I can reveal that our long-term goals include applying CRISPR technology to engineering personalised treatments for humans of a whole range of diseases that today are extremely difficult to treat. One of the things we are currently looking at is endometriosis, which affects millions of women the world over. Human DNA sequencing has already shown that rare variants of a gene known as NPSR1 are instrumental in the development of endometriosis. When we administer experimental inhibitor drugs which block the SPSR1 receptors and thus suppress that gene, a significant reduction in inflammation and pain occurs. This is just one example of how it will be possible in the not-too-distant future, to develop personalised gene therapy for sufferers of a whole range of diseases.'

'Another illness is cystic fibrosis, which affects tens of thousands of people. It is caused by a mutation in a single gene called the CFTR gene which results in a dysfunctional CFTR protein expression. This in turn causes the main symptoms of cystic fibrosis. Illnesses such as these which are purely the result of very specific genetic mutations, could potentially be eradicated in the future using our proprietary CRISPR technology at the early pre-embryonic stage of development. And last but not least, cancer. Around half of all cancers are caused by a damaged or missing gene called the P53 gene. As I am sure you're aware, a long list of cancers are hereditary, passed on unwittingly from parent to child. Imagine if these genetic predispositions could be edited out and cancer could be prevented from ever developing.'

He paused.

'Just imagine.'

Balfour scanned the faces of the crowd from one side of the lobby to the other. At that moment he held them in the palm of his hand.

'Now allow me to zoom back out for a moment and attempt to put this into a context that will perhaps allow you to appreciate the significance of what we are endeavouring to accomplish.'

Balfour cleared his throat and looked up at the ceiling, as if pondering an important question.

'Alexander the Great's beloved dog Peritas was by his master's side through years of military campaigning. This pet probably travelled further with

its master than any before or since. He was loyal to a
fault and even fought alongside Alexander. Having
been brought along from Greece, this pet was by
Alexander's side as he conquered most of what was
then the known world in just ten years. The story
goes that during Alexander's campaign into what is
today the Punjab, the great commander was trapped
by enemy forces, at which point Peritas ran to
Alexander and attacked them. Alexander had just
been badly wounded by a javelin, but Peritas'
intervention allowed Alexander's troops to reach him
in time, thereby saving his life. In saving Alexander,
however, the dog had itself been wounded, and it later
died in his master's lap.'

Balfour paused again for dramatic effect.

'Now, why am I telling you this story?' he asked
rhetorically. 'I am telling you this story because,
among the many theories about why Alexander the
Great died at the age of just 31, some have suggested
that he was suffering from congenital heart disease or
perhaps even leukaemia. Others propose that he died
of a malaria infection. Still others contend that he was
poisoned. Imagine for a moment that it was the
former.'

Balfour re-centred himself on the stage.

'As I hinted at earlier,' he continued, 'we at ZOE
Technologies, using CRISPR technology, are
developing techniques that can effectively eradicate
such congenital diseases. Alexander's conquests ended
up spreading Greek ideas such as philosophy,
empirical science, and even democracy to a huge part
of the world. Without it, the world we know would
most likely be almost unrecognisable to us now.

Imagine if a technology such as CRISPR had been available at the time of Alexander the Great's birth in 356 BCE, and imagine if his genetic predispositions had not been part of his genome. What if Alexander had lived to become an old man, never suffering from a weak heart or from leukaemia? Or, if he really did suffer a lethal malaria infection, contemplate the fact that right here in this city at University College London, there are efforts underway to eradicate malaria through the application of CRISPR technology to mosquito DNA. Now imagine the impact on the world if Greek culture and science had continued to spread throughout Arabia, India and perhaps even the Far East. The whole world would have been different.'

Balfour clenched his fist in front of himself.

'This is just a small glimpse of the immense power of CRISPR technology and the difference we envisage it will have on the future of mankind. And the future of our company is equally bright, especially with regard to the many ways in which we envisage the application of our patented technology to the treatment of hereditary diseases in humans. At ZOE Technologies, we believe that in a matter of just a few decades only treatments tailored to the individual will be offered to patients, and many of those will be based on CRISPR technology. This is nothing less than a watershed moment in human evolution. Needless to say, the profit potential of these sorts of products is vast. Ladies and gentlemen, we are on the cusp of a new age in medicine and pharmaceuticals, and ZOE will be at the very forefront of it.'

The hall was silent, except for the sound of a few SLR cameras clicking away as they captured the image of the CEO on the stage.

'And now, I would like to invite you to ask questions,' he said, calmly, taking half a step back and thereby signalling the partial handover of the stage to his audience.

'Mr Balfour,' said a journalist, raising his hand. 'What will be the retail price of one of your pets?'

'Good question,' replied Balfour. 'It all depends of course, but we currently estimate that the average price that consumers will be prepared to pay for what we call an *enhanced* pet, will range from five thousand dollars to as much as fifty thousand dollars, depending on the geographical region and the number of individually tailored traits. This may seem like a lot of money, but compare it with what consumers spend on cars or boats, or holidays, and you begin to get a sense of the potential here.'

'Could you be more specific about your future earnings potential in the context of these products?' the journalist followed up.

'For obvious reasons, I cannot reveal the cost to us of creating and then breeding each pet to the point at which it can be handed over to its new owners, but we envisage net profit margins of several hundred percent. For those of you in the audience today who are financial analysts or investors, I would encourage you to do a few simple back-of-the-envelope calculations yourselves to acquire a sense of the possible earnings potential here. We will of course retain a brokerage house to manage our stock market flotation in due course, and when that happens you will have precise valuation models. In the meantime, our own internal forecasts indicate an annual market size of at least one trillion dollars as we roll out the Peritas range over the next five years.'

Balfour smiled his winning smile and held it for a few seconds, allowing the photojournalists to get the perfect pictures for their various publications.

'Mr Balfour,' asked a female reporter as she took half a step towards the front of the pack of journalists. 'What do you say to people who claim that we should not meddle with nature and that changing the building blocks of life is an attempt to mess with God's design. At the very least, do you accept that there are serious ethical questions attached to this type of technology?'

Balfour took a moment to consider his reply, and for a fleeting moment he looked as if he would be unable to hide his contempt for the basis of the question. He quickly regained control over his facial expression and smiled benignly at the journalist.

'As I said earlier,' he began. 'Humans have been engaged in genetic engineering for thousands of years already. We used to do it by breeding crops and animals. What we are doing now is essentially the same thing, except we are not doing it blindly the way our ancestors did. When they interbred different types of cows to get offspring that produced more milk, they were relying on chance to give them the outcome they wanted. Sometimes the DNA from the mother combined with the DNA from the father to produce offspring with what we considered more desirable characteristics. In other words, sometimes it worked and sometimes it didn't. All we're doing now is using our knowledge of an animal's genome to target specific areas that govern certain traits that we would like to encourage. We are essentially doing the exact same thing that they did then, but we can do it in just one generation with no uncertainty involved, whereas our ancestors might have to wait many hundreds of generations before perfecting an animal.'

Balfour paused as if pondering his next words carefully.

'There is one other thing I would like to say in reply to your question. By definition, everything we humans do is a natural part of evolution. When a predator species hunts another species to extinction, we call it a natural event. When an animal becomes out-competed in its quest for food by another slightly different variant of that same species and ends up becoming extinct, we call it natural selection. When a certain type of animal breeds beyond the capacity of its ecosystem to support it, diseases often emerge, and those have the effect of reducing the population back to a more sustainable level. All of these things are natural phenomena, and the same logic applies to human beings. We are as much part of this world as any other species. We can't be separated from the world we have evolved from, so whatever we do is by definition natural and simply a part of the evolution of life on this planet. And we should not limit ourselves based on misconceptions about evolution, or indeed based on superstitious beliefs about disapproving deities.'

'Mister Balfour,' asked another journalist. 'Could you explain what might be the first disease you will attempt to treat in humans, and when you might begin clinical trials?'

'I am afraid not,' smiled Balfour benignly. 'At this stage, we will not be…'

Suddenly there was the noise of a scuffle somewhere near the back of the crowd. Hardly anyone moved or turned around, so transfixed were they by Balfour's performance. Andrew was the exception. The speed and force of the movement he sensed behind them, as well as the sound of surprised grunts from some in the crowd, was enough for his instincts to kick into gear. These were not natural sounds in a setting like this. They were far too forceful. Something bad was about to happen.

'No!' shouted a man in the audience as he forced his way violently towards the front of the crowd. 'He's lying! He's lying to you all.'

Andrew was already moving forward through the crowd and in parallel to the tall man, but the man was several metres away and quickly approaching the stage. Andrew only sensed him to his left as he tried to make it through the crowd towards Balfour as fast as he could. The man burst out of the front of the crowd and raised a gun, pointing it at Balfour who stood frozen to the spot.

'She must be stopped!' yelled the man, and then he pulled the trigger three times.

As the shots rang out, Andrew was just clear of the crowd, but he was too late to stop the shooter. The gun was less than an arm's length from Balfour when the shots were fired, and all three bullets smacked audibly into the CEO's chest and knocked him back.

He staggered backwards a few steps, and then fell onto his back whilst pressing his hands to his chest.

Just as Balfour fell onto the stage with a loud thud, Andrew threw himself at the shooter and they both crashed to the floor. People were now screaming and running away in panic at the surreal display of violence in front of them.

The shooter was tall but slim, and Andrew easily managed to disarm him, pin him down and restrain him in a chokehold. Seconds later, the museum's own security guards, along with two guards from ZOE Technologies, arrived and took charge of the shooter. At the same time, someone from the audience who looked like he had medical training, jumped up onto the stage and knelt beside Balfour. He ripped open the CEO's shirt and placed his hand on the side of his neck.

As he did so, the Museum's security team tied the shooter's arms behind his back with zip ties, and Andrew rolled away to one side and stood up. He then took a step back as the security team began frog-marching the shooter away.

'It's an abomination! You have to stop them!' shouted the man, and looked imploringly at Andrew, sweat pouring off his forehead. 'You people don't understand. This is not what it seems.'

At that moment, a couple of police officers came running into the lobby with handguns drawn. The security team quickly made clear that the shooter was detained, and the officers holstered their weapons and took charge of him.

Andrew glanced at the stage where the man tending to Balfour slumped down, hands bloody and now looking towards Andrew. He shook his head slowly. Balfour was dead.

Andrew sat down on the edge of the stage and lowered his head. This was somehow all too familiar. Not for the first time had someone expired right next to him after the sound of gunshots had rung out. He had never met Alistair Balfour until today and he had no idea what sort of man he really was, but a death was a death and this man probably had a family. Children. Perhaps his parents were still alive. Had they been here today? This was a tragedy whichever way you looked at it.

At that moment Fiona came hurrying over and sat down next to him. The exhibition hall was now virtually empty, with most people having fled as soon as the shooting had started.

'Are you alright?' she asked.

Andrew shrugged and grimaced. 'If only I had been a couple of seconds quicker, then…'

Fiona placed a hand on his shoulder and shook him gently.

'Hey,' she said sternly. 'Don't do that to yourself. You were the only one here who even saw this coming. Nobody else did anything. At least you tried to stop it, and no one else got hurt.'

'I guess,' said Andrew, and pressed his lips together. 'It's just difficult not to think *what if*.'

'I understand,' replied Fiona sympathetically. 'But there's no point. It's over. Come on. We should get out of here.'

'No,' said Andrew and shook his head. 'We need to stay for a bit. I am sure the police will want to have a word with me, and since we arrived together, they'll probably want to talk to you too.'

'I guess you're right,' said Fiona and took his hand. 'Well, let's at least find a more comfortable place to sit. There is a bench over this way. Come on.'

★      ★      ★

An hour later, the two of them were in a cramped, sparsely furnished and tired looking meeting room at the nearest police station. The walls were painted a dull green and there were scuff marks aplenty around the door where the chairs had been pulled out hundreds of times by police officers uninterested in looking after their surroundings. In the ceiling were cold neon lights that looked like they had been installed when Margaret Thatcher was still prime minister, and the only wall decoration in the room was a badly faded colour photo of Queen Elisabeth II, which hung ever so slightly askew.

'I guess police budgets really have been cut down to next to nothing,' said Fiona in a hushed voice, even though she and Andrew were alone in the room.

There was something about the setting that felt oppressive and slightly claustrophobic.

'I know,' said Andrew in a hushed voice. 'I think I'd be prepared to confess to just about anything just to get out of here.'

At that moment the door opened, and the two of them involuntarily pulled away from each other and sat up straight, as if they had been pulled into the principal's office for a dressing down.

Into the room walked a middle-aged female police officer wearing dark blue trousers and a white shirt with a name badge and chevrons on her shoulders. Her hair was dark brown with a few grey streaks, and it was trimmed neatly into a style that somehow harked back to the 1990s when she would have been a young woman. Oddly, she was also wearing a bowtie, and she appeared strangely androgynous being dressed in a female uniform that seemed to have been lazily adapted from a male template several decades ago.

'Right,' she said in a tired voice as she slumped down in front of them. 'My name is Chief Superintendent Emma Worthington. Thank you very much for waiting. As you can imagine, this murder has got a lot of people riled up and we don't exactly relish the attention around here.'

'Not a problem,' said Andrew. 'How can we help?'

'I'd like to start by asking a few questions,' said Worthington, and began methodically going over what had happened during those minutes when the elegant business setting inside the exhibition hall at the British Museum had been transformed into a bloody murder scene.

Worthington took them through what the police had managed to piece together, asking them various questions and attempting to verify the sequence of events as she understood it. Andrew and Fiona answered her questions and tried to assist as well as they could, but they could not contribute much given that the whole thing had been over in just a few moments.

'There's something else that we need to discuss,' said Worthington and closed the folder in front of her where she had been taking notes. 'This is a bit unorthodox, but my superiors have persuaded me that we should proceed this way.'

Andrew and Fiona glanced at each other and then returned their attention to the police captain.

'You're with the SAS, correct?'

'Yes,' replied Andrew hesitantly.

'Right. Once we found out about your attachment to the SAS, we obviously reached out to them. My section chief then received a call from a Colonel Strickland just over an hour ago, and he suggested that we should let you two have a crack at this. And the higher-ups here at the Metropolitan Police decided to go along with it. We will of course carry out our own interviews in due course, but let's first see what information you can extract from the murderer.'

'Right,' replied Andrew with an uncertain smile on his face. 'No pressure then.'

'To be blunt,' said Worthington. 'We would like your help in investigating this matter. It is obviously not standard operating procedure for us to involve the military in these sorts of civilian investigations, but apparently, Colonel Strickland was most emphatic that you two would be able to support the investigation.'

'Alright,' replied Andrew hesitantly. 'We'd be happy to help if we can. You don't mind our involvement?' he asked sceptically.

'Let me be honest with you,' said Inspector Worthington with a tired sigh. 'We have very few resources as it is, and this investigation, being extremely high profile, will pull an unreasonable amount of those resources away from other investigations. As you know, gang-related knife crime has exploded in London over the past decade, but our budgets have remained the same. Is it fair that we should divert a significant portion of our investigative officers to this case, just because the victim was wearing an expensive suit? The parents of all the teenagers stabbed to death in this city over the past several years deserve the same level of attention from us in the murders of their children, don't they?'

Worthington's last sentence was clearly a rhetorical question, so Andrew and Fiona sat impassively and waited for her to carry on.

'The other aspect of it is that we feel that there is a chance that perhaps your presence might elicit more information from the murderer. He would recognise you from the British Museum. Who knows? It might just exert enough pressure to make him tell you what he knows and why he resorted to murder to make whatever point he was trying to make. He spoke to you, didn't he?'

'Very briefly, yes,' replied Andrew. 'He said something about things not being what they seem.'

'So how can we help?' asked Fiona.

'For starters, I'd like you to go to Saint Bartholomew's Hospital and interview the man. His name is Peter Lambert, and he is currently being held in a secure room guarded by two police officers.'

'A hospital?' asked Andrew surprised.

'Apparently, he broke a couple of ribs when you tackled him,' replied Worthington. 'He is quite literally chained to his bed as we speak.'

'Alright,' nodded Andrew, trying to take in what was being asked of them. 'Anything in particular you want us to try to dig into? Do we know who he is?'

'Well,' said Worthington. 'This may surprise you, but his name is Lambert and until last week he was an employee of ZOE Technologies.'

'What?' said Fiona perplexed. 'You're saying he's one of theirs?'

'Apparently so,' replied Worthington and shrugged. 'He was a senior researcher at their main facility in California. In charge of some of the most advanced genetics research in the world. So, the obvious question is this. Why would a senior and probably extremely well-paid employee suddenly want to murder the CEO of the company he works for? It is probably not because the coffee machine in the cafeteria is broken.'

Worthington's expression was deadpan, and neither Andrew nor Fiona was sure whether this was a poor attempt at a joke.

'What have ZOE Technologies said about this?' asked Fiona.

'Well,' replied Worthington. 'They put out the usual lawyer statement, saying that Lambert is a mentally unstable disgruntled ex-employee. This might all be true, but we need to make sure we understand all the facts of the case.'

'Alright,' replied Andrew finally. 'If you give us the details of his location, we'll be on our way as soon as possible. I assume we need to move as fast as we can on this.'

'Yes. Like everything around here,' sighed Worthington, 'we would ideally like to have it done by yesterday.'

'We understand,' said Andrew and looked at Fiona. 'Are you alright with this?'

Fiona hesitated for a moment but then nodded.

'Sure,' she replied. 'We were eyewitnesses, and if it can help clear up why this happened then I will be glad to help. Just as long as there's no risk to us.'

Andrew and Fiona both looked at Worthington, who spread out her hands in front of her.

'As I said, we have two experienced officers, Boyer and Simmons, currently guarding Lambert, and he is chained to his bed with two broken ribs. You will be perfectly safe. So, is that a Yes?'

'Sure,' replied Andrew. 'Whatever we can do.'

'Great,' said Worthington and placed her hands flat on the table. 'I'll have my assistant hand you the particulars of Lambert's location. And she will also provide you with credentials to let you past the guards.'

A few minutes later, they had said goodbye to Inspector Worthington and were making their way back down the stairs to the ground floor of the police station and towards the double doors leading outside.

'Well,' said Andrew as they exited onto the street outside. 'Although that didn't exactly inspire a lot of confidence in the Metropolitan Police, I'm actually glad they have decided to follow Strickland's advice and put us on the case.'

'Really?' asked Fiona. 'Why? I mean, it seems like Inspector Worthington has her heart in the right place, but I haven't got the first clue about these sorts of investigations.'

'I guess I feel partly responsible for what happened,' replied Andrew. 'If nothing else, I want to understand the motivation of the shooter. This Lambert character.'

'I can't imagine what could possibly make someone do something like this,' said Fiona. 'Do you suppose it could be some sort of mental breakdown?'

'Who knows?' said Andrew. 'There's no point in speculating at this point. We'll have to see what he has to say. If he will even talk to us, that is.'

'I am guessing he will,' said Fiona. 'He was clearly keen on letting people know what was on his mind just after the shooting. I think once he sees you again, he'll probably want to talk.'

'Hopefully,' replied Andrew. 'Come on. Let's grab some food before we go.'

# THREE

'Ackerman here.'

'Doctor Ackerman, it's Stone.'

'Stone. Thanks for coming back to me so soon. Is this line secure?'

'Yes sir.'

'Good. The shit has really hit the fan. I assume you've seen the news?'

'I have, sir.'

'Then you know what to do. We were concerned that those three men might try to monetize their former relationship with ZOE Technologies, but this is on a whole different level. As it stands, the entire management team of the company is now in lethal danger, and the risk of unauthorised disclosure of sensitive corporate data remains. We need to make sure nothing like this can happen again, do you understand what I am telling you?'

'Absolutely sir. Our asset in London is already in place to deal with Lambert. We'll track the two others down soon enough.'

'Good. Keep me updated.'
'Will do, sir.'

★          ★          ★

As the sun was setting over London, Andrew and Fiona arrived at Saint Bartholomew's Hospital, just north of St Paul's Cathedral. Showing their credentials at the front desk, they were then shown to an elevator that would take them to the 5th floor of a private wing where Peter Lambert was being kept under armed guard. Entering the elevator, Fiona looked over her shoulder towards the receptionist who was now walking back to the front desk.

'She seems awfully casual considering they have a deranged murderer in the building,' she said, looking slightly bemused.

'I guess they see just about everything here,' replied Andrew. 'I am sure a single 24-hour cycle in a large hospital like this puts almost every aspect of the human condition on display. Life. Death. Joy. Despair. And almost certainly all sorts of mental illnesses.'

'I guess you're right,' said Fiona. 'Perhaps I was just expecting some sort of escort. Haven't they sealed off the floor where Lambert is being kept?'

'Supposedly so,' replied Andrew. 'We'll find out.'

Just then the elevator stopped, and after a short pause and a distant metallic clang the doors slowly slid open to reveal another hospital corridor. Grey, drab, badly lit and not at all conducive to recovery, either mental or physical. Somewhere in the distance was the sound of a door slamming shut. It echoed along the empty and unfurnished corridor.

As they stepped out, Andrew grimaced. 'Now I remember why I hate hospitals. Which room was he supposed to be in?'

'508,' replied Fiona and pointed along an empty corridor bathed in cold white neon light. 'It should be this way.'

The corridor had an eerie feel to it, not least because there was no sign of anyone else being there. It seemed completely abandoned, and there were no sounds other than those of their shoes on the grey linoleum floor. A reception desk near the elevators where nurses would usually have been sitting was empty, and none of the computer monitors were switched on.

'Do you suppose they have cordoned off the whole floor?' asked Fiona.

'It's possible,' replied Andrew. 'This is such a high-profile case that I wouldn't be surprised if they went to great lengths to keep the media away.'

They began walking along the seemingly deserted corridor, checking the room numbers as they went to work out where 508 would be. As they approached the end of the corridor, Andrew began to feel uneasy. There was something off about the whole thing. If Lambert was under police guard, at least one of the officers should have been outside the room, but there was no trace of anyone on the whole floor.

'Fiona, I don't like this,' said Andrew in a hushed voice as they arrived at the closed door to room 508. 'Something's wrong. Where's the police?'

'Inside?' replied Fiona and gently jerked her head towards the door.

'Someone should be out here too,' replied Andrew and gripped the door handle, his face now looking troubled. 'We need to get inside. Ready?'

Fiona nodded silently. Andrew then pressed the door handle and opened the door to reveal a truly nightmarish scene inside the room. It was approximately four by five metres in size, with large windows with drawn blinds on the wall opposite the door. In the far corner was a bed with Lambert lying in it, but he was motionless and covered in blood.

The first thing that Andrew and Fiona saw, however, were the bodies of two Metropolitan Police officers splayed on the floor, both of them lying in dark red pools of blood. Andrew immediately noticed that one of the pools was still expanding slowly across the floor.

'Shit,' he breathed and pointed at one of them. 'See if that one is still alive. I'll check this one.'

He quickly knelt down next to the officer closest to the door. He was lying on his front and Andrew could see small entry-holes in his uniform from where bullets had struck him from behind. He had been shot twice in the back.

Andrew placed two fingers on the officer's neck and waited for a few seconds. The neck was still warm, but there was no pulse. Andrew shook his head and pressed his lips together.

'He's gone,' he said bitterly and looked over to where Fiona was kneeling next to the other officer. 'What about him?'

Fiona was frozen next to the other officer, her hands in her lap and an ashen look on her face.

'His…,' she stammered. 'His head. There's a big hole. I can see his brain.'

'Damn it,' grimaced Andrew. 'This is bad.'

As he rose and made his way towards Lambert, he had a sinking feeling that whoever had done this was almost certainly a trained killer. Walking over to Lambert, he was finally able to take in the horrifying sight that had met them when they first entered the room. Lambert was lying on his back, the bed having been raised slightly. He was motionless and staring into space with dead eyes and one arm flopped over the side of the bed, small drops of blood running from his chest down along the arm and dripping onto the floor.

But what really got Andrew's attention was the man's chest. His white hospital shirt seemed to have been ripped open, and on his skin, the shape of a star seemed to have been crudely painted with blood.

'Oh my God,' whispered Fiona as she came over to stand next to Andrew, looking agog at the grisly scene in front of them, involuntarily placing her right hand over her mouth and looking like she might be sick. 'Andrew, what *is* this madness?'

'I don't know,' said Andrew grimly, 'but whoever did this must still be close, perhaps still in the building.'

He started walking towards the door, still looking at Fiona and pointing at Lambert.

'Stay here with him, and call the police now,' he said. 'There is only one elevator to this floor, and we just came up in it. Either the killer is still here, or he made it out using the fire escape. I am going to find him.'

'Andrew, be careful,' pleaded Fiona with a trembling voice. She looked terrified at the prospect of being left alone in the middle of a blood-soaked triple murder scene.

Andrew slipped out of the room and started walking briskly along the corridor and away from the elevator. The fire escape was likely to be as far away from the elevator shafts as possible.

At the end of the corridor, he found what he was looking for. Without hesitating, he pushed his way through the door to the stairwell, but then immediately stopped while holding the door open, trying to listen for noises. Much further down the stairwell, he could hear the sound of feet, not quite running but clearly not moving at the slow pace that one might expect from someone calmly making their way down.

He moved quickly to the railing and looked down the roughly twenty-metre drop to the bottom of the stairwell. He could see no one, but he could now clearly hear the sound of brisk footsteps descending the stairs.

Andrew grabbed the railing and propelled himself forward and down the first section of stairs as fast as he could. After a couple of floors, he was able to take several steps at a time and he was now quickly making his way down towards ground level. However, he was making a lot of noise. He had to assume that the killer had heard him already, and so there was no point in stopping to listen for footsteps again or trying to be quiet.

On the ground floor was a long, dimly lit corridor that led to the hospital interior at one end, and an exterior fire exit at the other. As Andrew reached Level 1, he heard the fire exit slam shut. The killer had already made it out onto the street outside.

Andrew took the last sections of steps in long leaps and jumped the final several steps to the corridor in an effort to make up time. His feet landed with a loud thud onto the painted concrete floor, the noise reverberating up through the staircase, and then he bolted for the door with the red glowing fire exit sign above it. As he crashed through it and out into an alley, a taxi was driving along just in front of the door. He lurched back to avoid being hit and the taxi jerked to a halt, the driver shouting a couple of angry but unintelligible words at him from inside the cab.

Panting hard, Andrew looked quickly to the right and further down the alley but saw no one. Then his head whipped to the left, just in time for him to see a black-clad man with short black hair running to the end of the alley, and then turning the corner south onto King Edward Street in the direction of the Thames.

Andrew immediately started sprinting up the alley towards the corner where the man had now vanished. When he reached it, a white van was just pulling off the road and into the alley blocking Andrew's path. Instead of slowing down, Andrew sped up and jumped with one foot onto the hood of the van and then continued up onto its roof, where he stopped to look for the man in black.

'Oi!' shouted the van driver angrily as he bolted out of his van and gesticulated at Andrew. 'Get off my bleedin' van ya wanker!'

Andrew stood still for a few moments, trying to focus his gaze in the direction the killer had run.

'I said, get off, ya pillock!' shouted the man behind him, but Andrew ignored him, jumped down onto the pavement and started sprinting south along the street past the back entrance to Bank of America whilst scanning the pavements on both sides of the street. He quickly spotted the black-clad man who had now crossed over to the other side and was running in the direction of St Paul's tube station.

'Shit,' grunted Andrew as he looked over his shoulder for approaching cars and then followed the man to the opposite side of the road.

The London Underground was both loved and hated by tourists and locals alike. What to some was quirky, to others was old, run-down and a mish-mash of tube lines that had been constructed over the course of several centuries, none of them seemingly ever taking into account that London was a permanently growing city. Overcrowded trains had been the norm for as long as anyone could remember, and the tube stations across the network were not exactly in contention for the most aesthetically pleasing subway in the world. Their crowded entrances, narrow escalators, and cramped passageways between both platforms and adjacent tube stations made it the perfect place to lose someone in the crowds.

Andrew was gaining on the killer as he ran down the stairs after him into the interior of St Paul's tube station. He was just in time to watch the man crash through the ticket barrier and barrel into a group of youngsters, knocking two of them over. At first, it looked as if the group was about to pounce on the man, but something about him made them hold back. Instead, they resorted to shouting obscenities and gesticulating angrily as he ran on towards the escalators that led down to the platforms.

As Andrew approached the barriers, the shouting and general confusion allowed him to jump unnoticed over another ticket barrier and head towards the same escalators where the killer had just disappeared. As he arrived at the top, he was just in time to see the man run off the final section of the escalator down below, and at that point it was obvious to Andrew what had happened and what he would have to emulate in order to catch up.

'Bloody hell,' he groaned, and then he jumped onto the flat metal section between the two escalators going up and down, respectively.

Using the metal section as a long slide just as the killer had done, he arrived at speed at the bottom of the escalator a few seconds later and was able to leap off and transition perfectly into a run. Having just watched another man come down the escalator in a similar fashion, the commuters down below hurried aside to clear a path for him.

The wide corridor at the bottom of the escalator had two sets of narrow corridors leading off to the right and to the left, allowing access to trains heading either east or west on the Central Line. Andrew to make a snap decision and so he ran down the first corridor on the right. A couple of seconds later, he emerged onto the platform where the tube train going east was just pulling in. Amid the loud screeching noise from the brakes and the pre-recorded voice on the PA system asking commuters to allow people off the train before boarding, he made his way as fast as he could along the platform trying to spot the killer. It was as crowded as usual and he was unable to run, instead having to skip, dodge and weave his way through the throngs of commuters moving in and out of the tube carriages.

Just as a shrill noise sounded, indicating that the doors on the train were now closing, he spotted the man near the far end of the train. He was still moving along the platform and away from him. But then, as he turned his head and looked in Andrew's direction, he lurched to the right into the last carriage of the train. Andrew bolted for the nearest double doors, and managed to launch himself through the air and inside the carriage just as the doors closed.

He landed hard on the metal floor of the carriage and quickly got to his feet, watched by the otherwise famously unimpressed but now bemused London commuters. He straightened his clothes and brushed himself down with an apologetic shrug and a smile. Everyone went back to reading their books and tablets or continued their conversations as if large men launching themselves into tube carriages was something that happened on a regular basis.

As the train picked up speed, Andrew started to move in the direction of the killer's carriage. Now sweating profusely, he grimaced as he remembered that it was often not possible to move between carriages on London Underground trains. He would be unable to reach the killer's carriage until the train pulled into the next station. He did not need to check the overhead tube map to know that the next stop was Bank Station, which had the same narrow platforms and corridors as St Paul's.

Andrew moved to the single door at the end of the carriage and waited, trying to second-guess what the killer might do next. If he stayed in his carriage after enough stops, Andrew would eventually be able to reach him by swapping carriages at upcoming stations, and since he had to assume that the man had spotted him it was likely that he would try to make a run for it at Bank Station. Andrew took a couple of deep breaths to oxygenate his blood and then exhaled slowly. He had to be ready.

As the train pulled into Bank Station, it seemed to take forever for it to slow down, come to a complete stop and for the doors to finally open. When they eventually did, Andrew bolted out and immediately started running along the platform trying to dodge other commuters, mostly succeeding but occasionally grazing or hitting some of them, which elicited various shouted insults.

Suddenly he spotted the black-clad man exiting a carriage with his face turned towards Andrew. As soon as they spotted each other, he immediately raced towards the platform's exit. It was yet another narrow corridor leading to an escalator going up towards street level. Andrew was now close behind him, and as the two of them raced up the escalator past other commuters, the gap closed even further as the killer had to push people out of the way, whereas Andrew was simply able to follow in his wake.

The killer quickly realised this and grabbed a large woman by her coat as he passed her. He then hurled her violently down the moving escalator towards Andrew. She barged into several other commuters, who in turn were knocked over and started falling down towards him. Seeing the human avalanche coming towards him, Andrew jumped up onto the handrail whilst leaning away from the escalator itself. He narrowly avoided being swallowed up by the mass of bodies tumbling down the escalator and grimaced as he resumed his run upwards. He did not like leaving behind such chaos, but at this moment catching a triple murderer was more important than being a good Samaritan.

The mayhem had allowed the killer to extend his lead by around ten seconds, but that was enough for him to make it up to the ticket barriers and out of sight of Andrew, who was now beginning to feel the burning sensation of the lactic acid building up in his legs. He was fit, but so was the killer, and he was beginning to worry that his time behind a desk at SAS HQ might cost him this race.

As the killer jumped over the ticket barrier, he turned around briefly and pointed behind him.

'Stop him. He has a knife,' he shouted in broken English, and then he raced for the exit.

Several commuters turned to see Andrew coming up the escalator, panting heavily and looking agitated. A couple of uniformed transport police officers immediately started moving towards him, one of them with one arm outstretched and his palm extended towards Andrew.

'Listen, mate,' he said in a tense but placating voice. 'Just calm down now, alright?'

The other officer was reaching for his baton and began moving off to the left and around to the side of Andrew who stood still, scanning the area for the killer. When he spotted him, he only just caught a glimpse of him heading around the corner towards the station's exit onto Lombard Street. Andrew sprinted towards the ticket barrier and adeptly jumped over to continue his chase before either of the two officers could stop him.

Emerging onto the street above, he spotted the killer running south-east along Lombard Street and he immediately began running after him. As his legs pounded the pavement and his arms were pumping through the air, his lungs were now stinging, and he knew that he would not be able to keep this up for much longer.

Another couple of minutes of running later, the man suddenly veered to the right into an alley that led towards the river at the back of the Tower of London and Tower Pier, where river cruises and shuttles make their stops.

The black-clad man sprinted along the first section of the pier and then jumped off it onto a small speedboat that was moored near the ticket gates. The occupant of the boat gave a panicked shriek and was then shoved violently into the river by the killer, who clearly possessed significant physical strength as well as no qualms whatsoever about what he needed to do to get away from his pursuer.

The engine sprang to life just as Andrew arrived at the pier, and as he began running towards the boat it leapt forward in the water, leaving a fine spray in the air behind it. As it did so, the killer, who was now gripping the wheel and pushing the throttle as far forward as it would go, turned his head back towards Andrew and produced a disdainful grin as the boat sped away from the pier.

Andrew continued running even though he knew that he would be unable to catch the killer now. Eventually, he reluctantly slowed down and stopped, bent over with his hands on his thighs and panting heavily. His pounding heart was threatening to burst out of his chest, and sweat was running off his forehead. He could hear the sound of the boat picking up speed as it made its way across the water under Tower Bridge and east along the Thames in the direction of Canary Wharf.

'Fuck!' Andrew swore between laboured breaths. Then he stood up and reached inside his pocket for his phone.

★        ★        ★

As the sound of Andrew's footsteps receded down the 3rd-floor corridor in Saint Bartholomew's Hospital, Fiona had turned back to the gruesome scene in front of her.

Lambert was lying motionless on the hospital bed, his eyes closed and his mouth open. His exposed chest had at least three wounds from where he had been shot. She felt sure that one of the bullets must have gone straight through his heart.

She leaned in slightly to look at the bloody pattern on his chest. It was the size of a hand, and it had clearly been painted using Lambert's own blood. It resembled a star, although it was of an irregular shape, possibly because the killer had been in a hurry. But who would murder two police officers in cold blood in order to be able to kill a scientist and then take the time to paint this symbol on the dead man's chest?

Suddenly Fiona froze. Out of the corner of her eye, she realised that Lambert's eyes blinked. An instant later, the blood-covered scientist inhaled with a sickening gurgling wheeze, and Fiona shrieked and leapt backwards, almost tripping over one of the murdered police officers.

Lambert blinked again, his eyes now moving to look at Fiona, and then his lips trembled. Fiona took a cautious but terrified step closer. His eyes were pleading with her as he attempted another breath, but the gurgling sound made it clear that his lungs were filling up and that he was drowning in his own blood.

Fiona took another step, and as his lips moved again, she could just make out his words.

'Stop her,' he whispered as he exhaled. 'It is Alexander. Dubois. He…'

Fiona stood still like a statue, waiting for the next words. But they never came. Lambert inhaled slowly one more time, seemed to hesitate, and then exhaled again, producing the sound of liquid gurgling in his oesophagus. As he did so, Fiona's heart sank. It felt as if Lambert's life was leaving him as the air was leaving his lungs. His eyes turned slowly to look upwards as if gazing at something in the far distance. Then he was still.

Fiona stood dumbfounded for a few moments, half expecting Lambert to breathe again. She eventually dared to place a finger on the side of his neck, but she could feel no pulse. Then she took a slow step backwards and turned to look at the two dead police officers. Her hand found its way up to cover her mouth, and she gave a small muffled sob. The pools of dark red blood around the bodies of the two officers were now much larger.

'What the hell is happening?' she whimpered quietly and put her head in her hands.

At that moment her phone rang, making her jump with fright.

'Andrew? Where are you? Are you alright?'

'I am fine,' replied Andrew, sounding out of breath. 'Bastard got away from me. He's on the river, heading east in a boat. There was no way for me to follow him. He's gone.'

'Lambert spoke to me,' said Fiona meekly.

'He what?' exclaimed Andrew, sounding astonished. 'Is he still alive?'

'No,' replied Fiona. 'He died a few moments ago.'

'What did he say?' asked Andrew.

'I will explain later,' said Fiona. 'Just get back here as soon as you can.'

'Alright,' said Andrew. 'I will put a call through to get a tactical police unit to you as soon as possible. Just stay there. Lock the door if you can, and don't leave. I should get to you before they do.'

'Ok. Hurry please.'

# FOUR

Mike Stone was sitting in his 22nd-floor office in downtown San Francisco, looking across to Oakland on the other side of San Francisco Bay. The office was rented under the name Samson Private Investigations, named after the road he grew up on. But Stone had not actually carried out any proper investigative work for anyone for a long time. Whenever he was approached by potential customers, he would tell them that he was booked up many months into the future and then proceed to recommend other genuine private investigators in the San Francisco Bay area.

In reality, he currently had only one client and that was ZOE Technologies, which paid him a substantial monthly retainer. His only point of contact at ZOE Technologies had been Fabian Ackerman, whom he had been introduced to through a mutual friend several years ago.

He was not officially on the payroll, and only a handful of people at the very top of the company even knew he existed and what he did for them. He thought of himself as a fixer. Someone who could step in to take care of problems when the usual procedures for conventional solutions to problems proved unfeasible.

Reclining in his large office chair wearing a dark pinstriped suit and a shirt, he had come a long way from the dreary housing estate in Plaistow in London's East End where he had grown up in the 1980s. The so-called Second Oil Crisis in 1979 and its effects on the British economy for several years after that, as well as his less than stellar performance in school, meant that the only real career option he had ever had was to join the army.

He signed up at the age of 16, and after his basic army training, he eventually made it into the Parachute Regiment, the UK's airborne infantry, where after three years he became a sergeant. He was a natural warfighter and was deployed on two tours during the Iraq War, where he was decorated twice for bravery. His downfall was his pathological hatred of the English ruling classes and by extension the officer corps of the army, since army officers are almost exclusively drawn from those echelons of British society.

As far as Stone was concerned, officers represented everything that was wrong with the faltering British Empire, and there were countless examples throughout history of the incompetence and ignorance of the 'toffs' in the officer corps being directly responsible for the deaths of hundreds, sometimes even thousands of British servicemen. Stone's loyalty lay not with the officers, but with the military as an institution and with his comrades in arms that fought by his side.

This only amplified the anger, humiliation and resentment he had felt after being dishonourably discharged after a bar fight in a pub in Gibraltar. He and his squad-mates had been on a night out when an argument had ended with Stone landing a right hook on the jaw of one of his superiors. In the ensuing brawl, Stone had been hauled away by police, grinning maniacally at his squad-mates who were cheering him on as he was placed in the police van.

As he was sitting in a holding cell at the local police station several hours later, he struggled to remember what the argument had even been about. Instead, his overriding memory was of the satisfaction of his right fist connecting with the jaw of the officer, and the buzz from watching his legs give way under him as he slumped to the floor like a ragdoll. It later turned out that the officer's jaw had been broken in two places, and that he had suffered a concussion as the back of his head had hit the floor. Stone had been left with only a light tingling sensation in his knuckles, and the feeling of having put something right that had been wrong for too long.

After he was brought back to the UK, Stone had been shocked to find himself unceremoniously discarded during a rushed military court proceeding, from which he remembered very little, apart from the words "zero tolerance" and "dishonourable discharge". The day after the verdict had been handed down, he was back on the streets, stripped of all purpose in life. He had forfeited his military pension, and his prospects were looking even more bleak than before he had joined the army many years earlier.

It was at that time Stone had decided that there was no such thing as loyalty to country or army. It was all an illusion, designed to keep the grunts in check as they were marched out to die on the battlefield. Loyalty was something a man could bestow on another man, but it could only ever be earned. The only true loyalty was to himself. Ultimately, he himself was the only person he could rely on. Everyone else was just a tool, like an extra in a scene in a movie.

He moved to the United States shortly thereafter and set himself up as a private eye. This quickly turned out to be a successful venture, and his military background garnered him instant credibility with the American civilians who were impressed with his no-nonsense demeanour, as well as his gruff East London accent.

After almost a decade of working for paranoid CEOs and business leaders, as well as husbands and wives suspecting their partners of infidelity, he had been approached by a man named Fabian Ackerman. The elegantly dressed Swiss doctor had said that a friend had recommended Stone to him, but he had provided no detail as to who that friend was, and Stone had not asked.

Ackerman had proceeded to offer Stone a retainer to work as Ackerman's personal private eye and general fixer. Initially, Stone had been reticent since his business was going well and he enjoyed his work. However, the money Ackerman had offered had made his proposal impossible to turn down.

The two men were like chalk and cheese, but despite that a mutual respect quickly developed between them. Ackerman valued Stone's scrupulous attitude to completing the tasks he had been set, whatever it took and without asking unnecessary questions. Stone in turn appreciated Ackerman's directness, as well as his ruthlessness in dealing with issues or people that were creating problems for the company. Stone's role had eventually evolved into much more than just being a private eye for the company. He had eventually taken on a role as an unofficial and more or less off-the-books corporate security consultant, with a remit as broad as Ackerman needed it to be.

As Stone picked up his mobile phone from the table, he walked over and stood next to the floor-to-ceiling windows looking east over San Francisco Bay. Behind Oakland, on the far side of the bay, he could see the hills rising up above the city, and if he had looked through a pair of binoculars, he would have been able to make out the top of ZOE Technologies' corporate headquarters.

'Hello?', said Stone, having noted that the call came from a withheld number. He was expecting a call from a disposable phone.

'Moscow is cold now,' said a voice on the other end of the line. It had a heavy Russian accent and sounded like that of a man in his thirties.

'Yes, but Gorki Park is always pleasant,' responded Stone, thereby completing the mutually agreed codewords to indicate that no one else was listening and that both ends of the call were encrypted.

'The target has been terminated,' said the Russian.

'Good,' replied Stone. 'Collateral?'

'Two police officers,' said the Russian.

'What?' Stone blurted out, struggling to control his temper. 'Two bleedin' officers? What the hell happened?'

'It was the only way,' replied the Russian calmly, his voice laced with the weariness of a pragmatist. He appeared entirely unmoved. 'They were both inside the hospital room, so they would have covered each other unless I moved fast on both of them. If one of them had been outside I could have completed the mission without killing them, but this is just how it had to happen this time.'

Stone took a moment to compose himself. He would just have to try to tidy up the situation. After all, that was his job.

'Alright,' he said. 'Have you left the country?'

'Yes,' replied the Russian. 'I am already out.'

'Ok,' said Stone. 'Go to the safe house and stay there until I contact you again. We have another matter that needs to be dealt with. I will update you shortly.'

'Fine,' sighed the Russian, sounding like he was leaning back in a chair and lighting a cigarette. 'And what about the two others?'

'I will take care of them,' replied Stone. 'And I'll make sure to make a whole lot less noise than you have.'

Stone terminated the call, slipped the phone into his inside suit pocket and looked out towards the bay where a container ship was heading towards the Golden Gate Bridge.

He took a deep breath and exhaled in a deliberate way, focussing his mind on the task ahead. It was rare that he had to dig down into his bag of hands-on military training, but this time he would have to take things into his own hands.

*Sometimes you just have to sort things out yourself,* he thought, shaking his head as he turned and walked towards the door.

★          ★          ★

It was early afternoon as Andrew and Fiona entered the non-descript office building on Sheldrake Place in Kensington in London's West End. Andrew greeted the receptionist as they walked through the lobby towards the elevators, and the two smartly dressed guards nodded to indicate their recognition of both him and Fiona.

Arriving in Colonel Strickland's office, they sat down on the comfortable leather chesterfield sofas, and a couple of minutes later Strickland arrived and joined them.

'How are you two?' he asked sympathetically as he sat down and poured them all a cup of tea. 'Quite the mess at the British Museum yesterday.'

'We're alright, mostly,' replied Andrew and glanced at Fiona.

Fiona smiled uncertainly, but it was obvious that she had not yet recovered from the traumatic events of the previous day. Witnessing a murder just a few metres away and then finding herself in the middle of another gory triple murder scene had clearly taken a toll on her. The rings under her eyes told the story of how badly she had slept.

'I'm ok,' she lied. 'Rough night, but I'll be fine.'

'I understand,' said Strickland. 'Seeing death up close like this is upsetting, especially so in the middle of a supposedly civilised city like London. I must say I was shocked to hear what had happened when Inspector Worthington from the Met rang me a couple of hours later.'

'She mentioned to us that you had suggested we join the investigation,' said Andrew, sipping his tea.

'Yes,' replied Strickland. 'I took the liberty of suggesting you two assist them. I hope that's ok.'

Andrew gave a wry smile. 'Worthington told us that you were quite insistent.'

'Well,' said Strickland. 'I genuinely think that you two could contribute a lot to their investigation. It would be an understatement to say that you have already proven your investigative prowess. On more than one occasion, I might add. And since you were both eyewitnesses, I thought you should be able to provide your input and help wherever you can.'

'What does the word *help* mean in practice?' asked Fiona, her demeanour suggesting that she was still reticent about their involvement, at least until it became clear what they were dealing with.

'To put it bluntly,' said Strickland. 'Anything you can dig up would be appreciated. You really have a free hand to pursue any leads you might be able to find. Given the nature of this case, there is a good chance that the investigation will include efforts abroad, and you two working under my direction will be able to more quickly and easily chase down those leads. If the Metropolitan Police were to do that, they would have to go through official channels and seek approval from the police forces of other nations. This would be time-consuming and probably quite complicated, and there is always the risk of running into police corruption which would obviously hamper our efforts. You two will be able to do this under the radar, so to speak.'

'I see,' said Andrew. 'Cloak and dagger then?'

'In a manner of speaking,' replied Strickland. 'Nothing illegal, you understand. But let's just call it a more *flexible* approach.'

'And backup and support?' asked Andrew.

'Not officially, no. Essentially you will be on your own,' said Strickland and spread out his hands. 'But I might be able to bring in specialised assistance should you need it. We would have to discuss that in the event it becomes required.'

'Alright,' said Andrew, nodding. 'Fair enough.'

'What about the killer?' asked Fiona. 'Has anyone been able to trace him?'

'That is something I wanted to discuss with you actually,' replied Strickland. 'As I am sure you are aware, London has a very extensive CCTV network. Between the Metropolitan Police, Transport for London and the huge network of private and corporate CCTV, there are thousands of cameras all across the city. In addition, the government's communications headquarters GCHQ can pipe virtually every private CCTV feed through to their own operations centres at Cheltenham if needed, so access to footage is never an issue.'

'Don't they need warrants for those sorts of things?' asked Fiona suspiciously.

'Technically yes,' replied Strickland hesitantly. 'But with the right sign-off from the Home Secretary they effectively have full access to all electronic communications in this country. And because of the often time-critical nature of these things, the sign-off is really only ever a rubber-stamping of their request, no questions asked.'

'That's appalling!' exclaimed Fiona and looked aghast, first at Andrew and then back at Strickland. 'Are you saying there is effectively no oversight?'

'Let's just focus on the task at hand, shall we?' smiled Andrew, trying to sound placating. He could sense Fiona's fiery temper stirring.

'Well,' said Strickland, attempting to move the conversation along, and for a moment looking slightly uncomfortable. 'I think the important thing right now is that we are quite sure that we have a positive ID on the killer.'

'How?' asked Andrew. 'And who is he?'

'Well,' replied Strickland. 'Going back over all the available CCTV footage from all the different sources across London, we managed to piece together what he did next. Having stolen the boat from the pier at Tower Bridge Quay, he proceeded east along the Thames past the Isle of Dogs and down to Greenwich Pier. Because of the low tide, he simply rode the boat onto the bank and jumped out, climbing over the railing and onto the footpath next to a pub called the Trafalgar Tavern. This was picked up by a security camera on the pier, and we also have several witnesses who saw him climb up from the river bank.'

'And I guess nobody thought much of it at the time,' said Andrew. 'They wouldn't have had any reason to think that there was anything particularly strange about it, other than perhaps a boat running out of fuel.'

'Exactly,' replied Strickland. 'The next images we have are of him walking up the road towards the Naval College. At this point, we no longer have CCTV coverage, but he is picked up again about forty minutes later at St. Pancras Station boarding a Eurostar train to Paris.'

'He's no longer in the country?' asked Andrew.

'Almost certainly not,' replied Strickland. 'The train does stop at Ebbsfleet and Ashford before crossing over to France, but it is extremely unlikely that he would have remained in the UK. We don't yet know whether he might have got off the train in Calais or Lille, or whether he went all the way to Paris. GCHQ is currently liaising with French police intelligence to determine that. Anyway, GCHQ was able to identify him using their state-of-the-art facial recognition AI. Apparently, it can match people in real time against an extensive database of people that are already of interest to the intelligence services.'

'So, who is he then?' asked Andrew impatiently.

'He is a Russian national by the name Yevgeni Morozov. Former Spetsnaz, or special forces under the auspices of military intelligence, also known as the GRU.'

'Shit,' said Andrew, clearly taken aback by this revelation. 'Are you saying that this was sanctioned by the Russian government?'

'Very unlikely,' replied Strickland. 'As far as we can tell, Morozov left the service about six years ago. We do not have any information on what he has been up to since then, but he does not appear to be affiliated with military intelligence anymore.'

Andrew leaned back in the sofa with a troubled look on his face.

'I am not sure if that is a good or a bad thing,' he said. 'On the one hand, it would be really bad if this turns out to be some Russian intelligence operation. On the other hand, a highly trained rogue special operations asset on a murder spree in London is not exactly an ideal scenario either.'

'I know,' said Strickland, and shook his head ruefully. 'We need to tread a bit carefully on this one, Andrew. At least until we know exactly what we are dealing with. But if anything, this is just another reason why an under-the-radar effort from you two could prove helpful.'

'Any other indications as to his movements in the city?' asked Fiona. 'Surely you must have been able to track him entering the hospital, and then work out how he got there and where he came from.'

'We do have footage of him entering the hospital,' said Strickland. 'But so far they have been unable to trace his movement before that. There are somewhere between two and three million people using the underground network in London every day, so as you can imagine it is a bit like finding a needle in a haystack. But the chaps at GCHQ are still working on it.'

'I guess we'll just have to wait for that,' said Andrew. 'But I agree that we should do what we can to uncover his movements before he arrived at the hospital. We might get lucky and find out who he might have met with. It might help us uncover what is really going on here.'

Strickland nodded sagely. 'I will let you know if GCHQ manages to dig anything up. Now, I would like to move on to talk a bit about the murder scene at Saint Bartholomew's Hospital, if you don't mind,' he said and looked at Fiona. 'What did you make of the motif that was painted on Lambert's chest?'

Fiona took a deep breath and looked up at the ceiling, as if trying to recall the scene that had met them in the hospital room.

'I am not entirely sure,' said Fiona. 'It is clearly some sort of star shape, but an unusually elaborate one. It's all a bit odd, actually. If someone had wanted to leave some sort of sick calling card in the shape of a star, you would think that it would be a simple one, right? But that star was anything but simple.'

'What do you mean?' asked Strickland.

'Well,' replied Fiona haltingly, looking slightly queasy. 'It was crude and messy of course, because of the… blood.'

She paused for a second, swallowed, and then steadied herself for a moment as the gory memory flashed through her mind.

'But it was an unusual star,' she continued. 'It had a lot of rays coming out from the centre. Not just four or five as you might expect if someone wanted to draw a stylised star in a hurry.'

'So, what does that mean?' asked Strickland. 'Could this be some sort of ritual killing?'

'Impossible for me to say at this stage,' replied Fiona. 'It could be something like that, or it could be that the killer, this Morozov character, simply left it there for us to find, as a way to send us down the wrong trail. I just don't know.'

Strickland nodded again.

'Well, hopefully we will be able to uncover more information about this chap soon. The other thing I wanted to talk to you about was Lambert's last words. Could you remind me what they were please?'

Fiona creased her forehead, trying to remember.

'It was something along the lines of "It is Alexander Dubois." And then something about a *she*. I couldn't make out anything else.'

'Alexander?' asked Andrew, looking puzzled.

'Might be the obvious one,' replied Fiona. 'But I have no clue what he meant by "she".'

'There's clearly a lot more to uncover here,' said Strickland. 'I suggest you two take the rest of the day off and perhaps spend tomorrow pondering what we have talked about here. Who knows? You might be able to come up with something neither the police nor GCHQ have thought of yet.'

'Sounds good,' said Andrew, and rose. 'We'll be in touch.'

★     ★     ★

It was becoming dark as Samuel Hicks walked south across Snow Park next to Lake Merritt. It was one of the few green spaces in Oakland, and even though it was small, he had enjoyed coming here during his time in the city. Originally from Sacramento, he had moved down to Oakland to Study at the University of California Berkeley, and he had lived in his apartment on Waverly Street ever since he took the job at ZOE Technologies.

The pay was great, but joining Peter Lambert's team straight out of university had been the most exciting thing he could have wished for. Soon after starting his degree in bio-engineering, he had become convinced that gene-editing was a game-changer for the world. And not just in traditional medical science. It would soon pervade everything from medicine to food production. Anything in the world that was organic and alive would eventually be genetically edited and tailored to human needs, and it represented a huge opportunity for ambitious entrepreneurs and visionaries. And as far as Hicks was concerned, Lambert was one of those visionaries. Extremely bright and single-minded, Lambert was forging ahead with his own version of the CRISPR technology, and it had already shown impressive results in animal test subjects.

But now Lambert was dead. Hicks had only managed to glean a few details from the news of what had happened in London, but everything about it seemed completely out of character for his former boss. Lambert was usually calm and thoughtful, but the revelations about the alternate research program at ZOE Technologies' New York facility had shaken him to his core and apparently caused some sort of mental breakdown.

Hicks pulled his coat tight around himself and flipped up the collar. The rain was starting to come down hard, and the wind was picking up. He stuck his hand inside the coat and pulled out his phone, quickly selecting Tim Dawson's number on the speed dial. It rang only once before being picked up.

'Hello,' said a voice.

'Tim, it's me,' said Hicks.

'Jesus Christ, Sam,' said Dawson, sounding as if he was relieved to hear his colleague's voice. 'What the hell is going on? Did you see what happened to Lambert?'

'Yes,' replied Hicks grimly, as he turned to look over his shoulder. Behind him, a man was walking along, also talking on his phone. 'Tim, I am freaking out. This whole thing is totally messed up. Where are you?'

'I am at home in my apartment,' replied Dawson. 'Do you want to come over?'

'No,' said Hicks. 'I don't think we should meet up. I don't know. I feel like something bad is going to happen. Do you remember I once told you about an old cabin on the other side of Folsom Lake?'

'Back in Sacramento? Sure,' replied Dawson. 'The log cabin with the open fireplace? You went there with your granddad, right?'

'That's right,' said Hicks. 'I am going up there now. After what happened to Lambert, I honestly don't know what they are going to do to us. I really think you need to get out of there too, Tim.'

'Hold on a second, buddy,' said Dawson. 'Don't you think you're overreacting?'

'Overreacting?' Hicks blurted out, sounding agitated. 'First our boss tells us about a secret program that is totally fucked up, then we all get fired and threatened with a mountain of legal problems if we talk, and now our boss has killed the CEO and is lying dead in a fucking morgue somewhere in London having been brutally murdered along with two cops. And you think I am overreacting?'

Dawson sighed. 'Alright, listen, maybe you're right. But this was all Lambert. We didn't do anything wrong!'

'At this point, I don't think they care,' said Hicks. 'Whoever *they* really are. As far as they're concerned, you and I are loose ends, and you know what happens to those when billions of dollars are at stake, right?'

'Well, let's go to the police then,' said Dawson, beginning to sound anxious.

Hicks produced an incredulous, almost mocking laugh. 'Are you insane? ZOE is bound to have tentacles reaching inside the police. And San Francisco PD is right up there with the NYPD in the corruption league tables.'

'Shit,' said Dawson, hesitating for a moment. 'What do I do?'

'Just get out of there,' replied Hicks. 'Leave your apartment. Disappear. At least for a while until we can figure out what is really going on here. Do you have somewhere you can go?'

'Yes, I think so,' replied Dawson. 'I have some friends that might be able to help me. Do you really think this is necessary?'

'Look man,' said Hicks. 'It's up to you, but I am not taking any chances. We both know what Ackerman is capable of now, ok? We all pretend to play nice at the office because it gets us what we want, but that guy is a fucking sociopath. And just think about what Lambert found. That shit is so far out there that we ought to go to the police if they weren't on the take. If that stuff became public, it would be the end of ZOE Technologies. So do you really think they'll just let us walk away, especially after what Lambert did?'

'You're right,' sighed Dawson. 'Shit.'

'I don't know about you,' said Hicks. 'But until I find someone I think I can really trust with this information, I am staying well out of sight, and so should you.'

'Damn it,' said Dawson reluctantly. 'Alright. I'll pack up my stuff and leave. You take care of yourself, ok?'

'Yeah, you too man,' replied Hicks and tapped the End Call icon. Then he stopped walking and just stood there for a few seconds, staring down at the phone in his hand. As he did so, the man walking behind him caught up and walked past.

'Fuck!' whispered Hicks bitterly to himself. 'I should have thought of that.'

Then he looked around to make sure no one was near him, dropped the phone on the cement footpath and stomped down on it with his right boot. There was a crushing sound and as he removed his boot, he saw the phone's plastic case cracked open and some of the electronic parts spilled out onto the ground. He then picked them up, walked onto the grass and hurled the broken phone as far as he could into the lake.

Exiting the park and walking along the street in the rain, traffic was flowing normally but Hicks felt himself studying each car for a moment as if he might be able to tell if any of them were following him. He was walking towards the taxi stand at the Lake Merritt subway station a couple of blocks away, intending to hire a taxi for the long drive up to Sacramento, and as he did so his mind was racing. Maybe Dawson was right. Maybe he was overreacting and being paranoid. But then he shook his head and continued walking.

*Get out*, he thought to himself. *Just fucking get out.*

He turned down an alley to take a shortcut from Alice Street to Jackson Street both of which run parallel to each other, towards the Lake Merritt subway station. At the end of the alley was a parking lot, and as he approached it he saw a black van with tinted windows pull in from the road and slowly make its way towards the back of the lot and stop in the bay nearest to the point where the alley met the parking lot. As he approached it, the van's wipers remained switched on and so did its headlights and engine.

Hicks had to make an effort to keep walking and not turn back. There was justifiable caution, and then there was irrational panic. If he was going to make his way to the cabin on Folsom Lake, he needed to calm down and act normal.

*It's just a damn van.*

When he was about ten metres from the vehicle, the driver's side door opened and a large man stepped out. He was wearing a dark boiler suit and a cap, and before he closed the door he leaned in and extracted a toolbox from behind his seat. The rain was falling hard now, but he did not seem to care as he slammed the door shut and started walking towards Hicks.

'Sorry mate,' said the man in a deep voice as he approached. He had an accent that Hicks could not place. 'Is this Jackson Street?' He was pointing towards the street on the other side of the parking lot.

Taking a step to one side and away from the man, Hicks stretched out his hand behind him.

'No, buddy,' he said, not sure what to make of the situation. His nerves were getting the better of him. 'Jackson Street is that one.'

Hicks instinctively turned his own head in the direction he was pointing, and that is when the man pounced. In a split second the man had dropped his toolbox, moved up behind Hicks and wrapped a strong arm around his neck, putting his head in a headlock. He smelled of burgers and chips. As soon as the man had secured a tight grip around Hick's neck, he started dragging him towards the van.

Hicks panicked and started clawing at the man's arm, but it was like an iron vice pressing in on his throat. As Hicks attempted to shout, the man pressed even harder, making it impossible for Hicks to breathe. He started retching and felt as if he was going to throw up.

The man placed his other hand on the side of Hicks' head and pressed hard. First, there was excruciating pain. Then Hicks felt something snap inside his own neck, producing the sound of an ice cube being crushed between teeth.

'Night night,' whispered the man in his ear. 'Time to go to sleep.'

Hicks' body immediately went limp, and he lost all sensation as the man dragged him the last few metres to the van. It took a few seconds for him to realise that he was no longer breathing. Had his heart stopped beating too?

*Oh God*, he thought, as his life flashed before his eyes. *It's happening.*

His last conscious thought before he died was of his parents back in Sacramento. Then darkness closed in.

# FIVE

Fiona was reclining in one of the comfortable white linen sofas in Andrew's living room while he was in the kitchen making them cups of tea.

'Sugar?' called Andrew.

'No thanks,' replied Fiona. 'I am sweet enough.'

'Very funny,' said Andrew and smiled at her.

A few minutes later Andrew came into the living room carrying a tray with tea and a box of chocolates.

'How are you feeling?' he asked as he sat down.

'I'm OK,' said Fiona. 'I guess I am not as used to seeing dead people as you are.'

'It will pass,' said Andrew, and placed a hand gently on her shoulder. 'But trust me, the day you get used to seeing dead people is not a good day.'

'I suppose,' replied Fiona and reached for her tea cup. 'Have you managed to find out anything more about Lambert?'

'Nothing we didn't already know,' replied Andrew. 'Super bright. No history of mental illness. Seemingly a loyal employee of the company. As for what exactly he was working on, we have come up empty. ZOE Technologies is infamous for being extremely tight-lipped about its research. All we know is that Lambert was an exceptionally talented geneticist and that he was heading up the company's main research lab.'

'The whole thing is just baffling,' said Fiona. 'But clearly *something* was going on that made him snap.'

'About the star painted in blood on his chest,' said Andrew. 'Any idea what that might mean?'

'No,' sighed Fiona. 'My first thought was that it might have been the Star of David, but Lambert is not Jewish and there is no other Jewish connection to this whole affair that I have been able to find.'

Andrew shook his head. 'I am as confused about that as I am about the name Alexander Dubois. I have asked our spooks to look into it, and there is literally not a single person of interest to the intelligence services by that name.'

'Sounds French,' said Fiona.

'We already asked the French,' said Andrew. 'They are also not looking for anyone by that name. Apparently, our French liaison officer said that the only person currently known to French police is a chap in Marseilles who set fire to his ex-girlfriend's house. I still can't decide whether he might have been joking or not.'

Fiona raised her eyebrows and looked dubiously at Andrew.

'Either way,' continued Andrew. 'So far, we have nothing useful on that name.'

Fiona tilted her head to one side and furrowed her brow as she put down her tea cup.

'Andy,' she said. 'Do we have access to the photos from the crime scene at the hospital?'

'Sure,' replied Andrew. 'I have been given full access to everything in the police database that relates to this case, so that includes photos from the crime scenes at the British Museum and Saint Bartholomew's Hospital.'

'Could I see those please?' asked Fiona and rose.

'Of course,' said Andrew. 'Let me get my laptop.'

A couple of minutes later, they were sitting down on the sofa, looking at the images on the laptop. There were hundreds of photos, covering virtually every inch of the two crime scenes, especially the three victims, from every possible angle. The detail of it was stomach-churning. The two dead police officers. The pools of blood on the floor reflecting the ceiling lights. Apparently, the officer nearest Lambert's hospital bed had drawn his firearm but was shot and killed before he had a chance to defend himself. The gun was lying on the floor close to his dead body. Something Andrew had not noticed at the time.

'How come crime scene photos are always in black and white?' asked Fiona. 'I always wondered about that.'

'It has to do with people's emotional responses, especially in the context of a criminal trial, replied Andrew. 'Apparently, jurors are less likely to be emotionally affected by any evidence presented to them if it is black and white. Gruesome evidence presented with colour photos supposedly increases a juror's emotional response, which makes them less impartial. Something along those lines.'

Fiona shrugged. 'I suppose that makes sense.'

'Anyway,' said Andrew. 'The killer must have entered the room and more or less immediately shot the first officer in the back. The second officer must have attempted to draw his weapon, but he was clearly unsuccessful.'

Andrew flicked through another few images, studying the details. The revulsion was written all over Fiona's face.

'Look at this,' said Andrew, pointing to an image showing Lambert lying dead in the hospital bed. The scientist's face looked gaunt and in agony, and his left arm was flopped over the side of the bed, with a trail of coagulated blood tracing a path from his chest to his fingertips. 'There are bruises on his right wrist from the handcuffs. He must have attempted to break free and defend himself during those last moments.'

Fiona leaned in and studied the star painted in blood on Lambert's chest. As she did so, she tried to mentally block out the rest of the image of the dead man, focussing only on the star-shaped motif.

Andrew rubbed his chin, looking closely at the image.

'Look,' he said and pointed. 'His shirt has been pulled away from his chest, but there are bullet holes in it here and here. That means the shirt was covering his chest when the shots were fired, and then pulled back to expose his chest afterwards.'

'Why would the killer do this?' asked Fiona. 'To send some sort of cryptic message?'

'Perhaps,' replied Andrew. 'But it didn't exactly have the desired effect. The only people who have seen this are us and a handful of people at the Met.

And none of us are able to decipher what it means. Either way, I am not convinced by the idea of it being a ritual killing. It just seems too far-fetched.'

Fiona looked pensive, staring at the image for a moment.

'What if it wasn't the killer who drew the motif?' she said, without taking her eyes off the laptop's screen. 'What if Lambert did it himself? He was still alive when we got to him.'

'Are you serious?' asked Andrew, looking sceptical. 'Why would he do that?'

'Well, I know it sounds macabre,' said Fiona. 'But he was handcuffed to a bed, losing blood and clearly close to death, and he was unable to communicate with anyone. He must have known those were his last moments. Perhaps this was a final attempt to point someone in the direction of his killer.'

'I see what you mean,' said Andrew. 'It is not as if he could have written a long message. A simple motif like that was all he would have been able to do. But what is it, and what does it mean?'

Fiona had closed her eyes and bowed her head, rubbing her temples with the tips of her fingers. Suddenly she looked up at Andrew.

'Wait,' she said. She switched to an internet browser on the laptop and typed in a search term. 'Look at this,' she said, and pointed at the screen. It showed a stylised depiction of a star.

'What am I looking at?' asked Andrew, looking closely at the image.

'This is the Vergina Sun,' said Fiona. 'Also known as the Star of Vergina. It was the royal symbol of the Argead dynasty.'

Andrew looked at her with a puzzled expression on his face. 'I'm sorry, but I have no idea what you are talking about.'

'It was the symbol of Alexander the Great, his father Philip II and of their bloodline for several centuries before that. Alexander's troops carried it on their shields during his campaign.'

'I see,' said Andrew. 'That's all very interesting, but why was it on Lambert's chest? And if you're right, why would he draw that as the very last thing he did in this life?'

'I don't know,' replied Fiona. 'But for some reason, references to Alexander the Great seem to be popping up all over this whole affair. The mysterious Greek private owner of ZOE Technologies is supposedly obsessed with Alexander. The genetic engineering project was named after Alexander's dog. And now this strange reference to his bloodline. What's going on here?'

Andrew shook his head. 'No idea, but Lambert clearly wanted to draw attention to Alexander the Great, so it is up to us to work out how that fits into all of this.'

Fiona rubbed her eyes. 'I guess a place to start would be to learn as much as we can about ZOE and its owner. This mysterious Alex Galanis.'

'Ok,' said Andrew. 'I will ask Strickland to liaise with our American counterparts about this. ZOE Technologies' main research facilities are in the US, so perhaps they have some useful intelligence on the company which might assist us.'

'We also need to get to grips with this whole topic of genetic engineering, especially CRISPR technology.

It is clearly at the heart of what Lambert was working on, so we need to at least understand the basics.'

'I agree,' said Andrew. 'I will see what I can set up for us.'

'Great,' said Fiona and yawned. 'I don't know about you, but I am really tired. I need to go to bed.'

'Good idea,' said Andrew. 'I will send an email to Strickland and join you in a bit.'

★      ★      ★

*Пантера. Pantera.* The Russian word for panther. That was his callsign in the Russian special forces division called Spetsnaz. It is the equivalent of the U.S. Navy SEAL teams or the British SAS, and he had spent most of his adult life there. He had even had a small black panther claw tattooed onto his lower right arm. He had earned the callsign as a result of his unrivalled ability to sneak into enemy facilities undetected and often under cover of darkness, either to retrieve information or to assassinate enemy commanders.

His skills had been deployed numerous times in Chechnya and Ukraine over the past decade, where he and other special forces commandos had carried out countless missions behind enemy lines, and he had been decorated several times for his exploits there.

But those days were behind him now, and military honours never meant very much to him anyway, except as a sign of respect from his fellow soldiers. Going private was the best thing he had ever done, and once he had offered his services to private individuals and so-called PMCs or private military contractors the first couple of times, he had never looked back. It was a lot more interesting and infinitely more profitable. His parents were still stuck in the old ways of communist Russia, where profit was a dirty word. But Yevgeny Morozov had embraced the philosophy of free enterprise once he had left the army.

His latest mission in London had been a thrill, and it had paid extremely well, since capture could have meant a life-long prison sentence. But he knew he would be able to carry it out without problems. He had realised something important that most people simply did not understand. If someone is prepared to place themselves completely outside the norms of human behaviour, then there is very little that so-called civilised societies can do about it. If he was prepared to kill an unlimited number of people to carry out his mission, then there was simply no way for him to be captured. To Morozov, this was why terrorism was impossible to defeat. Terrorists don't play by the rules, and most societies are simply not set up to deal with those types of individuals. And he himself had found that if he simply dispensed with all convention and conducted himself as if no rules applied to him, then he existed outside of normal society and could more or less do as he pleased.

He was not sure exactly when, but somewhere along the line he had lost his capacity for compassion with his victims, whether they had been legitimate targets or simply bystanders caught in the wrong place at the wrong time. He guessed that if you kill enough people, you simply stop caring. He never intentionally set out to hurt or kill anyone not designated as a target, but sometimes it was unavoidable.

Having made his way up the fire escape at Saint Bartholomew's Hospital, he had then walked calmly towards room 508 where he knew Lambert was being detained. To his surprise, there was no one in the corridor guarding the door. Rookie mistake. He had not been able to ascertain how many officers were guarding the scientist, but he felt completely confident in his ability to deal with them. They were probably well trained, but he was certain that their actual field experience was lacking. The absence of an external guard only reinforced that suspicion. In addition, he would have the element of surprise, which more often than not decided the outcome of an engagement.

Moments before he entered the room, he had pulled out his silenced Yarygin MP-443 pistol and chambered the first round. As he silently moved closer to the door, he heard the voices of two men talking. They sounded relaxed. English accents.

Holding the pistol in his right hand and pointing upwards, ready to extend and aim, he grabbed the door handle, turned it counter-clockwise and pushed open the door.

The two officers were caught completely off guard. One was by the bed where Lambert was lying, and the other was in the middle of the room, facing away from the door. As the door swung open, Morozov quickly aimed and fired two shots into the back of the closest officer. He instantly went limp and dropped to the floor, as if he had been a robot with the power suddenly switched off.

In a panic, the other officer had reached for his holstered firearm, but before he could pull it out and aim, Morozov had put a bullet in his forehead. The officer's head had snapped backwards, and his body had then slumped to the floor in a messy heap.

Finishing off Lambert had been easy. Three bullets to the chest and it was all over. The entire hit had taken less than a minute, and it had been clean and efficient. As Morozov left the room, he heard the bell of the elevator at the far end of the corridor, so he hurried back to the fire escape and slipped through the door, making his way down the stairwell towards ground level.

When he heard the door above him open again and the sound of footsteps coming down, he had been surprised. He did not think anyone would have had the courage to chase after him, but he quickly sped up and exited out into the alley outside. His pursuer had been stubborn, but he was never in any doubt that he would be able to lose him. Giving him the slip by stealing a speedboat had been thrilling, and he simply couldn't resist turning back and flashing a victorious grin at the man in the suit. He had taken a brief moment to study him before accelerating away down the river, and there was something about his demeanour that seemed familiar. A fearlessness and determination that surely indicated military training. Definitely not a police officer.

Morozov had slipped out of the country on a Eurostar train and made it to a safehouse in Paris, where he had contacted Mike Stone to say that he was now awaiting further instructions. After two days there, he had a visit from Pierre Dubois who had given him the details of the item he had been tasked with retrieving, as well as its approximate location inside the huge mansion.

The building was an enormous 18th-century colossus set back from a private road on a large well-groomed estate in an exclusive Paris suburb. The estate was situated next to a woodland area southwest of the city, which afforded it an excellent degree of privacy. However, it also allowed Morozov access to the grounds without being seen from any public roads.

Clad entirely in black, Morozov was crouching behind a large tree just outside the estate, waiting for darkness to fall. The only sounds he could hear were the leaves in the tree and a few crickets optimistically chirping their mating noises. The whole estate was calm and serene, and from his current vantage point, he could see no sign of any people. He had been told that the owners were out of town, but that a team of three security guards were always present.

As he expected, there were security cameras along the perimeter, and the tall hedges surrounding it were in fact barbed wire fences that had been expertly masked by various bushes that had grown to cover them.

Somehow, Stone had obtained and forwarded him a complete and detailed map of both the estate and the mansion's interior as well as the placement of its security cameras, and Morozov had spent several hours studying and memorising the information. Dubois had given him very little information about the occupant of the mansion, except that he was some

Russian oligarch with a predilection for obscure ancient artefacts.

Morozov had no qualms about breaking into the house of a fellow countryman. He understood that the Russian economy was a ruthless dog-eat-dog kleptocracy, and people simply took whatever they could get for themselves. The only thing Morozov cared about was getting paid, and Dubois' benefactors seemed to have very deep pockets.

Morozov cut a hole in the fence, slipped through and made his way around to the left, using the bushes as cover. If the schematics he had received were correct, there would be a small CCTV blind spot near the rear service entrance to the house. He made his way as close to the door as he could, while remaining inside the camera blind spot, and then he pulled out his silenced pistol. Tilting his head slightly to the right, he brought up the gun and aimed down the sight at the security camera covering the back entrance and mounted high on the exterior wall some fifteen metres away. He held his breath for a moment, aimed and fired. There was a pop from the gun, and a bullet slammed into the camera shattering its housing and sending a couple of sparks flying out of it.

Morozov lowered his gun and waited, listening for the sound of approaching guards. After about a minute he decided that the coast was clear, and then he moved quickly but silently to the door. He knelt down next to the security panel and punched in the correct code. Somehow Dubois had managed to get his hands on that, too. Morozov guessed that someone at the company installing the security systems for the mansion had been compromised or perhaps simply paid off. Either way, the alarm stayed silent and Morozov pushed open the exterior door and entered a small hallway with two doors leading to the kitchen and the wine cellar. If all went to plan, Morozov would not have to enter the upper floors of the mansion, and he might even be able to steer clear of the guards altogether. His instructions were to remain undetected and only use force if absolutely necessary.

Taking a moment to make sure there were no sounds of anyone moving around inside the mansion, he then snuck over to what he knew to be the door to a winding staircase. It was unlocked, and he quickly slipped inside closing the door behind him. He then made his way down one flight of stairs to the wine cellar.

Here he paused for a few seconds, recalling the layout of the room from the schematics he had been shown, and matching it up with what he saw in front of him. The room was approximately three by four metres in size, and the walls were covered with faux brickwork to make it look like an authentic French wine cellar. Each wall was full of wine racks brimming with what were no doubt extremely expensive bottles of wine. The back wall of the room was the exception. It had a small section in the middle, perhaps a metre wide, where no wine racks had been mounted. Instead, there was mounted a wooden rack with four clothes pegs. There were no clothes on any of them.

Morozov moved quietly to the back wall, grabbed the two outer pegs and pushed them towards each other. There was a small metallic click, and the wooden rack popped out about a centimetre from the wall. Mounted on two rails, the rack could be slid to the left, revealing a digital keypad whose display glowed a faint green in the dark room.

Morozov pulled a small screwdriver from his tactical vest and unscrewed the four tiny screws holding the front panel in place. Inside was a number of thin wires and a green circuit board. He reached into his backpack and extracted a small device with a display and two wires with clamps at the ends. He connected the clamps to the two wires linking the keypad to the circuit board and switched the small device on. It quickly ran through its initialisation procedure and then began prodding the internal memory of the circuit board. Somewhere in the local memory was hidden an encrypted file with the correct combination. It took less than ten seconds for the device to extract the combination and decrypt it.

Morozov placed the panel back in its housing, quickly screwed the four screws back in and then entered the numbers 2-0-1-5 on the number pad. The display panel produced a faint double beep, and immediately the entire wall section around the coat hanger receded into a hidden room, and then it swung open into the room beyond, allowing Morozov to enter.

The walls of the room were painted black and small spotlights in the ceiling gave off a warm yellow light. It was empty, except for a display case at the centre, which sat raised on a grey granite pedestal. One of the ceiling spotlights was mounted directly above it.

The display case was large, around one square metre across, and made from aluminium except for the top which was made of non-reflective glass. As Morozov stepped closer, he could see the item he had come for. It was a book, but not in the conventional sense. Its pages, measuring roughly forty by twenty centimetres, were very obviously extremely old, with the paper yellowed and blotchy, and in some places it was worn thin and even missing small parts here and there. Each page had been hermetically sealed between two hard panes of thin but toughened acrylic, with the air having been replaced with the inert gas argon. This ensured that the pages would not be bent or otherwise disturbed, but more importantly, that they would not decompose by being subjected to oxygen, or degraded by exposure to moisture and harmful bacteria or fungi. Theoretically, they could remain safely preserved in their current state indefinitely.

The display case contained a stack of around seventy such pages placed in the middle of the case. On either side were placed the book's original cover and back cover, respectively, both made of leather but with no discernible writing or other symbols on them. Morozov was not particularly interested in history, but he still found himself admiring the sight in front of him, and reflecting on what the world had been like when these pages were first written more than two thousand years ago.

Morozov opened the display case and pulled out a small camera from his backpack. He then extracted another item from his backpack. It was a small square metal plate with four telescopic legs attached to it. He extended each leg and placed their feet just inside the case in its four corners. Then he mounted the camera on the metal plate pointing downward to allow the camera to take the highest quality pictures with no risk of blurring due to motion.

He then carefully and methodically began taking high-resolution pictures of each page, gingerly lifting each acrylic pane to one side after shooting, and then proceeding to the next one until he was done. The pictures were meant as an insurance policy in case the book's pages were damaged in transit, or worse still, in the unlikely event that he was caught leaving the mansion. He had initially resisted the idea since he was completely confident that he would be able to retrieve the book undetected, but Dubois had insisted, also and reminded him of how much he would be paid upon successful completion of the mission, so in the end, Morozov had agreed.

The whole process of photographing all the pages took almost ten minutes, during which time he regularly paused to listen for movement upstairs. After finishing taking all the pictures, he gently lifted the acrylic panes up and out of the display case and put them inside a tailormade padded hardcase which he retrieved from his backpack. The panes were surprisingly heavy, hard and completely inflexible. Whoever had placed the pages inside the panes clearly knew what they were doing.

Morozov exited the secret room, closed the door, walked back through the wine cellar and proceeded quietly back up the winding staircase. At the top, he turned left towards the door to the outside, from where he had entered less than half an hour earlier.

'Stop right there, buddy,' said a tense voice behind him.

Morozov's head snapped round to see a guard standing in the doorway to an adjacent room at the end of the hallway. He was holding a sandwich in his left hand and had a surprised and nervous look on his face.

In one lightning-fast movement, Morozov whipped out his pistol, cocked it and pointed it at the guard. The guard instinctively began reaching for his firearm, which was sitting in a holster strapped to his chest.

'Don't,' said Morozov tersely, and took half a step forward, aiming his pistol at the guard's head.

The guard seemed to hesitate, but then decided to take his chances on the intruder's gun being a harmless replica meant to scare off people like him. In a split second his hand darted to his gun and he pulled it out in front of himself to open fire.

Morozov's pistol produced two pops in quick succession, and both bullets found their mark on the guard's forehead. His head jerked backwards, and then he collapsed onto the floor. Morozov quickly moved to where the guard had fallen and stood over him with his gun pointing down at him.

'Stupid bastard,' he whispered and shook his head.

His mission had been to enter undetected and to leave no trace of his presence. Clearly, that was not going to happen now. He turned his head slowly from one side to the other, attempting to pick up the sound of anyone else approaching. Apparently, no one else had heard their altercation or the sound of the guard hitting the floor.

Morozov briefly considered dragging the body outside, but there was no way of disposing of it, and there was already blood all over the floor, so he instead decided to leave. He had accomplished his main objective, so there was no reason to hang around any longer.

He exited the mansion, and as soon as he was outside he initiated the upload of the image files from the camera to a secure server via the local mobile phone network. He then retraced his steps to the back of the estate and slipped back out through the hole in the overgrown barbed wire fence. Less than an hour later he was back at the safehouse, where he would be paid a visit by Pierre Dubois the next morning.

★          ★          ★

George Frost and Emily Scott were inside the underground ZOE Technologies research facility in upstate New York. Sitting in Frost's windowless office, they were observing real-time footage of an embryo on his computer monitor. The embryo was created using the DNA they had extracted from their latest specimen, and by far the most prominent feature was the small but clearly visible rhythmic contraction at the centre of the screen.

'This is incredible,' said Scott. 'Are you seeing this?'

'This is exceptional,' Frost replied, barely able to take his eyes off the screen. 'Much better than we had hoped for.'

Scott nodded. 'I never imagined this would carry over so seamlessly from the Peritas program. How old is it now? Something like forty hours?'

'Yes,' said Frost. 'Thereabouts. During normal development, this would have taken at least four weeks, but the change to the RX-7 gene has accelerated growth by a factor of at least twenty, perhaps even more.'

'Holy shit,' breathed Scott. 'We actually did it.' Then she looked at Frost. 'I mean, *you* did it.'

Frost sat back in his office chair, eyes still locked on the screen.

'Well. I suppose it was a team effort,' he said, sounding preoccupied.

'It's a shame we can't go public with this,' smirked Scott. 'It has Nobel Prize written all over it.'

Frost immediately turned his head sharply and looked sternly at her, his eyes narrowing and his lips pressed together. His demeanour had changed in an instant.

'Don't even think about that,' he said tersely. Then he seemed to relax somewhat again. 'We're not here for accolades. Plus, we're not even halfway there. We need the specimen out of the artificial womb and into the vat if we're going to grow it to full size. And after that, the real work starts. No one has ever even attempted this, so we're going in blind. There are literally hundreds of things that can go wrong, and there's no guarantee that the end product will even be useful. We have a long way to go.'

'Understood, sir,' said Scott sounding contrite. 'I'm sorry for being flippant. I fully understand where we are and what we need to do to succeed. I won't let you down.'

'You had better not,' said Frost and rose. 'Now get back to your desk. We need to get the next one ready.'

'Yes, sir,' replied Scott and nodded. 'I'll get right on it.'

Then she left Frost's office and returned to her cubicle to ready the next sample. Frost sat back down and picked up his phone, dialling a number he only ever called when he really needed to.

'Mr Ackerman?' he said. 'It's Frost. I have some good news. The embryo is performing significantly better than expected. RX-7 seems to be the key. Yes, sir. We will continue as planned, but we may have to bring forward our schedule. The rate of growth is unprecedented. I think we've cracked it. Yes, sir. I will keep you updated. Thank you, sir. Goodbye.'

# SIX

It was a bright and sunny but slightly chilly day in London when Andrew and Fiona got out of their cab at University College London, where a meeting with Professor McIntyre had been arranged. McIntyre was a leading researcher at the UCL Genetics Institute, and as Andrew and Fiona entered his office on the 3rd floor of the main building facing the university courtyard, he was barely visible, sitting at his desk behind stacks of books and research papers.

He was a short portly man with spectacles and a moustache, and his hair had long ago given up the fight against baldness. He was wearing a white shirt with thin blue stripes and a dark blue tie with white spots. His trousers were a light beige colour and quite baggy, and his brown leather shoes had clearly seen better days.

As he spotted the two guests entering his domain, he jumped up and shuffled around the corner of the desk with an outstretched hand and a wide smile.

'Dreadfully sorry about the mess in here,' he said, sounding like this was his standard opening remark whenever anyone entered his office for the first time.

'It looks like chaos, but I know where everything is. Not a big fan of computers, I must admit. I like to keep things up here,' he smiled and tapped the side of his head. 'Anyway. I'm sorry to be waffling. I am Professor McIntyre, and you must be Mr Sterling and Miss Keane.'

Andrew smiled and took the professor's hand. It was warm and slightly damp.

'Professor,' said Andrew. 'Thank you for seeing us.'

'Please,' said McIntyre and motioned towards a small seating area opposite his desk. 'Sit. Can I get you anything? A cup of tea perhaps?'

Andrew was about the decline when Fiona cut in.

'I'd love some coffee,' she said, and smiled.

McIntyre pointed at her jovially. 'One coffee. And for you?' he said, looking at Andrew.

'Coffee is fine, thanks,' said Andrew.

'Great,' said McIntyre, and stuck his head out into the corridor. 'Brenda, could we have three coffees, please? Thank you so much.'

'Right,' said McIntyre and sat down across from them, his hands clasped together. 'What can I do for you?'

Andrew looked at Fiona and smiled. 'I'll defer to you on this. You're the scientist here.'

'Well,' said Fiona. 'In a nutshell, we're here in the hope that you could provide us with some insights into genomics and genetic engineering, specifically the CRISPR technology. We're working on a case which requires us to have some basic understanding of what those things actually are, and how they might be used.'

'We're not at liberty to reveal very much about the case itself,' said Andrew. 'But I think I am permitted to say that we are involved in an investigation of a company that may be utilising genetic engineering in a way that may not be legal and could potentially put people at risk. Although to be frank, we're still trying to discover exactly how they might be breaking the law. You might consider our visit here a basic factfinding mission. Something to help us put the results of our investigation into some sort of context.'

Professor McIntyre nodded pensively.

'I see,' he said. 'Well, my area of expertise is mainly in applied genetic therapeutics, but that does require me to keep abreast of the latest research in other areas as much as I can, especially in the field of genetic sequencing and gene editing. And it is a very exciting area, I can tell you.'

'So, what are genomics and genetics exactly?' asked Fiona.

'In a nutshell,' replied McIntyre 'Genomics is simply the study of the body's genes, in terms of their biochemical role and the way they influence and govern how the body develops and functions. Genetics, on the other hand, is concerned with understanding heredity in living organisms through the study of gene variations and mutations.'

'If you don't mind,' said Andrew. 'Could you just explain what a gene actually is?'

'Certainly,' replied McIntyre. 'But let me first begin by explaining what a genome is, and then I will move on to genes. It makes more sense that way.'

'Thank you,' smiled Fiona. 'Whichever way you think is best.'

'Ok,' said McIntyre. 'Essentially, a genome is the entire collection of genes that an animal or a plant or a human being possesses. It is an organism's complete set of DNA. It contains all the genetic information that is required to make a particular organism. Taking us humans as an example, inside the nucleus of each of our cells are a set of 23 chromosomes, which are basically coiled up structures made from long DNA molecules. These chromosomes dictate how a human body is constructed, how it looks, and how it functions at a biochemical level. The DNA molecules themselves are extremely long and complex, yet simple structures. They are made of two twisting paired strands, famously referred to as the Double Helix, which I am sure you have heard about.'

Fiona nodded. 'Yes.'

'Good,' said McIntyre. 'Each of the two DNA strands is made up of just four very simple and very tiny chemical units, called nucleotide bases. They each consist of just a handful of atoms joined up in these nucleotide molecules based around a simple sugar molecule, and you can think of them as the genetic alphabet. The four nucleotide bases are adenine, which we just call A, thymine called T, guanine called G, and cytosine called C. These four bases on opposite strands of the double helix pair up in a very specific way. An A always pairs with a T, and a C always pairs with a G. The order of these letters of the genetic alphabet determines the meaning of the information encoded in a specific section of a DNA molecule, in the same way that the order of Roman letters in our alphabet determines the meaning of a word. And each unique section, which determines a specific trait in a living organism, is what we call a gene.'

'I see,' said Fiona. 'And those genes or sections of DNA decide everything about us?'

'Well,' said McIntyre. 'Pretty much everything in terms of physiology and biochemistry. Of course, there is much more to a person than that, but basically, you're right. Now, I said that all of this was simple yet complex. And the reason is this. There are about twenty-five thousand genes in the human genome, and each one of those genes directs the production of proteins. The way this works is that an enzyme in a cell's nucleus copies the information contained in a gene into so-called messenger ribonucleic acid or mRNA. This mRNA then travels out of the nucleus into the cell's cytoplasm, which is a solution that is enclosed by the cell's outer membrane. Here, something called a ribosome reads the information that it contains. The ribosome then pieces together small amino-acid molecules to make complex proteins, which make up the structures in our bodies, such as tissue and organs. They also regulate how the body functions and are essential for the body to develop and grow.'

'I see,' said Fiona. 'It really is rather complex, isn't it?'

'And there's another reason why this ends up being quite a complex area,' said McIntyre. 'Even though there are only four types of nucleotides or bases, and even though these bases pair up in a very limited way, each DNA strand is incredibly long. Again, taking the human genome as an example, Chromosome 1 alone contains some 249 million base pairs.'

'Wow,' said Fiona. 'That's a lot.'

'Yes,' chuckled McIntyre. 'And that is just one out of 23 chromosomes needed to construct a human being. For a sense of scale, imagine if you were to write a book that contained just the information encoded into Chromosome 1. If you were to fill the pages with the letters A, G, T and C, with no spaces between them, you could fit around 1500 characters on one page. In order for the book to encompass all the information contained in just Chromosome 1, the book would have to be 166,000 pages long. That is equivalent to eighty Bibles. Or almost as many characters as are contained in the latest edition of the entire Encyclopaedia Britannica. And again, that is just one out of twenty-three chromosomes. In total, there are around 3.2 billion base pairs in the human genome, and a copy of that information sits inside every single cell in our bodies.'

'That's really incredible,' said Fiona, visibly impressed. 'And an absolutely staggering amount of information. How on earth do geneticists know which gene does what? Surely, that knowledge must be a prerequisite for doing any sort of meaningful genetic engineering, right?'

'Very good question,' smiled McIntyre. 'It took scientists a very long time to map out the human genome. And both before and since, the entire genomes of many plants and animals have been mapped out. And as for what each base pair in each gene inside each chromosome actually does, and what might happen if that base pair was changed, that is often a trial-and-error process, although there are various techniques for determining these effects. For starters, we often know which gene or section of the DNA's double helix a particular base pair belongs to, so already there we have some sense of what we are dealing with.'

'I suppose that brings us neatly on to gene editing,' said Fiona. 'And CRISPR in particular. Could you help us understand precisely what it is, and what is possible with that technology?'

'Of course,' said McIntyre. 'Gene editing is exactly what it sounds like. It is the deliberate editing of certain genes in a DNA molecule, in order to change the way those genes operate. We basically change the way the gene functions, in terms of what protein it produces. This is called a gene's protein expression, and a change to this has the potential to completely change the way an organism looks and functions.'

'And CRISPR is just a technique for editing genes?' said Fiona.

'That's correct,' replied McIntyre. 'Specifically, the so-called CRISPR/Cas9 technique has proven incredibly powerful over the past several years. The acronym CRISPR stands for Clustered Regularly Interspaced Short Palindromic Repeats, meaning repeating sequences of DNA found in certain bacteria, which those bacteria have obtained from previous viral infections, and which they themselves then use in order to detect and destroy future viral infections. It is a type of acquired viral immunity. You can think of it as a library of remedies that certain bacteria have included in their own DNA, which holds recipes for how to defeat infections from specific viruses in the future. Every time a bacterium is invaded by a virus, a new book is slotted into the long bookshelf that is the bacterium's DNA, thereby allowing the bacterium to remember how to defeat that particular virus. So, bacteria have this adaptive immune system that stores information about previous viral infections. The term Cas9 just refers to the protein inside the bacterium that actually performs the editing.'

'That sounds intriguing,' said Fiona. 'How exactly does it do that?'

'Well,' said McIntyre, clearly relishing the opportunity to explain his passion to an attentive audience. 'Imagine if a bacterium, which on the scale of proteins and DNA molecules are huge things, becomes infected by a virus, which itself is a tiny molecular structure by comparison. These bacteria have evolved methods that copy the virus' genetic information and insert it into its own DNA. This may sound strange, but as I mentioned it allows the bacterium to effectively combat future infections from that particular virus. And it is this ability of the bacterium to copy foreign DNA and insert it into its own DNA that we can leverage to target and edit the DNA inside a living cell in any organism. The CRISPR/Cas9 technique simply uses the DNA manipulation abilities of these bacteria to cut, edit and stitch together sections of DNA in an extremely precise manner. They effectively allow us to modify individual genes by precisely editing specific base pairs in those genes. Without going into too much detail, the essence of it is to feed the Cas9 protein a tailored RNA sequence, which then functions as an instruction to the Cas9 protein to edit a specific strand of DNA in a particular way.'

'Fascinating,' said Fiona. 'Could you give us an example of how this has been applied?'

'Of course,' said McIntyre. 'I think it is important to reflect on the fact that virtually every human ailment has some basis in our genes. Even if an illness isn't directly caused by hereditary genetic factors, there are many people who are predisposed to developing certain illnesses because of their particular genetic makeup. But some of the most promising areas for genetic engineering with CRISPR/Cas9 in which there are already clinical trials under way, are in the treatment of various viral infections, cardiovascular diseases, immune system disorders, hemophilia, as well as several cancer-related immunotherapies.'

'Has anything progressed to actual treatment,' asked Fiona.

'Yes,' replied McIntyre. 'As an example of the application of this technology, I can briefly mention how a team of scientists have already applied it to the correction of disease-causing mutations, specifically sickle cell anaemia which you may have heard about. The disease is caused by something as simple as a single base pair, where the two bases A and T have been swapped. This results in the wrong protein expression, which causes red blood cells to be misshaped. This in turn causes blockages of blood flow to nerves and organs, and it can actually end up being fatal. By reversing the position of the two bases A and T in the double-stranded DNA molecule inside the embryo, which is easily done using CRISPR/Cas9, the mutation is corrected and the disease is effectively cured. Or rather, it will never develop once the embryo matures into a fully grown human being.'

'That is astonishing,' smiled Fiona, clearly taken with what McIntyre was presenting.

'It is,' smiled McIntyre. 'And with the emergence of the field of pharmacogenomics, which basically involves using information about an individual patient's specific DNA make-up to tailor treatments, there really does seem to be an almost limitless number of applications.'

'I guess some of the diseases you mentioned are some of the really big-ticket items in terms of health care expenditure,' said Fiona.

'That's right,' said McIntyre. 'Combined, they afflict hundreds of millions of people across the world, so the potential public health impact from these efforts is enormous. And as you mention, it could possibly save billions on national health care budgets.'

'I am assuming the potential for profits is similarly enormous,' interjected Andrew.

'We try not to pay too much attention to that here,' said McIntyre demurely. 'But I am sure that whoever develops these drugs first, stand to make significant amounts of money.'

'We recently attended a talk at the British Museum,' said Fiona. 'And someone mentioned that UCL is involved in an anti-mosquito effort using

CRISPR technology. What exactly was he talking about?'

'Well, it is a slightly novel and unusual approach to the whole thing, but basically, it revolves around so-called gene drivers, which ensure that a genetic modification is inherited by all subsequent offspring. In this case, we introduced a gene into the type of mosquito that is responsible for carrying the malaria parasite, rendering it unable to lay eggs. During trials, we found that if both parents of a mosquito carried the gene then the entire population was wiped out after seven generations.'

'Crikey,' said Andrew. 'So, in effect, it is less about actually treating an illness than it is about wiping out the carrier of that illness. Parasite genocide, you might call it.'

'Yes,' replied McIntyre. 'As effective as it is, or perhaps precisely because it is so impactful, there are some serious ethical implications of the gene driver approach.'

'Yes,' said Fiona, looking disturbed. 'Just so I understand. You're saying any changes to DNA in an embryo will become a permanent trait of that organism, and therefore be carried over to its offspring?'

'That is correct,' said McIntyre.

'So, if tomorrow I was able to introduce a change to all of the world's embryos currently in the wombs of their mothers so that their eye colour would be blue, then suddenly all future generations of the entire human race would have blue eyes.'

'Theoretically, yes,' replied McIntyre. 'At least until some mutation occurred naturally that then caused an embryo to develop brown or green eyes.'

'That is fascinating,' said Fiona. 'And also terrifying. We're really talking about changing the very nature of what it means to be human. Taken to its extreme, we're effectively able to completely re-design our own species. I shudder to think about what the Nazis would have done with genetic engineering and gene drivers if those technologies had been available to them. Both in terms of breeding new traits into the Aryan race and in terms of suppressing the procreation of other races. It does make me worry about who might employ these technologies in human populations in the future.'

Andrew nodded sagely. 'I think it is also fair to say that, at least theoretically, it could have some extremely worrying military applications. Imagine if a nation decided to go all-in on this and push this technology to its limits in just a generation or two.'

McIntyre began to look uncomfortable. 'Uhm. Let me just stress that we're not involved in anything remotely like that here,' he said, smiling nervously. 'It is also worth mentioning that it takes considerable time, effort, and funding to fully develop and roll out new therapeutic drugs. Most commercial products stemming from genome-based research are probably at least ten to fifteen years away. And even after a drug has been developed, the regulatory approval process itself often takes many years. But clearly, all of these issues leave this particular field of research with a very profound philosophical question. What are the limits to the way we should allow ourselves to change the very nature of the human race? If we start editing human DNA and the human beings that result from those changes have children of their own, where do we draw the line? At what point, if any, will we find ourselves in a situation where a legitimate question could be raised as to whether the being in question is still really human? We do very much share those concerns here, and you might remember that just a few years ago a Chinese scientist used CRISPR to edit DNA in the embryos of what was to become two girls, in order to essentially knock out the gene called CCR5. This particular gene plays a key role in HIV infection, and the girls' father was HIV positive.'

'I think I read something about that at the time,' said Fiona. 'What do you think about that whole affair?'

McIntyre seemed to wince as he considered how to reply.

'There is no doubt that part of the motivation for going ahead with the edit of CCR5 was noble,' he said. 'But the reality is that the consequences of changes to this gene are not well understood, either in humans or other primates. So, there could easily have been serious unintended consequences. And I think the wider point here is that there has to be some sort of global regulation. The World Health Organization has been pushing for a moratorium on the editing of human embryos, sperm or eggs, the so-called germline editing, and for the creation of a register of anyone engaged in the application of CRISPR to human genetics. But I think it stands to reason that it will be difficult if not impossible to effectively police and enforce control of this field of research, simply because of the power it holds and the potential for profit it represents.'

'On that point, Professor McIntyre,' said Fiona. 'If for a moment you could imagine yourself as a researcher, not at a university but in some sort of commercial entity. And if you had no constraints on your work, either financial, legal or ethical. What would you be able to do?'

He smiled uncertainly as his eyes darted to Andrew and then back to Fiona.

'You're talking about ZOE Technologies, aren't you?' he said, looking concerned. 'I saw what happened on the news, by the way. Dreadful business.'

'Possibly,' said Fiona hesitantly and glanced at Andrew. 'As Andrew said earlier, we're not really in a position to give you any details, but yes, we are looking into the deaths of Alistair Balfour and Peter Lambert.'

'Yes. I see,' said McIntyre.

'Are you familiar with the research of Peter Lambert?' asked Fiona.

'Yes, I am,' replied McIntyre. 'I didn't know him personally, but both he and the ZOE research director Fabian Ackerman have been well known in the field of genomics and genetic engineering for several years now. By all accounts, they were developing some of the most advanced gene-editing techniques we've ever seen. Although I must admit that the transparency of their research efforts was some way off what would normally be expected from a university or even a company listed on the stock exchange. I suppose that's part and parcel of being a privately held company. You're not really accountable to anyone, and you can't be compelled to reveal anything about what you are doing.'

'Do you know anything about the owner of ZOE Technologies?' asked Andrew. 'Supposedly a man by the name Alexis Galanis, sometimes referred to as Alex.'

'Not at all,' said McIntyre and shook his head. 'That is to say, nothing beyond what one can read in the gossip columns.'

'Are you concerned about what private entities like ZOE Technologies are doing?' asked Fiona.

Professor McIntyre sighed and hesitated for a moment before replying.

'To be honest,' he said. 'Some of us have had our eye on ZOE Technologies for a while. They are clearly pushing the boundaries of genetic engineering and by all accounts their work is impressive, but transparency as far as what exactly it is they are doing is lacking, and their ultimate research goals remain quite opaque.'

Fiona nodded. 'If what their CEO said turns out to be true, they are on the cusp of actually launching bespoke pets as a commercial product.'

'Yes, I read about that,' said McIntyre. 'It is entirely possible that they have indeed managed to genetically tailor various types of pets, although it is likely to be a limited number at this stage.'

'Why do you say that?' asked Andrew.

'Simply because a prerequisite for this sort of thing would be a complete mapping of each animal's genome, and then significant research into discovering which genes actually govern what trait.

And after that, I would imagine a significant amount of work would have to go into perfecting the deliberate tweaking of those genes, without inadvertently triggering other side effects.'

Andrew cleared his throat and brought up his hand in front of himself, fingers outstretched as if grasping for a way to verbalise his thoughts.

'So, if we can just step back for a moment,' he said. 'What you're saying is that we humans now have the ability to target and edit at will any base pair in any gene in any living being.'

'Basically, yes,' replied McIntyre.

'But,' continued Andrew, 'we don't know exactly what each base pair does, is that correct?'

'That's right,' said McIntyre. 'Although we have mapped out the entire genome of humans and many other species, we are still a very long way from understanding precisely what each base pair, or even each gene actually does. And we are even further away from mapping out precisely what a change to one of those genes will mean for the organism.'

'And I suppose,' said Fiona, 'by extension, that means that if we do start playing around with these base pairs and genes using techniques like CRISPR, the results will invariably be unpredictable.'

'In many cases, yes,' replied McIntyre. 'But just to reiterate, there are no efforts underway to edit human DNA in the way that ZOE Technologies is currently editing animal DNA. And certainly, here at UCL our focus is entirely on therapeutic goals.'

'But as you just said,' interjected Andrew. 'ZOE Technologies has already gone down this road with the editing of the genes of pets. What's to stop them from moving on to human DNA?'

McIntyre shifted uncomfortably in his seat. 'Look,' he said, and spread out his hands. 'Theoretically, and apart from the ethical constraints that any good scientist would place upon themselves, there is nothing to stop someone from editing the genome of a human embryo. But the implications are obviously potentially huge, and I am not aware of anyone even contemplating doing that at this point in time. On top of that, there are practical reasons why this is not as straightforward as it might seem.'

'What do you mean?' asked Andrew.

'Let me give you an example,' replied McIntyre. 'Several years ago, scientists discovered a gene in mice that is linked to memory. By modifying this gene, the scientists were able to greatly improve the memory of mice, but it also caused a significant and unexpected increase in their sensitivity to pain. So, simply identifying some function of a gene and then beginning to edit it can have significant and unpredictable negative side effects.'

'But if someone did in fact decide to proceed with the editing of the human genome,' said Fiona, 'what would you then say would be possible in terms of attribute changes?'

McIntyre shrugged. 'Honestly? The only limit is your imagination. In some ways, you could say that these gene-editing techniques have given humanity, for the very first time, almost limitless power to control the evolution of a species, including us, Homo Sapiens. But in answer to your question, theoretically you could tweak a human embryo's

DNA to cause it to develop larger muscles, better memory, higher IQ, better emotional control or the suppression of emotions altogether, edit out susceptibility to diseases, make people taller, change their hair colour, make their hands larger and their feet smaller, their necks longer, possibly extend life spans or speed up the growth of a foetus. There is virtually no limit. But I think we can all agree that we don't want to live in a world where that sort of thing happens as a matter of course. And I feel confident that governments around the world will be only too keen to legislate and regulate this area.'

Fiona paused for a brief moment, contemplating the full implications of what McIntyre had just said.

'Well, I am sure the three of us here can agree on that,' she said. 'But I am also convinced that there are people or governments or organisations out there that would love to have a free hand in the application of these tools.'

'I agree,' said Andrew. 'I would be very surprised if there aren't already efforts underway to fully leverage these techniques to achieve political or military goals. And I am willing to bet that some of those efforts are completely free of things like moral or ethical considerations, or even government oversight.'

McIntyre sat for a moment looking as if somehow the meeting had not gone the way he had expected.

'I am sorry,' smiled Andrew finally. 'I don't mean to be such a cynic, but I am afraid I am slightly damaged by the nature of my job. I am sure our concerns are probably overblown, at least in the short term. I hope you understand that it is part of our responsibility to consider all angles in relation to our investigation.'

'Of course,' exclaimed McIntyre, now appearing somewhat appeased. 'I understand fully. I do hope I have been of some help to you today.'

'Oh, absolutely,' said Fiona placatingly. 'This really helped us a lot. I think we now have at least some context for evaluating the results of our investigation, so thank you very much.'

'Yes, thank you, Professor,' said Andrew, and rose to shake McIntyre's hand. 'This has been extremely useful.'

Ten minutes later, Andrew and Fiona were back outside in the cold crisp air. They walked along the pavement for a few moments before speaking, both of them pondering what the professor had said.

'Crikey,' said Andrew. 'That was intense. I feel like I need to lie down.'

Fiona smiled. 'Yes, that chap really knows his stuff. And it was quite a lot to take in, but it was so interesting, don't you think?'

'Absolutely,' replied Andrew. 'Although I am not sure if it brings us any closer to understanding what ZOE Technologies' role in this whole mystery might be. I guess we need to find out more about the company and its enigmatic owner.'

'By all accounts, that is going to be difficult,' said Fiona. 'Apparently, he is quite the recluse. I haven't even been able to find a photo of him anywhere.'

'We might have to see if we can apply a bit of pressure,' said Andrew. 'As tragic as the murders of Balfour, Lambert and the two police officers were, we might just be able to use that as leverage. I'll have a word with Strickland and see what we can do.'

# SEVEN

Tim Dawson slowed down slightly as he approached the San Ysidro border crossing into Tijuana, Mexico. One of the busiest border crossings in the world, it processes around fifty million people per year, which equates to tens of thousands of vehicles and pedestrians every day, and today was as busy as any other day. Hundreds of cars were filing slowly into six southbound lanes that snaked their way towards the inspection point, where border police were carrying out vehicle spot checks at random, and checking the passports of everyone intending to cross into Mexico.

Dawson had spent the last four hours in the car driving south along Interstate 5 out of Oakland through Los Angeles and San Diego, to arrive at San Ysidro just after 5 pm. He had spent most of the journey trying to come to terms with the way in which his life had been turned upside down over the past few days. When Peter Lambert had initially asked him and Hicks to the bar for a drink, he had no idea what he was about to be told. Part of him now wished that he had never gone to that bar. If he had remained blissfully ignorant of Lambert's findings inside the secret ZOE Technologies servers, then perhaps everything would have been alright. He would have been at home in his comfortable apartment, watering his plants, sipping cups of tea and watching Netflix.

It all seemed completely surreal, but here he really was, attempting to escape into Mexico and away from ZOE Technologies and what was likely to be a corrupt police force. If he was completely honest with himself, he had to admit to having had his reservations about joining ZOE Technologies to begin with. There was no doubt that the company was one of the hottest places to work in the field of genetics, but he too had heard all the rumours about how the frantic pace of research at the company was at the expense of employee health and sanity, with exceptionally long working hours expected of everyone. Meeting Fabian Ackerman had also given him cause for concern. The Swiss national had seemed completely devoid of emotion, and he had a cold calculating look to him that Dawson had found deeply uncomfortable. Like a spider eyeing up prey trapped in its net.

In truth, the only reason Dawson had decided to quell the internal voices telling him to pass on the opportunity to work for ZOE Technologies was his meeting with Peter Lambert. His prospective boss had come across as highly ambitious and probably with a slightly inflated ego, but Dawson had felt that deep down Lambert was a decent human being who he would be able to trust and who could provide an exceptional career path to the right candidate. On his first day, he had been surprised to discover that Lambert had actually hired two candidates, himself and Sam Hicks. But the two junior team members had jelled instantly, and the team of three had quickly made huge progress in their joint research. All of that seemed like a distant memory now.

As he pulled up to the small shack at the end of lane 6, he was greeted by a surly-looking middle-aged official from the Mexican border police.

'Hey. How's it going?' asked Dawson, trying to sound relaxed and cheerful.

'Passport,' said the man, barely looking at Dawson and beckoning with his hand for the passport. Inside the shack, a small TV was showing a baseball game.

Dawson handed over his passport, cleared his throat and ran his fingers through his hair, but then suddenly felt very self-conscious. The border official looked at his passport and then glanced up at him with a suspicious look on his face.

'Are you ok, sir?' he asked.

'Yes, I am fine,' said Dawson, doing his best to sound calm. 'Just had a busy day. I need to get to a wedding later this evening, and I am a little late.'

'I see,' said the guard, taking another look at Dawson's passport. 'Well, I hope you make it, sir. Have a nice evening.'

The guard then handed Dawson his passport back and waved him through.

'You too, sir. Thank you,' said Dawson, putting the car into gear.

He found himself looking at the small shack in the rear-view mirror as he slowly pulled away and headed into Tijuana, a city of more than one and a half million people. It was known for its violence and drug dealing, but right now Dawson would rather be on this side of the border, even though he did not have a plan for what to do next.

After a few seconds, he involuntarily breathed a sigh of relief and switched on the radio. It was CBS News Radio, and he had dropped into a world news segment. What he heard immediately made his ears prick up.

'… and this is not just something that is relevant to California,' said the female reporter. 'This story has reverberated around the world where many global companies have now been forced to ask themselves whether their security measures are sufficient to protect senior management from violent attacks from people with mental disorders. There has also been a reaction in the financial markets where several other pharmaceutical and biotech companies saw a brief sell-off, but most have now recovered their losses. ZOE Technologies, which has its headquarters right here in California, was expecting to go public on the New York Stock Exchange later this year, but those plans could possibly be shelved. We'll have to wait and see what the company says. Meanwhile, the spokesperson for the Metropolitan Police in London, Chief Superintendent Emma Worthington, told reporters today that there had been no arrests yet, but that police were pursuing several leads. And that's the end of news from around the world, so let's move on to sports. Jimmy, what have you got for us today?'

'Worthington,' said Dawson, as he switched off the radio and stared blankly out through the windscreen.

Then a plan slowly began forming in his head.

★          ★          ★

The apartment in the elegant yet quaint 5th Paris arrondissement known as the Latin Quarter, was on the 4th floor of a building on Rue Valette, just across from the Bibliotheque Sainte Genevieve. The 18th-century building had tall solid oak double doors leading to a courtyard from where most of its apartments could be accessed.

It was just after 8 pm in the French capital, and a light drizzle was falling on the city, making the streets and the cars glisten under the streetlights. As Dubois pressed the buzzer next to the door, a gaggle of students exited the library across the street and made their way noisily south towards Place de Panthéon and the enormous mausoleum building bearing the same name and housing the remains of notable French citizens. Inspired by the churches of St. Peter's Basilica in Rome and St. Paul's Cathedral in London, the imposing domed building holds the tombs of such famous figures as Voltaire, Rousseau, Alexandre Dumas and Marie Curie. Dubois had passed it on the way to the safehouse, and it never failed to instil in him a sense of pride in his French heritage.

'Oui?' said a gruff voice on the intercom.

'C'est moi. Pierre Dubois. Open up.'

A few seconds later, the door buzzer growled angrily as the person in the apartment on the 4th floor unlocked the heavy oak doors to let Dubois inside. He pushed them open and entered. Inside, he made his way to the staircase on the left and proceeded up to the apartment as the oak door slammed shut behind him with a loud thud that reverberated through the courtyard. There was only one apartment on the 4th floor, and it was owned by a chain of offshore holding companies somewhere in the Caribbean, making it virtually impossible for anyone to trace the real owner.

As Dubois approached the landing on the 4th floor, he heard the reinforced door to the apartment unlock. As he looked up, he saw that the door had been opened just a crack, and that a pair of dark eyes were looking out at him.

Upon recognising the Frenchman, Yevgeni Morozov opened the door fully to let him in. Dubois could see that the Russian had a silenced pistol in his hand, which he was holding pointing down and behind himself as he opened the door.

'Come on,' said Morozov. 'Hurry up. Get inside.'

Dubois didn't like taking instructions from Morozov, who was technically beneath him in the informal hierarchy of their joint venture, but given that the Russian was holding a gun, he decided to bottle his irritation and let it slide.

Once inside, Dubois and Morozov walked into the living room where Dubois sat down on one of the plush dark purple velvet sofas and pulled out his phone. He pretended to check his messages, but quickly switched on the voice recorder and then placed the phone on the low brass and glass coffee table in front of him. If there was one thing he had learnt in this business, it was to never trust anyone and to make sure he was always covering his back. If some disagreement should arise between them, potentially jeopardising his relationship with his benefactor, he wanted to make sure that he could prove what had been said.

'So,' he said, and smiled vacuously at Morozov. 'You managed to retrieve the items?'

'Of course,' said Morozov, and sat down across from the Frenchman on the sofa opposite.

'And did everything go according to plan?'

'Mostly, yes,' said Morozov and shrugged. 'The entry codes worked and I got the book, but one of the guards got stupid and tried to play the hero. I had to take him out.'

Dubois looked at him disapprovingly and furrowed his brow. 'Take. Him. Out,' he repeated slowly. 'What does that mean exactly?'

The Russian took out a packet of cigarettes from his shirt pocket, slotted one of them in the left side of his mouth and shrugged. 'Let's just say he is done stealing oxygen from the rest of us.'

Dubois frowned. 'That was not part of the plan. You understand that, right?'

Morozov looked at him frigidly. 'Just because I am a soldier doesn't mean I don't have a brain. The guy was going for his gun, so it was him or me. And if I had not ended him right there, you would not have acquired the book.'

Dubois sighed. 'Right. Well, just as long as they can't connect you to the scene. I can't say I care whether you spend the next ten years in prison, but if the police somehow find a way to nail you for this, then I would also be at risk.'

'How touching,' smirked Morozov sarcastically.

'Anyway,' said Dubois, now sounding more placating. 'I doubt this particular gentleman would consider inviting the police into his house, if you know what I mean.'

Morozov chuckled. 'I had a feeling that might be the case.'

'Ok,' said Dubois and rose. 'Let's not waste time. Show me the item, please.'

Morozov nodded and walked to a shallow cupboard mounted on one of the walls of the living room. Here he opened the two wooden doors to reveal a safe with a digital lock embedded into the cement wall. He quickly entered a six-digit combination, after which a brief beep could be heard. Then he opened the safe's door and extracted the small metal suitcase that had been specially constructed for Morozov's job. He carried it over to a table and placed it there, turned the dials on the locks to the right combination and snapped the two locks open. Then he opened the lid of the case.

'There you go,' he said, and took a step back. 'Knock yourself out.'

Dubois approached the table slowly with an expectant look on his face. Moments like this never got dull. Although he had partly lost his reverence for antique items, the thrill of seeing and perhaps even possessing an item that very few people had ever laid eyes on was undiminished.

Inside the foam-padded case was a cut-out where the panes of toughened acrylic containing the yellowed pages fit neatly. Even though the pages were well protected inside the vacuum-sealed acrylic, Dubois lifted the first encased page out as gingerly as he could and placed it carefully on the table next to the case. Then he leaned over it, studying it silently for a couple of minutes. Then he used his phone to take a picture.

'Everything ok?' asked Morozov, hovering over Dubois's shoulder.

Dubois's turned his head partly towards the Russian, his reverie momentarily interrupted.

'Patience,' he said, sounding irritated. 'You'll get your money if everything checks out. Don't worry.'

'Fine,' said Morozov, and walked over to the sofa where he sat down again.

Dubois extracted the next page, placed it on top of the first one and took another picture. He methodically kept inspecting and photographing the ancient pages in this manner until he got to one near the bottom of the case, which had a blotchy dark brown stain of some sort that covering much of the lower righthand corner.

'There you are,' he whispered as he put the page on the table and looked closely at the stain. He took another picture, and then put his head right down to the page, studying it for a long time. Then he smiled.

'Beautiful,' he finally said, and then he stood back up.

'What is this thing anyway?' asked Morozov, only sounding vaguely interested.

'This *thing* is a diary,' said Dubois, a hint of derision in his voice. 'Very old. Which why its pages have been placed inside these panes of hardened plastic. They have been completely sealed in there in order to prevent damage to them, and to stop the pages from decomposing.'

'How did you get the information about the location of the diary,' said Morozov lazily, and lit a cigarette. 'Seems like a strange thing for someone to keep hidden behind a wall in a wine cellar.'

'Well, it's potentially extremely valuable,' said Dubois. 'Our mutual benefactor attended a dinner party there, and the owner of the house, this oligarch who collects ancient relics, was apparently keen on showing it off. Human vanity is such a weakness. So easy to exploit.'

'Have you met him?' asked Morozov.

'Who?' replied Dubois.

'This *benefactor*,' said Morozov and waved his hand. 'The one who finances all this?'

'Yes, just once, several months ago,' said Dubois.

'Who was it? What was the meeting like?'

'Well,' said Dubois, suddenly seeming slightly on edge. 'We're not supposed to share information about this, but let's just say it wasn't what I had expected. The less you know, the better.'

'Alright, fine,' said Morozov. 'So, anyway. Who wrote the diary?'

Dubois glanced back at the Russian. He suddenly did not like all the questions.

'That's above your pay grade,' he said, and returned to inspecting the final pages in the case.

Morozov smirked indifferently.

'Suit yourself,' he said in his thick Russian accent, and shrugged. 'As long as the money keeps coming, I don't really care anyway.'

A few minutes later Dubois stood up again and placed his hands on his hips whilst looking at the stack of pages.

'Everything we need seems to be there,' he said. 'I will request the transfer now.'

He then pulled out a small laptop from his bag and placed it on the table next to the diary pages. After a few seconds it had booted up, and then he opened a secure account transfer app that had been coded for this specific purpose. He entered the passcode on the tiny keyboard, and after verifying an authentication message on his phone, he then proceeded to transfer the specified amount to an account in a private bank in Macau.

A few seconds later, Morozov's phone pinged. The Russian extracted it from his pocket and studied it for a few seconds.

'Excellent,' he said, and looked at Dubois. 'Pleasure doing business with you.'

Dubois grunted. *The pleasure was all yours,* he thought.

He neither liked nor trusted Morozov, and it seemed pretty obvious that the feeling was mutual. But he had to admit that the Russian was very good at what he did. And as long as the money from their benefactor kept coming, trust never really entered the equation. Dubois walked over and sat down across from Morozov again.

'I have another job for you,' he said. 'A job that requires your particular field of expertise, but something slightly more delicate this time. Retrieval of an item from a public place. A museum, to be exact.'

Morozov sat up and leaned forward, clearly interested. How could he not be, considering the amount of money he was being paid for these jobs?

'I am listening,' he said, and lit another cigarette.

'We need you to go to Cyprus,' said Dubois. 'There is a museum in Nicosia called The Cyprus Museum, and they hold in their basement a mummy that was unearthed on the island just a few years ago. I need you to enter the museum, make your way to the mummy and take a sample.'

Morozov looked dubiously at Dubois and tilted his head slightly to one side. 'A sample?'

'Yes,' said Dubois. 'Ideally a bone fragment, but if that is not possible then a tissue sample would do as well.'

'Ok,' said Morozov. 'Fine. I am not even going to ask what you need it for.'

'Good,' said Dubois, 'Because I wouldn't tell you anyway. I will be contacting you again via the usual channel to provide you with all the information you need about its location and what it will look like, so you'll be able to recognise it when you see it.'

'Fine,' replied Morozov. 'And when do you need this done?'

'Ideally without delay,' said Dubois. 'The museum is closed on Mondays, so you should attempt to retrieve the sample then.'

'Two days then?' asked Morozov. 'Not much time to prepare.'

'You'll find a way, I am sure,' smiled Dubois acerbically and tilted his head towards the bedroom. 'You should probably start packing.'

Morozov gave him a cold stare, and for a brief moment Dubois thought he might have crossed the line. Looking at the Russian's eyes, he could feel a cold chill running down his spine, but he reminded himself that Morozov was in it purely for the money. He was not going to blow his chances of another big pay-out just because he didn't like someone.

'I'll get there,' said Morozov with a hint of amusement in his voice. 'Don't you worry.'

Dubois rose and returned to the table where he carefully placed all of the pages back inside the foam padded case. The next step would be to have a small fragment of the diary carbon dated, and if the age of the diary fit with his assumptions about its provenance, he would then carefully extract a section of the bloodstained paper, after which his benefactor would proceed to perform DNA sequencing on the blood.

After leaving the safehouse on Rue Valette ten minutes later, Dubois decided to take a small detour towards the Pont de Sully bridge across the river Seine. It took him past the Sorbonne University campus, which was only a couple of hundred metres from Rue Valette. As he walked past the dark buildings with their lit-up windows, he spotted a couple of people walking in and out of the main entrance. They seemed to him strange mirrors of his past. After all, he used to be one of them. The archaeology department was just behind the main building, and he had spent more time there than he liked to think about.

As he watched the silhouettes of his former colleagues in the windows, he almost felt sorry for them now. Here they were, busily going about their lives, writing research papers for scientific journals, teaching students, doing fundamental research to advance their respective fields, and all of them no doubt convinced that they led interesting, fulfilling, and perhaps even meaningful lives. Yet, he now understood that they lived an existence in dull shades of grey, whereas he had opened the door to a world in full vibrant colour where there were no longer any limits to what he could do. No conventions to hold him back and no rules to keep him down.

Walking over the Pont de Sully and looking out over the Seine, he took a deep breath, greedily inhaling the chilly evening air. He felt so alive. More so than ever before.

*This is what most people never come to understand*, he mused to himself. *If you ignore the rules, the rules cease to exist. You are truly free.*

Liberté was what he had taken for himself, and once that had happened, he had never looked back.

As for Égalité, and Fraternité, that was something for ordinary people. They could have those. He was not interested.

# EIGHT

Andrew was walking through St. James's Park in London's West End when his phone rang. He pulled it out from the inside pocket of his dark navy-blue coat and saw that it was Colonel Strickland, so he quickly walked over to a bench.

'Sir,' he said, and sat down.

'Andrew,' said the colonel, sounding mildly distracted. 'How are you?'

'Not bad, sir,' replied Andrew. 'Is everything alright?'

'Yes,' said Strickland. 'There has been a bit of a development. As per your suggestion, we decided to lean on ZOE Technologies on account of the murders and the general PR fallout for the company after recent events, and they have now offered us a meeting. With the owner, Alex Galanis, no less.'

'Really?' said Andrew, sounding surprised. 'That is a bit unexpected.'

'Yes, I agree,' replied Strickland. 'But I suspect the pressure of the sudden media attention as well as the police investigation has put the company into damage control mode.'

'Yes, I think you're probably right there,' said Andrew. 'Especially with the company aiming for a stock market listing later this year. This whole debacle is really the last thing they need.'

'Precisely,' said Strickland. 'So, in the spirit of their newfound openness and cooperation, Alex Galanis has apparently offered us an in-person meeting, according to one of his assistants. But there's a catch.'

'Oh?' said Andrew. 'What is it?'

'They only want to meet with us off the record and the meeting has to take place in Galanis' private residence in Athens.'

'I see,' said Andrew. 'Well, I guess we will get ourselves down there then. When has it been arranged for?'

'The day after tomorrow, at 10 am local time.'

'Right,' said Andrew. 'We had better get packing then. I am assuming both Fiona and I are attending?'

'That is completely up to you,' said Strickland. 'But I suspect Fiona would be none too impressed if you went off on your own.'

Andrew could hear the wry smile in Strickland's voice, and couldn't help smiling himself. 'Yes, sir. I suspect you're probably right. I will get in touch with her right away.'

'Good stuff,' said Strickland. 'You'll have full use of the jet of course, and you'll be flying out of RAF Northolt again. I will have my secretary send you the details.'

'Excellent,' said Andrew. 'Thank you, sir.'

'The other development I wanted to mention to you is that we have some more colour on our former Spetsnaz friend Yevgeni Morozov.'

'Oh really?' said Andrew and leaned forward, pressing the phone against his ear. 'What have you got?'

'Using their facial recognition software our chaps at GCHQ managed to track him from the moment he entered the hospital and back in time for just under an hour before the murders. Our first sighting is from a CCTV camera at the end of a street in Holland Park, which caught a couple of seconds of footage of him leaving a house there.'

Andrew involuntarily turned his head to look across the park towards the west.

'You think he was staying there before hitting the hospital?' he asked.

'It seems that way,' replied Strickland. 'We are looking into it in further detail now, but we have already uncovered something interesting. The house is owned by a property investment company by the name Apex Realty which is registered in the Cayman Islands. There is nothing particularly unusual about that, but some more digging by a very bright chap at GCHQ revealed that the investment company is located in a building which is owned by a small ZOE Technologies subsidiary.'

'You're kidding,' said Andrew. 'He stayed in a house which is effectively owned by ZOE Technologies?'

'It seems that way,' replied Strickland. 'We are not entirely sure what is going on here, but it does seem rather peculiar and certainly very unlikely to be a coincidence.'

'Are you attempting to get a warrant for a search?' asked Andrew.

'We did consider that,' replied Strickland. 'However, that may be premature. I think we should walk softly for now. The reality is that this link is very tenuous, and we don't have any actual proof of foul play on the part of ZOE Technologies. On top of that, we don't want to risk our investigation by making them aware that we have this particular piece of information. I would rather have you and Fiona meet this Galanis character first, and then we can discuss how to proceed afterwards.'

Andrew nodded. 'I guess that makes sense. And I will keep this to myself for now.'

'Very good,' said Strickland. 'There's one final thing that I would like to discuss with you.'

'Yes, sir?' said Andrew.

'It's about Fabian Ackerman, the head of research at ZOE Technologies. We have been doing a full background check on him, aided by our partners in Five Eyes and in Europe, and you might be interested to hear what we have found.'

Strickland was referring to the intelligence-sharing alliance between Australia, Canada, New Zealand, the United Kingdom, and the United States. Combined, the intelligence gathering capabilities of those five nations were unmatched, and Five Eyes had already assisted Andrew and the SAS on several occasions in the past.

'Fire away,' said Andrew.

'It turns out he is a rather more colourful character than you might expect from a research director at a genetics firm,' said Strickland. 'He is a Swiss national who got his doctorate degree from the University of Lausanne's Faculty of Biology and Medicine, where his research mainly focussed on the growth cycles of mammalian cells, specifically the role played by growth hormones. So far so ordinary. He then took up a research position at a Swiss Army biological research facility, from which he was eventually fired for what was termed *unethical conduct* in relation to genetics research. We're still trying to find out exactly what happened.'

'Do we know what he was working on at the time?' asked Andrew.

'Something to do with cell cycle regulation and genes that function as suppressors of cell division speed. I haven't got the faintest idea what that actually means, but that is what the report from GCHQ says. You might want to read it yourself.'

'And I am guessing this is when he joined ZOE Technologies?' asked Andrew.

'Correct,' replied Strickland.

'He sounds like a bit of a maverick,' said Andrew. 'How long has he been with the company?'

'At least ten years, as far as we can tell,' replied Strickland. 'Indications are that he was instrumental in setting up the whole thing to begin with. But again, it has proven difficult to obtain very much information about the company. It has operated under the radar for most of its existence, and the people there guard their secrets extremely well. Anyway, I will forward you the provisional report from GCHQ, and you can have a read yourself. You might understand it better than I do. All this genetics jargon is beyond me, I am afraid.'

'Thank you, sir,' said Andrew. 'I will certainly have a look at it.'

'And don't forget to tell Fiona about the trip as soon as possible,' said Strickland.

'I won't,' smiled Andrew. 'For my own safety, if nothing else.'

'Good man,' chuckled Strickland. 'I will talk to you soon. Cheerio.'

★          ★          ★

Mike Stone was back in his office, standing in his favourite spot and looking out over San Francisco Bay. He had an unlit cigar in his mouth and was absentmindedly rubbing his stubbled chin with one hand, while the other was fishing for the Zippo lighter he kept in the inside pocket of his suit jacket. Wearing his usual office attire, which consisted of a plain white shirt and a dark blue tie, a dark grey pinstriped suit and a vest, all of which he now thought of as his uniform, he was pondering how to tie up the loose end that was Tim Dawson. Having scoped out the scientist's apartment in the leafy neighbourhood of Berkeley Hills just north of Oakland, he had eventually concluded that Dawson must have done a runner. Breaking into his apartment had been easy, but he had found no clues as to where Dawson might have gone. In fact, all of Dawson's electronic devices had been removed from his apartment, including backup drives or thumb drives that people tended to have lying around in drawers. It seemed as if Dawson had deliberately attempted to obscure any sign of what he was planning and where he was going.

But there were still ways around those sorts of problems. One of the benefits of being a private eye was that it gave him an opportunity to cultivate a wide network of sources from many different walks of life. From bankers and insurance claim processors to local law enforcement personnel and bail bondsmen, to security system installers and IT professionals, the number of people he could draw on had become large and varied. His network even included a couple of US congressmen. Most of them had been enticed by promises of discreet cash payments for their various services, but some had been persuaded to assist him by other means.

The man Stone was about to meet a short walk from his office in the small and neatly manicured Mariposa Park, belonged to the latter category of people. His name was Geoffrey Turner, and he had already been a useful asset on a couple of occasions in the past. He had initially found his way into Stone's Rolodex the same way as most of his assets.

It had all started four years ago, when Stone had been hired by Turner's wife. She thought he was an employee of a San Francisco-based think tank, and she had become convinced that he was being unfaithful and so had hired Stone to find the evidence.

As it turned out, using covert listening devices and with the assistance of a freelance hacker, Stone had discovered that the man was actually working for the

Department of Homeland Security, where he had top-level security clearance in one of their domestic intelligence-gathering operations. The entire office complex was masquerading as a foreign policy think tank, and if Turner ended up divulging the presence and nature of the operation, he was likely to get fired or at least reprimanded. But that was not what Stone had ended up using as a pressure point.

It became clear that Turner had indeed been having an affair, but it was with another man. Stone personally did not care about who Turner slept with, but the revelation had provided him with significant leverage over the seemingly respectable Catholic father of two. Ever since then, Turner had effectively been bound to Stone against his will. But Stone knew that a man like Turner would never try to do anything stupid to turn the tables. He would only ever keep his head down and hope to never see Stone again. Turner was not going to enjoy today.

Half an hour later, Stone sat down on a bench in Mariposa Park just opposite Benioff's Children's Hospital enjoying the sunshine whilst watching people walk past. After a few minutes, Geoffrey Turner showed up, shuffling hurriedly along the footpath. He was in his mid-forties, remarkably ordinary and lanky-looking, and as he walked along clutching his light brown leather document pouch, Stone wondered how this man had managed to keep an affair secret, never mind how he had been able to protect the secrets of the DHS.

Turner did not greet Stone but sat down nervously next to the impeccably dressed but imposing-looking ex-soldier.

'Hello Geoff,' said Stone cheerfully, in his thick East London accent. 'What a lovely day it is.'

Turner gave Stone a surly glance and leaned back with his document pouch on his knees.

'Forecast says it's going to rain all afternoon,' he said.

'Yes,' said Stone. 'Lovely. How's the wife and kids?'

Turner looked at him with an acidic expression on his face.

'Alright, you've made your point,' he said tersely whilst fiddling nervously with the clasp on his document pouch. 'Let's just get this over with.'

'Easy now, sunshine,' chuckled Stone calmly. 'Just making sure you and I are both clear about where we stand. So, tell me, what have you got for me? And stop fidgeting, mate. You look like you need to go to the bloody toilet.'

Turner took his hands off the clasp and cleared his throat.

'Ok, fine,' he said. 'I pulled the location data from Dawson's phone company, and it showed him driving from his home in Berkeley Hills to the Mexican border in Tijuana. From there he proceeded to Tijuana International Airport where we lost the signal. He probably switched his phone off there. At first, I thought maybe he had done so as part of a ruse to dump his own car and hire a new one, so I checked all the car rental places at the airport. None of them had his name in their systems and I am pretty sure he doesn't have a fake ID. So, I put in a request to Mexican Border Police, and they came back and said that Dawson had left on a flight with KLM to

London Heathrow Airport via Mexico City and Amsterdam. His flight landed in London late last night.'

'Old Blighty, eh?' mused Stone, sounding mildly surprised. 'Well, I never.'

'What?' said Turner, looking at Stone with a confused look on his face.

'Never mind,' replied Stone. 'Is that all you've got?'

'Yes,' replied Turner, sounding partly impatient, partly exasperated. 'Are we done here? Can I go now? Don't take this the wrong way, but I really don't want to spend any more time with you than I absolutely have to.'

'Oh, I do like you, Geoff,' chuckled Stone. 'Yeah, alright then. Be off with you.'

Turner stood up and was about to walk off, when Stone spoke again.

'Oh, and Geoff. Say hello to the wife, will you?' he said and winked.

'Fuck you,' sneered Turner, disdain dripping off every syllable. Then he walked away.

★        ★        ★

'What a cute plane,' said Fiona excitedly as she and Andrew walked towards the small bull-nosed twin-engine jet parked on the tarmac at RAF Northolt in west London. It had the standard dark grey-green livery typical for RAF planes that were used as VIP transports, but with just four seats for passengers, it was much smaller than anything else flown by 32 - The Royal Squadron, which operates the VIP jets.

'Cute?' said Andrew.

'It's just so small,' said Fiona and smiled at him. 'I like it a lot better than that big one we borrowed last time we did this.'

She was referring to the much bulkier BAE 146-200 which had taken them through Egypt, Israel and Ethiopia on their previous outing for the SAS's investigative unit. This newly acquired Honda HA-420 was just 13 metres long and had a wingspan of 12 metres which was less than half of its BAE predecessor. It had a slim design, two powerful engines mounted at the rear of the fuselage, and swept-up winglets making it look like something that really wanted to go fast.

'Yes, I suppose it is a lot smaller,' said Andrew. 'But I am told it has about the same range. Just under 3000 kilometres. And it cruises at around 700 kilometres per hour, so it will do very nicely for what we need.'

'How long is our flight time to Athens?' asked Fiona.

'It should be around three and half hours,' said Andrew as they ascended the small staircase to enter the passenger cabin.

'Oh wow,' said Fiona upon seeing the comfortable-looking interior. 'This is lovely. It feels like a lounge in a swanky bar in central London.'

The interior of the aircraft was not at all like most commercial aircraft. It had large reclining white leather seats, two on each side facing each other. There was gold effect metal trim on the edges of the armrests, and the floor was covered in a soft blue-grey carpet.

'It is quite a pleasant way to travel,' said Andrew. 'It certainly beats sitting in the back of an AC-130 cargo plane waiting to be dumped out of the back at ten thousand feet. No flight attendants though, so we will have to get our own drinks.'

'I think I can just about live with that,' laughed Fiona.

A few minutes later, the aircraft made its way slowly out along the taxiway towards the runway where it stopped, awaiting permission to take off. Then the whine of the two GE Honda HF120 turbofan engines increased in pitch, and when the pilot disengaged the breaks, they immediately began pushing the aircraft forward along the runway using their combined four thousand pounds of thrust to quickly accelerate it to its take-off speed of 220 kilometres per hour.

Once in the air, it quickly and quietly retracted its landing gear and banked left to head south over the European continent. Ten minutes later it was at cruising altitude, streaking across the sky towards its destination just north of Athens.

'So, what is our strategy for the meeting with Galanis?' asked Fiona as she made herself comfortable. 'What are we trying to get out of him, and how do you want to go about it?'

'I suppose we need to pin him down on whether he knew of anything that might have caused Peter Lambert to kill Balfour. And I would like to probe exactly what ZOE Technologies is working on. Lambert was clearly upset about something he had discovered, so we have to assume that Galanis knows what that was. And we need to understand the role of Fabian Ackerman in the company too.'

'I would really like to try to understand Galanis' psychology,' said Fiona. 'Particularly this supposed fascination with Alexander the Great. I can't shake the feeling that somehow it is key to this whole thing. I have already been reading up on that topic, and it really is very interesting.'

'I guess we will have to wait and see what he is prepared to divulge,' said Andrew. 'It isn't strictly speaking part of our remit, but I agree that it could be relevant.'

'Let's play it by ear and see what we can get out of him,' said Fiona and leaned back in her seat with a book. 'I am going to read up some more on Alexander the Great. It is fascinating stuff.'

# NINE

The Honda HA-420 touched down just after midday at the Tatoi military airport just north of Athens, which was a relatively small single-runway airport used by the Hellenic Air Force. Twenty minutes later, Andrew and Fiona were in a taxi heading for Alexis Galanis' estate on the southern outskirts of the ancient city. As they drove through it, they caught occasional glimpses of some of its ancient monuments, most prominently the huge temple on top of the Acropolis in the centre of the old city.

'Did you know that the name Acropolis is made from two ancient Greek words,' said Fiona and glanced at Andrew. 'Akron, which means summit, and Polis, which means city. So, it literally just means the top of the city.'

'You're going to be doing this a lot, aren't you?' said Andrew, and gave her a smile.

'Hey, you might actually learn something,' replied Fiona and elbowed him gently on the shoulder.

'I honestly don't mind,' said Andrew and held up his hands. 'I like learning new things.'

Ten minutes later their taxi weaved its way through the southern suburbs of the city. The large estate belonging to Alexis Galanis was located on the Megalo Kavouri headland, which is a part of the suburb of Vouliagmeni extending west from the mainland south of Athens and into the Saronic Gulf next to which the ancient sprawling metropolis was built. It was an enormous mansion set back on large well-manicured grounds where several gardeners were busy watering plants and flowers and trimming elaborately sculpted hedges and bushes.

Andrew and Fiona got out of the taxi and walked the sixteen steps up to the massive black-painted front door, which was flanked by two large pillars that were clearly made to look like ancient columns found on the Acropolis itself.

There was no doorbell, so Andrew grabbed the large brass knocker that was shaped like a lion's head and knocked twice, glancing at Fiona as he stepped back from the door and waited.

'I bet you anything there's a butler,' whispered Fiona, and just then the door opened.

They were greeted by a well-groomed, middle-aged man in a black suit and tie. Andrew was about to introduce himself to what he thought was Alexis Galanis, when the man opened the door fully and beckoned them inside.

'Please come in,' he said in heavily accented English. 'Would you like to just wait here,' he continued, his words making it clear that he was asking a rhetorical question.

The man disappeared into an adjacent room and the foyer fell silent. It was grand by any measure, being at least six metres to the ceiling, with black and white marble floors, intricate cornicing and black wrought-iron bannisters on a huge sweeping staircase leading upstairs to the first floor and sitting directly opposite the front door. Along the walls were what appeared to be statues of various Greek gods. Fiona noticed two in particular that she recognised.

One was a winged man standing upright whilst emerging from an egg with a serpent wrapped around him. Fiona knew him to be Phanes, the god of creation and life. Phanes, whose name means "to bring light" or "to shine", was also hailed as the deity of light and goodness.

The other statue was a young man, also with wings, but with a sword at his side and holding a torch upside down, signifying a life extinguished. This was Thanatos, the god of death.

Life and death, side by side.

An inscription on the wall above them read 'Ζωὴ απὸ θάνατο', or *Zoe apó thánato*, translating roughly to 'life from death', analogous to the Latin term Vitam Mortem.

As Andrew and Fiona waited in the imposing foyer of the mansion, they suddenly heard the sound of approaching footsteps up above them, and then a woman appeared on the landing at the top of the wide sweeping staircase.

She was tall and slim, with jet black hair arranged in a ponytail that reached down to her lower back. She was wearing high heels and a very low-cut black silk dress that hugged her figure and which seemed more appropriate for a glitzy award ceremony or a high society dinner party. It had a long slit on its left side, beginning at her ankle and extending upwards to the middle of her thigh allowing her left leg to briefly slip into view when she walked. Around her neck was a gold necklace with a circular pendant containing an intricate motif.

She descended the stairs gracefully and slowly, her long legs extending down to the steps below as she placed one foot deliberately in front of another. As she came down towards them, she was seemingly unphased by the two visitors waiting patiently for her in the foyer. She was clearly used to being in control.

As she approached them, it became more and more apparent how arrestingly beautiful she was. Her face was slender and elegant with immaculate makeup, and her eyes were so dark and clear that her irises and pupils seemed to blend into one, giving the appearance of a deep well of blackness.

She extended her hand towards Andrew in a manner that for a moment made him wonder whether to shake it or bow and kiss it. He struggled to take his eyes off hers, and she smiled coyly as she held his hand.

'Mr Sterling?' she said, her voice soft and calm but also measured and with a hint of authority.

'Yes,' said Andrew, and cleared his throat. 'Call me Andrew. This is Fiona Keane, my assistant.'

The woman glanced sideways at Fiona and smiled. 'Miss Keane.'

Fiona nodded, her eyes momentarily darting down to look at Andrew's hand still locked in greeting with the woman.

'Hello,' she said haltingly.

'We are here to see Mr Galanis,' said Andrew.

The woman tilted her head slightly to one side, an expression of amusement moving fleetingly across her face, and then she beckoned towards two enormous open double doors that led to an opulent sitting room beyond.

'Please follow me,' she said and began walking towards the doors, her heels clanging against the polished marble floor.

Andrew glanced briefly at Fiona who looked decidedly unimpressed with him. Then she started walking after the woman, tugging at his sleeve as she passed him.

'Come on!' she whispered as if she had been addressing a naughty schoolboy.

The woman led them into the sitting room. It was at least ten by fifteen metres in size, with a vaulted ceiling around five metres from the floor. From the centre of the ceiling hung an enormous gold and crystal chandelier. Giant replicas of Greek Ionic limestone columns were placed at each of the four corners of the room, and the four large windows along the wall facing out to the lush gardens beyond were dressed with long purple velvet curtains. The floor was white marble and the walls were painted a soft off-white colour and were decorated with paintings in gilded frames. All of the motifs seemed to be from classical Greek mythology. One of the walls was decorated with an intricate mosaic of a young man wearing light armour and a helmet with a plume of red trimmed feathers running along its centre. He was holding a spear and a shield, seemingly ready to throw the weapon at an unseen enemy.

The woman gestured for them to sit on a luxurious sofa that was placed roughly in the middle of the room, and then she started to walk towards its far end. Andrew subconsciously expected her to go and fetch something to drink, but instead she proceeded to a large tufted armchair made from white velvet and a gilded wooden frame. Facing the sofa Andrew and Fiona were sitting on, the chair was unusually large and high off the floor, and it seemed more akin to a throne than anything else.

In front of the chair was what at first appeared to be a rug made from a complete lion pelt, but on closer inspection, Andrew noticed that the impressive feline's incisors were exceptionally long.

As the woman sat down and crossed her left leg over her right, the slit in her black dress allowed the silk fabric to slide ever so slowly down to reveal the outside of her lower left leg, at the end of which was one of her black gloss stilettos.

Andrew was struggling not to be distracted, and he began to get the unpleasant feeling that he was being manipulated at an embarrassingly basic level. He hesitated for a moment, trying to work out what was happening, and he was about to ask a question when the woman smiled benignly at him.

'So, tell me,' she said. 'What can I do for you?'

Andrew and Fiona glanced briefly at each other.

'I am sorry. You are Alexis Galanis?' asked Andrew hesitantly. 'The owner of ZOE Technologies.'

'I am,' said the woman and gave a slow and measured nod. 'Is there a problem?' she smiled sweetly and almost mockingly, tilting her head to one side, clearly amused by the puzzlement of her visitors.

'No, not at all,' said Andrew, suddenly feeling slightly self-conscious. 'I think we were expecting a man, but now that I say that I can't really justify why that would have to be the case. I do apologise. Miss Galanis, thank you for seeing us. Is it Miss?'

'You are very welcome,' said Alexis with a cat-like smile. 'And yes, it is Miss.'

Fiona knew that her reaction was petty, but she could not help feeling a strange pang of envy in the presence of this woman. Alexis was utterly gorgeous, sexy, elegant, obviously highly intelligent and supremely self-assured. She was pretty much everything Fiona had ever aspired to be. Fiona and more or less every other woman she had ever known. Still, there had to be a chink in her armour somewhere. Some weakness. Something she kept hidden from the world.

At that moment, Fiona spotted something. The necklace around Alexis' neck had a pendant in the shape of a star, with sixteen rays extending out from its centre. The Vergina Sun. The symbol of the ancient Argead dynasty and of the house and lineage of Alexander the Great. The same symbol she had seen drawn crudely in blood on the chest of a dying Peter Lambert just days earlier in London.

'Your English is impeccable,' said Fiona, trying to conceal her momentary loss of focus. 'Did you grow up in the UK?'

'I was sent to boarding school there,' replied Alexis, 'but I always had English tutors even as a young child. My parents wanted the best for me, and they thought I ought to be proficient in at least two other languages besides Greek. I suppose they could not have known back then that perhaps I should have been taught Mandarin instead,' said Alexis, and winked at them, clearly implying that English influence and culture were on the decline across the world, increasingly replaced by Chinese soft power.

'Quite a place you have here,' said Andrew, gesturing to their opulent surroundings. 'I guess the genetics business is a lucrative one.'

Alexis chuckled and smiled. 'No, sadly it isn't. Not for the moment anyway. This house has been in my family's possession for almost two centuries. And I should tell you that ZOE Technologies is currently just breaking even. Research and development in this field is extremely costly, and as you may know we are only in the very early stages of rolling out our first commercial retail product, so revenue is minimal at this point in time.'

'You're talking about the Peritas programme, right? The tailored pets?' asked Fiona.

'Correct,' replied Alexis.

'So, ZOE Technologies is not making money at this time?' asked Andrew.

'No,' replied Alexis. 'It has been operating at a loss since it was founded, but I have been fortunate enough to be able to fund it myself without having to turn to banks or the equity markets.'

'May I ask how you managed to do that?' asked Fiona. 'I am assuming we are talking about hundreds of millions of dollars over the past decade in order to fund a company as large and technologically advanced as yours.'

'It is closer to a billion at this point,' said Alexis blithely, seemingly unfazed by the wealth that such a number would represent to the average person. 'But it's just money. I am the heir to the shipping conglomerate Diakos Marine Transport. I took full control of my share of the business on my eighteenth birthday. My parents were both killed in a plane crash when I was thirteen, and I was named as sole heir.'

'So, are you actually a Diakos?' asked Fiona. 'I have read about your family. Diakos Marine Transport is one of the largest global shipping firms if I am not mistaken.'

'I am,' said Alexis. 'And yes, DMT is in the top five. I have never been involved in running the business myself though. I do hold a minority share of the company's equity. But I have never taken up the position on the board which I am entitled to do, or otherwise allowed myself to influence the company. It was built by my father, and it was and still is run by very capable people. I have simply never had any passion for it.'

'So, your holding in DMT has financed ZOE Technologies?' asked Andrew.

'That is correct,' said Alexis. 'I felt I could do much more interesting things with that money than simply carry on with the family business.'

'Well,' said Andrew. 'I think it is fair to say that you have succeeded. ZOE Technologies seems to have made quite a name for itself in the world of genetics research.'

'It has,' said Alexis cautiously. 'But we are not content with research just for the sake of it. We intend to keep pushing the boundaries of practical applications of those technologies. There are many others around the world who have advanced the field of genetics over the past several years, but what good is a great discovery if it remains in the laboratory? I think what sets us apart from most others out there is simple ambition. Some seem content with tinkering in their university labs, going to conferences and writing research papers for prestigious medical journals. We, on the other hand, want to apply these powerful new tools to affect our reality.'

'You want to change the world,' said Fiona, partly as a question, partly as an observation.

'Yes, I suppose you could say that,' replied Alexis, seeming to briefly study Fiona. 'If we don't do it, someone else will. And I trust myself above anyone else to lead this effort.'

Fiona glanced at Andrew, momentarily taken aback by the unbridled self-confidence of this relatively young woman sitting in front of them.

'And you are the sole owner of ZOE Technologies, is that correct?' asked Andrew.

'I am,' replied Alexis.

'So, I have to assume that you knew Alistair Balfour quite well?' asked Andrew.

'Of course,' said Alexis. 'When I first appointed him a couple of years after founding ZOE Technologies, he had gone through the most rigorous interview process you could imagine, and he came out head and shoulders above the rest of the pack. Alistair was a great asset to the firm. He will be extremely difficult to replace, but I do have someone in mind that will be able to drive the business forward as our interim CEO. At least until we appoint a new permanent one.'

'And that person is?' asked Fiona.

'I obviously can't divulge that at this stage,' said Alexis, clasping her perfectly manicured hands. 'We will make an announcement in due course.'

'When did you first hear of Balfour's death?' asked Andrew.

'Along with everyone else, I suspect,' Alexis replied, looking genuinely pained. 'After all, it was being broadcast live on several financial news channels. I did not see it myself as it happened, but my assistant phoned me immediately after. It was quite awful.'

For the first time during their meeting, Alexis' mask of perfect composure seemed to slip for a moment, hinting at the loss she had clearly felt at Balfour's murder. Or was there something more to it than that? Fiona studied her face, but the moment was gone as quickly as it had arrived.

'What about Peter Lambert?' asked Andrew. 'Did you know him well?'

'No,' replied Alexis. 'I only dealt with Balfour and our research director, Fabian Ackerman. I believe I once met Lambert at a corporate drinks reception, but only for a couple of minutes. He did not seem like much of a socialite, to say the least. Typical scientist.'

'Can you think of any reason why anyone might want Balfour dead, and were you aware of any animosity between Balfour and Lambert?'

'The answer to your first question is no,' said Alexis. 'None whatsoever. And as for your second question, I honestly wouldn't know. We have several hundred employees across several research and production facilities. I really have no insights into those sorts of interpersonal relations between individual employees, but Lambert would have reported directly to Ackerman, and I have never heard Fabian mention him in anything other than a strictly professional context.'

'What about Lambert's co-workers?' asked Andrew. 'Can you tell us anything about them? Could they be involved in Lambert's actions? And if so, what might their motive be?'

'I am afraid I can't offer any help there at all,' said Alexis. 'I have never met any of them. I'm not even sure what their names are.'

'As I am sure you are aware,' said Andrew. 'Two special protection officers from the Metropolitan Police were murdered whilst watching over Lambert in a hospital. That makes this an extremely serious affair. Not to be too crass here, but I would imagine that the reputational risk to your company would be significant if it turned out that this whole thing was somehow connected to work that the firm is doing.'

Alexis studied Andrew for a couple of seconds without moving a muscle. Then she looked down and produced a reticent smile.

'Mr Sterling,' she said slowly. 'I am fully aware of the potential impact of this tragic event on my company. Do not doubt that for a second. As I have said, I have no insights into why this might have happened, but I am here and at your disposal to assist in any way I can.'

Andrew shifted in his chair, briefly glancing at the furry rug on the floor. It clearly still had part of the feline skull attached, and the fang-like teeth were resting their tips on the marble floor, holding the head up at a slight angle and giving the pelt a menacing look.

'What is that thing, if you don't mind my asking?' asked Andrew, and gestured towards the fanged floor ornament.

'This *thing* was a sabretooth tiger,' said Alexis, seemingly enjoying Andrew's curiosity.

'But they went extinct thousands of years ago, didn't they?' said Fiona.

'They did indeed,' said Alexis, and shifted her legs to now have the right leg crossed over her left. 'This was a Smilodon which went extinct very close to ten thousand years ago. It was closely related to modern tigers and other cats, and I think you can see why it is such a famous animal. The name Smilodon literally means *scalpel-tooth*.'

'It looks decidedly dangerous,' said Andrew.

'It certainly was,' said Alexis. 'These were powerful predators that hunted herbivores such as bison and antelope. This particular one belonged to the subfamily that roamed what is now the western United States. Several of them have been retrieved from the tar pits around Los Angeles where a particular type of heavy crude oil called gilsonite seeps up from deep inside the earth's crust and has been doing so for tens of thousands of years. These tar pits have trapped countless pre-historic animals like this one over the millennia. Because of the absence of oxygen as the gilsonite encased the animals, the tar was able to preserve the bones and sometimes even organic matter like tissue. Many pre-historic plants have also been preserved this way.'

'But how did you retrieve this one?' asked Fiona, nodding towards the pelt on the floor in front of Alexis. 'Did you find the skull in a tar pit and attach a lion's skin to it?'

Alexis produced a sweet, but ever so slightly condescending laugh.

'No,' she said. 'Not a bad guess I suppose, but this was obtained in a much more interesting way.'

'How then?' asked Andrew.

'Let me show you,' said Alexis, and reached over to the side table next to her plush chair, where she picked up a tiny brass tube with a slim varnished wooden handle. She briefly licked her lipstick-covered lips and placed the tube between them. Then she blew air through it, but there was no sound. The whistle produced a sound frequency above the spectrum audible to the human ear, but at a point where many animals can hear it.

A few moments later, the soft clattering sound of approaching feet on the marble floor could be heard from an adjacent room behind Alexis' chair. They were clearly not human feet but sounded more like claws.

Andrew and Fiona could barely believe their eyes. Advancing slowly on either side of a smiling Alexis, were two huge sabretooth tigers who strode calmly into the room and continued towards the visitors. Fiona gasped, and Andrew instinctively moved to the edge of his seat, grasping the sofa's armrest as if ready to either fight or leave quickly.

With sharp pointy incisors as long as Fiona's forearm the two hulking cats lay down on either side of the rug made from one of their own kind, seemingly entirely unaffected by the presence of the pelt on the floor between them. One of them began leisurely licking one of its enormous paws.

Alexis smiled calmly. It was impossible not to notice the air of complete mastery over life and death that this remarkable scene afforded her as she sat there behind the two pre-historic predators in her throne-like chair, smiling her perfect and charming smile.

'What in God's name is this?' breathed Fiona.

Alexis shook her head faintly and creased her forehead.

'There's no need to invoke deities, Miss Keane,' she said, looking vaguely amused by their reaction. 'What you are seeing is the result of solid human science and technology, with a little bit of help from a couple of Bengal tigers who served as surrogate mothers for the incubation of the sabretooth embryos.'

'How did you do this?'

'We simply extracted enough DNA from enough recovered cells in the specimen we found in a California tar pit. This allowed us to piece together a complete genome for an animal that roamed what is today Los Angeles just over ten thousand years ago.'

'Are these two made from the same DNA?' asked Andrew.

'Yes, said Alexis. 'For all intents and purposes, they are identical twins, even if they were grown in two separate wombs. By which I mean to say that they are clones. They are one hundred percent identical, right down to the genetic level. But they are so much more than that. They are each also completely identical to an animal that lived in the wild around twelve thousand years ago, when the most advanced humans in North America were just learning to use a bow and arrow. We have only introduced a few very limited changes to their DNA.'

'So you have, what do you call it, *enhanced* them, right?' asked Fiona.

'Yes, we have,' replied Alexis. 'In a number of important ways. We have strengthened their immune systems to allow them to deal with animal pathogens that have evolved after they went extinct. We have also edited their DNA to make them much more docile and to suppress their otherwise aggressive impulses, even when faced with a highly stimulating or threatening external environment.'

The two massive predators were licking their paws and producing a low growling noise that in a cat would have been called purring, but in these beasts seemed distinctly menacing. Andrew could even feel the soundwaves in his chest.

'Well, that's good to know,' said Andrew, hesitantly moving back into his seat again.

'When did you do this? How old are they?' asked Fiona incredulously.

'They are seven months old,' said Alexis.

'Seven months?' asked Andrew, looking perplexed. 'But they look fully grown.'

'Oh, they are,' said Alexis. 'We have discovered a way to accelerate cell growth. This was a prerequisite for the success of the Peritas program and an essential component in our ability to deliver products to our prospective customers quickly. After all, who wants to order a bespoke pet if they have to wait several years for it.'

'I have never heard of this being done before,' said Andrew.

'I should hope not,' said Alexis. 'This is a proprietary technology that we have invested significant resources into developing. It will become public knowledge once we launch the Peritas program.'

'Just to be clear,' said Fiona. 'You are only performing these…' she hesitated and gestured at the two predators on the floor, '*experiments* on animals, correct? You haven't actually tried any of this on humans?'

'Oh no,' said Alexis, looking slightly affronted at the question. 'Our goal at the moment is to fully develop our Peritas range. We have no plans to try to develop a commercial product based on editing of the human genome. In time we would like to move towards applying our technologies to human therapeutics, possibly even replacement organs, but that is some way off at this point. And as I am sure you know, there are significant regulatory barriers in that field. But we can potentially do such good with our technologies.'

'Do you mean CRISPR/Cas9?' asked Andrew.

'Among others, yes,' replied Alexis. 'Did you know that there are in the region of ten thousand genetic diseases, and only about one hundred of them currently have a cure? That leaves the other ninety-nine percent which now at least have a chance of having a cure developed. This equates to hundreds of millions of people whose suffering could potentially be alleviated. And we are going to have to keep working at this for as long as the human species exists. DNA is so much more than just a blueprint. It is a living and evolving entity which our bodies are beholden to.'

'What do you mean by the word "*beholden*"?' asked Fiona.

Alexis looked at Fiona, her eyes alight with passion for the topic. 'Are you familiar with the notion of the Selfish Gene?' she asked.

'No, I am afraid I am not,' said Fiona. 'What is it?'

'According to this somewhat philosophical characterisation of our genome,' said Alexis, 'our genome is in complete control either directly or indirectly of our bodies, our minds and our lives.'

Fiona remained silent, a look of slight confusion on her face, waiting for Alexis to continue.

'Ok,' said Alexis and looked at her. 'When you, Fiona are attracted to you Andrew,' she said and shifted her gaze to Andrew. 'It is simply the DNA in your bodies having developed to respond with endorphins to each other's scents. These, in turn, are expressions of your DNA, which are interpreted by both of your brains as being mutually compatible. This mechanism exists for a multitude of physical and intellectual traits that humans are subconsciously attracted to in potential mates. It is all a program run by your respective genomes through your brains and through your bodies, and you have absolutely no say in it whatsoever. You are simply attracted to each other, and there is nothing you can do about it. Your respective genomes have each found a compatible match for breeding and therefore self-replication, and self-replication is as close to the definition of life as you can get. The genomes are in control, and your brains and bodies are simply extensions of those genomes. They are merely tools that have evolved to enable your genomes to survive and replicate.'

As Andrew and Fiona listened to Alexis, they were both feeling slightly taken aback by her indirect assertion that they were romantically involved.

'This obviously begs the question,' continued Alexis. 'What is love really, other than sufficiently strong mutual responses to pheromones, which in turn are dictated by the specifics of a person's DNA? And if the human body is simply just a vessel for ensuring the continued survival of the molecule we call a genome, and if it is just a large water balloon controlled by deep impulses dictated by instincts which in turn are determined by a person's genes, then the real question becomes this. What is the perfect vessel to propagate DNA? What is the perfect human specimen to ensure the continued survival of a particular double helix of nucleotides?'

At this point, Alexis appeared to have drifted off into her own philosophical reverie, seemingly oblivious to the presence of Andrew or Fiona.

'Are you saying that ZOE Technologies will eventually proceed with human genome engineering?' asked Andrew. 'And if so, who would set the ethical boundaries for those efforts?'

'As I mentioned earlier,' replied Alexis. 'Not for the moment. But let's be honest. If we don't do it, someone else will. Who knows what the Chinese are up to this very moment in some secret government lab somewhere?' she asked rhetorically. 'Anyway, let me give you a couple of examples of ways in which genetic engineering has already been used.'

'Human-induced climate change and habitat loss for hundreds of species is already a reality. With small tweaks, we could make species threatened by extinction more tolerant of our changing climate and better able to adapt and survive. The black-footed ferret is an animal that almost went extinct. There used to be millions of them across North America, but the conversion of habitats to farmland meant that just one small colony in Wyoming was left by 1981. Using a combination of genome sequencing, genetic engineering including artificial increases in the DNA variation of individual animals, and also In-Vitro breeding, there is now a population of 600 ferrets there, and they are all the descendants of just 7 ancestors. With these technologies, we can compensate for the lack of genetic diversity which would normally lead to inbreeding and non-viable offspring. Imagine if we could do the same for the woolly mammoth, or for these two sabretooth tigers. We would be able to breathe new life into hundreds of extinct species, and using CRISPR we could ensure that they were adapted to the state of current habitats and that they were not susceptible to diseases that have evolved over the past ten thousand years after they went extinct. Another example is the American chestnut tree of which there were an estimated 4 billion back in the 17th century. For millennia it was the most abundant tree in North America. But then a blight was inadvertently imported to the continent by humans, and it spread rapidly, quickly killing off almost all the trees and leaving the species virtually extinct by 1950. The deliberate insertion of a single gene from wheat made them blight-resistant, and they are now able to thrive once again.'

Andrew and Fiona were both listening intently.

'The way I see it,' said Alexis. 'We simply must embrace this technology. We don't have a choice now that it is here.'

She held out her hands in front of herself, fingers outstretched and palms towards the ceiling.

'We now have the power to control evolution,' she said, lost in her own thoughts. 'This is the greatest power ever wielded by Homo Sapiens. In the beginning, we had simple tools like rocks and sticks. Then we made clubs and bows. Then we constructed guns and machines. Then we learned to master electrons in silicon substrates allowing us analytical powers that are orders of magnitude above those of the human brain. Then we produced Artificial Intelligence, and now we are at the final step of our journey. Complete control of biological evolution at a genetic level. And by evolution, I don't just mean our own. We now have the power to redesign the entire biome of this planet to suit our needs. Every plant, every animal, every microorganism. Humans will be like gods. We are finally taking the reins of our own destiny. Defeating cancer will be the first major step, but in comparison with what will come next, it will seem like a small one. We will eventually be able to completely control the characteristics of our progeny, enhancing the traits that make us stronger and suppressing the traits that make us weaker.'

Listening to Alexis say those words, Fiona felt a chill running down her spine.

'If you don't mind,' she interjected. 'Words like *stronger* and *weaker* are highly subjective in this context. And what you are talking about is in some respect the same as eugenics, isn't it? Suppressing supposedly weaker parts of humanity and cultivating those that are stronger. And the wealthy will always be stronger than the poor. Surely there is a strong argument that this is unethical.'

'Unethical?' retorted Alexis in a surprised and almost condescending tone of voice. 'Miss Keane, I predict that there will come a point in human history when a consensus will emerge that says it is unethical *not* to use this technology to alleviate suffering.'

'How do you mean?' asked Fiona, standing her ground against the sudden outburst from Alexis.

'Have you ever been to a hospital ward full of children dying from leukaemia?' asked Alexis pointedly, leaning forward and fixing Fiona with an intense stare from her dark eyes. 'Children dying!'

'Uhm, no,' admitted Fiona.

Alexis composed herself and leaned back in her chair, taking a deep breath before she spoke again.

'With this technology we can cure illnesses, extend the human lifespan and eradicate some of the biggest killers such as cancer. We can hugely increase the yield of crops thereby alleviating malnutrition and starvation in the world's poorest nations, and at the same time we can cut energy usage and carbon emissions. We can engineer bacteria to break down polluting chemicals and make other bacteria that can process organic waste and produce carbon-neutral biofuel. This is a genuine revolution and it will all happen within the next couple of decades. In the past we had to wait for hundreds or even thousands of generations of a plant or animal, hoping that a random mutation would initiate the change we desired. Now we can literally do it by flicking a base-pair switch inside the genome of that organism. The same will be true for most illnesses. By preventing the application of CRISPR technology to extending a person's life, you would effectively be letting that person die even though there was a viable way to keep them alive. I would argue that this runs counter to the Hippocratic oath, the very foundation of the application of medical science. Are you capable of making such a decision?'

Alexis pinned down Fiona with her stare. 'Preventing the application of CRISPR to ridding the human genome of congenital diseases will absolutely kill people. Would you be prepared to take responsibility for making that decision?'

Fiona hesitated. 'I haven't had the opportunity to think about this as deeply as you have,' she said. 'I do see your point.'

'People are very limited in their capacity to think beyond their immediate reality,' said Alexis. 'One day humans will colonise Mars and probably several of the moons in our solar system. That might not happen for several decades or even centuries. But the human race will persist for tens of millennia, and I guarantee you that the humans that end up on the moon Enceladus, or on Europa or even on Mars, will not look like you and me and their biochemistry will not be like ours. They will be genetically engineered to be stronger, capable of breathing air with tiny levels of oxygen or perhaps be capable of breathing an entirely different gas to sustain their bodies. All of these things are inevitable. They *will* happen. So, what is the point in trying to stall or delay? Let's grasp this opportunity and run with it. Let's take control of it. It is our destiny as a species.'

'Miss Galanis,' said Andrew. 'As you can appreciate, we are not here to discuss genetics as such, although I respect your passion. Our job is to try to ascertain whether what your company does could in any way have had a bearing on the murders of Alistair Balfour and Peter Lambert as well as the killings of two Metropolitan Police officers.'

Alexis smiled. She was once again perfectly composed.

'And I, in turn, respect your focus on the job you have been tasked with,' replied Alexis. 'I commend you for taking it so seriously, but I can tell you honestly that I am as much at a loss as to why those murders happened as you are, and I am as keen as anyone to see the perpetrator brought to justice.'

Andrew nodded. 'I really appreciate that,' he said.

There followed an awkward few seconds, where no one moved and the only sound was of the purring sabretooth tigers, who seemed oblivious to the tension between the three humans a few moments earlier.

'Is that a mosaic of Alexander the Great?' asked Fiona finally, pointing to the huge image of the young man holding a spear.

'No,' replied Alexis. 'This is Achilles, the greatest of all Greek warriors. But he was without question

Alexander's favourite mythological hero, according to every source there is about the matter. Apparently, Alexander brought a copy of Homer's Iliad with him at all times. He was a great student of philosophy and forever hungry for knowledge, as well as being perhaps the greatest military commander that has ever lived.'

'You seem to have a real interest in Alexander,' said Andrew. 'And the same could be said about the late Alistair Balfour. He mentioned Alexander repeatedly during his presentation in London, just before he was killed.'

'I am afraid my enthusiasm for Alexander the Great eventually rubbed off on Alistair,' smiled Alexis sadly. 'He and I came up with the name Peritas for our genetically engineered pet program together. He too was fascinated by the great man.'

'We overheard some people who called it an obsession,' said Fiona, trying to sound as un-antagonistic as she could.

'Little people say all sorts of things,' shrugged Alexis. 'But, yes. Alexander was without question the greatest Greek that has ever lived,' she said matter-of-factly. 'Possibly the greatest that will ever live. His life, even though it was cut short at a young age, might just turn out to be the most impactful of anyone before or since. Perhaps his impact on history is yet to be fully felt.'

Alexis rose suddenly before Andrew and Fiona had time to respond to her cryptic statement.

'Please,' said Alexis. 'Let's go outside and get some fresh air. Our grounds are lovely at this time of year.'

She walked over to a set of tall glass-paned double doors leading out to a veranda overlooking the perfectly groomed garden. The gentle sounds of sprinklers mixed with birdsong lent a pleasant and relaxing feel to the scene. Andrew and Fiona followed Alexis down a few steps to a lower section covered by large flagstones. At the end of it were two life-sized statues. One of a man. The other of a woman.

'This one here is Alexander,' said Alexis, glancing back at them and gesturing at the semi-naked white marble statue of an Adonis-like figure. His face was unmistakably that of Alexander the Great. 'And this is Hypatia,' continued Alexis, gesturing to a statue of a female.

'She's very attractive,' said Andrew looking at the statue and noting the similarities between it and Alexis.

Alexis scoffed. 'Mr Sterling, you disappoint me. This woman's strength was not just her beauty but her mind. She was a philosopher, a mathematician and an astronomer. A true scientist before science as we know it really existed. She lived in the 4th century CE in the Egyptian city of Alexandria, which of course was founded by this great man,' she said, and pointed at the statue of Alexander. 'When I was a child, I wanted to be just like her.'

'What did she do in Alexandria?' asked Fiona.

'She was a force of nature,' said Alexis. 'She lectured on the writings of Plato and Aristotle. She made great advances in algebra, and she revolutionised astronomy. She was instrumental in developing the Astrolabe, which is a handheld mechanical device constructed from metal cogs and dials. It can determine the time of day and the observer's latitude or altitude above sea level. It was the smartphone of its day. And Hypatia did all these things despite being a woman in a world that was dominated by men and by thoughtless superstition. Predictably, perhaps, it ended tragically for her.'

'What happened?' asked Fiona.

'Alexandria was an important centre of knowledge and wisdom at that time. Its open-minded and inclusive culture, which was a mix of Egyptian and Greek cultures and philosophies, encouraged the sharing of new ideas and thoughts. Because of this, it also became a place where the followers of the new and fledgling religion called Christianity would congregate. One of the people who had arrived there was the gospel writer Mark, who is credited with bringing Christianity to Africa and who was later sanctified. Once it had established itself there, the tensions between the existing tolerant multi-faith environment in Alexandria and the new monotheistic faith of Christianity eventually spilt over into violence. The tolerance that had permeated Alexandria vanished after a new bishop by the name of Cyril began inciting violence against what he considered to be pagans. He also circulated rumours that Hypatia's astrolabes were instruments of divination, designed to try to know the mind of God by predicting the future. This was seen as witchcraft, and the result was an atrocity. Hypatia was hunted down and killed by the Christian mob during Easter of 415 CE. They hunted her down through the streets of Alexandria, ripped off her clothes, flayed her alive and then tore her limb from limb. Finally, they carried her dismembered body to the edge of the city, and there they burned her mutilated remains on a pyre.'

'That's terrible,' said Fiona, visibly shocked.

'Yes,' said Alexis bitterly. 'This is what happens when superstition gains power over free thought. Whenever mindless religion is allowed to trump science, chaos and destruction follows as sure as night follows day. She was a light as bright as any that has ever shone in that part of the world, and she doesn't even have a grave where she can be remembered.'

'That's really awful,' said Fiona. 'I am glad the world has moved on from those things.'

Alexis looked at Fiona, studying her for a moment. 'Has it?' she asked with a quizzical look on her face. 'There are still many places in this world where women are forbidden from meaningful work, where women are treated as property that can be brutally killed like animals for petty transgressions against the religious dogma, and where books that are not scripture are burned as a matter of routine.'

'But what those religious fanatics did to Hypatia could have happened without religion,' said Fiona. 'Are you suggesting that it was religion per se that killed her?'

'That is exactly what I am saying,' replied Alexis emphatically. 'And your notion of religion as being separate from people simply does not stand up to scrutiny. It is no different from when the gun lobby in the United States promotes the idea that guns don't kill people, but that it is people who kill people. It is just nonsense. Monotheistic religion is a weapon. It is a loaded gun, and its inherent intolerance of so-called unbelievers or heretics or pagans or whatever the buzzword happens to be this century, can easily be turned into violence, and it will only ever bring misery to the human race, especially the female half.'

Alexis paused for a moment and took a deep breath, seemingly calming herself down. Then she gently took Fiona's hand and continued in a sorrowful and almost despondent tone of voice.

'We as a species have not moved on so very much since the 4$^{th}$ century, and we can easily regress to those terrible days in Alexandria if we are not careful. Cherish what you have, Fiona. It may not last.'

Alexis let go of Fiona's hand and walked a few steps towards the statue of Hypatia. Fiona pressed her lips together, pondering Alexis' words and having to admit to herself that what she was saying rang true. Uncomfortably so.

'I noticed a book lying on the coffee table in there,' said Fiona, trying to steer the conversation in a different direction.

She turned her head briefly towards the enormous room where they had sat in virtual audience with Alexis a few minutes earlier. 'It was the complete works of Homer.'

'He was a remarkable writer,' said Alexis. 'As I mentioned, Alexander always kept Homer's works by his side. He adored the great philosopher and he attempted to emulate the bravery and cunning of Achilles throughout his life. With some success, you might say.'

Fiona tilted her head to one side and smiled as she studied Alexis' necklace.

'What a lovely necklace,' she said casually. 'What is that symbol?'

'It is the Vergina Sun,' replied Alexis. 'It is the symbol of the Greek region of Macedonia where my family is originally from.'

'Really?' asked Fiona. 'That was also where Alexander was from, right?'

'Yes,' said Alexis. 'That is correct.'

Fiona turned and looked out over the blue ocean about a hundred metres away, beyond the pale brown rocks of the Megalo Kavouri headland.

'What a stunning view,' she sighed. 'If I lived here, I don't think I would ever leave.'

'Look out there,' said Alexis and pointed. 'There to the southeast beyond this bay is the Aegean Sea. For centuries, and with the help of its unrivalled navy, these waters allowed the city-state of Athens to project its power toward the Persian empires. Most people do not realise that the power of ancient Greece was in large part due to its dominance of the sea.'

'It looks like someone has cast anchor right on your doorstep,' said Andrew, pointed at a huge superyacht several hundred metres out to sea, beautifully framed by the golden sunlight reflecting and glistening off the calm ocean.

The yacht looked to be almost 100 metres long with a black hull and a white superstructure. With its tiered design, Andrew guessed that it had at least four separate interior levels.

'Oh, that one is mine,' said Alexis casually. 'It is one of my little guilty pleasures in life. I love being on the ocean. Such freedom and solitude.'

'That's a gorgeous ship,' said Andrew. 'What is she called?'

'The Hypatia,' replied Alexis.

'Of course,' smiled Andrew. 'Do you spend much time sailing? I know if I had one of those, I would spend as much time on it as I could.'

Alexis shrugged. 'Not as much as I would like. I am often needed elsewhere and I travel a lot. But I do have an office on the yacht, so I can work from there if I need to. And I also have the occasional visitor there. Some people are easily swayed by trinkets like that.'

'Some trinket,' said Fiona. 'That must cost a bomb.'

'Once again,' said Alexis. 'It's just money. Anyway, I do not mean to be rude, but I really must be getting on with my day, if there is nothing further you would like to ask me?'

'I think we're probably done here,' said Andrew, glancing at Fiona who nodded. 'We are very grateful for your time. Thank you for answering our questions so forthrightly. I prefer directness any day of the week.'

Alexis smiled. 'A man after my own heart,' she replied, and held Andrew's gaze for a few moments.

As they were walking back up the steps to the mansion, Fiona glanced sideways at Alexis.

'Do you have a partner?' she asked Alexis. 'Children perhaps?'

For the briefest of moments, Fiona thought the mask of perfect composure cracked almost imperceptibly. Was there a fleeting moment of sadness flashing across Alexis' face? If there was, it was gone now.

'No,' replied Alexis in an even and matter-of-fact tone of voice. 'My work consumes all of my time. I have not yet had that opportunity.'

'I didn't mean to pry,' said Fiona apologetically. 'I just thought it would be lovely to have a child play in these wonderful surroundings.'

'Perhaps one day,' said Alexis and smiled benignly. 'Who knows what the future holds?'

# TEN

Having said their goodbyes, Andrew and Fiona exited Alexis' mansion and entered the back seat of a waiting taxi.

'Holy smokes,' said Andrew, letting out a long sigh. 'That woman is on a whole different level. I don't think I have ever met anyone that impressive before. Her IQ must be off the charts.'

'Or perhaps she is just so detached from reality that what you think of as intelligence is actually just incoherent waffling. Did you hear what she said about the future of humanity?'

'Well, I am pretty sure she is extremely bright,' said Andrew. 'She supposedly laid the whole research foundation for ZOE Technologies more or less on her own, and given her sole ownership, I guess she personally holds the patents for most of their advanced genomics technologies.'

'You're really taken with her, aren't you?' asked Fiona, watching Andrew somewhat suspiciously. 'I mean, she *is* extremely attractive.'

Andrew glanced probingly at Fiona. 'Well, yes, she certainly is. But that is not what I am talking about. Although, I am sure she uses that to her advantage on a regular basis.'

'That's a very sexist thing to say,' protested Fiona.

'Alright,' said Andrew holding up both hands in surrender. 'I am sorry. I just think that there must have been many occasions where she has used her good looks to get what she wants. I mean, wouldn't you?'

'Are you saying you don't find me attractive?' asked Fiona.

'No-no,' blurted Andrew. 'Not at all, I just…'

'Alright,' chuckled Fiona. 'Relax. I am just messing with you.'

Andrew shook his head and laughed. 'Crikey. You really know how to make a chap feel like he's digging a giant hole for himself, and then make him dig even deeper.'

'I am just keeping you on your toes,' smiled Fiona.

'Anyway,' said Andrew. 'What was all that about as we were leaving?'

'What do you mean?'

'That stuff about a partner and children. That was a bit too personal, wasn't it? Not exactly the reason we are here.'

'I disagree,' replied Fiona. 'We are here to learn as much about her and ZOE Technologies as possible, and her personal circumstances are highly relevant to who she is and how she behaves.'

'Well, whatever she is, she is one of a kind,' said Andrew. 'Did you see what she was wearing? I mean, who dresses like that in their own home?'

'People with more money than they know what to do with,' replied Fiona. 'I would wager everything I own that this woman has never cooked a meal in her life. Anyway, I find it extremely interesting that she wears the Vergina Sun around her neck. For whatever reason, she definitely feels a connection to Alexander the Great.'

'Yes. That much is obvious,' said Andrew. 'The question is whether there is a link to that symbol being left on Peter Lambert's chest. I guess it's too early to tell. It could just be a coincidence.'

'I doubt it,' said Fiona. 'Anyway, are you up for an interesting anecdote about Alexander the Great and the Vergina Sun?' said Fiona.

'Sure,' said Andrew. 'Let's hear it.'

'Well,' began Fiona. 'According to the ancient historian Herodotus, the kingdom of Macedonia and the Argead Dynasty started in the city-state of Argos where three brothers named Galiane, Aeropas and Perdiccas lived in the early 6th century BCE. The three brothers were the descendants of Temerus, a legendary warrior who himself was a direct descendant of Heracles. Heracles is perhaps better known as Hercules, son of the god Zeus. After being exiled from Argos, the brothers travelled north and settled in the tribal lands of Macedonia where they worked as shepherds. After being presented with an omen that Perdiccas would end up as a powerful king, the local chieftain ordered the brothers to leave. Perdiccas asked for payment for their work but the chieftain mocked him by saying he could have as payment the ray of sunlight that was coming in through the window. Instead of becoming angry, Perdiccas calmly walked over to the sunlit patch on the floor and drew a circle around it with his cane, claiming it for himself. The brothers were chased out of the chieftain's lands and eventually settled at the base of a mountain overlooking what later became the Macedonian kingdom, where they would eventually unite all the disparate tribes and become rulers of all of Macedonia. Perdiccas ascended as the first king of the Argead dynasty, taking the image of the sunlight he had claimed for himself as the emblem of his dynasty. And Alexis was wearing this emblem on a chain around her neck.'

'Ok,' said Andrew tentatively. 'That's all very interesting, but what does that have to do with anything?'

'My point is that Alexis' fascination with Alexander the Great goes well beyond normal curiosity. She is clearly somewhat obsessed with him. But why?'

'She could just be interested in the history of her own country?' suggested Andrew. 'There's nothing strange about that.'

'But virtually everything in that house has some relation to Alexander,' insisted Fiona. 'I am telling you, there is a lot more to this than meets the eye.'

'So, what do you think it is then?' asked Andrew.

'Your guess is as good as mine,' shrugged Fiona. 'Perhaps Alexis believes that she belongs to the lineage of the Argead Dynasty. And because Alexander was of the Argead dynasty, Alexis could potentially be a direct descendant of Alexander the Great.'

Andrew looked at her sceptically. 'Really? That would be a bit difficult to prove, wouldn't it? I have never seen a family tree go back that far.'

'Neither have I,' said Fiona. 'But imagine if it really were true.'

'Well, if it really were true,' said Andrew. 'Alexis would then be the descendant of Zeus, right? Alexander was a descendant of Macedonia's first king Perdiccas, and he was supposedly descended from Zeus. Wasn't that what you just told me? I am not sure I like the sound of that, by the way. Alexis already has a huge ego without some vague claim to divinity on top of it.'

'Did you notice her reaction when our talk strayed onto the notion of terminally ill children?' asked Fiona. 'I must admit that I was taken aback by her then. Again, I feel like there is more to this story than some theoretical idea about sick children. I think we should look into this.'

'I agree,' said Andrew. 'By the way, while you were talking to her about the ethics of genetic engineering, I sent a quick email to McIntyre at UCL in London with a couple of questions. He has just replied to say that they have no record of an Alexis Diakos having studied at UCL, but they did have a PhD student called Alexis Galanis, and McIntyre remembers her very well, he said. Apparently, she was one of the brightest and most talented students he has ever had. He also says she finished another doctorate at Berkeley in record time before coming to UCL.'

'I told you she was bright,' he said, and looked at Fiona. 'I guess she picked the name Galanis as a way to be anonymous when she was studying. The Diakos name might bring her more attention than she would have liked.'

'Galanis actually means *pale blue eyes* in Greek,' said Fiona.

Andrew looked pensive for a moment. 'Let me guess,' he said, and looked at her. 'Alexander had pale blue eyes?'

'Bingo,' replied Fiona, 'which means that her fascination with Alexander goes back many years, at least to her student days. I am not sure what to make of that exactly, but I am sure it has some sort of bearing on this whole affair.'

'Right. Well, let's just get to our hotel now,' said Andrew. 'I think we both need a rest. I will tell Strickland to hold the plane at the airport until further notice. We might need to stick around for a few days.'

Andrew instructed the taxi driver to take them to the King George Hotel on Syntagma Square, just a few hundred metres from the Acropolis. As they arrived at the hotel and got out of the taxi, they could see the Hellenic Parliament on the eastern side of the square. Limousines were coming and going at the many hotels located there, and black chauffeur-driven cars with tinted windows and diplomatic plates were parked around it waiting to pick up dignitaries. Milling around on the pavement was a disparate mix of men in business suits and garishly dressed tourists returning from excursions in the ancient city.

'This place has a great vibe,' said Fiona, looking out over the square. 'It makes me want to just walk off in a random direction and see what I find.'

'Well, there might be time for that,' said Andrew. 'But first, let's get some rest.'

As they entered the lobby, a concierge greeted them and carried their luggage through the sumptuous cream-coloured marble foyer to the front desk where Andrew got them a room on the $4^{th}$ floor facing out to the square. Ten minutes later they were slumped on a comfortable sofa in their room.

'I am going to give Strickland a call in a few minutes,' said Andrew. 'I need to give him a quick update on what we've found so far. He might have something for us, too.'

'Alright,' said Fiona and rose slowly from the sofa. 'Sounds good. I am going to take a shower. Let me know what he says.'

★          ★          ★

George Frost was in his office in the secret underground laboratory near Rhinebeck in upstate New York. It was for obvious reasons a windowless room, but one of the walls had a giant display on it which mimicked a window looking out onto a garden. The artificial view followed the day-night cycle of the real world some fifty metres above him, and it came complete with a suite of different weather options and ambient sounds such as birdsong, the pitter-patter of raindrops and the soft rustling of leaves on trees, giving the impression of the window being partly open to the outside. Even though it was an illusion, it was a remarkably convincing one, and Frost often found himself looking absentmindedly 'out of the window' when pondering things related to his research at the lab.

Today he was preparing for a call with Fabian Ackerman. The research director wanted an update on the upcoming stage of their next-generation CRISPR program, specifically the effort to control cell growth. Ever since he had been a medical student Frost had been interested in the mechanisms that govern cell proliferation, particularly the speed with which cells divide. Conventional wisdom held that there were static switches in the genome that at some point simply stop an organism from growing any further, but Frost had discovered something much more elaborate which could have huge potential for commercial food products.

The basic problem was that growth in animals is rapid in early life but then progressively slows down, which imposes a limit on adult body size. This deceleration of growth is the result of suppression of cell division and is driven by local tissue mechanisms, rather than systemic ones. The decline in division results from a genetic program that occurs in multiple organs and involves the down-regulation of a large set of growth-promoting genes. But what is more important is that this program is not simply driven by time but depends on growth itself, and it is tied to the cell cycle, which is a complex cycle of chromosome duplication, cell division and chromosome error checking. This means that the limit on adult body size is imposed by a negative feedback loop whose impact grows ever larger the more times a cell divides. It also means that if cell division could be accelerated, it would result not in run-away growth, but in exactly the same amount of growth but over a much shorter time span.

Frost's PhD thesis had investigated ways to use the initial versions of CRISPR to edit a couple of base pairs in a specific gene in chickens, in order to accelerate growth, which would result in larger chickens that could reach full maturity in a fraction of the time it normally took to grow one. His initial idea had been to start a company that would license this technology to livestock producers, but those plans had been shelved when one day he received an unannounced visit. The visitor was a Doctor Fabian Ackerman, who had been working on a similar technique, and who offered Frost a job that he simply could not turn down. Frost did not know of ZOE Technologies at the time, but Ackerman had persuaded him that his future would be much better served if he joined the company. There was a catch, though, as Frost found out during their second meeting. He was to live in a company-owned house on the outskirts of Rhinebeck and work from an off-site research location, effectively hidden from public view as well as company and public records. His research would also not be shared or publicised to the wider world, including to scientific journals. This meant that any breakthroughs he might manage to achieve would never be credited to him. However, the condition for employment that had given him the most pause had been the fact that Ackerman was asking him to join a research effort into the editing of the human genome.

This area was a virtual taboo in genetics research circles, but Ackerman had convinced him that this was the future and that this future was coming, whether he elected to participate in it or not. When Ackerman had slid a contract across the table with a dizzying number of zeros in the line pertaining to remuneration, Frost had not hesitated. He had gone all-in. Now, several years later, as the head of Ackerman's off-the-books research facility, Frost and his team had achieved some spectacular results. He was just going over his notes when the phone rang.

*Right on time as always*, thought Frost.

'Frost here' he said as he picked up the phone.

'Frost,' said Ackerman, in a slightly Germanic-accented voice. 'Fabian here. How is it going? Do you have the results?'

'Yes, sir,' replied Frost. 'They are very encouraging. Transposing the new editing technique from the primate genome into our sample human genome caused a significant increase in growth rates.'

'Very good,' said Ackerman.

'Importantly,' continued Frost, 'the speed increase seemed to be uniform across the organism, so no unintended variation in size was observed. I think we are on the right track here. The only anomaly was an unexpected gene expression which resulted in the production of a protein that turned out to inhibit oxygen uptake through otherwise healthy lung tissue.'

'Excellent news,' said Fabian. 'Shame about the anomaly though. What about the test subject?'

'Didn't make it,' said Frost matter-of-factly. 'But we didn't really expect it to survive. And even if it had lived, we would have had to terminate. As you know, we can't allow growth to full term at this stage. It would jeopardise everything.'

'Of course,' said Ackerman. 'Good work, Frost. Keep pushing ahead. This was only phase one. In phase two we will progress to much more ambitious goals. Make sure the new larger growth vats are up and running well ahead of time. Have Rosetta run a test using primate germ cells first. We need to do what we can to make sure the procedure will work before we commit to the final human trials. This is an expensive program. We can't afford any screw-ups.'

'Yes, sir,' replied Frost. 'I will do that. I have every confidence that this methodology will translate to germ cells in human embryos. The first tests should be ready in a matter of days.'

'Very good,' said Ackerman. 'Let's talk again soon. You're doing great.'

'Oh,' said Frost, sounding uncertain. 'One more thing.'

'Yes?' said Ackerman, impatiently.

'This is a bit delicate,' said Frost.

'Well, spit it out man,' said Ackerman brusquely.

'It's just that we have all seen the news,' said Frost. 'The team here obviously think that this has nothing to do with them since none of them know they are really working for ZOE Technologies, but I am wondering whether this will have any impact on me. I mean, will it affect our program?'

'I am handling this,' said Ackerman, resolutely. 'I have my people on it, and we are busy cleaning up that particular mess. We have already tied up a couple of loose ends, and we should be done soon. After that, there is nothing to worry about. Your part of the program is safe. Just keep doing what you're doing. Ok?'

'Alright. Thank you, sir,' said Frost. 'I will keep you updated. Goodbye.'

★        ★        ★

The Cyprus Museum in the Cypriot capital of Nicosia, or Lefkosia as it is called in Greek, is located just outside the ancient city walls, across the road from the Cypriot Parliament and the Municipal Theatre. It was constructed in 1908 as the result of a petition by the Cypriot people in response to vast amounts of ancient artefacts being illegally removed from the island. Chief among the perpetrators was the United States Ambassador Luigi Palma di Cesnola, who was responsible for as much as thirty-five thousand pieces being smuggled off the islands and into the hands of black-market dealers, if they were not destroyed in transit.

The simple but elegant design of the large building clearly harked back to the golden age of ancient Greece when Athens was one of the wealthiest and most cultured cities in the world. With a gable roof pitched at around fifteen degrees, red roof tiles, light cream-coloured walls and tall majestic pillars arrayed in a colonnade on its façade, it was built to closely resemble the Temple of Athena Nike which had been built on the western-most point of the Acropolis in Athens around 420 BCE.

It was late on a hot and sunny Monday afternoon when an old white Ford Fiesta drove along the road called Mouseiou, where the Cyprus Museum is located. The car pulled into the car park at the Municipal Theatre diagonally across from the museum, and a man stepped out and reached inside the back seat to retrieve a large black holdall. The bag appeared light as he slung it over his shoulder and began walking casually along the road. He was wearing a dark blue boiler suit with a label velcroed to the left breast pocket. The label had the logo of a large and well-known plumbing company called Thalia, which serviced central Nicosia.

The man glanced over his shoulder to check for traffic and then jogged lazily across the road waving a thank you to a car that had slowed down to allow him to cross safely. Once on the other side, he continued walking at a leisurely pace along the pavement towards the Cyprus Museum which was closed as it was every Monday.

As he calmly strolled onto the museum grounds glancing up at the tall pillars from under his dark blue cap, he spotted a gardener tending to some small palm trees growing in an arrangement of pots along the wall to the far left of the building. The gardener waved briefly to him, and he waved back. As he did so, he caught sight of his own tattoo of a panther claw on his lower right arm, and he quickly pulled the sleeve of the boiler suit down to cover it. The gardener was already back to busying himself with his palm trees.

Morozov had arrived the night before on a fake passport, flying from Paris Charles de Gaulle Airport to Larnaca International Airport, and he had then taken a taxi to an address in a rundown part of town where a plumber named Kostas, who worked for the company Thalia, lived by himself in a small apartment. Morozov did not like Pierre Dubois, but he had to admit that he knew what he was doing. He suspected that Dubois had friends in low places, and that the Frenchman could source hackers at will to work for him to gather this type of information. In the right hands, it could be very valuable indeed.

Incapacitating the plumber with a dart gun had been quick and easy, and Morozov had taken the opportunity to have a sleep in the man's armchair. The effects of the tranquiliser would last at least twenty-four hours, but after that, Kostas would slowly come to again, probably feeling like he had been on a spectacular night out. In fact, he was likely to convince himself that that was actually what had happened. Either way, Morozov would be long gone by then. In the morning he had taken the plumber's car and driven the short distance to the Cyprus Museum, wearing the plumber's boiler suit.

Morozov followed the path to the right around the main museum building and walked down alongside it to the back of the building. Using bolt cutters he quickly forced his way inside a small service building the size of a large closet, where he had been informed the power and phone lines came into the building. He spent a few minutes disabling the alarm system by accessing the dedicated signal line and feeding the remote-control centre a continuous false 'All Clear' signal. Then he exited the service building and walked to the nearest back entrance to the main building, where he unzipped his holdall and pulled out a battery-operated drill. Placing the drill on the lock of the door and quickly looking around to make sure no one was approaching he then used the weight of his body to lean into the drill as it started grinding its way through the lock. Within seconds the lock had been drilled out, and Morozov calmly placed the drill back in the holdall and stood back up. He grabbed the door handle and pushed the door open. Nothing. No sound. No alarm. No guards.

Once inside, he closed the door behind himself and walked calmly down the corridor towards another door that he knew led to the central part of the museum. Initially designed as a quadrangle of large high-ceilinged exhibition rooms with an open courtyard in the middle, the museum had eventually built over the courtyard in order to use the space for storage for its ever-growing collection of artefacts. The museum now has fourteen large exhibition rooms holding artefacts found on the island of Cyprus from as far back as the Neolithic period. Since the earliest evidence of human habitation on Cyprus is 11,000 years old, and because of the island's generally dry climate, which tends to preserve artefacts well, there is a very long period from which to collect archaeological finds. This means the museum is only ever able to exhibit a small fraction of its possessions.

It was towards the back of this storage facility that Morozov was headed. He knew that there was a stairwell there that led down to the underground storage space, and that was where his target was supposed to be located.

Reaching the end of the corridor he grabbed the door handle and opened the door to what he knew was another corridor leading to the back of the museum. But what greeted him was not an empty corridor. As he pulled the door towards himself, he was suddenly faced with a single museum guard leaning lazily against the wall, smoking a cigarette and looking at his phone. Morozov could hear the faint sound of football commentary emanating from it. The guard looked up. He was a big man with a thick moustache and large hands.

*Fuck*, thought Morozov. He had screwed up and become complacent. He should have been more careful moving through the museum instead of simply assuming that it was empty.

The guard looked at Morozov's face, and that was when the ex-Spetsnaz operative knew what he had to do. He gave the guard a quick nod as a greeting and began walking past him, but the big man's hand came up and blocked his way. As it did so, Morozov's left hand slipped inside a pocket in his boiler suit and extracted a small metal cylinder not much larger than a ballpoint pen. It was a medical grade pressurised atomiser injection pen containing a powerful sedative.

Still moving forward, Morozov used his momentum to first grab onto the guard's arm with his right hand, and then turn himself towards the big man. At the same time, he swung his left arm up and around to bring his hand up right next to the guard's neck, where he jammed the pen hard against his skin and pressed the button on the end of it.

There was a click and a very brief hiss, and then the guard's eyes went wide, partly in shock at the lightning-fast movement of what looked like a simple plumber, and partly because he immediately sensed something entering his body.

He instantly let go of Morozov, taking a step backwards and away from him and holding his right hand up to press against the side of his neck, whilst at the same time looking at his assailant with a wild look in his eyes. Then his knees began to wobble, and he partly lost his footing. Slumping down with his left hand bracing his fall, he groaned and held himself up for a couple of seconds, but then he finally sank to the floor, exhaling noisily.

Morozov observed him for a couple of seconds and winced. This was not how he had planned for this to go. But as he knew better than anyone, no battle plan survives contact with the enemy, and this was no different. He would just have to adapt and improvise.

Shoving the pen back into his pocket, he then bent down to grab the large man under the armpits. He proceeded to drag his unconscious body a few metres down the corridor to what looked like a stockroom for office and cleaning supplies. Here he pulled out two sets of zip-ties, which he used to tie the guard's hands and feet together. He would probably be able to break free from them eventually when he came to, but that would be several hours from now. Morozov placed him in an upright position leaning against the wall, and he then left the stockroom and closed the door.

*Not good enough*, thought Morozov, chastising himself for allowing things to get this messy. *Am I getting sloppy?*

Still, at least he hadn't killed the man, which would have been standard operating procedure during his time in the Russian special forces. But Dubois had asked him to do what he could to keep things clean and tidy, so this was how it had to be, even if the guard would probably be able to recognise his face. Morozov winced again and shook his head as he walked the final few metres to the stairwell leading down to the basement level.

He descended the stairs, and after opening the door to the large storeroom below the museum, he was greeted by several long aisles of metal mesh cages, each one containing lots of artefacts organised neatly on shelves, and each one locked behind padlocked doors.

Morozov had memorised the layout of the storage room and walked straight to the mesh cage near the back, where a wooden box sat atop a metal table. Along the back wall was an elaborate granite sarcophagus with its lid placed on the floor next to it. Along the sides of the cage were several shelving systems, each containing what appeared to be hundreds of smaller items.

Morozov broke open the padlock, pushed the door open and headed straight for the wooden box. It was exactly as he was expecting. A simple box made to hold a body in transit from a dig site to the museum where it could be examined. But this was not just any body. This was the mummified corpse of an ancient Egyptian royal, with its ornate granite sarcophagus placed on the floor next to the table.

As Morozov approached, the mummy contained in the box came into full view. Wrapped in long, partly decomposed strips of linen that had gone from a crisp white appearance to a blotchy faded brown over the two millennia since the tomb was sealed, it looked bone-dry and extremely delicate. Near the head several pieces of linen strips seemed to be missing, possibly completely decomposed, or perhaps they had fallen off during the transportation from the dig site in Paphos to the museum's storage room in Nicosia.

Underneath the loose strips on the neck, Morozov could see the corpse itself, or rather, what was left of it. As he reached in and lifted up part of the brittle linen, the skin and muscle tissue on the corpse appeared shrivelled up like a raisin, and it seemed possessed of a paper-like fragility. What was also noteworthy was the size of the mummy. It was appreciably smaller than a grown man or woman, much less than 1.5 metres tall.

Morozov studied it impassively for a few seconds. Then he knelt down and reached into his holdall, extracting a small metal case similar to the one he had used in Paris. He placed it on the table next to the wooden box and popped open the clasps. Inside was a neatly arranged set of different types of metal tweezers, a couple of scalpels, one of them with a slightly serrated edge, as well as several small foam-padded plastic containers.

Morozov stood up and leaned in over the mummy. Then he reached down and started cutting a small piece of withered tissue from the neck of the ancient corpse. He then got the tweezers and placed the tissue carefully in one of the foam-padded plastic containers and pressed the lid down carefully until it clicked shut. After that, he used the serrated scalpel to shear a tiny piece of bone from the jawbone of the corpse. He placed that in a different container. He repeated the procedure twice more, placing the samples in separate containers and returning all four of them to their designated places inside the small metal case.

Had it all been up to him, he would have simply broken off a leg and carried it out of there, but Dubois had been very specific about which types of samples to take and where to take them from.

Having finished his task, he quickly packed up his equipment and walked towards the stairs leading back up to ground level. As he was walking up the stairwell, he heard footsteps. He stopped dead in his tracks, his ears straining to hear where it might have come from and whether someone was approaching or moving away.

'Hello?' said a female voice.

'Fuck,' whispered Morozov to himself, wincing. This was not part of the plan.

After a few seconds, the voice came back, closer this time.

'Hello? Anyone there?'

Morozov decided to take the bull by the horns and simply play the part of the plumber. He resumed walking up the stairwell, and as he exited into the main artefact storage room in what used to be the museum courtyard, he spotted a middle-aged woman standing just a few metres away. She was holding a broom and wearing clothes that indicated that she was almost certainly a cleaning lady.

'Hello,' said Morozov coolly. 'Nice evening.'

'Oh,' said the woman, and smiled uncertainly. 'Yes. Working late. The museum opens again tomorrow.'

Morozov shrugged. 'Problem downstairs. Water pipes.'

'Oh,' repeated the woman. 'Have you fixed it?'

'Yes, all fixed now,' replied Morozov, and then he began walking back towards the rear entrance, where he had entered the museum less than an hour earlier.

'Goodnight,' called the woman after him.

Morozov didn't reply but simply waved briefly as he walked away.

*She saw my damn face*, he thought. *Maybe I should just kill her. But better not to leave a mess this time. I will be gone by tomorrow morning anyway. She will never know how lucky she was.*

# ELEVEN

The next morning, Andrew and Fiona were sitting at a table in the roof-top restaurant of the hotel. It was shaping up to be a clear sunny day, but for now the temperature was still pleasantly cool. A few hundred metres away to the southwest, the Acropolis rose up from the rest of the city, its ancient temples bathed in the golden morning sunlight.

'What a view,' said Andrew. 'This city really has character.'

'I know,' smiled Fiona. 'I love it here. You can practically feel the history in the air.'

'Speaking of history,' said Andrew. 'Would you mind refreshing my memory on Alexander the Great? I remember being taught about him in school, but that is a very long time ago. I think the army actually uses his long campaign and his battles to teach strategy and battlefield tactics.'

'Well,' said Fiona. 'I would imagine that if you were to teach those particular topics to anyone, using Alexander as an example would not be a bad place to start. His campaign from Greece to India lasted over a decade, and he never lost a single battle. He is arguably one of the most successful tacticians and field commanders of all time.'

'So, tell me his story,' said Andrew, and leaned back in his chair, shifting slightly to face Fiona. 'You're a good storyteller.'

Fiona nodded. 'Alright then,' she smiled and made herself comfortable. 'This is going to take some time. You have been warned. So, first a bit of context. From around 480 BCE, after seeing off an attempted invasion by the Persian Empire, Greece and its great city-states were able to establish themselves as some of the most prosperous and powerful players in the ancient world. This period was the golden age of classical Greece. But increasing internal strife and tension, particularly between the two major city-states of Athens and Sparta and their respective allies, eventually dragged the entire Greek world into a civil war that lasted almost a century. This opened the door for the small, mountainous and previously weak and irrelevant kingdom of Macedonia in the north to assert itself. It was ruled from the city of Pella by the Argead dynasty which became more and more powerful and influential over the decades, so when Philip II took the throne in 359 BCE, things really started to take off for the Macedonians.'

'This was the dynasty using the sixteen-pointed star as its symbol, right?' asked Andrew. 'The one you found on Lambert's chest?'

'Correct,' replied Fiona, looking uncomfortable at the memory of the bloody hospital room coming back to her. 'The Vergina Sun.'

'Something just occurred to me,' said Andrew. 'How did the ancient Greeks keep track of years? I mean, if someone was born when Philip II took the throne in 359 BCE, they wouldn't have known that it was the year 359 BCE, because *Year 0* had not happened yet.'

'That's a good question,' smiled Fiona. 'In ancient Athens, there was always a so-called *Archon*, which literally means ruler but which equates to a chief administrator of the city. Initially, an archon sat for ten years but that was later changed to one-year periods, and there was an unbroken sequence of archons going back centuries. So, if you wanted to refer to a particular year, you might say "In the year of Archon so-and-so", and then everyone would have a chance of understanding what year you were talking about.'

'I see,' said Andrew. 'Interesting.'

'Anyway,' continued Fiona. 'Philip II developed entirely new battlefield units and tactics, most famously the Macedonian Phalanx which carried unusually long spears and operated in tight and highly disciplined formations. This quickly allowed him to begin to dominate his weak rivals. He was also a highly skilled diplomat who navigated and exploited interpersonal relations, bribery, assassinations and marriage alliances to his advantage. Eventually, he subdued the city-states of Thebes and Athens, establishing the so-called Hellenic League in 337 BCE which made him the undisputed ruler of almost all of Greece. Only the proud warrior city of Sparta remained independent.'

Fiona took a sip of her glass of orange juice.

'At this point in time, the Persian Empire was the superpower of the day, but it was ailing and beginning to lose its influence. Philip II was seeking to exploit this weakness and was preparing for an invasion of Asia Minor, also known as Anatolia in Turkey. This invasion was intended as the beginning of a campaign to subdue the entire Persian Empire. But at a grand feast for his allies, Philip II was assassinated by one of his own bodyguards, and suddenly his young son Alexander was catapulted into the role of almost omnipotent king and ruler of ancient Greece at the age of just twenty.'

'Crikey,' said Andrew. 'Was a motive for Philip's murder ever established?'

'There has obviously been an enormous amount of speculation about that ever since,' said Fiona, 'and there are many different theories. But what is certain is that Philip II would not have been able to attain such power without making many mortal enemies. One intriguing theory however, is that it was Alexander's mother Olympias, who was behind the assassination. She was known to be highly ambitious for her son, and she supposedly harboured some serious animus towards Philip because of his polygamy and arrogance.'

'And Alexander was twenty years old?' asked Andrew incredulously. 'How was he even remotely ready to rule?'

'That is exactly what a lot of people were asking themselves at the time,' replied Fiona. 'But Alexander was under the personal tutelage of the great philosopher Aristotle, who in many ways was the father of modern reasoning and the logical deductive way of thinking that we take for granted today in all the sciences.'

Fiona leaned in slightly towards Andrew with a sly look on her face. 'By the way. Would you like to know where the word philosopher comes from?' she asked.

Andrew laughed. 'I can see that you are just dying to tell me, so let's hear it then.'

'Alright,' said Fiona. 'We think of the word philosopher as meaning a person engaged in deep existential thought, but the word philosophy simply means lover of wisdom, from the ancient Greek words Phil, meaning loving, and Sophos, meaning a wise man, since the noun Sophia means wisdom.'

'That's really interesting,' said Andrew.

'It is, isn't it?' beamed Fiona. 'I have taken an interest in etymology lately. The origin of words. There are so many words that have their origin in ancient Greek, and I kept coming across them as I was studying the life and death of Alexander. Anyway, back to the story.'

'Yes. So, let me guess,' said Andrew. 'With a military already gearing up for an invasion, Alexander simply took over where his father had left off and got ready to start his campaign?'

'More or less,' replied Fiona. 'Except that he had to spend some time beating a couple of would-be rebellions into submission. But it wasn't long before it became apparent to everyone that Alexander was easily as capable and ruthless as his father, and any opposition to his rule evaporated very quickly. After that, the scene was finally set for what was to become the largest and most significant military campaign in history, and in 334 BCE he and his army of forty thousand men crossed over into Asia Minor. I won't bore you with all the details, but there really is an enormous amount of information preserved about this campaign, right down to the names of the commanders of individual phalanx units.'

'I guess they would have brought scribes and historians with them to chronicle the king's exploits,' said Andrew.

'Absolutely,' said Fiona. 'In fact, one of the most important generals and the subsequent ruler of part of Alexander's empire after his death, Ptolemy, himself became a famous historian. He wrote very extensively about Alexander's campaign as well as more broadly about his life and death. I think it is fair to say that Ptolemy's writings are one of the most reliable sources we have since he was there himself for the duration of the campaign.'

'Do Ptolemy's writings still exist?' asked Andrew.

'Sadly, they don't,' said Fiona. 'But we do have the writings of a historian by the name Arrian of Nicomedia who wrote in great detail about Alexander's military campaign, and who himself cited Ptolemy's writings as one of his main sources. Arrian's work of seven books is called The Anabasis of Alexander, and it is 113,000 words long, about the same as a long novel. I have read it myself, and it is remarkably detailed. Anyway, after Alexander had crossed over into Asia Minor at the Hellespont on the peninsula of Gallipoli, the Persian armies decided to face the Greek army at the river Granicus, which flows north towards the ocean in what is now north-western Turkey.'

Fiona rummaged around in her bag for a few seconds and then produced a tablet which she switched on. She tapped on its screen a few times and then handed it to Andrew.

'Have a look at this map,' she said. 'It shows Alexander's entire campaign, beginning in Greece in 334 BCE until his death in Babylon in 323 BCE. You can see the location of the battle of Granicus there on the left.'

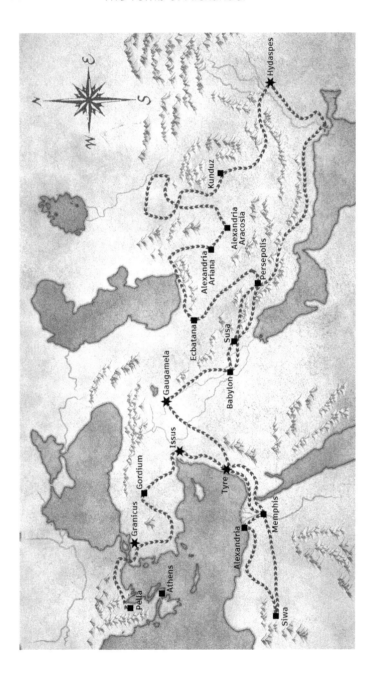

'The Persian ruler, Darius III, apparently considered Alexander to be nothing more than an upstart, so he decided not to command his armies himself. Instead, he left it to his most senior general Memnon of Rhodes who was a Greek mercenary. There is obviously some uncertainty about the number of troops involved, but most estimates say that Alexander's armies totalled roughly 18,000, men whereas the Persian army could have been as many as 80,000 strong. This included thousands of Greek mercenaries that were positioned at the back of the army because Memnon of Rhodes did not fully trust them to fight against their fellow Greeks. In other words, Alexander was at a huge numerical disadvantage.'

'Those do sound like almost insurmountable odds,' said Andrew. 'I bet those phalanx units proved their worth there.'

'Yes, they certainly did,' replied Fiona. 'As I said, the battles are described in amazing detail in Arrian of Nicomedia's work, thanks largely to Ptolemy's earlier historical writings. And the Battle of Granicus is a good example of that. It provides an almost blow-by-blow account of how the battle unfolded, including a moment where Alexander was almost killed.'

'Really?' asked Andrew. 'What happened?'

'Well,' said Fiona. 'Before the battle, Alexander donned a helmet with a large plume of white feathers so that everyone including the enemy soldiers could clearly see where he was. Already at this early stage in his life he seemed to hold an absolute conviction that he was invincible, and that he was destined to be ruler of the world.'

'Confident young man,' said Andrew, and smiled wryly. 'I remember feeling like that when I was twenty years old. Minus the ambitions to become ruler of the world, of course.'

'I think he was trying both to project and instil confidence in his men,' said Fiona. 'And it seems to have worked, because against the advice of some of his generals, especially Parmenion, he led the charge forward across the river, flanking the left side of the Persian army. As they crossed the river, the Greeks initially suffered heavy losses, as Memnon of Rhodes along with his sons was trying to prevent Alexander's forces from climbing the opposite river bank. Eventually, the Greek army established a foothold on the river bank, but at that point Alexander's spear broke and things almost went very badly for him. Let me read you a small section from this chapter. This is from Book 1, Chapter 15 of Arrian's account.'

Then Demaratus, a man of Corinth, one of his personal Companions, gave him his own spear; which he had no sooner taken than seeing Mithridates, the son-in-law of Darius, riding far in front of the others, and leading with him a body of cavalry arranged like a wedge, he rode on in front of the others, and hitting at the face of Mithridates with his spear, struck him to the ground. But hereupon, Rosacea rode up to Alexander and hit him on the head with his scimitar, breaking off a piece of his helmet. But the helmet broke the force of the blow. This man also Alexander struck to the ground, hitting him in the chest through the breastplate with his spear. And now Spithridates from behind had already raised aloft his scimitar against Alexander, when Cleitus, son of Dropidas, anticipated his blow, and hitting him on the arm and cut it off, scimitar and all.

'Wow,' said Andrew. 'So, Alexander almost died there?'

'That's right,' said Fiona. 'If Alexander's general, Cleitus the Black had not spotted the danger and cut off the Persian nobleman's arm with a single blow, Alexander could well have been killed in that moment.'

'Can we assume that this is an accurate account?' asked Andrew.

'There is really not much reason to doubt that this actually happened precisely the way it is described,' said Fiona. 'As I mentioned, Arrian based his writings on the very detailed account written by Ptolemy, and as Arrian wrote in his introduction, he trusted Ptolemy's account mainly because Ptolemy later became a historian and a king, and as Arrian said, it would be shameful for a king to lie.'

'I suppose that makes sense,' said Andrew.

'But just think about this for a moment,' said Fiona. 'I find it interesting to reflect on the fact that had this small skirmish in the very first battle of Alexander's campaign gone just slightly differently, Alexander might have been killed and his campaign of conquest would have collapsed. Who knows what the world might have looked like now if that had gone differently Anyway, Alexander's flanking attack gave his phalanx units in the army's centre the opportunity to cross the Granicus River, and once on the other side they completely dominated the Persian army. Faced with a wall of deadly spears, most of the Persian cavalry and foot soldiers fled, and then Alexander surrounded Darius III's Greek mercenaries and slaughtered them without mercy.'

'I guess he didn't trust them either,' said Andrew dryly.

'It was a bloodbath,' said Fiona. 'But it was also a decisive victory, and it left Asia Minor wide open for Alexander to take from the Persian Empire. He marched his army south across Asia Minor to the ancient city of Sardis which was the capital of the province of Lydia, and here the local Persian commander surrendered the city without a fight. Alexander then turned his attention to the Persian navy which was a formidable force at the time. Instead of fighting it at sea, Alexander moved on the main coastal cities that held its naval bases. By the winter of 334 BCE those cities had been taken, and the Persian fleet in the Mediterranean was now effectively neutralised.'

'Clever move,' said Andrew. 'Like neutralising an entire tank division by stealing their fuel. I don't think I would have thought of that.'

'Alexander was by all accounts a military genius,' said Fiona. 'This type of outside-the-box thinking was a hallmark of his approach to warfare and conquest. By the spring of 333 BCE he had swung his army back north to the ancient city of Gordion. The city was on the royal road first established by Darius I, and it stretched all the way from Sardis in the west to Persepolis in present-day Iran in the East, and so it was an important link into the very heart of the Persian empire. It was here that one of the most famous episodes of Alexander's life unfolded.'

'The Gordian Knot,' said Andrew expectantly.

'That's right,' replied Fiona. 'Gordion was founded four hundred years earlier by the Macedonian King Gordias, who was the father of the well-known King Midas. Gordias had supposedly arrived in an oxcart at the place where the city was later built, and the cart's shaft was tied to the yoke with a giant knot made from thick rope. When Alexander arrived, the city threw open the gates for him, and he settled in with his army to wait for reinforcements from Macedonia. Legend held that whoever could untie the knot would be the ruler of all of Asia. As most people know, Alexander unsheathed his sword and struck the knot with such force that it was cut open, thus fulfilling the prophecy. This was yet another example of Alexander's ability to dispense with convention and think outside the box.'

'I've always loved that story,' said Andrew. 'There is something about the sheer irreverence of it that I really enjoy.'

'Same here,' smiled Fiona. 'Anyway, after receiving his reinforcements Alexander headed south again. He was intending to take his army along the coast through the Levant to Egypt, which the Greeks viewed with some reverence as a centre of culture and history, but which at the time was part of the Persian empire. However, when he arrived at the ancient town of Issus at the foot of the Nur Mountains in what today is the southern-most province of Turkey on the border with Syria, the Persian army suddenly appeared behind them. Cut off from their supply lines and trapped on the narrow coastal plain between the mountains and the Mediterranean Sea, Alexander's only option was to fight. This time Darius III had taken command of the Persian army himself, and it outnumbered Alexander's two to one. Estimates vary hugely, but it is likely that Darius had around 100,000 men, against Alexander's 40,000. Either way, what Darius had not fully grasped was that the terrain favoured the tight formations of the Macedonian phalanx, and it left his cavalry-heavy forces at a disadvantage, as well as preventing him from exploiting his numerical advantage. The two forces lined up on opposite sides of the Pinarus River in battle formations quite similar to those of the Battle of Granicus. Once again, Alexander led his men on horseback across the river and charged. In an effort to keep up, gaps started to open up between the phalanx unit at the centre of his army. Alexander swung round to assist, and soon the Persian army was in disarray, with Alexander in the thick of the fighting. He fought his way straight towards King Darius with such ferocity and recklessness, hacking and slashing his way towards the Persian king, that Darius turned his chariot around and fled the battlefield.'

'Crikey,' said Andrew. 'He ran away?'

'That's right,' said Fiona. 'The great king of the largest empire in the ancient world was so spooked by Alexander's unpredictable and effective tactics that he must have concluded that there was a real chance that he might be captured or even killed. It is worth noting that Alexander was wounded in the thigh in this battle, but it clearly didn't dent his appetite for fighting.'

'So, what happened next?' asked Andrew. 'Did Alexander pursue Darius?'

'Initially he attempted to give chase, but he received word that his left flank under the command of Parmenion was in serious trouble against the Persian cavalry, so he decided to turn around and come to his general's aid.'

'Good man,' nodded Andrew. 'That's the sort of battlefield leadership you need if you're a soldier and you're up against it on the battlefield.'

'And that is exactly why his men loved him so much,' said Fiona. 'He was always at the front leading the charge, and he did not needlessly sacrifice his own troops.'

'Another resounding victory then,' said Andrew.

'It was,' replied Fiona. 'General Ptolemy apparently told Alexander that there had been so many dead Persians that his men had used their bodies to fill a ravine so they could cross. And in fact, it was enough to make Darius III send a letter to Alexander effectively suing for peace. He offered Alexander all of the land west of the Euphrates River in present-day Iraq, as well as one of his daughters in marriage if he would enter into an alliance.'

'Quite a turn-around,' said Andrew. 'I guess Darius could see which way the wind was blowing.'

'Probably,' said Fiona. 'But Alexander said no. The story goes that the seasoned general Parmenion, who was already a commander when Alexander was born, advised him to accept the offer by saying: "I would accept this offer, if I were Alexander." To which

Alexander rather scathingly replied: "So would I, if I were Parmenion." And then he sent a letter back to Darius, declining the offer and instead telling the ruler of the largest empire in the world to address Alexander as his king in future letters. He also told him that everything he owned was now Alexander's, and that if he wished to dispute this claim he should stand and fight rather than run away.'

'Such hubris,' chuckled Andrew. 'He really was beginning to think of himself as invincible, wasn't he?'

'Absolutely,' replied Fiona. 'In fact, this might have been around the time when he decided to go to Egypt, not just to conquer it and take it from the Persians, but to visit a famous oracle there that he wanted to ask some important questions about his future destiny. But I will get back to that in a bit. For now, let's continue with the story of the campaign. Alexander's next stop was the rich coastal city, trading hub and naval harbour of Tyre in present-day Lebanon. Founded around 2750 BCE, it is one of the oldest continually inhabited cities in the world, and it was then part of the Persian empire but formerly an independent Phoenician city-state. All other such city-states had surrendered to Alexander as he made his way south through the Levant along the Mediterranean coast towards Egypt, but Tyre would not surrender. Situated on a heavily walled island several hundred metres out into the sea, it was a natural fortress and virtually impregnable to assault from land or sea. From 585 BCE the city had withstood a siege by Nebuchadnezzar II which lasted 13 years, so they probably thought they could deal with Alexander too, when he arrived in January 332 BCE.'

'I can see where this is going,' remarked Andrew wryly. 'How did he do it?'

Fiona smiled knowingly. 'An artificial causeway, or mole, stretching out from the mainland all the way to the island. Using this mole, Alexander's army was able to transport huge siege towers out to the walls of Tyre and eventually conquer it. It was a mammoth engineering project that took seven months, but it cemented Alexander as an unstoppable force which it was wiser to bow down to than to oppose.'

'Irrepressible, is the word that springs to mind,' said Andrew. 'He just wouldn't take no for an answer, would he? Like a dog with a bone.'

'Exactly,' said Fiona. 'His sheer force of will drove him inexorably forward, and anyone who stood in his way was eventually made to regret it. What is amazing is that if you go to Tyre today, you will see that the island is now completely landlocked with the mainland, and that is partly to do with geological events but also partly a product of the causeway that Alexander built. You can literally walk on the land that started out as the causeway to Tyre.'

'I am guessing most would-be opponents thought better of the notion of resisting Alexander from then on,' said Andrew.

'Yes,' said Fiona. 'From this point on it was relatively easy for Alexander to sweep south along the coast, although the great city of Gaza was besieged and taken in late 332 BCE as well. Eventually, Alexander made it to Egypt. He arrived at the gates of Pelusium, which was where the Persian governor of

Egypt surrendered the entire province to Alexander, and then he proceeded to the great city of Memphis.'

'So, Alexander took control of all of Egypt without a fight?' asked Andrew.

'Indeed,' replied Fiona. 'I doubt even Alexander had dared to hope that he would one day be able to so easily conquer that ancient land and crown himself pharaoh.'

'Wait a minute,' said Andrew, sounding sceptical. 'Alexander became pharaoh?'

'Of course,' replied Fiona. 'Egypt effectively became his personal property. In fact, by some accounts, many Egyptians were quite pleased to see the Persians booted out. But Alexander did not dawdle. He moved back out to the coast of the Mediterranean, coming across a place where he had a vision of creating a great city. And this was where in April 331 BCE he founded what we know today as Alexandria. He ordered the beginning of its construction on the coast directly across from the nearby island of Pharos, intending it to become a gateway to Egypt from the Mediterranean. Apparently, he designed the layout himself, including the city's outer defences, the position of the market square, several temples around the city, and he also stipulated which gods they should be dedicated to. As a trading port Alexandria became very successful, and it eventually superseded the ancient Egyptian port city of Canopus, which was slightly further along the coast to the north-east. Alexandria would become one of the most important cities in the ancient world, not least because of its huge library. But also because of its enormous lighthouse on Pharos Island, which was one of the Seven Wonders of the World. By the way, it was Alexander's general Ptolemy who took charge of this part of the empire after Alexander's death. He founded the Ptolemaic dynasty in Alexandria which lasted for almost three hundred years, and it was Ptolemy who oversaw the building of the library and initiated the construction of the lighthouse.'

'A man after Alexander's own heart then,' observed Andrew.

'In some ways, yes,' smiled Fiona. 'But I will come back to that in a bit, because having founded Alexandria, Alexander was off into the western desert to see the oracle of Siwa.'

'Siwa?' said Andrew, and sat up. 'You mean, *the* Siwa? The one we sent McGregor to, in order to take out that rogue Egyptian general?'

Andrew was referring to their previous trip to Egypt, where they had helped to avert an Egyptian general getting his hands on nuclear material and using it against civilian populations in the Middle East.

'The very same,' nodded Fiona. 'It is a strange coincidence that we are talking about that place again in the context of something completely different. But I guess that is a function of the fact that many of these places have been around for thousands of years. Eventually, things are going to happen in the same places at different times in history. Anyway, after an arduous and perilous journey several hundred kilometres into the desert, they finally arrived at the temple of Siwa, which still stands today 2,300 years later.'

'Who was this oracle?' asked Andrew.

'The Oracle of Siwa was actually several people who, like the oracles that Alexander and his father before him had consulted in Delphi in Greece, were thought to be able to see into the future. This was a time in history when there was no such thing as science in the way we know it today. Even though ancient Greece was in many ways the birthplace of logic and reason as cornerstones of the way people thought, actual scientific theories and hypotheses tested by rigorous empirical evidence and analysis simply did not exist in the way they do now. Most things were grounded in superstition and mythology. Things like omens and prophecies were taken extremely seriously, and Alexander had several questions that he wanted answers to.'

'Such as?' asked Andrew.

'The first question he wanted an answer to was "Am I the son of a God?",' said Fiona.

'Really?' asked Andrew, looking dubious. 'How did that come about? Why would he believe that?'

'Apparently, Alexander's mother Olympias had hinted to Alexander that King Philip II was not actually his father and that instead he was the son of Zeus. Olympias was known for her strange esoteric rituals and what some would have considered witchcraft, and Alexander seemingly thought that perhaps what she had told him might be true.'

'I am not a parent,' said Andrew. 'But that surely can't be a healthy way to raise a young boy.'

'I agree,' said Fiona. 'But it was a very different time then, and Olympias was desperate to ensure that her son would come to rule Greece one day. As it turned out, she got her wish.'

'So, what did the oracles say then?' asked Andrew.

'Well. Alexander entered the inner chamber in the temple alone and asked his three questions,' said Fiona. 'And the answer to the most important one was, yes. He was indeed the son of Zeus, King of the gods, or as the Egyptians called him, Amun.'

'What were the other questions?' asked Andrew.

'The second question was, "Will I conquer the world?",' said Fiona. 'The answer to this question was also yes.'

'And the third?' asked Andrew.

'The final question was. "Have all my father's murderers been punished by the gods?".'

'That was a bit of a strange one,' said Andrew. 'What did he mean by that?'

'Well,' said Fiona. 'The theory goes that if Alexander's mother Olympias and perhaps even Alexander himself had been part of a plot to kill Philip II, thereby effectively making Alexander king, then Alexander would want to know if the gods had imposed justice on them all, in which case he and perhaps his mother were now safe from divine wrath.'

'And the answer?' asked Andrew.

'Yes again,' said Fiona. 'So, presumably, Alexander would now have thought that the gods favoured him and that he really was invincible.'

'Not that his ego needed a boost,' said Andrew. 'What happened next?'

'Having been reassured that he was indeed the son of Zeus-Amun, Alexander returned east to travel back to Tyre. From there he set out to finally vanquish Darius III. Alexander realised that he could never claim to be the ruler of the world for as long as King

Darius III was alive. Similarly, it was clear to Darius that he would never take back control of Asia without first defeating Alexander.'

'A final show-down then,' said Andrew.

'Something like that,' replied Fiona. 'Alexander set off with his army into the Persian heartland in what today is Syria, and he eventually entered present-day Iraq where he finally encountered Darius near the village of Gaugamela just north of the city of Mosul in northern Iraq. Darius and his army were waiting for Alexander there, and this is where the final battle took place.'

'How many men were involved in this battle?' asked Andrew. 'Presumably, they both brought as many as they could possibly muster?'

'Our best estimates are that the Persian army totalled at least 120,000 men, but it was possibly several times that,' said Fiona. 'Even by today's standards, that is a significant number of soldiers involved in one battle. I think it is worth remembering that the total population of the world back then is estimated to have been somewhere around 150 million compared with today's almost eight billion, so the sizes of these two armies relative to how many people actually lived in the Greek and Persian empires at that time were absolutely enormous. If Darius had managed to bring an army with the same proportion of the global population today, it would have numbered in the region of seven million.'

Andrew shook his head. 'That is mind-boggling. But even with just 120,000, the supply logistics for such a force would have been staggering.'

'Again, no one knows exactly how many fought that day, but Ptolemy later wrote that Alexander's army consisted of just under 50,000 men. In any case, it was almost certainly the largest battle in history at that point in time. And once more, Alexander was severely outnumbered.'

'Yet, once again he won, right?' smiled Andrew, anticipating Fiona's next words. 'So how did he do it?'

'As before at the Granicus and at the Pinarus, the two armies lined up facing each other,' said Fiona. 'Because of Alexander's numerical disadvantage, a simple head-on confrontation would not work. He had to be creative, so he ordered his phalanx in the centre to advance while he moved to the edge of his own right flank, thereby drawing Persian cavalry to him. The plan worked and a gap opened up in the centre where a decisive blow could then be dealt. As the Persians advanced to the Greek flank in an attempt to hold back Alexander and his companion cavalry, he filtered in his rear guard and then disengaged himself and his cavalry. He then formed his units into a wedge, swung back around to his own centre, and with himself at the front he charged into the weakened Persian centre. He and his cavalry units fought their way towards Darius himself, defeating the Persian king's royal guard. At this point Darius apparently panicked yet again and rode off after which his army collapsed. Listen to this. This is from Arrian's Anabasis of Alexander, Book 3, chapter 14.'

For a short time, there ensued a hand-to-hand fight; but when the Macedonian cavalry, commanded by Alexander himself, pressed on vigorously, thrusting themselves against the Persians and striking their faces with their spears, and when the Macedonian phalanx in a dense array and bristling with long pikes had also made an attack upon them, all things together appeared full of terror to Darius, who had already long been in a state of fear, so that he was the first to turn and flee.

'So, once again King Darius fled?' said Andrew.

'He did,' replied Fiona. 'And at that moment on a plain outside the village of Gaugamela, the Persian Empire effectively ended.'

'Amazing tactics,' said Andrew. 'What happened to Darius?'

'Alexander didn't give up trying to catch him,' said Fiona. 'After the battle, he took his army to the Persian Empire's capital Babylon which opened the gates for him as their new ruler. He then moved on to the ancient city of Susa which was the former capital of the Persian Elamite empire. It also offered no resistance, and Alexander made a point of going to sit on the royal throne of Persia there. Then he moved on towards Persepolis the empire's ceremonial capital, but he was held up for a month in the mountains before defeating the last remnants of the Persian army. When he reached Persepolis, he ordered it burnt and pillaged as retribution for the Persian invasion of Greece and the burning of the temples of Athens in 480 BCE.'

'And Darius?' asked Andrew. 'Presumably, he kept running?'

'He did,' replied Fiona. 'He was making for the empire's provinces of Parthia, Bactria, and Sogdia, which today roughly correspond to northern Iran, western Afghanistan and southern Turkmenistan, where he intended to raise a new army. But he never got there. Just as Alexander was drawing near, he was murdered by one of his own governors, a man by the name of Bessus, who immediately made the mistake of proclaiming himself the new ruler of Persia. He even changed his name to Artaxerxes V, taking on the royal name of past Achaemenid Persian rulers.'

'Oh dear,' said Andrew. 'I guess that wasn't the cleverest thing to have done.'

'That's right,' said Fiona. 'Upon hearing this, Alexander instantly set out to track Bessus down and kill him. He simply could not accept any resistance to his rule. When he arrived at the place where Darius III had been killed, Alexander lay his own cape over him as a sign of respect, and then ordered that his body be buried with his ancestors in the royal tombs of Persepolis. As for Bessus, he fled to the ancient city of Ecbatana which was halfway between Baghdad and Tehran. When Alexander approached, he fled further east into Bactria but was eventually hunted down after a chase lasting months and covering incursions as far north as Khujand in Tajikistan, which was founded by Alexander as Alexandria Eschate. This name literally means *Alexandria the furthest*, because as far as anyone in Greece knew, this was the very edge of the world. Anyway, when Bessus was finally caught more than two thousand kilometres to the east in what is today Kunduz in northern Afghanistan, his body was torn limb from limb in a particularly gruesome act that Alexander deemed befitting of a traitor and a kingslayer. After that, there were no more pretenders to the Persian throne.'

'Brutal,' said Andrew, and winced. 'Alexander absolutely refused to give up, didn't he? I guess that was the end of Alexander's Persian conquest.'

'Yes,' replied Fiona. 'But it was not the end of his campaign. He was possessed of seemingly limitless ambition, and he spent several years playing a game of whack-a-mole with local rulers and tribes in the large mountainous area of central Asia that today forms part of Tajikistan, Uzbekistan and Kyrgyzstan. None of those rulers seemed to fully grasp who they were up against. There was a slew of battles and skirmishes, but eventually, Alexander dominated them all, and then he began taking his armies back south and east towards what is today Pakistan and India. He had heard tales of great kingdoms there and simply could not resist trying to subjugate them. On the way, he conquered Bactria and founded the cities Alexandria Ariana, which is modern-day Herat, and also Alexandria Arachosia, which is now called Kandahar. You can actually hear it in the name. Alexander was known as *Iskander* in Asia, and over time the name Iskander became Kandahar.'

'That is fascinating,' said Andrew.

'Yes,' said Fiona. 'He really left his mark on history, and this huge campaign of his had a profound impact on the world. But in some respects, he was now also overplaying his hand. Ever since the defeat of Darius III, many of his men particularly the ones that had been with him since leaving Greece around eight or nine years earlier, were growing tired of endless conquest. As far as they were concerned, they had fulfilled their mission to conquer the Persian Empire, and many of them simply wanted to go home to their farmland and their families. There was also unhappiness with the way in which Alexander increasingly took on Persian customs and began to dress like a Persian king, which the Greeks thought was effeminate. And when he finally insisted that his men prostrate themselves in front of him, which means to lie flat in deference before him as if he really was a god, it became too much for some of them. Several times over the next few years there was almost mutiny in the ranks, and a couple of times Alexander executed suspected mutineers including the experienced general Parmenion and his son Philotas who had been in charge of Alexander's own companion cavalry. Both of them had played crucial parts in Alexander's campaign, but when he suspected them of plotting against him, he had them executed. In another incident in the royal city of Maracanda, which today is the city of Samarkand in Uzbekistan, there was a drunken row with Cleitus the Black, who as you will remember, had saved Alexander's life during the Battle of Granicus by chopping off the arm of an attacking Persian nobleman. Cleitus had already expressed his dislike of Alexander's increasing affinity for Persian clothes and customs, and given their shared history Cleitus perhaps felt that he could speak freely. This turned out to be a mistake. During an argument, Alexander was so incensed by Cleitus suggesting that Alexander's success was mainly due to his father Philip II, that Alexander ran him through with a spear and killed him.'

'Jesus!' exclaimed Andrew. 'Cleitus was an old friend. He was the reason Alexander was even alive at that point. Without him, there would have been no campaign. No empire.'

'It was a great shock to everyone in the royal court,' nodded Fiona. 'And by all accounts, Alexander was stricken by remorse for days afterwards. This is what Arrian wrote about the incident in Book 4, chapter 9.'

Directly after he had done the deed, he recognised that it was a horrible one. Some of his biographers even say that he propped the pike against the wall with the intention of falling upon it himself, thinking that it was not proper for him to live who had killed his friend when under the influence of wine. Most historians do not mention this, but say that he went off to bed and lay there lamenting, calling Cleitus himself by name. He did not cease calling himself the murderer of his friends, and for three days rigidly abstained from food and drink, and paid no attention whatever to his personal appearance.

'So, he was clearly distraught by what he had done,' continued Fiona, 'but he eventually regained his composure and pushed south through present-day Afghanistan across the towering mountain range of the Hindu Kush and through Pakistan towards India, taking several cities along the way. Eventually though, after a particularly bloody battle at a river the Greeks called the Hydaspes in the Indus Valley, he finally had to concede that he could command his men to go no further. At the Hydaspes in 326 BCE they simply refused to go on, and Alexander reluctantly gave the order to return to Babylon. On the way there he did manage to conquer several more cities, but he was also wounded by an arrow to the chest and nearly died. The voyage back towards Babylon through the hot and barren southern desert of Gedrosia in present-day Pakistan and Iran was gruelling and took many months, and large numbers of his men died from illness and exhaustion. When they finally reached Persepolis and Susa, Alexander arranged for mass marriages between his generals and the daughters of local Persian nobles in order to consolidate his power. But then another event happened that was even more momentous for Alexander. His childhood friend and confidant Hephaestion died from suspected typhoid after several days of fever in the city of Ecbatana in 324 BCE. This was a huge blow to Alexander. He had lost his most trusted companion and he apparently refused to eat or drink for many days following his friend's death. He also ordered a period of mourning across the entire empire. After finally returning to his royal seat in Babylon, Alexander received emissaries from all across his giant empire who had come to recognise him as their ruler.'

'This was where he died, right?' asked Andrew.

'Yes,' replied Fiona. 'The circumstances are vague, but he fell ill with a fever and died on the 11th of June 323 BCE. And of course, this immediately led to the wars of succession between his generals, since no successor was ever appointed by Alexander. The ambiguity of the situation was made worse by the fact that Alexander had married a number of times during his campaign and had fathered several boys, most recently Alexander IV whose mother was Roxana, Alexander's Bactrian wife.'

'So, there were actually blood-line successors out there when Alexander died?' asked Andrew.

'Yes,' said Fiona. 'But none of them had come of age yet, so when he died it left the open question as to who would be capable of taking over and ruling his empire. It is generally accepted amongst historians that when asked who he would appoint as his successor, Alexander replied "To the strongest". This enigmatic answer left the door open for ambiguity and strife between the possible successors. The empire was in many ways easier to conquer than to rule, but without Alexander it would be impossible to keep it together. The empire would have to be broken up and divided between his generals. Anyway, that has to be a story for another day. I think I have talked at you for long enough now.'

'Fascinating,' said Andrew. 'That was really interesting.'

'If you were to sit down and read the seven volumes of Arrian of Nicomedia's Anabasis like I have, you would find an extremely detailed account of all of Alexander's military exploits.'

'He was quite the narcissist though, wasn't he?' said Andrew. 'I mean, he was clearly a great commander, but that whole thing about trying to force old friends to lie down on the ground in front of him and to treat him like a god. That is just not something a normal person with a healthy mind would do. He seemed to have been an absolute megalomaniac.'

'You are probably right,' said Fiona. 'If not when he started out from Greece, then certainly increasingly so as his campaign progressed. By the end of it he was one of those men who simply could not abide waking up in the morning knowing that somewhere there were people who did not accept his greatness. And he seemed pathologically compelled to either make them submit or to kill them. But then again, in an age where gods were real things that people absolutely believed existed, a young man from a lineage like his could probably easily be swept up in the belief that perhaps he himself was divine. Especially since the gods seemed to favour him in almost everything he did. But all of what I have just said is more or less inferred from the written sources, because the emphasis in the accounts of people like Arrian was on the facts of what happened during the various battles. There is very little context either in terms of the state of the world outside of Alexander's bubble, or in terms of what Alexander might have been thinking privately about this or that. The most detailed view we get from these writings of Alexander as a person was in the sections related to the mysterious death of Hephaestion, and when Alexander killed Cleitus the Black.'

Andrew nodded, gazing towards the Acropolis, seemingly lost in thought.

'What's on your mind?' asked Fiona.

'I keep thinking about Alexis,' replied Andrew. 'She is quite a remarkable woman, and the things she said about where the human species is going are difficult to wrap my head around. I have to admit that there was very little she said that didn't ultimately ring true in some sense. But I can't help thinking that somehow ZOE Technologies is playing a much more active role in those things than she admitted. We need to get to the bottom of it. Four people have already lost their lives over this, and we need to find out what Lambert thought he knew that would make him want to kill Balfour.'

'I agree,' said Fiona. 'We have to come up with a plan for getting closer to Alexis. I swear she is hiding something. We need a way into her mind so we can find out what she really knows.'

Andrew nodded pensively, looking out over the ancient city for a few moments.

'You're right,' he finally said. 'And I think I may have an idea.'

# TWELVE

Standing in front of the white-painted double doors made of solid oak with his right hand raised, Dubois hesitated for a few seconds before knocking. This was going to be an important meeting and he was taking a brief moment to steel himself. The truth was that he found his benefactor highly intimidating, but he knew he was bearing good news. He knocked three times in quick succession.

'Come in,' said a female voice on the other side.

Dubois grasped the door handle, turned it and opened the door.

'Monsieur Dubois,' said Alexis, and rose to greet him, smiling warmly.

She had been sitting in a purple velvet armchair by the fireplace. Her hair was flowing loosely over her shoulders, and she was wearing an elegant cherry-coloured dress, silver earrings and a silver necklace. The colour of the dress created a stunning contrast with her ink-black hair and caused Dubois's eyes to linger for a brief moment.

He closed the door behind him and approached her with his hand out. As they met, he took her outstretched hand, bowed slightly and kissed it.

'Mademoiselle,' he said nervously. 'A pleasure to meet with you again.'

'I am sure the pleasure will be all mine,' replied Alexis, and beckoned him towards a small antique mahogany table with two upholstered brass-studded chairs on either side of it. The table was placed in a sunlit spot by a window overlooking the garden of the estate. 'Please, sit.'

'Thank you,' said Dubois and sat down in one of the chairs. Alexis sat down opposite him and placed her hands on the table, loosely clasped together.

'How have you been?' she asked, her mouth smiling, but her eyes studying his face in a slightly detached manner.

Dubois had felt nervous about the meeting all morning, and now that he was here that nervousness had not abated. Alexis was both stunning and terrifying all at the same time. His hands were sweaty, and sitting there in a light beige suit with a white shirt and black tie he could feel his own pulse in his carotid arteries. She, on the other hand, seemed entirely relaxed and comfortable sitting there in her chair, confident and effortlessly beautiful, her inscrutable eyes meeting his. He knew he would never have a woman like this, and it ate away at him. Part of him wanted to leave, but another part wanted to stay here in the company of this captivating woman for as long as he could.

'I am well,' said Dubois, putting on a laboured smile and shifting slightly in his chair. 'In fact, I am better than just well. I have been looking forward to this meeting and to showing you what I have come up with. But first, may I ask about the diary? Was everything as expected?'

'Yes, it was,' said Alexis. 'The courier company sent it to Athens with a specially chartered jet, and it was brought here under guard from the airport. I have spent a lot of time examining it and it all appears to be entirely undamaged and in incredible condition considering its age.'

Dubois nodded. 'I am glad,' he said. 'May I… May I see it?'

Alexis gave him a curious smile as if she was trying to figure out why he had asked that question, but then she rose and began walking towards the opposite wall from the windows in the large sumptuous sitting room.

'Come,' she said. 'Let me show you.'

Dubois rose and followed her towards the wall in the high-ceilinged sitting room where an enormous painting of the Acropolis hung. It was at least three metres wide and about as tall. Alexis walked close to the painting and placed a finger on a small concealed button on the gilded frame. There was a short beep, and then Alexis stepped back, glancing at Dubois with a mischievous smile.

Amid the barely audible whirring of electrical motors, the painting slid slowly upwards on rails along the wall to reveal a set of steel double doors with a digital display shining faintly blue next to a keypad on the door on the right.

'I had this specially constructed a couple of months ago in anticipation of the arrival of the diary,' said Alexis.

'Very impressive,' smiled Dubois. 'And well hidden.'

'So, now you know one of my secrets,' said Alexis with a playful smile. 'Just keep it to yourself. Remember, we know secrets about you too.'

Dubois looked alarmed and involuntarily brought up his hands in front of him, palms facing Alexis. 'Mademoiselle, I would never…,' he began nervously.

'Relax,' laughed Alexis placatingly. 'I am sure you wouldn't. I was just teasing you.'

'Oh,' said Dubois, feeling foolish. This woman had him wrapped around her finger, and he hated it and loved it all at the same time.

'Would you mind looking away?' she asked.

It took him a couple of seconds to register what she had asked him, but then he turned around.

'Oh! Of course not,' he said, waiting patiently with his back to her.

He heard the sound of an eight-digit passcode being entered, followed by the clack of a metal lock disengaging.

'Come,' said Alexis.

As Dubois turned around, he saw the double doors swing open to reveal a number of steel shelves. Alexis pressed a button on the top shelf and it immediately began extending itself into the room. As he approached, Dubois saw rows of the diary pages arranged neatly in a grid and still inside their protective casings. Covering the shelf was a thick pane of glass.

He gently placed the fingertips of his right hand on the glass whilst leaning in over the shelf to get a better look. The glass was cold to the touch. The entire wall safe seemed to be kept at a low temperature.

'I see you have taken good care of them,' he said.

'They are quite literally invaluable to me,' said Alexis. 'I have already begun analysing their content.'

'I see,' said Dubois. 'How did your oligarch friend get his hands on the diary to begin with?'

Alexis moved her head to one side, and gently tossed her hair away from her face.

'Interesting story,' she replied. 'He apparently bought it from a private collector in Egypt. This person had himself acquired it as part of a lot coming from an "unofficial" dig site in Alexandria in a location thought to have been part of the royal palace of the ancient city.'

'Incredible,' said Dubois. 'Sounds almost too good to be true.'

'I know,' said Alexis. 'It was only ever thought to be a forgery. It is amazing to think that it might well be the real thing.'

'And the oligarch?'

'Probably happy to take the insurance pay-out,' replied Alexis. 'I am sure he does not suspect me, and I doubt he ever fully understood what he was sitting on. My sense was that he bought it just because he could, and to own something to impress his dinner guests.'

'Well, he certainly succeeded in the latter,' observed Dubois. 'Have you been able to make much sense of the contents of the pages yet?'

'As you know,' said Alexis. 'I am a keen student of my country's great history, and I have spent many years researching ancient writings. Its form is not dissimilar to modern Greek writing, but there are many differences in the vocabulary, the use of words and even in the meaning of those words. And conjugations have also changed, all of which often render the text quite ambiguous. But I have so far managed to conclude that the contents of the diary marry up very well with the second-hand account from Arrian of Nicomedia, and I now feel quite confident that this is the personal diary of Ptolemy.'

'One of Alexander the Great's most important generals,' said Dubois.

'Yes,' said Alexis. 'The man who came to rule all of Egypt after Alexander's death. His descendants ruled after him for centuries in the Ptolemaic dynasty, and his writings, through the work of Arrian, form most of the basis of what we know today about Alexander the Great.'

'Have you performed chronometric analysis on these?' asked Dubois, gesturing to the ancient pages.

'We have carried out carbon dating on fragments of each individual page, and their results all concur. This reinforces our belief that they are all clearly part of a whole, and that just one author wrote the entire thing. The carbon dating yielded results in a range around 300 to 250 BCE, so that also fits perfectly with what we had hoped for. But as you and I have discussed, there is really only one way to be sure, and that is to match the DNA from the stains of blood and sweaty grime that is embedded into several of the diary's pages to the DNA of Ptolemy himself. We have already extracted and sequenced the entire genome from the blood on the pages, but we obviously need to match it against a known source to verify their identity.'

'Correct,' said Dubois, nodding.

'When we last spoke, you said you believed you had come up with a way to achieve that,' said Alexis. 'So, have you?'

'Well,' said Dubois, clearing his throat. 'The basic problem is that the location of Ptolemy's tomb is unknown, making it impossible to directly acquire a sample from his body. But I came up with a way that was almost as good.'

'Tell me about it,' said Alexis, sounding both intrigued and eager.

'Well, as you know better than anyone,' began Dubois. 'During conception, and unlike the other 22 chromosomes, the male Y chromosome is passed on from father to son virtually unchanged. This means that if we could find just one confirmed male descendent of Ptolemy, we would be able to compare the Y chromosome of that descendant with the Y chromosome of the blood samples we have retrieved from the diary.'

'And if they match,' interjected Alexis, now visibly excited, 'we would know for certain that the blood on the diary did indeed belong to Ptolemy himself.'

'That is correct,' said Dubois. 'And we would not have to do a complete sequencing and comparison of the two genomes. We could just focus on the Y chromosome.'

'Monsieur Dubois,' said Alexis, her eyes gleaming with delight. 'That is an inspired idea. I must say I am deeply impressed.'

'Thank you,' said Dubois calmly, but inwardly basking in the unbridled attention and praise from Alexis.

'So have you done it?' she asked expectantly. 'Have you located a known descendant?'

'Yes, I have,' replied Dubois, savouring the moment. 'A Ptolemaic prince buried in an elaborate tomb that was part of a large necropolis just north of the harbour in Paphos in southwestern Cyprus. It was unearthed in the Tombs of the Kings complex in that town just a few years ago, and I have concluded that it must be the tomb of Ptolemy Eupator, the son of Ptolemy VI Philometor and Cleopatra II, who reigned for a very short period as co-ruler from 152-150 BCE. He was the great-great-great-great-grandson of Ptolemy, who as you know renamed himself Ptolemy I Soter, when he took the throne of Egypt and became pharaoh. Soter meaning *saviour*.'

'Yes,' said Alexis. 'I am aware. And you are certain that the tomb belongs to that prince?'

'Absolutely,' replied Dubois. 'There is a whole range of factors that taken together leave me in no doubt that this prince was Ptolemaic. Firstly, the tomb itself had several structural differences from other tombs in the necropolis, all indicating Egyptian links. It was elevated and sitting on a podium indicating that it was constructed for a deified person, which is exactly what Ptolemy Eupator was. In addition, bronze coins were found inside the tomb kept next to the sarcophagus in a badly decomposed sheepskin pouch with drawstring, and they had the unmistakable image of an eagle on a bolt of lightning on the reverse. This was the case for all Ptolemaic coins minted during the reign of that dynasty. This particular symbol was also present on the sarcophagus itself, along with other elaborate decorations.'

'Anything else?' asked Alexis. 'This sounds promising but perhaps not definitive.'

'Well, there's more,' said Dubois. 'Two eagle sculptures were found on the tomb itself, which would never have been the case had it not been built for a member of the Ptolemaic dynasty. And finally, the mummified body was young. Around 12 years old, which is exactly the age at which Ptolemy Eupator died. It all fits perfectly.'

Alexis nodded, clearly impressed. 'I must say, that is as convincing a set of evidence as we could hope for. Where was the boy's mummy being kept?'

'His remains were kept at the Cyprus Museum in Nicosia,' replied Dubois.

'But you managed to find a way in,' smiled Alexis knowingly.

Dubois nodded. 'Stone's man, *Pantera*, as he is called, managed to enter when the museum was closed, disguised as a plumber. He was able to retrieve a number of tissue samples from the mummy.'

'And you have them with you?' asked Alexis, raising her eyebrows.

'I do,' smiled Dubois and gestured towards his briefcase. 'Let me show you.'

Dubois walked to the briefcase, placed it on the small antique table, set the dials on the locks and popped it open.

Alexis joined him, standing close to him and leaning in over the case to look at the tissue samples, that were safely stored in small plastic containers and kept in form-fitted cut-outs in the foam that lined the inside of the case. She was so close to him that Dubois could smell the subtle and flowery perfume in her hair.

'Marvellous,' she said, and straightened back up. 'I will have them sent to our lab today. If we are right about this, the pages in that safe will be one of the most important finds in the modern era of my country.'

'You plan to keep them, right?' asked Dubois.

'Of course,' said Alexis, seemingly surprised that he would even ask. 'I don't trust anyone else with something as important as this, and that includes the supposed Greek authorities. There is no amount of money that could make me part with them.'

'Speaking of which,' said Dubois and cleared his throat once again. 'I trust my bonus will be sent shortly?'

Alexis smiled at him coyly.

'Mr Dubois,' she purred. 'Pierre. You will get your payment as soon as I have verified that the two sets of DNA match. A little patience, please.'

'Of course, mademoiselle,' replied Dubois obsequiously and bowed slightly. 'I will wait.'

'Excellent work,' said Alexis, and placed a hand gently on Dubois's shoulder. 'I will get this to our lab for sequencing immediately. We should have the result within a couple of days.'

She took her hand off his shoulder and started walking back to the antique table with the two chairs.

Dubois's eyes lingered on her as she walked away from him.

'In the meantime,' said Alexis casually. 'I would like you to prepare for a trip to northern Greece. Come and sit down. Let me tell you the details.'

# THIRTEEN

The Atene-Vouliagmeni Marina is a couple of kilometres south of the Megalo Kavouri headland on the outskirts of southern Athens where Alexis' estate was located. As the sun approached the horizon towards the west and pleasure boats were returning to the marina after an afternoon out on the water among the islands of the Saronic Gulf, Andrew was loading the diving equipment into the small boat he had rented a couple of hours earlier. The boat was just under four metres long and had a single outboard engine that was powerful enough to propel the boat along the coastline near a harbour, but not designed to enable the boat to cross the open sea or go island-hopping. However, for Andrew's purposes, it was just right since he was planning on hugging the coastline and he never intended on taking the boat much further than fifty metres from the shore.

Wearing tight-fitting shorts and a T-shirt, which would make wearing a wetsuit easier, he had just picked up the underwater scooter from the small pier where the boat was moored. The scooter was about a metre long and shaped like a small torpedo with a caged propeller at the rear. It also had a top-mounted handlebar similar to those on a motorcycle, which allowed a diver to grab on and be towed through the water. Andrew had some experience with these from the SAS already, although only ever in a simulated amphibian insertion behind enemy lines. It was not the way he and his platoon had usually been deployed in the past, even on a mission that involved an approach to a target from the sea, but they had all received training to allow them to use this type of equipment.

The scooter's maximum depth was 100 feet or around 30 metres, and its top speed was just 5 kilometres per hour. That equates to a fast walking pace and does not initially sound like much. However, over a distance of several hundred metres, it represents a huge saving in both time and energy expenditure versus having to swim that distance underwater.

He grabbed the buoyancy vest with the chest-mounted mini breathing apparatus. It consisted of a small pressurized metal tank that sat in a Velcro-locked pocket and was connected to a mouthpiece via a short tube. This would allow him to remain submerged for up to twenty minutes which would be more than long enough for what he was planning.

Finally, Fiona handed him the utility belt, which had several pouches attached to it containing various equipment that he expected to need. It also held the device he was planning to place once the sun had gone down and darkness had fallen.

'Remember the spot?' asked Andrew, looking up at Fiona, who was standing on the pier.

'The big rock next to the B&B on the way back towards Athens,' replied Fiona. 'Got it.'

'Good,' said Andrew. 'Just climb up there and keep a lookout for anything that might mess things up for me. It should provide a good view of the whole bay. I'll set my phone to vibrate, so just send me a message if you spot anything.'

'Will do,' said Fiona.

'Great,' said Andrew, pulling the chord on the small outboard engine which sputtered to life and then settled into a gentle growl as it idled.

'Be careful, ok?' said Fiona, looking uneasy. 'We don't know who is on that boat. There might be guards.'

'I know,' said Andrew. 'Don't worry. I promise I won't do anything reckless.'

Fiona looked unconvinced. Then she turned around to look at their rental car parked nearby.

'I think I will get going then,' she said. 'I need to spend some time buying an ice cream and walking up and down the beach first. I want to make sure I look like a tourist.'

'Alright,' said Andrew. 'I will see you in a couple of hours if the sharks don't get me.'

Fiona smiled and shook her head. 'Not funny. Good luck.'

Then she walked towards the car, got in and drove away.

Andrew twisted the handle on the outboard motor and the small vessel started to gently move through the water. He steered it out of the harbour and then revved up the engine to nearly full throttle, making the prow of the boat rise up slightly as it cut its way through the gentle seas of the Aegean. As soon as he was out of the harbour, he turned right to sail west around a small rocky headland, and then he made his way north towards the bay where the Hypatia lay anchored. He followed the coast at a distance of around thirty metres and soon had the yacht in view. Continuing around the headland along the rocky coast, he could clearly see the yacht to his left around 400 metres out into the bay. He also spotted the large rock Fiona was heading for a few hundred metres further along the coast to his right.

Once he had reached a somewhat isolated location away from beaches and people, he killed the engine and allowed the boat to drift silently forward using its own momentum. Then he got up and lifted the heavy anchor from the front of the boat and tossed it over the side. The water was roughly three metres deep and the anchor quickly wedged itself into the sand at the bottom.

He slipped into a thin black wetsuit, and then sat down and strapped on the buoyancy vest along with the mini breathing apparatus. Then followed the goggles and the belt, after which he slipped into the water and hauled the underwater scooter over the side after him. The scooter had almost perfectly neutral buoyancy and bobbed calmly in the shallow waves that were gently caressing the hull of the small boat.

As he pulled away, he swung the scooter around in front of him and pointed it out toward the bay. Then he gripped the handlebars, pressed the dual triggers mounted on both sides of the handlebars and twisted them slightly towards himself. The small but powerful electric motor instantly sprang to life, making the propeller churn the water in front of him, and then it began dragging him forward through the water. Using the handlebars he tilted the scooter downwards, and within a few seconds, he was several metres below the surface, gliding effortlessly through the water.

Having reassured himself that the mini breathing apparatus worked as intended, he descended to around five metres and checked the small compass that was mounted on the top of the scooter. He knew he had to head roughly northeast, and he expected to reach the Hypatia after no more than ten minutes.

As he proceeded further out into the bay, the seabed dropped away under him, and all he could see were shades of greyish blue, penetrated by the shafts of light from the setting sun. It was now virtually sitting on the horizon, and darkness would begin to fall very soon.

He checked his wristwatch several times along the way, and after around five minutes he ascended towards the surface and slowed the scooter down to a slow crawl as he briefly lifted his head above the water to orientate himself. Seeing the 100-metre-long yacht ahead of him in the distance, he adjusted his course slightly and then descended again.

Another four minutes later he spotted first the heavy anchor chain reaching down at a slight angle towards the seabed, and then after that the underside of the hull of the Hypatia.

He eased off on the throttle and slowed to a couple of kilometres per hour as he carefully approached the huge vessel. He tried to peer up through the surface to see if anyone was out on the front deck or on the sundeck at the top of the superstructure, but the refractions caused by the waves made it impossible to make out any details. The light was also fading fast, but that would now begin to work to his advantage.

As he approached the rear of the boat he spotted the two giant propellers, which at full speed could push the ship forward through the water at an impressive rate of knots. He suddenly had gory visions of what would happen if the captain suddenly fired up the engines and decided to relocate the ship. Pushing those images out of his mind, he approached the rear platform just above the propellers and then switched off the underwater scooter. Using the high-strength magnet that he had glued to the scooter, he brought it right up close to the hull and the submersible snapped onto it with a muffled clonk.

Slowly and carefully, he poked his head out of the water just behind the large open deck at the rear of the ship that was almost level with the waterline. It was less than half a metre for him to climb up, but he spent a few seconds making sure that no one was around.

Placing his hands on the edge, he hauled himself up and out of the water, careful not to make too much noise, and suddenly conscious of his actual weight after having spent the past ten minutes floating weightlessly underwater. He quickly took off his mask and his breathing apparatus, and then he unzipped his wetsuit and pulled it off, hiding all three of them behind a large plastic trunk sitting on one side of the boat's rear platform. Then he approached the door to the rear lower level of the vessel. His shorts and T-shirt were still wet, but they were so thin and fit so snugly to his body that he knew that the lightweight polyester material would be dry within a couple of minutes.

As he looked around, he could see why this was called a *super*-yacht. It was more akin to a floating house than a boat, although its long sleek shape was clearly designed to look like something that wanted to move across the ocean at speed.

He suspected that Alexis' private quarters were probably on the $3^{rd}$ level, so as he made his way inside he immediately began looking for stairs. There were none in the rear-most room of Level 1 where he had just entered, so he carefully made his way further into the ship, approaching what sounded like the engine room. He skirted it and went further towards the front of the vessel, and roughly midships he found what he was looking for. Stairs leading up. There was even a small schematic showing which levels contained which rooms and facilities. Guest bedrooms on Level 1, bar, cinema and dining room on Level 2, and as he expected, private quarters on level 3.

He had no idea what the size of the crew might be, but he guessed that there would be a captain and possibly two more crew on the bridge on Level 4, two or three staff for cooking and serving, and perhaps another three for managing the rest of the ship, particularly during entry into and exit from harbours and marinas. However, all that mattered at this point was getting up the stairs to Alexis' private quarters.

He wanted to spend as little time on the ship as possible, so he had to move swiftly.

Reaching Level 2, he poked his head around the corner and saw a dining room that more than anything looked like a conference room in an upmarket hotel. Classical music was playing from hidden speakers, and the large table at the centre of the room looked like it had been set for four people.

He withdrew back into the stairwell and headed further up, emerging on Level 3 in what could best be described as a large comfortable sitting room, complete with a wide ethanol fireplace and a generous seating area with two sofas, two armchairs and a large smoked glass coffee table sitting on a deep and fluffy cream coloured rug. All the furniture was made of white leather, and a large number of spotlights in the ceiling were on but had been dialled down to provide a soft yellowish hue.

In the centre of the room was a large fish tank. It was at least three metres long and a metre wide, and it rested on a one-metre-tall glossy metal pedestal and extended all the way to the ceiling. Dozens of different and colourful tropical fish were languidly swimming along inside it as small air bubbles percolated up from the pebbles at its base.

The whole space looked exceedingly inviting, and when Andrew spotted the private minibar along a small section of wall, it was all he could do to resist the urge to pour himself a drink and slump into one of the sofas.

Towards the far end of the sitting room on the other side of the fish tank, were a set of dark wooden double doors with a large gilded Vergina Sun across them.

*Bingo,* thought Andrew. *That must be her office.*

Crouching down so as not to be spotted by anyone who might happen to be walking along the walkway outside the windows, he quickly made his way to the double doors where he paused for a few seconds. The only sounds he could hear were the distant low-level hum of the ship's engines and his own pulse throbbing in his still wet ears.

Gently and slowly, he pulled the sliding double-door apart revealing a large wood-panelled office with an imposing dark wooden desk by the far wall facing the entrance. On top of the desk and to one side was a large PC monitor. Above the desk on the back wall was a painting of the Hypatia in calm seas set against a lush mountainous backdrop. To one side, through an open door, was a small bathroom where the lights were still on.

Andrew slipped inside and quietly closed the double doors behind him. As he approached the desk he spotted something unusual. In one corner of the room was what at first appeared to be a spindly metal sculpture, but on closer inspection, Andrew recognised the shape. Just a couple of weeks ago he would have had only a vague idea of what he was looking at, but now he instantly saw that it was the double helix of a small section of the human genome, similar to what he had seen in Professor McIntyre's office at UCL in London. However, this model was almost certainly completely unique, in that the four nucleotides that make up the genetic code of the entire genome were represented by different coloured gems. Without being entirely certain, Andrew guessed that they were ruby, diamond, sapphire and emerald. The backbone of the structure looked to be made entirely of gold.

*That woman really has more money than she knows what to do with,* he thought. *Let's see what she has on her PC.*

Moving quickly but carefully, he walked around the desk and sat down in the black leather chair. Then he unzipped a pouch in his belt and extracted a clear plastic zip bag containing a USB stick. He took out the stick and inserted it into the laptop that was sitting on the desk and connected to the large PC monitor. Then he switched on the laptop.

Holding down the correct key combination, Andrew then forced the laptop to enter its pre-boot BIOS, where he changed the settings so that instead of going into its usual boot sequence from its local hard drive, the laptop had registered the presence of the USB stick and instead attempted to boot up and load its operating system from there.

Within a couple of minutes, the laptop had loaded a tailored Windows operating system from the USB stick which afforded Andrew full administrator rights over the entire computer, bypassing all security measures but still allowing him full access to all the data on the hard drive.

He quickly fired up a small application that he had been issued with from HQ in London, and set it to work. It immediately began copying all the data on Alexis' laptop onto the USB, and after a couple of minutes of tense waiting, it finished and auto-terminated, but not before erasing all traces of its activities. Then he ran a different application, which infiltrated the Audio-Visual drivers on the laptop and switched its microphone on, even if it showed as being off in the laptop's systems settings. This effectively turned the laptop into a listening device, but it was limited to working only when the laptop was actually switched on. The upside was that it would work regardless of where the Hypatia was located, as long as its satellite-based internet connection was up and running.

Andrew pulled out the USB stick, put it back into the zip bag and sealed it up again. Then he extracted another zip bag from a different pouch in his belt and emptied the content into his hand. It was a small matt black plastic box with an adhesive strip on one side. He peeled off the thin protective film and stuck it to the underside of the desk near the solid set of drawers on the right-hand side where no one would see it unless they were looking for it. The batteries in this listening device should be good for a couple of weeks and the transmission range was several kilometres, so as long as the Hypatia remained anchored in the bay he would be able to listen in on conversations Alexis might have in this office, even if her laptop was switched off.

Andrew was just about to make his way out of the office when he heard voices through the double doors leading to the sitting room. One male and one female. It sounded like Alexis, speaking Greek. For a brief moment, Andrew considered slipping into the bathroom, but he decided it would be too risky. Instead, he crouched down and crawled under the desk where there was just room for him to lie on the floor.

Through a small gap between the lower edge of the front of the desk and the carpet, he saw the double doors opening and the shoes of a person entering the room. They were high sandal-like shoes and Andrew immediately knew that they belonged to Alexis. Upon entering, she turned around and closed the sliding doors to the sitting room. Then she walked towards the desk. For a moment Andrew thought she was going to walk around it and sit down, but then her mobile phone rang and he watched as her feet stopped halfway between the sliding doors and the desk.

'Dr Ackerman,' said Alexis in a friendly but business-like tone of voice. 'Thank you for returning my call. I just wanted to let you know that I have decided to come to San Francisco for a quick visit the day after tomorrow.'

Brief pause.

'Yes, I realise this is short notice,' continued Alexis. 'But we need to meet in person to discuss the future of the company, including candidates for the new CEO. I am sure you're already fed up with taking on that role on top of your research responsibilities.'

Another pause. Then she spoke again, this time with a slightly harder edge to her voice.

'Dr Ackerman, if I didn't know better, I would have said that you aren't very keen to see me?'

Andrew strained his ears to pick up what Fabian Ackerman was saying, but all he could hear was an incomprehensible tinny warble from the phone's speaker.

'Alright,' said Alexis, now sounding relaxed and affable again. 'I will send you the details and give you a ring from the airport. Please make sure the Peritas presentation is ready to go in Meeting Room C when I arrive. Great. Thank you. See you soon. Bye-bye.'

A few seconds after the call had ended, Andrew could have sworn he had heard the sound of a small scoff coming from Alexis. Evidently, this Ackerman character was going to have a tough time in the upcoming meeting.

Andrew watched as Alexis shifted one foot slightly to one side, as if indecisive about where to go, but then the male voice from before came through from the sitting room. Alexis replied, once again in Greek, and then walked over to the sliding doors and proceeded through them, leaving them open.

Andrew watched her walk through the sitting room towards a set of stairs at the other end leading upwards, presumably towards the bridge. Deciding this was his moment, he slipped out from under the desk and continued cautiously back out into the sitting room. Whoever the male voice had belonged to was no longer there, so Andrew quickly made his way to the stairs leading down to the lower levels. Less than a minute later he was back at the yacht's rear platform, donning his wetsuit. The sun had now moved below the horizon, and the water was suddenly looking dark and menacing.

He slipped into the water, slotted the regulator mouthpiece of his breathing apparatus into his mouth, and then he yanked the underwater scooter loose from its magnetic grip on the hull of the Hypatia. Within seconds he had disappeared into the dark water.

Fifteen minutes later Fiona spotted him climbing back into the small boat a couple of hundred metres away. She quickly jumped down from the large rock and walked towards the pebbly shore. Soon after, Andrew's boat had reached her and he had jumped out, tying a rope attached to the boat to a large rock nearby.

'Everything ok?' asked Fiona anxiously.

'Yup,' replied Andrew, undoing the Velcro straps on his gear. 'I planted the bug and eavesdropping software on her laptop. And I managed to copy her entire hard drive onto the USB.'

'Any issues?' said Fiona.

'None other than the fact that I had to hide for a bit. Turned out she was actually there.'

'She's on the boat right now?' asked Fiona surprised.

'Yes,' replied Andrew. 'Looked like she was preparing to host some dinner guests. I had to disappear under her desk, would you believe.'

'Crikey,' said Fiona. 'Sounds like a close call.'

'You could say that,' said Andrew. 'But while I was there, I overheard her take a call from this Doctor Fabian Ackerman who runs their US-based research centre. Apparently, she is flying over to meet with him to discuss succession at the top of ZOE Technologies. I got the feeling he wasn't too thrilled by that prospect, but then Alexis is a bit of a ballbuster.'

'Well, I am glad you're ok,' said Fiona, placing her hands on his wet chest and reaching up to kiss him on the cheek. 'I think I would rather not have these cloak-and-dagger activities as part of my day.'

'Well,' shrugged Andrew, and gave her a quick smile and a wink. 'You know what they say. You can't make an omelette without breaking necks.'

Fiona shook her head. 'You're an absolutely atrocious comedian.'

'I know,' replied Andrew. 'Right. If you take my kit along in the car, then I will quickly sail the boat back to the harbour and meet you there. I will remote access the laptop tomorrow and then have it send me whatever it has picked up.'

'Oh look,' said Fiona and pointed out towards the superyacht.

A small speedboat had come round the headland from the north, slowing down and then approaching the Hypatia.

'Must be the dinner guests,' said Andrew. 'Looks like I got out just in time.'

'I wonder who they are,' said Fiona peering out across the water as the small vessel sidled up next to the rear of the giant yacht and stopped. They could just about make out the movement of people from where they were.

'Probably some business people from Athens,' said Andrew. 'Or perhaps a couple of local police chiefs coming to fetch their monthly bribes.'

'That's a bit cynical of you, isn't it?' said Fiona.

Andrew shrugged. 'At this point, I wouldn't be surprised by anything. One thing is for sure, though. This whole affair goes much deeper than a couple of genetically enhanced pets. What we need to do now is get the content of that laptop analysed and assessed. I might need to draw on London for this. Let's get back to the hotel so I can send it to HQ. The sooner the better.'

'Sounds good,' said Fiona. 'Let's go.'

# FOURTEEN

George Frost rose from his desk and walked out into the open-plan office space where the rest of his small team of researchers and lab technicians were sitting. As usual, the general volume of conversation in the space reduced to a murmur whenever he appeared.

Frost proceeded to the elevator and pressed the button. After a few seconds, there was a high-pitched electronic chirp and then the doors opened. He stepped inside and pulled out a small plastic keycard from his lab coat, inserting it into the narrow slit in the elevator's control panel. As he did so, a purple ring lit up around an unmarked button at the bottom of the panel, indicating that his credentials would allow him to access the lowest level of the underground complex.

As the doors slid shut, he checked the time. He had a few hours before another scheduled call with Ackerman. Enough time to do a thorough inspection of the new growth vats.

The elevator slowed down and stopped, and then the door slid open to reveal a long corridor with floor-to-ceiling mirrors on both sides and a large reinforced steel door at the far end which had a dull red LED glow around its edges. Frost walked briskly down the dizzying corridor and placed his hand on a green backlit glass panel with the outline of a human hand on it. The panel light pulsed twice as his fingerprints were analysed. Then it chirped and turned solid green. After that, Frost shifted himself to stand in front of a scanner that ran an infrared beam across his face, mapping out the complex structure of tiny veins inside both of his eyes. As soon as the scan was complete there was another chirp, the sound of locking pistons retracting and unlocking, and then the red glow around the reinforced door turned light green.

'Access granted. Welcome back Doctor Frost,' said a disembodied female voice.

Frost pressed a large black button on the steel doorframe and the door cracked open with a brief hiss of air. Then it slid inward and to the side, allowing him to enter. On the other side of the reinforced door was another short corridor that opened up into a vast space. Roughly 30 metres across, the circular vaulted room was bathed in soft blue light, and it had a walkway from the entrance down a few steps to the centre of the room, where a control terminal was placed on a slim steel pedestal.

Around the entire circumference of the room ran an intricate black steel lattice structure with 22 large elongated clear-glass vats that were shaped like giant medicine capsules. Each vat was hooked up to a number of tubes as well as a multitude of electrical cables for telemetry and power, and they were all held in place roughly one metre off the floor by an articulated steel cradle that allowed it to be moved around and positioned in different ways, depending on what was required for the different stages of the gestation process.

Frost walked calmly down towards the control terminal. He considered this his personal space in the Rhinebeck facility, even if one other person had access, but Fabian Ackerman rarely came down here. However, that might soon change now that the testing phase was ramping up.

This was a relatively small facility intended only for research purposes. A much larger production facility was currently being built in a small East-Asian nation with patchy regulations and a long history of lack of enforcement of legal structures. It was also characterised by an ingrained amenability to monetary persuasion amongst public officials. The capacity of that facility, which was expected to come onstream within a year, was orders of magnitude larger than the research facility in Rhinebeck.

'Rosetta,' said Frost in a loud clear voice as he walked up to the terminal.

'Good afternoon, Doctor Frost,' said the pleasant and somewhat ethereal voice of the artificial intelligence overseeing the operation of the underground vat complex.

Rosetta's neural networks ran the entire gestation process without human intervention. This involved measuring and adjusting the chemical contents and properties of the artificial amniotic fluids, as well as assessing the progress of the embryos using a separate convolutional neural network for image processing in both the visible and infrared spectrums. Unlike a human controller, it was able to perform these tasks thousands of times per second, 24 hours per day, indefinitely, or as long as the facility had power.

As Rosetta spoke, a strip of red LEDs on the terminal flashed and pulsated in unison with each word and syllable.

'Run deep systems diagnostics and generate status reports for all vats,' said Frost.

'Running diagnostics,' said Rosetta, and immediately a range of small LEDs on each of the vats started pulsing in different colours and at various speeds as the AI completed inspection and diagnostics of all 22 gestation attempts.

A few seconds later, the AI spoke again.

'Gestation successful in 19 vats,' Rosetta said. 'Growth targets achieved in 15 vats. Zero growth anomalies. Zero fatalities.'

Frost nodded approvingly, studying the data being presented on two screens embedded in the terminal.

'Rosetta, terminate all vats and purge,' he said in an even and unemotional voice.

'Please confirm termination and purge with biometric and voice identification,' replied Rosetta.

Frost placed his palm on another fingerprint scanner similar to the one he had used to access the gestation vault.

'Confirming termination and purge,' said Frost.

'Confirmed,' replied Rosetta dispassionately.

After a couple of seconds, the blue light in the vault gradually changed from purple to red, and then an alert in the form of a low repeating warbling noise filled the space.

Amid popping and hissing noises, the cables and tubes connected to each of the vats were then disengaged and all of the 22 articulated steel structures began raising the large glass vats whilst tilting them from a horizontal to a backward sloping position. Inside the vats, the artificial amniotic fluid sloshed around gently making their suspended contents visible from the terminal where Frost was observing proceedings.

Once the vats had been retracted close to the walls of the vault, each one had a wide tube inserted into a valve at the back. The valves then opened and their contents were sucked out amid sharp sloshing and gurgling noises. In a few of the vats, small streaks of blood could be seen swirling inside the fluid as it was being sucked out. Having been emptied, their contents would then be sent through a pipe system to a macerator, which would turn it into a semi-liquid pulp. After that, it would then be mixed with water and pumped to the surface, where it was funnelled through more pipes and fed into the local sewage system. The final step that the AI needed to complete was an internal cleaning process performed on all the vats, which involved various chemical solutions and then several rinse cycles using ultrapure water.

'Purge complete,' said Rosetta serenely.

Frost nodded, looking pleased.

'Initiate stage 1 of another round of gestation,' he said. 'This time with germ cells for sample H01.'

'Confirmed,' replied Rosetta. 'Preparing for H01. Human gestation. Trial One.'

Frost turned around and began walking back up the steps towards the reinforced door. On occasion, he had caught himself absentmindedly imagining what it would be like if for some reason the door wouldn't open and he was trapped in there.

He hit the button on the door, and it opened for him. Then he walked through the corridor towards the elevator that would take him back up to his office. If all went well, the gestation would take, and Project AnaGenesis would then have produced its first demonstrator products. Using the enhanced genome in the H01 germ cells, he was hoping to be able to achieve a gestation period of no more than 20 months after which the specimens should be fully grown.

*Brave new world,* he thought to himself.

★      ★      ★

Early the next morning as the sun was coming up, Andrew and Fiona were sitting down for breakfast in the rooftop restaurant of their hotel on Syntagma Square in central Athens. Fiona had insisted that they go early since she wanted a table overlooking the Acropolis. She wanted to watch the first rays of golden sunlight lighting up the more than 2500-year-old ruin.

While they waited to be served, Andrew flipped open his laptop and logged into the central server at Sheldrake Place in London using a secure VPN. Early that morning, Colonel Strickland had sent him an encrypted message to the effect that the digital forensics team had managed to decrypt some of the contents from Alexis's laptop, primarily the local email application folder. The team was still working on the rest of the files on the laptop, which were protected with multiple layers of 256-bit encryption, and so had to be chewed on by a supercomputer dedicated to that specific purpose. Strickland had said that this process could take anywhere from hours to days. They would just have to wait.

However, one of the things they had managed to decrypt so far was a large number of high-resolution images showing what initially looked like the pages of an old manuscript. The accompanying emails indicated that they were pictures taken of the personal diary of Ptolemy, one of Alexander the Great's generals who was later to become ruler of Egypt and a renowned historian.

Initially, Fiona was sceptical as to whether the images were genuine, but the more she looked into it the more she had to admit that purely based on their content they might be authentic. And judging from the correspondence between Alexis and a man named Pierre Dubois, Alexis certainly seemed to have been satisfied that these were the real thing.

'This Dubois character must be who Lambert mentioned?' said Andrew. 'Strickland said that he is a French archaeologist. Have you ever heard of him?'

'I have,' said Fiona ruefully. 'He is well known to the community. I should probably qualify that by saying that he is actually infamous.'

'Really?' asked Andrew. 'How so?'

'He is basically the poster boy for what greed and lack of morality can do to a person. He is like the fallen angel of archaeology.'

Just then their waiter arrived with their breakfast, and Andrew moved his laptop out of the way to make room for their food.

'Sounds serious,' said Andrew, as he poured tea for both of them. 'What did he do?'

'There was a big furore about him a few years back,' replied Fiona. 'He basically turned out to have broken pretty much every code of conduct there is for scientists and in this case, archaeologists. He dispensed with due care for artefacts, exploited work that fellow archaeologists had done to locate valuable artefacts in order to find and loot tombs and burial mounds. He has bribed local officials in several countries mainly in North Africa in order to get illicit access to a number of dig sites that were awaiting actual excavation by proper archaeologists. And those are just the sites we think we know about. There could be many more. He really went to the dark side and never looked back.'

'Wow,' said Andrew, taking a bite of his toast. 'I guess that sort of thing is a one-way street. Once you go down that road, you're never coming back.'

'Oh, he'll never work for anyone reputable ever again, even if he wanted to,' said Fiona, looking disgusted. 'But I suspect that would be the very last thing on his mind. Rumours have it that he is making obscene amounts of money whilst wrecking our collective history and selling off whatever he finds. And apparently, he was always a lecherous womaniser.'

'Well, whatever Dubois is, it seems that he is working for Alexis now,' said Andrew. 'What do you suppose that means?'

'I am not sure,' said Fiona. 'But it doesn't exactly give me warm fuzzy feelings about Alexis. From the decrypted correspondence I have seen so far, it appears that she has him on a retainer, and that she has already used that arrangement to acquire this diary. So, their involvement is already quite deep.'

'Yes, they have apparently been using an ex-military operative called *Pantera*,' said Andrew. 'The whole thing smacks of a clandestine endeavour to me. And clandestine, outside of the military world, invariably means criminal.'

'I am sure you're right,' said Fiona. 'But what exactly are they trying to achieve? And more importantly, what will be the next archaeological site that he trashes?'

'I guess that's what we should be trying to find out,' replied Andrew. 'Can we just briefly talk about the images we found on Alexis's laptop?'

'Ptolemy's diary?' said Fiona. 'Assuming that it really is his diary.'

'Yes,' said Andrew. 'What is the deal with this Ptolemy? What do we actually know about him, and why would Alexis go to such lengths to acquire his diary?'

Fiona took a sip of her orange juice and slowly placed it back on the white table cloth as she collected her thoughts.

'Well,' she said. 'In many ways, Ptolemy became even more influential than Alexander, although many people have never heard of him. He was born in 366

BCE and was a close childhood friend of Alexander, and like the great commander he was tutored by Aristotle which had a profound impact on him. By all accounts, he was naturally gifted and highly intelligent, and Aristotle's philosophy which centred around things like reasoning, logic, deduction and inference, and continuous learning throughout life, became embedded into the way in which Ptolemy conducted himself. He was the son of a Macedonian noblewoman named Arsinoe, and an Argead courtier by the name Lagus, so he was initially known as Ptolemy, Son of Lagus. He accompanied Alexander throughout his campaign to take control of the Persian Empire, and he was there at Alexander's side when the Macedonian king was lying on his deathbed in Babylon eleven years later. Being both a capable military commander and a shrewd political operator, he secured the province of Egypt for himself after Alexander's death, where he eventually declared himself Pharaoh and moved his capital to the new city of Alexandria on the Mediterranean coast. Throughout the rest of his life, and especially in the time immediately after Alexander's death, Ptolemy expanded his Egyptian empire so that it stretched far into present-day Libya in the west and to large parts of the Levant in the east. He oversaw the rapid growth of Alexandria as a commercial hub and also took control of Cyprus and Rhodes. At one point, during the so-called Wars of the Diadochi, which were the succession wars following Alexander's death, Ptolemy prevented a rout of the city of Rhodes by the forces of his rival Antigonus, after which he was apparently given the honorary title of *Soter*, meaning

Saviour. He also famously built the giant lighthouse on Pharos Island in Alexandria, and he founded its great library which had as its stated goal to acquire and hold all the knowledge that existed in the known world.'

'That's quite ambitious,' said Andrew. 'Especially for that time.'

'Absolutely,' nodded Fiona. 'You can think of it as an effort to establish the internet in the 4$^{th}$ century BCE. City officials did everything they could to hoover up as much written knowledge as possible, even going as far as sending out expeditions to the far corners of the world to retrieve documents and historical accounts. Another thing they did was to systematically confiscate anything in written form of any substance, typically books, from anyone visiting the city either by road or by sea. Those books were then taken to the library and copied by hand, and then the owner would get the copy returned to them so that the library could hang on to the original.'

'Quite astonishing,' said Andrew. 'It sounds almost manic.'

'It was in some ways,' replied Fiona. 'But it did achieve the goal it set out to achieve, and Alexandria became perhaps the most important centre for knowledge and progressive scientific thought anywhere in the world at that time.'

'There is actually an interesting anecdote related to this,' continued Fiona. 'In the modern city of Alexandria, the main public library has a separate section with a large number of computer servers that copy and store the entire contents of the internet every single day. I think that is quite a beautiful way of paying homage to the library of the ancient city.'

'Yes, that is actually quite touching,' said Andrew. 'But what happened to the old library?'

'As you probably heard Alexis talk about when we met her, Alexandria declined as a hub of knowledge, learning and free-thinking, partly as a result of the zealotry of the newly founded Christian sect that came to Alexandria with Mark the Evangelist. Then, during a Roman invasion of the city in 48 BCE, a number of ships in the harbour caught fire. The fire spread to the library turning a large portion of its contents into ashes. The final death blow happened much later in 272 CE when another Roman invasion laid waste to the so-called Broucheion quarter of the city where the library was located. It seemed to have been on the decline for several centuries by then as the fortunes of the city waned and the power and influence of other Mediterranean cities grew during the various stages of the Roman Empire.'

'That is a sad fate for such an amazing place,' said Andrew.

'Yes,' said Fiona. 'But anyway, getting back to Ptolemy. In his later years, he became a historian, and wrote the account of Alexander's exploits that formed the basis for Arrian of Nicomedia's history of Alexander.'

'Yes, I remember,' said Andrew. 'But what about these pages of Ptolemy's supposed diary? What are your thoughts on them?'

'Having seen the pages, and spent a bit of time trying to translate and make sense of some of them, I am becoming more and more convinced that this really is Ptolemy's personal diary. It actually also makes sense when you think about it. Arrian of Nicomedia's Anabasis of Alexander is extremely detailed with specifics about the number of different types of units that took part in different battles, who commanded what flanks, how the battles unfolded, the names of enemy battle commanders, names of local kings and their family members, locations they travelled through, including details of minor skirmishes with local tribes and so on and so forth. And this was for a campaign that stretched over more than a decade. There is so much information there that Ptolemy simply would have had to have taken notes. It is even quite likely that Ptolemy always intended to write the history of Alexander the Great, and so he would have used his diary for that specific purpose. If that is true, then it seems highly likely to me that he would have taken extensive notes along the way. And of course, as an old man in Alexandria, Ptolemy did indeed write the history of Alexander's campaign.'

Fiona took a sip of her orange juice before continuing.

'Anyway, as I said, I have only had a short amount of time to examine the images of the diary pages so far, but they seem to have been written in a very condensed shorthand which makes them quite difficult to make sense of. But from what I have seen so far, it could very well be the real thing, which is obviously really exciting.'

Fiona had an enthusiastic smile on her face, clearly excited by the possible implications of what the diary pages might hold.

Andrew smiled. 'Yes, I can imagine you would find that a thrill. And I must admit, it is fascinating to think that those pages were written by hand, by someone who had such a large impact on world history. The question is this though. What does Alexis want the diary for?'

Andrew took another sip of his tea, and as he did so he spotted a headline on the front page of the English language Greek newspaper that had been placed on their table by the waiter before they sat down. Below the headline was a blurry image that appeared to have come from a CCTV unit.

'Bloody hell,' exclaimed Andrew.

'What?' said Fiona perplexed.

'Look at this,' said Andrew, picking up the newspaper and placing it on the table in front of Fiona.

'Violent burglary at the Cyprus Museum,' she read out loud, and then looked up at Andrew.

'See this guy here?' asked Andrew, pointing to the CCTV image which had captured the side of the face of a man wearing a dark boiler suit.

'This is the man I was chasing in London. The Russian. Morozov.'

'Are you sure?' asked Fiona, leaning in over the newspaper for a closer look.

'Absolutely,' said Andrew. 'I won't forget the smirk on his face any time soon. It is definitely him.'

Fiona looked up at him again, now with a confused look on her face. 'So, the man who killed Lambert and the two Met officers also broke into a museum in Cyprus? Why?'

'No idea,' replied Andrew, shaking his head. 'But I am sure this is no coincidence. Morozov, Alexis, Dubois. They are all connected somehow.'

'Should we contact Strickland?' said Fiona.

'Yes, I will do that,' said Andrew. 'He might have something for us. They might even be able to track down Morozov's whereabouts if they are made aware that he flew into Cyprus a couple of days ago.'

'But if Morozov is working for Alexis, shouldn't we then contact the police?' asked Fiona. 'We know he's a murderer.'

Andrew shook his head. 'We don't have any solid proof of anything at this point. It could all be coincidental, although I don't believe that for a second. But also, if we want to try to extract information from Dubois somehow, we can't create a huge storm right now. If the police come after Alexis, which I am sure will yield absolutely nothing, then you can bet your life that both Dubois and Morozov will disappear into the ether, and then we will be stuck. We have to play this cool and let them carry on with whatever they are doing for a bit longer. All we can do for now is watch and wait.'

Just at that moment, Andrew's laptop produced a quiet chirp indicating that an email had come into his inbox. He opened it and read it silently for a few seconds.

'I just had another message from Strickland,' he said, looking intently at his laptop. 'You are not going to believe this. Pierre Dubois arrived in Athens three days ago from Paris. GCHQ got the French police onboard, and they tracked him. He is here right now.'

'What?' she exclaimed. 'He is here in Athens?'

Fiona involuntarily looked around the restaurant. 'Can you imagine if he is staying here too?'

'No such luck,' smiled Andrew. 'His travel records show him booked into the Athens Gate Hotel. It is supposed to be about one hundred metres southeast of the Acropolis. Not far from here, actually. He still hasn't checked out yet.'

Fiona turned her head to look out at the imposing ancient structure atop the rocky plateau jutting up above the rest of the city.

'We need to find out what he is doing here,' she said.

Andrew nodded pensively. 'That would be useful. He has almost certainly been to see Alexis already. But about what? If we could get close to him, we might be able to tap his phone or his laptop. That should tell us what we need to know.'

'I have an idea,' said Fiona. 'I will go and meet him.'

Andrew sat up and looked at her dubiously. 'What, just like that?'

'Sure,' said Fiona. 'Why not? He has no idea who I am. I will just chat him up, maybe tell him I am a fellow archaeologist and strike up a conversation.'

'And then what?' asked Andrew sounding unconvinced. 'Ask him what he and Alexis are up to?'

'Of course not,' scoffed Fiona. 'I will just gently prod him about his work. I can probably make him spill some of the beans. People like him like to brag. And I will try to distract him for long enough for you to do your James Bond thing and sneak into his hotel room. There is bound to be useful information in there.'

Andrew smiled, partly sceptical and partly impressed with Fiona's gumption and initiative.

'Are you sure it is a good idea for you to meet this chap?' he asked. 'You clearly loathe him. He might catch on.'

Fiona smirked. 'I will be fine. He won't be the first arse I have had to deal with, and at least this time there is a chance to do something about the chaos he is causing. Don't worry,' she continued, confidently. 'I can handle myself.'

'I know you can,' smiled Andrew. 'Alright. So, what do you propose then?'

'Let go back to the room and change clothes,' she replied, and waved at the waiter. 'I will tell you on the way.'

# FIFTEEN

In his room at the Athens Gate Hotel, Pierre Dubois had just come back from having breakfast in the restaurant that overlooks the Temple of Olympian Zeus on one side, and the Acropolis on the other. The ruins of the giant temple dedicated to Zeus, the head of the Olympian gods, which are located around 500 metres southeast of the Acropolis, were originally built of limestone in the Doric style. With its 104 columns surrounding its inner chamber, it measured 40 metres in width, more than 100 metres in length, and its roof would have been around 25 metres tall.

Dubois's room overlooked the site, and even now, after his career had taken what he liked to consider an unorthodox turn, he was still more than able to be impressed by a structure like this. If nothing else, it represented the sort of naked ambition that he admired.

Having had a change of clothes, he was planning on going for a walk in the city to have a think about how best to achieve what Alexis had asked of him. He was sure it would be possible, but he couldn't do it alone. He would have to work with Morozov again. He didn't like any of those people, but he needed the muscle and he was very keen to please Alexis, or Mademoiselle Galanis as he called her. She seemed to like that.

Dubois was supposed to make his way to a small heliport on the outskirts of Athens later that afternoon, after which he would be flown several hundred kilometres north to where Morozov was meant to meet him. Once there, he and the Russian would make their way to the site and attempt to retrieve the samples.

Dubois stood in front of the tall mirror by the door, adjusting his shirt collar and inspecting his light grey suit. He took pride in his appearance. He was not a particularly handsome man. He realised that. But most people could look impressive with the right clothes, and he always made an effort to look good with his tailored suits and expensive shoes.

Happy with his appearance, he left the hotel room and walked to the elevator. As he entered, he spotted another guest out of the corner of his eye walking down the corridor towards the elevator. He pretended not to see him, entered the elevator and pressed 'G'. A couple of seconds later he emerged on the ground floor and headed towards the revolving glass door leading to the street outside. As he walked, he reached inside his jacket pocket and pulled out his phone. He was going to need the map and its GPS function if he was going to go walking around the intricate web of narrow streets in central Athens.

The woman, who had just gotten up from her armchair in the small seating area in the hotel lobby, approached him from the left and was walking at a brisk pace. She had medium-length black hair and was wearing a smart business suit and black glossy high heels. A light grey scarf was wrapped loosely around her head, and she was wearing large black catlike Ray-Ban sunglasses. As she walked, she was rummaging around inside her handbag which she was holding close to her chest.

Dubois, who was holding his phone and attempting to type in the address of the National Archaeological Museum at number 44 on 28is Oktovriou, did not spot the woman until it was too late. She crashed into him, sending her sprawling on the beige marble floor, whilst he desperately tried not to drop his phone.

'Oh gosh! Oh no!' exclaimed the woman in a posh English accent. 'Look what I have done! Silly *silly* me.'

At first, Dubois did not understand what she meant, but then she approached him holding out her hands towards the right side of his elegant jacket. It had a streak of red lipstick smeared on it.

'Ah, *merde*!' said Dubois, visibly irritated.

'I am terribly sorry,' said the woman. 'And such a handsome jacket too. Was it expensive?'

'Of course it was expensive!' said Dubois brusquely. 'Tailormade in *Paris*.'

'Oh blast!' said the woman, looking distraught. 'Please sir, let me make it up to you. Can I buy you a drink?'

She gestured towards the opulent bar adjacent to the hotel lobby, where dark wood panelling, ochre-coloured leather furniture and warm lighting beckoned thirsty guests to come and relax for a few minutes with an expertly made cocktail.

Dubois looked towards the bar, and then back at the woman. She was really quite pretty. Not stunning like Miss Galanis, but pretty enough. And she had an enticing figure underneath her business suit. He hesitated for a moment, but then produced a reticent smile.

'Alright, Miss…?' he said, looking at her expectantly.

'Ward,' replied Fiona. 'Hazel Ward.'

She lifted her right hand slightly towards him, and on cue he took it in his and lifted it gently further up towards himself, as he bowed and gave it a brief peck.

'Nice to meet you Miss Ward,' he said. 'My name is Dubois. Pierre Dubois.'

Fiona tilted her head slightly to one side, smiled coyly and flashed her eyelashes twice.

'Ravi de vous rencontrer aussi, Monsieur Dubois,' she said and smiled.

'Tu parles français?' asked Dubois, smiling and now clearly impressed.

'Un peu,' she replied shyly. 'Je préfère parler anglaise.'

Dubois nodded, and then gently let go of her hand.

Alright,' he said. 'English it is then.'

'Let's go to the bar?' said Fiona.

'Fine,' said Dubois, and gestured for her to lead the way.

Fiona began walking ahead of him, and as she did so she could practically feel his eyes on her behind.

*Men really are terrifyingly easy to manipulate*, she thought.

She sidled up to a barstool and mounted it whilst tossing her hair back with a quick jerk of her head. Dubois followed and took the stool next to hers.

'What can I get you?' asked Fiona.

'A Mimosa,' replied Dubois with a smile. 'It is still early in the day.'

'One Mimosa and one Daiquiri, please,' said Fiona to the waiter, who nodded silently and began making their cocktails.

As he did so, Fiona spotted Andrew entering the bar and sitting down in a leather armchair with his back to them, but still able to watch them in a mirror mounted on the wall.

'Once again, I am *so* sorry,' said Fiona. 'I am not usually this clumsy. I was looking for my lipstick and didn't see you walking there.'

'Perhaps you should not wear sunglasses indoors,' replied Dubois in a slightly admonishing tone of voice.

Fiona giggled nervously, gave him a quick sideways glance and held up her right index finger.

'Perhaps you are right,' she smiled.

'So, what brings you to Athens?' asked Dubois.

'I am here for an auction,' replied Fiona. 'I am in the market for some ancient pottery for my collection.'

Dubois raised his eyebrows. 'Really?' he said. 'That is a coincidence. I am an archaeologist myself.'

'Are you really?' said Fiona, doing her best to sound impressed. 'You mean, you dig for ancient cities like Troy.'

Dubois chuckled. 'Sometimes,' he said. 'It depends on what my clients desire. I try to give them whatever they want.'

'Are you working on anything special right now?' asked Fiona in a hushed voice and looking starry-eyed and eager.

'Perhaps,' said Dubois reluctantly. 'My client and I are searching for something quite special. And if we can find it, it will change everything.'

Fiona stared at him with her mouth open in an expectant smile.

'So, what is it then? Tell me!'

Dubois shook his head dismissively and looked like he was about to speak. But then he hesitated for a couple of seconds.

'Miss Ward,' he finally said, looking at Fiona intently. 'Would you like to accompany me to my room? It has a lovely view out over the Temple of Olympian Zeus. We could call for room service to bring us cocktails. I am sure we would enjoy each other's company better there.'

For a brief moment, Fiona's eyes darted involuntarily towards Andrew, who was close enough to be able to hear their conversation.

'Uhm' said Fiona, looking nervously at Dubois. 'But we've only just sat down. We haven't even got our drinks yet. I think I would prefer to stay here.'

'I really must insist,' said Dubois with a friendly but ever so slightly assertive tone, whilst looking down at the lipstick stain on his jacket.

Fiona smiled at him anxiously, and out of the corner of her eye, she spotted Andrew moving his hand out to a clear area on the table he was sitting at, and then briefly giving a thumbs up. Fiona swallowed. This was not at all what they had planned.

'Alright then,' she said tensely. 'Just one drink.'

'Excellent,' said Dubois, clasping his hands together. Then he rose and called over the barman to arrange for their drinks to be brought up to his room.

The short elevator trip up to Dubois's room seemed like the longest trip Fiona had ever been on, and she breathed a sigh of relief when they exited out into the corridor on Dubois's floor. However, her relief was short-lived.

'Here we are,' said Dubois, and walked to a door diagonally opposite the elevator. He used his keycard to unlock it and then opened it whilst beckoning Fiona to enter first.

She smiled timidly, trying to maintain her composure despite feeling a rising sense of panic, and then she walked inside. As he followed her and closed the door behind them, Fiona was straining to hear if one of the other elevators was arriving, but she heard nothing. Where was Andrew? Then Dubois nonchalantly locked the door of the room.

'Right,' he smiled, walking back inside the room and making his way to the minibar.

On the way, he took off his jacket and hung it over the back of a chair by a small desk that had an old-fashioned landline phone and a brochure detailing the hotel's amenities.

'Let's have another little drink while we wait for our cocktails, shall we?' said Dubois. 'How about a Mojito?'

'Uhm, sure,' replied Fiona, sitting down apprehensively on the end of the bed.

Dubois turned around as he made their drinks, smiling at her. She felt like she was being assessed by a hungry predator. She suddenly had the horrible thought that perhaps he was about to spike her drink, rendering her incapable of resisting or perhaps even knocking her unconscious.

'Would you mind if I use the bathroom?' she asked. 'I would like to just freshen up a bit.'

'Of course not,' replied Dubois. 'Take as long as you like. I will be right here, making sure our drinks are just perfect.'

Fiona rose and had to make an effort to walk slowly and calmly to the bathroom where she closed the door behind herself. As soon as she was inside, she opened the taps at the basin, dug into her handbag and yanked out her phone. Then she hit the speed-dial for Andrew's number.

'How's it going?' asked Andrew calmly.

'What the hell do you mean?' said Fiona half whispering, half hissing. 'Our plan has gone to shite. You were supposed to be up here, not me!'

'I know,' said Andrew. 'Just calm down. Stall him. I am already busy making a new plan.'

'Well, whatever it is, do it fast,' she said. 'This guy is as lecherous as they come.'

'Alright,' said Andrew. It sounded like he was walking through a corridor with a concrete floor, his footsteps echoing slightly. 'Just stay put and stall him for another few minutes, alright? I will be there as soon as I can. I will bring the gadget.'

'Ok,' said Fiona. 'Just hurry.' Then she hung up, flushed the toilet and washed her hands.

*When this is over, I am going to need a long shower*, she thought to herself as she looked up at the mirror on the wall in front of her. *He gives me the absolute creeps.*

She straightened up and adjusted her hair and her necklace.

'You can do this,' she whispered to herself.

On the other side of the door, she could hear that Dubois had put on some Frank Sinatra. He was clearly expecting more than just a conversation.

Opening the bathroom door to the room, Fiona walked through it looking calm and confident, perhaps even a little bit flirtatious as she sat back down on the bed with an expectant look on her face.

'Drinks ready?' she asked.

'Oui Mademoiselle,' said Dubois. 'Right here.'

He came over with a drink in each hand and sat down uncomfortably close to her on the bed. She could smell his aftershave. It wasn't unpleasant, but she felt herself involuntarily holding her breath nonetheless.

Dubois handed her one of the Mojitos and was about to speak when there was a knock on the door. Dubois frowned, but then his eyebrows arched as he realised that it had to be the cocktails from the bar.

'One moment,' he said, standing up and walking to the door.

On the way, he put down his drink on the small desk. When the door opened, Fiona's heart leapt as she heard Andrew's voice, albeit in a different tenor to what she had ever heard before.

'Concierge service,' said Andrew in his best Greek-accented English.

He was wearing black trousers and a burgundy jacket with the hotel's logo on the front.

'I am here about the bed,' he continued.

Dubois looked perplexed, but before he could protest, Andrew had already made his way into the room. As he entered, Fiona rose from the bed and took a couple of steps towards him whilst raising her hand out in front of herself.

'I am very sorry to disturb you,' said Andrew, taking her hand and kissing it, whilst also passing her a small black plastic box the size of a matchbox with a short micro-USB cable attached. 'I will be as quick as I can. These beds can be a bit tricky.'

'Wait a minute,' said Dubois, clearly irritated both by being interrupted and at having the interloper kiss the hand of his new lady friend. 'There is no problem with this bed. I never asked for anyone to come up here.'

'I am so sorry,' said Andrew kneeling by the side of the bed and pulling out the sheets from under the duvet, dumping them unceremoniously on the floor. Then he began lifting up first one corner then the next corner of the mattress, as if he was looking for something.

As he did so, Fiona moved slowly towards the desk where Dubois's jacket hung over the chair.

'Listen to me, monsieur,' said Dubois angrily. 'I do not need anyone to come and look at my bed. You are interrupting what was a pleasant time with my girlfriend.'

It was all Andrew could do to not stand up and lamp the Frenchman, but he restrained himself and instead yanked one of the duvets onto the floor. As Dubois stepped further towards Andrew, remonstrating some more, Fiona reached into the jacket pocket, extracted Dubois's phone and swiftly plugged in the micro-USB cable. The gadget was a storage device, pre-loaded with firmware that initiated the transfer of a complete copy of the phone's contents. Depending on the amount of data, it should take just a few moments. After only a couple of seconds, a tiny LED lit up green on the device and Fiona was then able to quickly disconnect the device and slip it into her trouser pocket.

'Oh dear,' said Fiona, sounding both concerned and tired. 'I am suddenly not feeling very well.'

She took a couple of steps forward and then feigned a stumble that made her sit back down on the bed, the back of one hand on her forehead.

'I have barely had anything to drink,' she said, sounding confused.

At that, Andrew stood up and approached her.

'Are you alright, miss?' he asked. Then he looked at Dubois. 'Did you give her a drink?' he asked suspiciously.

'Well, yes,' stammered Dubois. 'But it was just a small one. And there was nothing in it. I mean, there was alcohol, but nothing else. I mean…'

By now Dubois looked positively ashen-faced as he attempted to impress on the 'concierge' that he had no hand in Miss Ward's sudden affliction. But the more he waffled, the more Andrew looked at him with increasing scepticism.

'I think I might need a doctor,' said Fiona weakly, and looked at Andrew pleadingly. 'Please can you take me to one?'

'Of course,' exclaimed Andrew. 'Let me take you to the hotel's resident physician at once.'

He offered his arm to Fiona who grabbed it and got to her feet with apparent difficulty. Then the pair of them began making their way towards the door. As they did so, Andrew shot Dubois a disdainful look and shook his head.

'Uhm, yes,' mumbled Dubois, now sounding like he was quite pleased to be rid of the young lady. 'That's probably a good idea. You should see a doctor.'

'Monsieur,' said Andrew contemptuously as he walked past him.

As the two of them left the room, Dubois just stood there, looking both horrified and relieved all at the same time.

# SIXTEEN

Mike Stone handed his fake passport to the UK Border Force official who glanced up at him for a couple of seconds, studying his face and comparing it to the photo in the passport. Stone was wearing a grey suit and a pair of glasses and was offering his most accommodating smile.

'Purpose of visit, Mr Douglas?' asked the official.

'Business,' replied Stone, doing his best to sound middle-class.

'And what business is that?' asked the official.

'Printer cartridges,' replied Stone. 'Universal cartridges for office printers.'

'Duration of visit?' asked the official.

'Shouldn't take more than a couple of days,' said Stone. 'I just need to finish a contract with a new client. He's dying to see me.'

The official looked down at Stone's passport again, glanced at his computer screen, and then handed back the passport.

'Welcome to the UK, Mr Douglas.'

'Thank you very much,' replied Stone, and tucked the passport back into the inside pocket of his suit jacket.

Ten minutes later Stone boarded a Heathrow Express train to Paddington Station in central London, where he hailed a cab for the ride across the city to his old stomping ground in the East End. He could have gotten to where he was going much more quickly by taking the underground, but he enjoyed sitting in the back of a cab looking out at his old home.

He got out on Plaistow High Street and walked across the road to his old pub, The Black Lion, where he approached the bar and bought a pint of Doom Bar, his favourite amber ale.

Sitting down at a small table away from the bar and the regulars that were milling around playing darts and arguing over football, he was amused to find that no one recognised him. He thought perhaps the pub landlord might have given him a second look, but despite having grown up just a stone's throw from the pub, he might as well have been a foreigner just passing through. Not that many foreigners ever found their way to this part of the city. The borough was run-down and tired, just like most of its residents.

*Some things don't change*, he thought to himself.

After finishing his pint he walked back outside and hailed another cab which took him back to the fashionable West End. On the way, he double-checked the notes on his phone, which he had received via an encrypted app the night before.

Stone's best hacker, a Lithuanian freelancer who went by the handle *Extr4xtor*, had worked his magic on a London-based law firm whose corporate computer servers Stone had asked him to hack into. The firm specialised in facilitating purchases of luxury London properties on behalf of wealthy overseas clients.

The Lithuanian travelled the world constantly, never staying in the same place for more than a few days, and only ever accessing the internet using a series of VPNs to mask his location and identity. He had spent just a few days on this job but had uncovered valuable information about one of the law firm's senior partners, which the man in question would probably do just about anything to prevent becoming public.

*Everyone has secrets,* thought Stone as he walked up the steps to the front door of an expensive townhouse in South Kensington. *If you dig deep enough, there's always something to find.*

He looked at his Bremont wristwatch and adjusted his tie. Then he pressed the doorbell. A few seconds later he heard the lock on the door being disengaged. The door opened to reveal a neatly dressed middle-aged man holding a wine glass with red wine in it. In the background, Stone could hear classical music playing.

'Mr Worthington?' said Stone.

'Yes?' said the man looking perplexed whilst inspecting Stone, seemingly examining the uninvited visitor for clues as to his reason for knocking. 'May I help you?'

Stone reached into his jacket under his left arm and calmly pulled out a small pistol with a silencer.

'You could invite me inside, chum,' said Stone evenly, but with a hard edge to his voice, now back to using his natural East London accent.

Locking eyes with Mr Worthington, he left him in no doubt that what he had said was not a request.

'I think you and I should have a little chat before your missus gets home,' he continued. 'We need to decide how to tell her what you've been up to, mate. And then we need to make sure it doesn't muck things up for you here in this lovely house of yours. You seem to have a very nice life here. It'd be a shame if something bad happened.'

★     ★     ★

After the successful retrieval of the complete contents of Pierre Dubois's phone, Andrew and Fiona had gone straight back to their hotel where Andrew immediately hooked up the small micro-USB storage device to his laptop. Within minutes the entirety of Dubois's emails, attachments, images and documents, were all laid out neatly in folders for easy access. All of the entries in his calendar were also there, mapped out in a grid at the bottom of the screen and spanning several months.

'Look here,' said Andrew, and pointed at the screen. 'There is a folder here that contains the same set of images of Ptolemy's diary as the one we got from Alexis's laptop.'

'Interesting,' said Fiona looking at the screen. 'I am guessing Dubois was the one who provided them to her to begin with.'

'Yes, most likely,' said Andrew. 'And it was almost certainly Morozov who acquired them for Dubois. They might even have managed to get their hands on the actual diary itself.'

'But that means they have had plenty of time to study it and press ahead with their plans, whatever they are,' said Fiona. 'Let's have a look at his calendar.'

Andrew clicked to maximise the calendar view across the whole of the laptop screen. There were lots of entries, but Andrew began by going through the ones that had already happened. There were several mentioning *Pantera*, including one in Paris that referred to "the package".

'Have a look at this,' said Andrew. 'Dubois went to meet with Alexis at her estate on the very same day that we were there. We just missed each other by a couple of hours.'

'Wow,' said Fiona. 'She really played it cool when she met us. There wasn't a hint that anything was amiss.'

'She'd make a great poker player, that's for sure,' said Andrew. 'There is another entry here that involves Pantera. Another "package" pick-up. This might have been whatever Morozov stole from the Cyprus Museum in Nicosia.'

'Have the authorities there released any information about what was stolen?' asked Fiona.

'I checked with Strickland,' said Andrew. 'Apparently, there is no trace of anything having been taken, but the museum holds so many thousands of artefacts that it might take them weeks to discover if something is missing.'

'I would kill to be able to find out what they were looking for,' said Fiona, sounding frustrated. 'The only thing that is certain is that it somehow has to do with Alexander the Great.'

'Here's something interesting,' said Andrew, pointing at an entry. 'Dubois is scheduled to go to a heliport just west of Athens later this afternoon. It looks like he will be flown to a place called Vergina. Do you know what that is? Is this *the* Vergina, as in the Vergina Sun?'

'Vergina,' breathed Fiona, her eyes widening and her mouth open. 'They are going to Aigai.'

'What?' said Andrew.

'Aigai,' repeated Fiona. 'The ancient royal capital of Macedonia and the seat of the Argead dynasty, Alexander's lineage. It is where it all started. It is where Alexander grew up and where all of the Argead royals were buried. They found the tomb of Alexander's father, Philip II there back in the 1970s.'

Andrew furrowed his brow and looked up at Fiona. 'You don't think…' he began sceptically.

'Oh shit!' exclaimed Fiona, sitting bolt upright. 'They are actually looking for Alexander's tomb. They think it is in Vergina.'

'But could that be true?' asked Andrew. 'I would have thought that the location of the tomb of such an important historical figure would be well known.'

'It is,' said Fiona. 'I mean, it was. Alexander was entombed in Alexandria by Ptolemy several years after his death in Babylon, and the tomb was definitely there for centuries according to a whole range of ancient Greek and Roman historians. It was quite famously visited by lots of Roman emperors who wanted to pay their respects or perhaps even absorb some of Alexander's power.'

'So, what happened to it?' asked Andrew. 'Is it no longer there?'

'It is a long story,' replied Fiona. 'But the short answer is that we just don't know.'

'What?' said Andrew incredulously. 'Are you saying it was lost?'

'Well, not exactly,' said Fiona. 'But in the fog of history somehow its precise location has been lost, and at this point in time no one really knows what exactly happened to it and where it is now.'

'That sounds quite incredible,' said Andrew. 'But come to think of it, I don't recall ever seeing or hearing anything about the tomb. Do you think Alexis and Dubois might have located it?'

'I doubt it, but I suppose it is possible,' replied Fiona musingly. 'They certainly might think that they have. Aigai, or Vergina as it is called today, contains a number of burial sites inside huge earthen mounds that have been excavated over the past several decades, most notably that of Philip II. There is an amazing museum there which has all of the artefacts on display.'

Andrew and Fiona looked at each other.

'Oh dear,' said Fiona, looking worried. 'I think they are going to attempt to break in there too.'

'But what for?' said Andrew, slowly scratching the side of his head. 'What do they want? Even if they did find Alexander's body, what would they do with it?'

Fiona shook her head. 'I'm not sure, but we can't let them wreck that place. It is of huge historical importance, and it is a UNESCO World Heritage Site.'

As they were talking, Andrew sifted through some more files to see if anything jumped out. At one point he opened a document containing a list of locations dotted throughout the enormous area that came under Alexander the Great's control during his campaign.

'What's this?' he said, glancing at Fiona. 'It looks like a list of places.'

Fiona leaned in and read them all out loud.

Granicus River, 334 BCE.
Battle of Issus, 333 BCE.
Siege of Gaza, 332 BCE.
Tanais River, 329 BCE.
Cyropolis, 329 BCE.
Chophen River, 327 BCE. *
Battle of Massaga, 327 BCE.
Hydraotes River, 325 BCE.

'Well,' she said, tilting her head slightly as she tried to make sense of the list. 'They are all locations where Alexander fought battles. But there are eight locations on this list and Alexander fought around twenty major battles and a huge number of smaller skirmishes during the course of his campaign.'

'So, what is special about these locations?' asked Andrew. 'What do they have in common? And why is one of them marked with an asterisk?'

Fiona ran her eyes slowly down the list once more, whispering them to herself as she went. The list read like an extremely abbreviated recounting of Alexander's decade-long campaign, with some major events present but even more of them missing. Then she suddenly turned to Andrew.

'I think I know what this is about,' she said excitedly. 'If I remember Arrian's account correctly, then these are all locations where Alexander was wounded.'

'Are you sure?' asked Andrew.

'Positive,' said Fiona. 'Look here. First entry. The Granicus River, where Alexander first clashed with the Persian army. Remember, he barely escaped with his life when Cleitus the Black cut off the arm of a Persian nobleman who was about to strike Alexander with a sword. In the moments before that, Alexander had been struck over the head with a scimitar. His helmet took the blow and shattered, but Alexander still received a wound to his head.'

'Second entry,' continued Fiona. 'At the battle of Issus, Alexander was injured by a sword thrust to the thigh. The third entry relates to the siege of Gaza, where a powerful dart pierced his shield and his armour and entered his body. This was apparently a very serious injury.'

'And so it goes on,' she continued. 'Every single entry on this list relates to a time when Alexander was wounded in battle.'

'But what could be the purpose of this list?' asked Andrew.

'I am not sure,' said Fiona, rubbing her fingertips gently against her temples. 'It seems like they might actually be trying to find the exact locations where Alexander was wounded.'

Andrew looked perplexed for a couple of seconds, but then his face betrayed a sudden realisation blooming inside his head.

'They are after his blood,' he exclaimed.

Fiona, who had simultaneously realised the same thing, grabbed his shoulder and stared at him for a moment.

'They are after his DNA,' she said, sounding both amazed, fascinated and confused. 'But what on earth does Alexis want with it?'

Andrew looked pensive, rubbing his jaw with his hand.

'What if Alexis thinks she might be related to Alexander?' he said.

'You think she would be prepared to almost literally move heaven and earth just for that?' asked Fiona. 'She is spending millions on this project, and her people are breaking laws and killing people over this. Is that really likely?'

'Who knows?' shrugged Andrew. 'She has more money than she knows what to do with. Ultra-wealthy people do the most eccentric things. Or perhaps she has political ambitions. I am pretty sure I read that there are rumours about her to that effect. If she could somehow prove that she is a direct descendant of Alexander the Great, that would be bound to catapult her up into the upper echelons of Greek politics. She could probably start her own party just based on that fact alone. Perhaps even become president. Head of state.'

Fiona looked unconvinced. 'I somehow doubt that it is that simple,' she said. 'It is too crass. She strikes me as someone who would have a much more sophisticated motive for doing something like this. But what?'

'Is it even possible to retrieve DNA from blood that is this old?' asked Andrew. 'If Alexander died in 323 BCE, then that blood is at least two-thousand three-hundred years old.'

'I have been wondering about the same thing ever since we met Alexis and saw those sabretooth tigers,' said Fiona, 'so I emailed Professor McIntyre, and he basically confirmed that under the right conditions, sections of DNA can remain more or less intact for thousands of years. He mentioned that just a couple of years ago the skeleton of a woman who died 7,200 years ago was found in a cave on the island of Sulawesi in Indonesia, and her genome was at least partly mapped out. But apparently, there is a big difference in how well DNA information is preserved, depending on which part of the body it came from.'

'How so?' asked Andrew.

'Well, the best chance of finding well-preserved DNA in an ancient body is in the teeth,' Fiona replied. 'Bones are also very good at keeping these tiny molecules undisturbed and relatively intact. After that it is tissue, and then blood.'

'So ideally, if Alexis is searching for Alexander's DNA, she would need his teeth or his skeleton,' said Andrew.

'That is correct,' replied. 'But since Alexander's tomb has been missing for almost two thousand years, the chances of finding any of those two are virtually nil. That must be why Alexis and Dubois are trying to track down places where Alexander was wounded. They are trying to recover his blood and then extract his genome from that.'

'Wow,' said Andrew. 'That really sounds far-fetched. Especially because blood is organic and largely made up of water, so wouldn't it decompose?'

'You would think so,' said Fiona. 'But according to McIntyre it is not entirely out of the question to find semi-intact DNA in ancient blood. He told me that a single drop of blood typically contains 250 million red blood cells, and remember that each of those blood cells has a complete human genome stored within them. That is a huge number, and if you have advanced gene sequencing and editing technology at your disposal in the way that Alexis and ZOE Technologies do, then it is perfectly conceivable that they would be able to map thousands or perhaps even millions of fractions of Alexander's genome, and then stitch them all together to recreate one complete genome. That was pretty much what they did with the sabretooth tigers, if I am not mistaken. The other alternative, which is tissue, also has potential if you can find any. Apparently, the human body consists of something like 30 trillion cells, each one containing a complete genome, and since we shed about one million of them per day, it gives you a sense of what might be possible if just a small amount of intact tissue could be recovered somehow.'

'Wow,' said Andrew. 'Perhaps this whole thing isn't nearly as fanciful as it first appeared.'

'The question is,' said Fiona. 'What do we do about it? We can't allow Dubois to pillage ancient burial sites if we can prevent it. What if they are actually right and they do manage to locate Alexander's tomb?

Then there is every chance that the tomb will be destroyed or have its contents sold off to the highest bidding private collector. Can you imagine if the tomb of Alexander the Great ended up in someone's basement? It would be completely abhorrent. Andrew, we have an obligation to do whatever we can to prevent that from happening.'

Andrew nodded. 'I agree,' he said reluctantly. 'That would be bad.'

'So, shouldn't we go to the police?' asked Fiona.

'As in, the Greek police?' asked Andrew sceptically.

'Obviously,' said Fiona with an uncertain frown.

Andrew winced and sucked his teeth.

'I am not sure that is a good idea, Fiona,' he said. 'Alexis has access to almost unlimited resources, not least ready cash. She is probably also well connected if the rumours of her political ambitions are true, and she almost certainly has at least part of the police force paid off.'

'Really?' said Fiona sceptically.

'I know this sounds uncharitable, but Greeks are notorious for taking bribes,' replied Andrew. 'We just can't risk it. We might even end up being locked up ourselves, and that would probably cause a diplomatic incident.'

'But worse than that,' said Fiona. 'Alexis and Dubois would steal a march on us and potentially do untold damage to the Vergina site and possibly other sites where they suspect there are traces of Alexander's DNA.'

'Well, then we have to go after them ourselves,' said Andrew determinedly. 'Are you sure you are up for that?'

'There is no other alternative,' said Fiona. 'If we can't go to the police, then we are the only ones who can do anything about it. And if we don't, then who knows what Dubois and his Russian psycho-friend might do to that place, or anyone unfortunate enough to get in their way. We should leave right now.'

'Well, it will take us a while,' said Andrew, whilst looking at a map on his phone of the area around the village of Vergina. 'We have a much faster aircraft, but we can't land anywhere near Vergina. We will have to land in Thessaloniki on the other side of the bay, some 60 kilometres away by road. Dubois, on the other hand, can set the chopper down pretty much on top of where he is going.'

'Can't we call on Colonel Strickland here?' asked Fiona. 'Wouldn't he be able to assist somehow? Perhaps get us a helicopter.'

'Normally he would probably be able to pull some strings,' said Andrew. 'But this is very short notice. The nearest RAF airbase is RAF Akrotiri in Cyprus, but that is several hours flight time away for a helicopter, and I am not even sure they have choppers with that sort of range stationed there. Akrotiri primarily hosts fixed-wing aircraft.'

'We should get going then,' said Fiona and rose. 'We can talk more on the way.'

'There just one other thing I need to show you,' said Andrew, and pulled out his phone. 'This might come in handy.'

He placed the phone flat on the table between them and tapped a small icon containing the SAS insignia of the vertical dagger with two wings spread out behind it and a banner at the bottom reading

"Who dares wins". It was an app called 5-Eyes Global Tracker.

'The boys back at the firm coded this up for me a few months ago,' said Andrew. 'It is basically a clone of a desktop PC application, transcoded to run on a phone.'

The app fired up and showed an animation of the earth slowly spinning. At the top was a drop-down menu where the user could enter a phone number or the unique serial and production number of any mobile phone produced anywhere in the world.

'When my little gadget extracted all the data from Dubois's phone, it also retrieved all the device-specific information that is used every time a mobile phone talks to any of the base stations in the network. It basically works a lot like the GPS on your phone by triangulating a position based on two or more base stations, except I can now track Dubois's phone almost anywhere.'

'So, we can monitor him where ever he goes?' asked Fiona.

'More or less,' replied Andrew. 'The app runs in the background even if his phone is on standby. The only time it won't work is if he is in the air or if he has his phone powered off completely. Apart from those instances, the phone is constantly talking to the mobile network base stations and snitching on his location.'

'So where is he now?' asked Fiona.

'Let's have a look,' said Andrew, and tapped the drop-down menu.

He then selected Dubois' mobile phone as the tracking target. Within a couple of seconds the view on the screen began gradually zooming in towards Europe, then Greece, then Athens, and finally settling on a red circle overlay that looked to be roughly 50 metres in diameter and centred on the location of the Athens Gate Hotel.

'In his hotel room, by the looks of things,' said Andrew. 'Seems like he hasn't left there at all today. He might have decided Athens was not as much fun as he had hoped, and now he is just waiting to leave for the heliport.'

'Right,' said Fiona. 'Let's pack up, get ourselves downstairs and check out.'

'Alright,' said Andrew. 'I will call ahead to the pilots and ask for the aircraft to be readied for us. Hopefully, we should be able to take off a couple of hours from now.'

# Seventeen

It was mid-afternoon when Andrew and Fiona made their way to the front desk of the hotel to check out. Andrew was sliding his credit card across the reception desk when his phone vibrated and produced a fast, high-pitched triple-ping. He pulled it out and swiped the screen.

'Seems Dubois is on the move,' he said quietly, turning to Fiona. 'I am tracking him heading east out of central Athens. Looks like he is heading for the heliport, just as we thought. He will probably be there in five or ten minutes.'

'Shit,' whispered Fiona. 'They are going to have a huge head start on us.'

'It looks that way, unfortunately,' winced Andrew. 'We will just have to get going and try to make up as much time in the air as possible. Could you try to arrange for a rental car to be waiting for us when we land?'

'On it,' said Fiona, quickly pulling her own phone from the back pocket of her dark blue jeans.

Andrew finished the check-out process, and as they walked through the hotel lobby to a waiting taxi, Fiona had her head buried in her phone trying to arrange for a hire car to be ready just a few hours later in Thessaloniki in the north of Greece.

About forty-five minutes later they were walking briskly through the small terminal at Tatoi Airport in northern Athens. The Honda HA-420 was waiting on the tarmac with its twin engines already running and the pilot signalling that the plane was ready to leave immediately. Andrew and Fiona climbed aboard and strapped themselves into the comfortable leather seats opposite each other by a window, and within minutes the small jet was barrelling down the runway and lifting off into the clear blue sky.

'The rental car is booked,' said Fiona. 'It should be ready in about an hour.'

'Good,' said Andrew. 'The pilot told me that he could make the trip in just under half an hour, but we still have to wait for a landing slot and then make our way from the private parking apron through the terminal to the other side. The biggest issue is the long drive. It is only about sixty kilometres, but we are forced to first head north through the city of Thessaloniki before we can take the E75 motorway southwest and down to Vergina. That is going to slow us down quite a bit. But there is no other way to do it.'

'Ok,' said Fiona. 'Oh, I wanted to ask you. Are you carrying a gun? I was just thinking. What if Morozov is there?'

'We will have to cross that bridge when we get to it,' said Andrew. 'But yes, I have a gun.'

He opened up his light grey suit jacket to let her see the matt-black semi-automatic Glock 17 pistol strapped to his chest in an underarm gun holster. With a full double-stack magazine it holds seventeen 9mm rounds, and its relatively low recoil means that it is surprisingly accurate even at medium range.

'Hopefully, I won't need it,' said Andrew and tucked his jacket back in close to his chest.

'Well, no,' said Fiona. 'Of course not. Vergina is a small village that just happens to have been built more or less on top of the Aigai burial mounds. We want to avoid any sort of violence if we can. But it is nice to know that we can at least defend ourselves. This Morozov character sounds like a proper psychopath.'

'I agree,' said Andrew. 'Better safe than sorry. Anyway, I wanted to mention to you that I have had an email from Strickland saying that the team back in London have decrypted a number of emails from Alexis's laptop. Most of them seem irrelevant, but there was one that I thought might be interesting. It was part of an email exchange between Alexis and Fabian Ackerman, and it had something to do with a new complementary approach to genetic sequencing. I won't pretend to understand all of it, but the gist of it is as follows. The human genome consists of 23 chromosomes, of which one is the gender chromosome which is either XX or XY. When a child is conceived, most of the Y chromosome is handed down from father to son entirely intact. This means that if you have the complete genome of a son as well as that of his mother, then you can assume that the Y chromosome of the son is the same as that of the father, and then reverse engineer the X chromosome from the father by mapping the X chromosome of the mother and examining the differences between that and the son. And as for the other twenty-two chromosomes, you can compare the mother's 22 remaining chromosomes with those of the son, and then infer which ones came from the father.'

'I am not sure I follow,' said Fiona.

'Basically, what it means is this,' said Andrew. 'If Alexis and Dubois could find the remains of a son of Alexander the Great, as well as those of his mother, they would at least theoretically be able to reconstruct the entire genome of Alexander. That is what Ackerman said he had trialled successfully in primates.'

'That sounds like something out of a science fiction novel,' said Fiona. 'I would love to hear what Professor McIntyre thinks about that, but I guess that will have to wait.'

'There was another thing I wanted to ask you,' said Andrew. 'In our hotel room in Athens you mentioned that Alexander's tomb had been missing for around two thousand years. So, what is the story around that whole thing? How could something as monumentally important as that simply go missing?'

'That is a great question,' said Fiona. 'And one that has kept historians and archaeologists busy for centuries. So, let's go back to the 11th of June 323 BCE. After the initial shock and distress of Alexander's death from a period of fever, a ferocious debate occurred among his top generals about who should succeed him. The basic problem was that none of Alexander's children had come of age, and

Alexander himself had not pointed to anyone as the man to take over the reign of his now vast empire. So, it was up to a small group of men, many of whom disliked each other, to effectively decide the fate of millions of people.'

'Sounds a bit like modern-day politics,' observed Andrew wryly.

'Well, yes,' shrugged Fiona. 'Sadly, that is true. Anyway, Alexander had a half-brother, Philip III Arrhidaios, who was three years older than him. The problem with Arrhidaios was that he was mentally impaired. It isn't clear from historical sources to what extent this was the case, but it seems to have been taken as self-evident at the time that he was unfit to rule. Alexander also had several children, but none of them were legitimate, and so they could not be proclaimed rightful heirs. However, Alexander's Bactrian wife Roxana was pregnant when Alexander died, but at that time no one was able to tell if it was going to be a boy or a girl, so it could not be assumed that Roxana was carrying an heir. The most senior general, Perdiccas, persuaded his fellow generals to wait for the birth, and as it turned out, a few months later, Roxana gave birth to Alexander IV who was technically the legitimate heir to Alexander's throne. However, he was obviously not able to rule yet, and the generals also decided that the fact that he was half Bactrian would not go down well with the Macedonians. As a compromise, it was decided that Perdiccas would be regent until Alexander IV came of age, and that the empire should be governed locally by the generals, who would be given a province each. Perdiccas put Alexander's signet ring on his finger and took for himself the central part of the empire, remaining in Babylon as ruler and local governor, with the support of a more junior general by the name of Seleucus. Ptolemy, Son of Lagus, a.k.a. Ptolemy I Soter, took control of the prosperous province of Egypt, and general Antigonus who was already an old man and who had served first under Philip II and then under Alexander himself, took Asia Minor. Another old general by the name Antipater eventually went back to Pella in Macedonia to take up the role of governor there, bringing with him both Roxana, Alexander IV and Arrhidaios.'

But what happened to Alexander's body?' asked Andrew. 'Was he buried in Babylon?'

'No,' replied Fiona. 'After his death, and supposedly on the express wishes of Alexander himself, his body was embalmed. This was carried out by Egyptian embalmers who would have been resident in Babylonia at that time. Apparently, Alexander had said that he wanted to be buried at Siwa in Egypt with his spiritual father Zeus-Amun, but the important thing to understand here is that Alexander's body, which in the minds of many was the body of a divine being, suddenly became a hugely important political asset. Having possession of the body of the great king would give the owner authority and legitimacy as successor to Alexander.'

'Slightly morbid,' said Alexander. 'But then on the other hand, I think dead Soviet leaders are still kept in an embalmed state in mausoleums in central Moscow, presumably for the same purpose.'

'Exactly,' said Fiona. 'If I am not mistaken, Lenin's body has been on display there for about a century now. So, great care was taken in Alexander's embalming to ensure that this incredibly important symbol of power over the vast empire could be kept safe. Despite Alexander's own wishes, Perdiccas decided that his body should be returned to Macedonia, and so over the following many months after his death, an enormous and elaborate funeral carriage was constructed, intended for returning his body to Alexander's royal ancestral home of Aigai, where we are going now. According to the Greek historian Diodorus who wrote about this in the 1st century, a solid gold coffin was prepared which had a purple gold-embroidered robe placed on it. Next to it were Alexander's personal weapons. The coffin was placed inside a vaulted golden structure roughly four by eight metres in size that was lined with columns and decorated with precious stones, and the whole thing was surrounded by gold netting to allow people to peer inside it. The carriage was pulled along by sixty-four oxen, each with a golden bell attached to a gem-studded collar.'

'That would have been quite a spectacle,' said Andrew. 'And a magnet for would-be robbers.'

Fiona nodded. 'The idea was for the cortege, which was heavily guarded by an army, to make its way slowly through Alexander's empire and back to Macedonia in a way that would be highly visible, so that everyone could pay their respects to the dead king. And in 321 BCE, almost two years after Alexander's death, the cortege set out from Babylonia on the long voyage towards Aigai.'

'I somehow sense that this didn't quite go according to plan,' said Andrew.

'That would be an understatement,' replied Fiona. 'As the cortege approached Damascus, it was intercepted and seized by a large army controlled by Ptolemy.'

'Ptolemy actually stole the body?' asked Andrew incredulously.

'He did,' replied Fiona. 'The cortege guard was simply not equipped to resist Ptolemy's forces. In addition, some money apparently also changed hands. In any event, Ptolemy took Alexander's body back to Memphis on the Nile, which was the traditional capital of Egypt. Here he had Alexander interred. But more or less as soon as Perdiccas heard of this disaster, he set out with his army for Egypt with the intention of defeating Ptolemy and recapturing Alexander's body. His authority had been severely undermined, and he was keen to re-establish himself as the primary caretaker of Alexander's empire.'

'I hear another 'but' coming,' smiled Andrew.

'Well,' said Fiona. 'Perdiccas was known as the most proper and regal of Alexander's generals, but he was not renowned for his prowess as a battlefield commander. Ptolemy, on the other hand, was widely regarded as highly intelligent and shrewd, and when Perdiccas arrived in Egypt, Ptolemy simply withdrew his forces to the western bank of the Nile and dug in. Perdiccas was impatient, and after several forced and badly planned and executed attempts to get his men across the river, he was assassinated by a group of his own generals. This group included Seleucus, who would later head back to Babylon and establish the Seleucid Empire which lasted almost three hundred years. As part of an agreement between the remaining generals, Antipater was named the new nominal regent until Alexander IV would come of age.'

'So, Alexander's body was buried in Memphis then,' said Andrew.

'Yes,' said Fiona, 'But only for about twenty years, because in 301 BCE Ptolemy moved it to his new capital Alexandria, where he constructed a magnificent tomb inside the royal quarters of the city.'

'Why the delay?' asked Andrew.

'Well, firstly Alexandria was a relatively young city when Ptolemy took control of the body, and he was still in the process of building it. Secondly, relations between Alexander's generals and would-be successors, known as the Diadochi, declined quite badly over the years following his death. Antipater died of old age and bypassed his son Cassander as ruler of Macedonia, instead handing over power to a man named Polyperchon who was one of his generals.'

'I am struggling a bit with all the names now,' said Andrew, rubbing the side of his head.

'I know,' said Fiona. 'It is a bit complicated but bear with me. The tensions between the Diadochi ended up in a full civil war where Ptolemy allied himself with Cassander in Macedonia, Antigonus who held most of Asia Minor, and also the wife of Alexander's enfeebled half-brother Arrhidaios, in order to attempt to defeat Polyperchon. They eventually succeeded, and while Ptolemy consolidated his power in Egypt and Seleucus returned to Babylon, Cassander took back control of Macedonia and installed himself as regent in Pella. This is important because in an effort to eliminate possible contenders for the Macedonian throne, Cassander then had Roxana and Alexander IV assassinated.'

'Crikey,' said Andrew. 'That was brutal. How old was Alexander IV?'

'Only fourteen,' replied Fiona. 'It was quite tragic really. His only crime was to have been born the son of Alexander the Great, a man he never even knew.'

'So, I guess you're saying that the lineage of Alexander ended there?' said Andrew.

'Yes,' replied Fiona. 'With no other legitimate sons the field was now wide open for the Diadochi to fight over the remains of the empire, and the result was almost forty years of civil war which ended in a climactic battle at Ipsus in Anatolia in 301 BCE.'

'What a mess,' said Andrew. 'Not exactly a dignified end to Alexander's empire.'

'No,' said Fiona. 'Not really. But I guess power, or the prospect of it, does that to people. Men in particular.'

Andrew looked at her sceptically but decided not to argue.

'So, what became of the tomb in Alexandria?' he asked instead.

'Well,' said Fiona. 'After the Battle of Ipsus where Ptolemy and his allies were victorious, Alexander's body was moved to a new elaborate tomb complex at the centre of the newly completed city of Alexandria. Ptolemy was probably the one general who came out on top after the Wars of the Diadochi. He established a long-lived dynasty in Alexandria, partly based on a new sect built around Alexander the Great, his tomb, and eventually also around himself. Among other things, he placed Alexander's image on the newly minted Ptolemaic coins, introduced a state cult of Alexander throughout Egypt, and he seeded the rumour that he himself was actually the illegitimate son of Alexander the Great's father Philip II, in effect attempting to make himself Alexander's half-brother. This wasn't true, of course, but it helped him and his successors to consolidate power in Egypt. When Ptolemy died of old age in 283 BCE, his son Ptolemy II Philadelphus had him deified alongside Alexander the Great.'

'No such thing as hubris back then, I guess,' said Andrew acerbically.

'It is not that simple,' said Fiona. 'In those days you could not be a ruler without some sort of divine link. Alexander's body was simply the tool Ptolemy used to achieve that link. Anyway, around 215 BCE Ptolemy IV Philopator had Alexander's body moved to a new and majestic royal burial complex known as the *Soma*, which by the way is the ancient Greek word for 'body'. Inside the Soma in the main mausoleum, which was contained in an underground chamber, Alexander's body was placed alongside those of the previous Ptolemaic rulers, starting with his old friend Ptolemy I. But of course, nothing lasts forever, and around three centuries and many Ptolemaic rulers later in 89 BCE, the Ptolemaic kingdom had become a shadow of its former self, and Rome was now becoming the dominant force in the ancient world. The kingdom was under military pressure from this new regional power, and at one point things became so dire that Ptolemy X had Alexander's gold coffin melted down in order to pay his mercenaries, and Alexander's body was then relocated into a glass coffin where it remained for several more centuries. But the decline of the Ptolemaic dynasty continued, and with the suicide of its last ruler Cleopatra VII in 30 BCE, the dynasty ended and the era of Roman Alexandria began.'

'Is this *the* Cleopatra?' asked Andrew.

'Yes,' replied Fiona. 'The one who was buried with her lover Mark Antony, possibly inside the tomb complex in Alexandria. Anyway, during Roman times Alexander's mausoleum became an object of pilgrimage, and over the next several centuries, dignitaries, including at least a handful of Roman emperors such as Julius Caesar, would come and pay their respects. The Romans had a particular fascination with Alexander because they saw him as the ultimate conqueror and the epitome of power, and so their emperors flocked to his tomb. Quite famously, when the Roman emperor Augustus came to visit the tomb, he was asked if he would like to see the tombs of the Ptolemaic rulers, to which he replied scathingly that he had come to see a king, not a bunch of dead corpses.'

'Harsh,' said Andrew and laughed. 'Still, a lot of people were clearly trying to bask in Alexander's reflected glory, so I understand the cynicism.'

'Well, the mausoleum stood for several centuries after that, surviving quite tumultuous times across a Roman empire riddled with conflicts and civil wars. The last mention of it can be found four centuries later in the writings of the Greek scholar Libanius in 390 CE, who mentioned Alexander's body being on display in Alexandria. But that is the last known reference to it. After that, there is just nothing.'

Andrew looked perplexed. 'How is this possible?' he asked. 'It seems completely absurd that it could just vanish from history.'

'Yes, it does,' nodded Fiona. 'But you have to look at the context. At the start of the 4th century CE, the new religion of Christianity was beginning to assert itself, often quite violently across the ancient world, and Alexandria was no exception.'

'This is what Alexis talked about,' said Andrew.

'Yes,' said Fiona. 'She certainly has a point. For a while Jews and Christians and pagans had lived in relative harmony in Alexandria, but when the Roman Emperor Theodosius I banned what he called paganism in 391 CE, Christian zealots basically went on a rampage through the cities of much of the ancient world burning down and destroying so-called pagan symbols and monuments. It is quite likely that Alexander's Mausoleum was destroyed during that time. It was without a doubt the main pagan place of worship, so it would almost certainly have been destroyed, and Alexander's tomb with it.'

'Quite an undignified end to such a huge historical figure,' said Andrew.

'Well, yes,' said Fiona and looked intently at Andrew. 'Unless of course, his body was removed and somehow brought to safety.'

'Is there any evidence to support that idea?' asked Andrew with a curious look.

'No hard evidence as such,' said Fiona. 'But there are lots of speculative theories about what might have happened to it, some more fanciful than others.'

'Have you ever seen anything to indicate that it might have been brought back to Vergina?' asked Andrew.

'No,' replied Fiona. 'But that doesn't mean it didn't happen. There was such chaos in Alexandria during those days that it is perfectly possible that someone loyal to the Ptolemies and the Argead house saw what was coming, and that they somehow managed to smuggle the body out. And what better place to bring it than the royal burial grounds in Aigai, Alexander's ancestral home.'

Andrew glanced out of the window. 'Well, we're coming in to land in a few minutes, so it won't be long until we find out if Alexis and Dubois are on to something or if it is a wild goose chase.'

'I really hope not,' said Fiona. 'Dubois would almost certainly cause damage to whatever he finds. He clearly has no respect for history anymore. The sooner we can put him out of business the better. Sorry about the barrage of information by the way. I know it is a lot to take in, but you did ask.'

'I did,' smiled Andrew. 'Anyway, let's see what we find in Vergina. We might still be able to stop him.'

# EIGHTEEN

'Are we encrypted?' asked Ackerman as he picked up his phone and sat down in his office chair at the ZOE Technologies research centre in California.

'Yes, sir,' replied Stone.

'Alright. Speak freely then,' said Ackerman. 'How did it go?'

'She's ours,' said Stone. 'Extr4ctor's information checked out. At least judging from the look on Jeffrey Worthington's face when I laid it out for him.'

'Go on,' said Ackerman.

'My Lithuanian friend was able to find some extremely useful Kompromat,' said Stone, using the Russian KGB term for damaging information, either personal or business-related, that could be used to blackmail someone and perhaps even force them to work for a foreign intelligence service.

'And what was that?' asked Ackerman

'The respectable Mr Worthington has been cultivating a client base of oligarchs from Russia, and Uzbekistan, and he has been creating offshore shell companies in a couple of Caribbean tax havens. He has then used these companies to launder criminal proceeds through property holdings in London. This amounts to tax evasion. But that's not the half of it. It seems the respectable Mr Worthington has been siphoning off significant amounts of that money for himself and putting it into a fictitious investment management firm located in the Cayman Islands.'

'I see,' said Ackerman. 'Silly boy.'

'Yes,' chuckled Stone. 'If those oligarchs ever found out, old Jeffrey would probably end up at the bottom of the Thames. Geezer went white as snow when I told him what we've got. Made things a bit awkward when the missus came home, of course. But then that was the idea.'

'I expect so,' replied Ackerman. 'How did Inspector Worthington take it.'

'Not too well to be honest,' said Stone. 'Well, she didn't say much. But I am confident she got the message alright. Seeing the evidence there in front of her made it difficult for her to deny it.'

'There is still the risk that she could wriggle,' said Ackerman. 'Perhaps she might try to get the intelligence services involved?'

'Oh, I don't think we need to worry about that,' said Stone calmly. 'She'd be out on her ear if the Metropolitan Police ever found out that her husband is as crooked as a barrel of fish hooks, and that she has been living off criminal proceeds for decades. Holiday home in Italy, expensive cars and two kids at posh universities. She won't be telling anyone anything, my friend. As I said to her, she has a simple choice. She can go to her superiors and stir up a hornet's nest trying to come after me, which will result in her losing her career, her family being disgraced and Mr Worthington being thrown in the nick. Alternatively, she can keep us updated on the Balfour investigation and let us know if they pick up Dawson, and then no one will ever know what we have on her and her husband.'

'Very good,' said Ackerman and chuckled. 'You really are a sneaky bastard, Stone. But you're my bastard.'

'We all just do what we need to do,' replied Stone languidly. 'It's just the way of the world.'

'Indeed,' said Ackerman. 'Excellent work, Stone. Your bonus will hit your account later today.'

*         *         *

The drive from Thessaloniki International Airport to Vergina took less than an hour, but to Fiona it felt like an eternity. Andrew more or less disregarded the speed limits and the motorway from Thessaloniki virtually goes in a straight line towards Vergina for most of the way there.

'I was thinking,' said Fiona, looking out of the window. 'If what you said about Ackerman's new complementary genome sequencing technique is true, then it really would be at least theoretically possible for Alexis and Ackerman to recreate Alexander the Great's genome, as long as Dubois can get his hands on the remains of Roxana and young Alexander IV.'

'Correct,' said Andrew. 'And they are both buried at Aigai, right?'

'That's right,' replied Fiona. 'The problem is that as far as I know they were both cremated, so there would be no DNA left to sequence, at least not from their bodies. Unless perhaps their teeth survived the cremation and could still yield enough genetic information to reconstruct their genomes. I don't know. Sounds tenuous to be honest, but this is just way outside of my field of expertise, and it is frankly beyond my ability to fully understand.'

'I know how you feel,' said Andrew. 'It is really complicated. Perhaps we should have a word with McIntyre as you suggested. But that will have to wait. Right now, we just need to get to Aigai as fast as we can.'

It was late afternoon when their rental car swung noisily into the gravelled parking lot and came to a stop. The village of Vergina, in which the Royal Tombs of Aigai are located, is situated on the southern edge of the huge Macedonian plain. Immediately to the south, the rocky foothills of the Pieria Mountains rise up, covered in the low vegetation that is able to survive the hot dry summer months. The fertile plain, which stretches away to the north towards Pella around 30 kilometres away, is surrounded on all sides by distant mountains, except towards the east where it meets the Aegean Sea along a silty coastline. Here, three major rivers come down from the mountains to the north-west, forming two large river deltas.

Andrew and Fiona got out of the car and looked around, but there was no sign of Dubois. In fact, there was no sign at all of anything untoward. A handful of tourists were milling around outside the museum, and quite a few were boarding a couple of tour buses. Fiona looked at her watch. The museum would be open for another hour.

'I am not sure what to make of this,' said Fiona. 'But then, I don't really know what I expected.'

Andrew opened the Global Tracker app and waited for the encrypted connection to the server in London to be established. When the map appeared, there was no sign of where Dubois might be. His last known location was somewhere north of Athens, seemingly heading out of the gulf of the Aegean Sea that provides access to what used to be ancient Macedonia. But that was several hours ago, and there was nothing since then.

'I don't have a fix on Dubois,' said Andrew. 'He might have turned his phone off.'

'Do you think he is on to us?' asked Fiona.

'Very unlikely,' replied Andrew, absentmindedly placing his right hand under his left arm where his pistol was strapped to his torso. 'If he was, he would probably never have gone to the heliport as planned. Anyway, let's get inside and have a look around.'

'Ok,' said Fiona scanning the surrounding area nervously. 'Let go.'

Just as they began walking away from the car, two elderly people, a man and a woman, were coming the opposite way. They seemed to be walking back towards a tour bus and Fiona overheard parts of their conversation as they passed.

'It's so lovely and peaceful here,' said the woman in an American accent.

'Yeah, except for the damn helicopter,' chuckled the man.

It took Fiona a couple of seconds to register what she had heard. She stopped and turned to face the two.

'I'm sorry,' she said in a friendly tone of voice. 'Did you say *helicopter*?'

'Yes,' exclaimed the woman. 'One flew over a couple of times and landed down that way.'

She pointed towards the east through a clump of trees and bushes. 'It made an awful noise.'

'What did it look like?' asked Fiona.

'It was black,' replied the woman. 'Looked like one of those corporate helicopters that important folks fly around in.'

'Did it take off again?' asked Fiona.

'I don't know,' said the man, looking at the woman who nodded her agreement. 'We have been inside the museum for over an hour. Are you here to see it?

'We are,' replied Fiona.

'Well worth the long trip here. We're from Idaho,' smiled the woman. 'Incredible history on display in there.'

'I guess we have something to look forward to then,' smiled Fiona. 'Have a lovely day.'

'You too,' said the man, and then the two of them smiled and continued walking to their tour bus.

'That has got to be them,' said Fiona turning to Andrew.

'You're probably right,' he said. 'Let's keep our eyes peeled.'

'Ok,' said Fiona. 'It's this way.'

She pointed towards an enormous earthen mound called a tumulus, which was on the other side of a large open space covered in light grey pebbles. The tumulus was huge, around 100 metres across and about ten metres tall. The museum was large and entirely underground, and it was accessible only through a 30-metre-long ramp flanked by large blocks of granite. The ramp sloped gently downward and extended all the way inside the tumulus.

'The museum has four royal tombs inside it, and it is located inside this tumulus which is really quite clever,' said Fiona. 'Instead of painstakingly cataloguing, disassembling and relocating the entire tomb piece by piece to a museum, they simply built the museum around the tomb that was inside the tumulus. Every block of stone is exactly where it was in the 1970s when it was excavated, which means they are precisely where they were in the late 4th century BCE when the tombs were first built. They have effectively remained untouched for 2300 years. However, this also means that, in a manner of speaking, the archaeological site was frozen in time in the 1970s. Anything they might have missed back then would have had a museum built around and on top of it, locking it in place perhaps unseen and unnoticed by archaeologists.'

'But surely they would have used ground-penetrating radar or something to ensure there are no more chambers?' asked Andrew.

'You would think so,' said Fiona. 'I am not sure if that is the case. But I reckon if the entire tumulus was dug up and removed, they would probably find more things buried in the ground.'

'Interesting. Anyway, let's just stay alert now,' said Andrew. 'We don't know what we are going to find down there.'

The two of them walked down the ramp and entered into a cavernous underground space painted entirely in black and lit by dozens of ceiling-mounted spotlights, which gave it a cosy and enticing atmosphere. Several of the spotlights shone down onto glass display boxes which were dotted around the interior of the space. A number of people were slowly walking around inspecting the artefacts, many of which were made of gold and shining brightly in the darkened space. Andrew and Fiona were still waiting for their eyes to adjust from the sunlight outside to the darkness inside, and Andrew was quickly scanning the huge room to see if anyone looked suspicious. All he could see were silhouettes against brightly lit display cases and artefacts.

'They can't possibly be down here,' whispered Fiona. 'Everything looks so… normal.'

'Hold your horses,' said Andrew quietly, his hand tucked inside his jacket. 'Let's look around.'

They moved deeper into the room, approaching a display case that was about four by four metres in size and placed near the centre. It contained a number of smaller sections that held jewellery and other items that had been found in the tombs inside the tumulus.

'Oh my god, look,' said Fiona suddenly and started walking.

'What?' said Andrew, now on guard and tightening his grip on his pistol still inside the gun holster under his arm.

But Fiona was already a couple of metres away and walking briskly towards a tall display case that was roughly one metre on each side. It contained what looked like the chest piece of a suit of armour, an imposing-looking iron helmet placed above it and greaves placed below. Next to the chest piece was an ornate bronze shield.

'Look at this,' said Fiona excitedly as Andrew caught up. 'This is Philip II's linothorax. The armour he would have worn in battle. And the helmet and shield are here too. These were found inside his tomb.'

'Alright,' said Andrew cautiously, looking around. 'You had me worried there for a second. I thought you had spotted them.'

'Sorry,' said Fiona. 'This is just so incredible. Look at this.'

She continued over to another display case which contained an elaborate golden crown. It was king Philips's diadem suspended above an ornate golden chest roughly thirty by forty centimetres in size.

'This is a so-called larnax,' she said, pointing at the chest. 'A container for human remains. It was found with Philip II's bones inside it. And look at the lid.'

Andrew peered inside the brightly lit display case where the larnax sat on four squat feet. On the lid was the unmistakable shape of a sixteen-pointed star.

'The Vergina Sun,' said Andrew. 'Amazing. But let's not lose track of why we are here.'

'I really don't think Dubois is here,' said Fiona quietly. 'It's too busy. There are too many people for him to be able to get away with anything.'

'I am not so sure,' said Andrew. 'I haven't spotted a single guard yet.'

'Let's just keep walking around calmly pretending to be tourists,' said Fiona. 'We can still keep an eye out. But I honestly don't think they are here now. They are probably waiting until the museum closes.'

'You might be right,' nodded Andrew.

'Come this way,' said Fiona and tugged at his jacket sleeve. 'This is the way down to the actual tomb of Philip II.'

They proceeded down another ramp and deeper into the tumulus, at the end of which was what appeared to be the façade of a mausoleum. It was around four metres tall and eight metres wide, and had a roof gable with a shallow pitched roof in classical Greek style. It also had four large pillars placed at the front in a mini-colonnade. At its centre was a large closed door. Above the pillars was a frieze of a hunting scene believed to depict Philip II, and possibly also his son Alexander.

'This style of tomb is actually known as a Macedonian tomb,' said Fiona.

'It's quite spectacular,' said Andrew. 'The museum has done an amazing job of this.'

'I can't believe this is the actual place that they found him,' said Fiona. 'Just in there beyond those doors were the remains of the man who in many ways laid the foundation for Hellenic culture to sweep across the known world. The father of Alexander the Great.'

They stood there in silence for a couple of minutes, taking in the view, and then they retraced their steps back up to the main room.

'Here's a model of the tomb,' said Fiona tugging at Andrew's sleeve again. 'It is quite typical of a tomb from that era.'

Set into a section of black-painted wall was a scale model of Philip II's tomb. It was about two metres long and stretched just under half a metre into the wall, and it consisted of two separate chambers. The first one was immediately behind the façade with the four pillars, and it then extended further back into another separate chamber where Philip II's remains had been found.

'Look at these chambers,' said Fiona. 'This tomb has just two of them, but some tombs have three chambers arranged consecutively like this, one behind the next. That's the antechamber there. The archaeologists would have entered that first, and behind it through a doorway is the burial chamber.'

'It must have been quite exciting to be the first people to lay eyes on those chambers for more than two thousand years,' mused Andrew.

'I can't even begin to explain how excited I would have been if that had been me,' beamed Fiona.

'Oh, and there it is,' she continued, pointing across the room to another ramp leading down to the façade of another tomb. 'That is the tomb where they found the remains of Roxana and Alexander IV.'

Andrew looked concerned. 'Could that actually be what Dubois is after?'

'Possibly,' replied Fiona looking around the room. 'As I said, it would only make sense if the teeth of both Roxana and Alexander IV were recovered. I am not even sure if they are kept here somewhere.'

'Listen, Fiona,' said Andrew. 'I am starting to get a bit nervous about this. I feel like a damn sitting duck down here in this dungeon. I think we should get out and try to re-assess what is going on. If they really intend to hit this place after dark then we need to be well out of sight by then.'

Fiona had a look on her face that said she did not want to leave just yet, but she quickly relented.

'Alright,' she said reluctantly. 'Let's go. We can park up somewhere discreet and watch the entrance.'

Just as they got into the car to wait for the sunset, Andrew's phone produced its now familiar fast and high-pitched triple-ping.

'It must have just picked up Dubois,' he said, and dug into his inside jacket pocket.

Bringing the phone out, he switched it on and waited for the app to fire up.

'Bloody hell,' said Andrew. 'He's close.'

Fiona leaned over to look at the screen. It was showing a map of the area around Vergina village, but there was no firm fix on Dubois's phone. Instead, it displayed a small semi-transparent circle that was overlayed onto the map near the bottom of the screen. The circle was moving around erratically in that area.

'I can't get a good fix on him,' said Andrew. 'He is somewhere south of here. Just a couple of hundred metres away. Possibly underground, so his phone can't maintain a firm link to the local mobile phone base stations.'

'Oh shit,' exclaimed Fiona. 'I think I know where they are.'

'Where?' said Andrew.

'That spot there is another archaeological site,' said Fiona and pointed to the centre of the red circle. 'It is a burial complex containing the tombs of Macedonian queens.'

Andrew and Fiona looked at each other for a couple of seconds, and without another word they then both got out of the car and started running across the road and south through a grass-covered field along the eastern edge of the village.

# NINETEEN

The air was cool and dry as Dubois and Morozov made their way down the ramp into the tomb complex inside the tumulus southeast of Vergina. Cluster B, or Burial Cluster of the Queens as it was officially called, was still an active archaeological site sitting under the cover of a temporary structure with open sides designed only to shield it from the elements. Three tombs had been uncovered, but only one of them was intact. The other two had been looted, most likely not long after their construction.

The intact tomb was that of Queen Eurydice, the wife of Amyntas I who was Philip II's great-great-great-grandfather. Next to her was one of the wives of Alexander I who was Amyntas I's son. In the same cluster, the mother of Philip II, who was also called Eurydice, was buried in a large Macedonian tomb. Inside was found her throne, which was still intact after more than 2000 years. The most recent tomb was thought to have belonged to the daughter of Philip II, Queen Thessaloniki.

As Dubois descended the final steps to the latter tomb, he peered up at the façade, with its distinct four pillars and the elaborately moulded cornice running across the top of it.

'Wait here,' said Dubois and looked over his shoulder to where Morozov was standing. 'I need to focus.'

'Suit yourself,' shrugged Morozov. 'Just be quick.'

At the centre of the façade was a doorway that led to the antechamber, and behind that Dubois could just make out the main burial chamber. He brought out his torch and shone it through the opening. This tomb had been looted long ago, so no definitive evidence had been found as to who it belonged to. The only thing archaeologists could agree on, based on the style of architecture and the friezes and wall decorations, was that it was a female member of the royal Argead dynasty.

Dubois proceeded into the main burial chamber with its dust-covered floor and its musty smell. Here he let the light from his torch sweep slowly across the walls and the ceiling. On the back wall was a badly faded mural of a scene depicting a woman with flowing hair and a long robe, wearing a diadem. She was standing in what appeared to be the Elysian Fields where only mortals related to the gods would spend the afterlife.

Dubois leaned in close and ran his fingertips slowly down the dry wall and over the frieze whilst studying the female figure closely. Around her waist and reaching up over her shoulder and down around her arm, he could just make out the faded form of a thin elongated shape coiled around her. A serpent.

'I knew it,' whispered Dubois. 'Olympias. The mother of a god.'

Dubois took a step back, fixing his torchlight on the image of the queen. He stood there for a few seconds without moving. Then he raised his right leg off the ground whilst leaning slightly forward, and then he kicked the wall as hard as he could. His heavy boot crashed into the false wall which immediately cracked and began disintegrating. Blocks of stone fell down inside the hidden space behind the wall with loud heavy thuds and a dry clatter as smaller pebbles fell to the floor.

'What the hell is going on,' shouted Morozov angrily.

The Russian ex-Spetsnaz soldier had hurried down to the doorway leading to the antechamber, and he was now peering through to the burial chamber, where a cloud of dust was slowly settling around Dubois. Behind the Frenchman was a gaping hole in the back wall.

'It's alright,' said Dubois, giddy with what he had discovered. 'Just a bit of excavation work. You wouldn't understand.'

'Do you have to make so much damn noise?' asked Morozov, sounding tense and irritated.

'Go over in a corner and sulk if you must,' said Dubois. 'But don't disturb me when I am working.'

Morozov retreated back out of the tomb, grumbling something in Russian.

'What have we here?' said Dubois as he knelt down and shone his torch through the hole into the concealed chamber, where a cloud of dust was still slowly whirling around in the air.

He squeezed himself through the hole which caused another block of stone to fall to the floor with a clonk. Inside was a chamber the same size as what had until now been thought to be the main burial chamber. The air inside was cool and had a powdery quality to it which he could taste when he breathed through his mouth. At the back, placed on a low but wide stone pedestal that ran along the entire back wall, was a richly ornamented open sarcophagus.

As he stood up and approached it, his torch revealed the skeleton of what appeared to be a queen. She was wearing a crown made of faded gold which had small gems set into it. Her elegant gold-threaded clothes, now almost completely decomposed, had clearly been the finest and most expensive that money could buy at the time of her burial.

Dubois knelt down next to the sarcophagus and smiled.

'Hello my queen,' he said, looking at the skull where the decomposed tissue now revealed her eye sockets and teeth in what looked like a crazed grin.

'And there it is,' said Dubois. 'Just as I expected.'

In her right hand, Queen Olympias was clutching a small metal box that had not yet lost all of its lustre, despite its age. As he pointed his torchlight onto it, it shone with a dull metal patina. He took a moment to visually inspect the box, and then he leaned forward and reached down into it.

'There is something that mothers never part with,' he mused as he reached towards the queen's hand.

'Something from their child that they never, ever throw away.'

He gripped the tiny metal box between his fingertips and wrested it away from the skeletal hands of Queen Olympias. As he did so, there was the sound of thin bones cracking as well as a very faint rustling sound, as if something was shifting inside the box.

'No matter how long they live,' whispered Dubois. 'They hang on to them until the day they draw their last breath.'

He brought the box closer toward himself, undid the tiny clasp and opened the lid.

'Their child's very first…'

He paused as a broad smile spread across his face.

'…baby teeth.'

Inside the box was a small collection of tiny baby teeth. As he shifted the box gently from side to side, the teeth slid back and forth inside the box, producing a gentle noise like little pebbles bumping into each other.

Behind him, he could hear Morozov come back down inside the tomb and peer through the hole in the wall. Dubois looked back out at him.

'These are the baby teeth of Alexander the Great,' he said triumphantly.

'That's great,' said Morozov tensely. 'Now can we get the hell out of here? This morgue gives me the creeps.'

Dubois stood and looked at the ex-Spetsnaz soldier with a mocking grin on his face.

'I thought you were a big tough special forces guy,' he said. 'The people in here are not dangerous. They are all very dead.'

'Yeah, well,' replied Morozov, who was out of his element having someone else along on a job, especially a civilian that he did not like. 'I am in no hurry to join them. If you have what you need, let's not waste any more time. Let's just go.'

Dubois crouched down and exited the hidden chamber, and the two of them then began walking out of the antechamber and up the ramp to the large covered area where the archaeological excavation was still incomplete.

They had just reached the top of the ramp and begun walking towards the helicopter, which was parked about one hundred metres away, when they heard the unmistakable click from a pistol being cocked.

'Stop right there,' said a man's voice. 'Yevgeni, drop your weapon. I know you're carrying.'

The two men instinctively raised their hands and began turning slowly towards where the voice had come from.

'You,' hissed Dubois when he recognised Andrew. 'And you!' he spat as he spotted Fiona next to him.

Morozov glanced at the Frenchman. 'You know these two?' he asked suspiciously.

'Yes,' replied Dubois, seething with anger. 'This man pretended to be a concierge at my hotel in Athens, and this lady…'

He didn't finish his sentence but instead looked at Morozov with a surprised expression on his face. 'You know them too?'

'Well,' grinned Morozov. 'I know one of them. This guy here tried to chase me down in London. Not quite as fit as you used to be, right?' he said and smirked at Andrew.

'Throw your damn gun over here, or I will put a hole where your kneecap is,' said Andrew, his intimidating voice laced with steely determination. 'I won't ask again.'

Morozov, seemingly unphased, shrugged and reached carefully inside his short black leather jacket to extract a pistol. Holding it by the grip, he tossed it a couple of metres towards where Andrew stood.

'Get that, please,' said Andrew and glanced at Fiona.

She approached the gun and carefully knelt down to pick it up, and then she aimed it at Dubois and Morozov whilst walking backwards to stand next to Andrew.

'And now the box,' said Andrew, shifting his aim to Dubois. 'Fiona, cover Morozov.'

Gripping the gun with two hands, Fiona nervously pointed it at the Russian whilst trying desperately not to shake so much that he would see it wobbling in her hands.

'We heard you in there,' continued Andrew. 'Hand the box over now! Place it on the ground in front of me.'

Dubois's eyes flashed with anger, but he knew he didn't have a choice. He was about to comply when Morozov suddenly took half a step towards him and violently shoved him sideways through the air to land behind a small mound of dug-up earth. As he fell, Dubois lost his grip on the small metal box and it tumbled through the air and down on the side of the mound that was facing Andrew and Fiona.

Immediately thereafter, the Russian reached down to his ankle and whipped out another pistol. Fiona pulled the trigger, but the gun just clicked. Morozov had slid out the gun's magazine just before he had tossed it over.

Just as the Russian was about to raise his other gun and shoot, Andrew quickly shifted his aim and fired twice in quick succession. One of the bullets missed by a hair's breadth, but the other slammed into Morozov's left shoulder, knocking him off balance and sending him staggering backwards. He quickly threw himself down behind another mound of dirt with a groan, and then looked over to Dubois, wincing from the pain.

'Run back to the chopper,' he shouted.

Dubois looked panic-stricken. 'What?' he yelled. 'Are you crazy?'

'If you don't get out safely,' Morozov shouted furiously, 'I won't get paid.'

'But the teeth!' shouted Dubois sounding desperate, and at that moment two more bullets from Andrew's gun slammed into the top of the mound of dirt right next to Morozov's head.

'Fuck!' spat the Russian. 'Forget the damn teeth, you idiot! Just get out of here. Do it or I swear I will shoot you myself. Go!'

Morozov sat up slightly, bringing his gun up and over the mound to aim at Andrew and Fiona who were now scrambling for cover. He fired six bullets in their general direction, but none of them found their mark.

In the confusion, Dubois leapt up and ran out from under the dig site's cover, and then he began sprinting through the darkness across the open field towards the waiting helicopter. It was a black four-blade Bell 407 corporate helicopter with room for four passengers in the back. The pilots must have heard the shooting because they had started the powerful turboshaft engine, its whine growing louder and higher in pitch as Dubois approached. For a moment he thought they might leave without him, so he began shouting and waving his arms frantically. He crouched down as he approached the chopper, pushing against the powerful downwash from the rotor blades.

Back at the dig site, Morozov had expended one magazine and was loading the next as he lay in cover behind the mound. Andrew and Fiona were taking cover behind a number of oil barrels that were used to store fuel for the site's generators.

'We need to move,' said Andrew hurriedly. 'There might be fuel in these barrels. They could blow if they are hit. Let's go.'

He grabbed Fiona by the arm and started running towards a neat pile of numbered stone blocks that looked like they had been extracted from the dig site and stacked up together. As they ran, Andrew fired three times towards where he had last seen Morozov. Then they crouched down behind the stone blocks.

As they did so, the helicopter lifted off and pitched down to quickly accelerate away from the dig site, the rapid thudding sound of its rotor blades receding towards the south.

'Fuck,' said Andrew. 'Dubois is gone.'

'But he didn't get the teeth,' said Fiona. 'The box is just there.'

She pointed at the small metal box which had come to rest at the bottom of the mound Dubois had been hiding behind.

'We need to get it,' said Andrew, and brought his gun up and over the stack of stone blocks. 'Stay here.'

He held his aim for a couple of seconds waiting to see if Morozov would appear, but there was no movement. Then, still aiming ahead of himself, he proceeded through the earthen mounds and the dig site equipment towards where Morozov had been hiding. It seemed like the Russian might have been out of ammo.

Moving cautiously sideways between objects that afforded him some cover and constantly training his gun at Morozov's last location, Andrew made his way in a flanking movement to a point where he could finally see the spot Morozov had been shooting from. It was empty. The Russian had gone. Taking another couple of minutes to clear the area, Andrew eventually returned to the mound and picked up the small metal box. The baby teeth were still inside.

'He bolted,' said Andrew, returning to Fiona with the metal box. 'Probably long gone by now. We need to get these to safety as soon as possible. Are you alright?'

'Kind of,' replied Fiona as she produced an anxious smile while at the same time trying to look brave. 'I have realised that I don't particularly like being shot at.'

'Good,' said Andrew dryly, taking a last look across the dig site and tucking the metal box inside his jacket. 'You don't want to ever get used to that. Anyway, we can't hang around here. The locals are bound to come and investigate the sound of the shots. We need to leave town as soon as possible. Come on. Let's get out of here.'

★          ★          ★

Ackerman was in his office awaiting the arrival of Alexis Galanis, ZOE Technologies's sole owner and his superior, as much as he hated to admit it. He had never warmed to her, but then he didn't really like most people. She had an arrogance about her that put him on edge, possibly because that arrogance was based on the fact that she was at least as intelligent as he was, and also because she was his boss. Like any boss, she could remove him by snapping her fingers, and he had never found a way to be relaxed about that.

Pacing the floor in front of the floor-to-ceiling windows, he caught his own reflection in one of the glass panes. He was wearing his usual office attire consisting of a dark grey pin-striped suit, a white shirt and a dark navy-blue tie.

*The image of respectability*, he thought, with a slightly disdainful look on his face. *If only they knew. The average person is a schmuck. Easily played and manipulated. Show them a well-groomed man with grey hair wearing a suit, and they snap their heels together like a bunch of trusting sheep.*

Ackerman thought back to the day he was dismissed from the Swiss Army's bio-chemical research facility. 'Unethical conduct', was what they called it. Ridiculous. His work was leading-edge research in the field of genetic engineering and the application of human growth hormones to embryos, but the army had been too squeamish to keep funding it. Now, though, he had access to more money than ever before. However, secretly funnelling a significant portion of it to the covert research facility in Rhinebeck had not been without challenges. It had required some creative accounting and a visit from Mike Stone to the most senior of ZOE Technologies's internal accountants. But it was all a small price to pay for what was in store.

*The world is about to undergo profound change, whether people like it or not,* he thought. *Better to be at the forefront and guiding that change, than to let the Chinese run away with it.*

Just then there was a knock on the door, and before Ackerman could say come in, the door opened and Alexis walked inside. Wearing a yellow business suit and black high heels, she looked striking with her long black hair tied into a ponytail that reached down to her lower back. Dark designer sunglasses perched on top of her head and her gold jewellery completed the ensemble.

'Fabian,' she smiled, offering him her hand. 'How very nice to see you again.'

'Likewise,' lied Ackerman, taking her hand and giving a small bow. His mouth was smiling, but his eyes were dead cold.

*What does she want this time?* he thought. *Does she suspect?*

'Please,' said Ackerman, gesturing towards the seating arrangement, which consisted of two sofas and a coffee table sitting on a large rug with a colourful abstract image weaved into it. 'Let's sit.'

Alexis walked over to one of the sofas and sat down, crossing one leg over the other, taking her sunglasses off and placing them on the coffee table. Then she ran her fingers through her perfect glossy black hair.

'Tell me,' she said, smiling endearingly at Ackerman. 'How have you been, my friend?'

*Nice try*, he thought. *You can't pull that shit on me.*

'Very well,' he replied evenly. 'Peritas is proceeding as planned. We're on target to launch by the end of the year. We are really just waiting for the final elements of the production chain to fall into place.'

'Excellent,' said Alexis, suddenly switching into a much more serious demeanour. 'Listen, Fabian. I had a visit from an investigative team from the UK. They seem to think we had something to do with Peter Lambert's murder.'

Her eyes were fixed on Ackerman's, but he did not flinch.

'It's a fishing expedition,' he said. 'They have nothing, because there *is* nothing. Whoever killed Lambert must have just been some lunatic.'

Alexis held her gaze on Ackerman for a couple of seconds, and then she leaned back on the sofa.

'Lambert was working on the AnaStasis project as well, was he not?' she asked. 'The woolly mammoths.'

'Yes,' replied Ackerman. 'After his success with the sabretooth tigers he was keen to push into other areas. And I think it was very valuable work. If nothing else, then simply as a technology demonstrator.'

'I agree,' nodded Alexis. 'Although, I could see several commercial applications as well. It really is quite shocking what happened to him.'

'Sometimes people snap for no reason,' said Ackerman matter-of-factly. 'We will find a replacement for him. Don't worry.'

'I also wanted to run something else past you,' said Alexis. 'I have been considering attempting to transpose the CRISPR/Cas12 methodology to human germ cells. I want you to start looking into this.'

*Fuck*, thought Ackerman. *Does she know? Has she found out about the New York facility?*

'Alright,' he replied, doing his best to sound intrigued but hesitant. 'You do understand that this is a bit of a legal minefield, as well as a potential PR disaster.'

'Of course,' said Alexis. 'Which is why I need you to keep it under wraps for now. Just get a couple of your best people to lay the foundation. I may have a complete genome soon which I will need you to attempt to transplant into the nucleus of a human germ cell. An egg, to be precise.'

'And you want us to attempt to grow it?' asked Ackerman.

'Yes,' said Alexis.

'That is… controversial stuff,' said Ackerman, attempting and mostly failing to look concerned. 'Can I ask what the goal is?'

'I will tell you in due course,' said Alexis. 'For now, the less you know the better for the firm.'

'Alright,' nodded Ackerman reasonably. 'I will pick a team, get the basics in place and also prepare a vat for seeding.'

'Excellent,' said Alexis. 'The last thing I wanted to tell you is that I have decided to hire a New York-based recruitment firm to run the search for a new CEO.'

Ackerman felt a knot in his stomach and a roiling heat rising under his shirt and up through his neck.

*You fucking bitch*, he thought. *You know I am the best man for the job.*

'I see,' he said as calmly as he could.

'They will get in touch with you within a week or so,' said Alexis. 'Please be as accommodating as possible. They will probably want to fly out a couple of consultants to meet with you and have a chat. I have obviously already provided my input on requirements, but I thought I would include you in the process. After all, you will probably be interacting more with that person than I will, whoever it ends up being.'

'Of course,' said Ackerman, biting back the impulse to be snarky. 'That is very considerate of you. I will help them as best I can.'

'Great,' smiled Alexis, flicking her ponytail back, and reaching for her sunglasses. 'I will let you know when we have a shortlist of candidates, and please do keep me updated on the progress of the vats for the human germ cells. I would like to know when they are ready.'

'Certainly,' smiled Ackerman, and rose to escort her out.

'Oh, don't worry,' said Alexis. 'I will find my own way out.'

Having taken a couple of steps towards the door, she suddenly stopped, hesitated for a moment, and then turned around to face him.

'One more thing before I forget,' she said as if pondering something. 'I may need to borrow one of your people. Your private eye. The ex-paratrooper.'

'Mike Stone?' said Ackerman looking slightly confused. This was highly unusual.

'Yes,' replied Alexis. 'Just for a couple of days. I have something important for him that should be just up his street.'

'Alright,' said Ackerman haltingly, looking like he was perplexed about the reason for this request. 'He's on a job right now in London.'

'Oh good,' smiled Alexis. 'That means he's halfway there. Please have him get in touch with me as soon as he is done.'

'I will ask him to do that,' said Ackerman.

'Perfect,' smiled Alexis. Then she left the office.

Ackerman stood there for a few moments with his hands on his hips, staring blankly down onto the floor. This was not how he had envisaged things going. Human germ cells? A new CEO from outside the firm? And what the hell was all that about Mike Stone?

Ackerman scratched his chin. He might have to take steps. Yes, he would definitely have to take steps. With a tense look on his face, he walked over to his desk, sat down and tapped a number on his speed dial.

'This is Ackerman, I need to speak to Frost immediately.'

Short pause.

'I don't give a shit what he is doing!' said Ackerman angrily. 'Get him on the line now.'

Another pause.

'Frost. It's me. Yes. Yes, shut up and listen. We may have a problem.'

# TWENTY

'How are you feeling?' asked Andrew.

'I'm ok,' said Fiona, sounding somewhat less than convincing.

The two of them were sitting in a coffee shop called Doufas in the southern suburb of Nea Elvetia south of central Thessaloniki, after having spent the night in a local hotel. Fiona was looking intently at the screen on her laptop, studying the images of the pages from Ptolemy's diary and writing up notes in a separate document.

'Find anything?' asked Andrew, nodding at her laptop.

'It is really tricky,' said Fiona. 'Just translating and making sense of this shorthand is hard work, but the real job here is to try to find things that did not make it into the historical account that Ptolemy wrote in Alexandria, and which therefore also did not find their way into Arrian of Nicomedia's writings about Alexander. But I have identified at least two instances so far. One which seems to relate to Bactria, or what is more or less eastern Afghanistan today, and another relating to Babylonia in the south of what is now Iraq. I am still working on the details though. Ptolemy clearly never meant for anyone else to read this, so it is extremely slow going.'

Andrew was taking a sip of his coffee when his phone chirped and vibrated, making it move ever so slightly across the hard marble-top table. He glanced at it and put down his cup.

'Strickland,' he said, looking at Fiona. 'I guess he got my short debrief from last night. I hope we haven't caused a major stink here.'

'Well, pick it up and let's find out then,' said Fiona jerking her head at the phone.

Andrew picked up the phone and cleared his throat. 'Gordon, sir. Are we secure?' he asked.

'Yes,' replied Strickland. 'Don't worry.'

'Alright. Sorry, sir,' said Andrew. 'At this point, I am working under the assumption that Alexis has everyone paid off. At least then we can't be surprised by anything. I know that sounds a bit paranoid, but she is a force to be reckoned with. If you ever met her, you would understand.'

'No problem,' said Strickland. 'That is probably wise. I trust your judgement.'

'You saw my report?' said Andrew.

'Yes, thank you,' replied Strickland. 'Quite the evening you two had. I considered inquiring with the Greek police about Morozov, but a man like him would never be stupid enough to get himself picked up by local cops, even if he had been shot. Wherever he is, he has probably already received medical treatment outside of normal civilian channels. As you said, these people have a long reach and plenty of cash.'

'And Dubois?' asked Andrew.

'I had someone here place a call to the Greek aviation authority to see if they had been able to track a helicopter at that location, but it seems like it must have had its transponder switched off, and none of the civilian or military radar stations picked up anything.'

'I am not surprised,' said Andrew. 'It was most likely an ex-military chopper pilot. Flying low, hugging the terrain and avoiding radar detection is just what they do.'

'You're most likely correct,' said Strickland. 'Either way, that is a dead end. What about the metal box with the teeth?'

'It will be locked away in the safe on the aircraft,' said Andrew. 'We will hang on to it until this whole thing is over.'

'Good thinking,' said Strickland. 'And you might as well head straight for the airport now.'

'Why is that?' asked Andrew.

'We've managed to decrypt a large cache of files from Alexis's laptop. The boys down in tech-ops told me there were multiple layers of encryption. Apparently, they damn near set fire to the supercomputer they were using for decryption.'

'So, what did they find?' asked Andrew.

'Mainly corporate communications including some interesting ones with the head of research, Fabian Ackerman.'

'The guy who was fired from the Swiss Army research lab?' said Andrew.

'Yes,' replied Strickland. 'First of all, we have some more colour on what exactly happened there.'

'Yes?' said Andrew. 'What was it?'

'It is slightly technical,' said Strickland. 'I won't pretend to understand all of it, but it seems that he had basically been given a free hand to pursue technologies for protecting soldiers on the battlefield against biological weapons. Part of this work involved methods designed to induce more rapid healing of wounds. Central to this was telomeres, which are sequences of molecules at the end of chromosomes. They are part of a mechanism that governs cell division and growth. At some point, Ackerman seems to have decided to follow his own agenda. He began developing techniques involving a variant of CRISPR-enhanced telomerase, which is a protein that extends telomeres to increase the number of times a cell can divide. Ackerman's variant also increased the speed of cell proliferation when used with a simple human growth hormone. This technique apparently had the potential to significantly speed up cell growth in mammals, including humans.'

'I don't think I understand,' said Andrew. 'What does all that mean?'

'It means that Ackerman's program, at least theoretically, had the potential to significantly shorten the time it takes for an embryo to turn into a fully grown foetus.'

'Crikey,' said Andrew. 'I can see why he was booted out. That crosses all sorts of ethical lines.'

'Indeed,' said Strickland. 'Our concern now is that he has carried over his research to ZOE Technologies. The emails indicate that the Peritas program clearly relies on very rapid production of tailored pets, which is what I believe Alexis told you as well. But our concern is that ZOE Technologies might be attempting to apply the same technology to human embryos.'

'Really?' said Andrew sounding alarmed. 'Do we have any actual proof of this?'

'No,' said Strickland. 'At the moment it is pure speculation on our part, but I thought I would at least let you know what sort of character Ackerman is. And the fact that he was hired as ZOE Technologies' head of research after what happened in Switzerland should make us all very suspicious about what that company is up to.'

'I agree,' said Andrew. 'It also puts our meeting with Alexis in a slightly different light, I must say. Who knows what she is hiding?'

'Well,' said Strickland. 'For now, make of it what you will. As I said, there is no direct proof of anything nefarious, but you should keep this information in mind in future dealings with those people.'

'I will,' said Andrew. 'Thank you for the heads-up.'

'Anyway,' said Strickland. 'Alexis has also had an email exchange with Ackerman following a meeting she had with him yesterday in San Francisco. Apparently, they are looking to replace him as acting CEO with someone from the outside. They have hired a head hunter firm to produce a shortlist.'

'I imagine Ackerman isn't too pleased,' said Andrew. 'Anyway, why do we need to get ourselves to the airport?'

'Ah, yes,' said Strickland. 'I was just coming to that. Some of the decrypted caches of emails were between

Alexis and Pierre Dubois. Apparently, Dubois is about to go to Iraq and possibly also Afghanistan.'

'Iraq?' asked Andrew. 'What for?'

'The emails are very vague, probably intentionally so, but they do mention the name Babylon several times. Dubois seemed to indicate that he had secured access to an archaeological site by paying off a local official. But as for what exactly he might attempt to do there, I have no idea.'

'And Afghanistan?' said Andrew.

'Same thing, I am afraid,' replied Strickland. 'Their communication is often extremely brief and lacking in detail. It is almost as if they are speaking in code. As if they suspect they might be watched.'

Andrew furrowed his brow and glanced across the table. 'I will need to have a chat with Fiona about this,' he said. 'She might have a hunch.'

'Very good,' said Strickland. 'The final thing I wanted to mention to you was concerning one of the late Peter Lambert's colleagues. A man named Tim Dawson.'

'Alright,' said Andrew and sat up. 'What about him?'

'Well,' replied Strickland. 'It is quite a peculiar thing. He worked with Lambert in the ZOE Technologies lab in San Francisco, but he walked into a London police station yesterday and insisted on speaking to Chief Superintendent Emma Worthington about Lambert's murder. As you know, she is coordinating the investigations into the murders of both Balfour and Lambert.'

'How did he know who to ask for?' asked Andrew.

'He must have seen her name on the news,' replied Strickland. 'There has been quite extensive coverage of this whole thing globally.'

'Did he say anything about what was on his mind?'

'No,' replied Strickland. 'He refused to speak to anyone else. All he would say was that he knew why Lambert was killed and that he had information that could bring down ZOE Technologies. He also said that he himself was in danger.'

'I see,' said Andrew. 'Where is he now?'

'He has been taken to a safehouse in Islington until a meeting with Worthington can be set up. It should happen within a day or two.'

'Is he really safe there?' asked Andrew. 'I mean, we already know what people like Morozov are capable of.'

'There are two officers inside the house with him at all times, and another two in a vehicle outside. He will be fine.'

'Ok,' said Andrew. 'Let me know what he has to say. I have a feeling he might be the key to understanding what Alexis is really up to.'

'I will get in touch as soon as I hear from Worthington. Stay safe,' said Strickland.

'Great. Thank you,' said Andrew. 'And I will keep you updated on what we decide to do. Goodbye, sir.'

Andrew placed the phone back on the table and looked up at Fiona.

'Iraq?' she said, looking curious. 'What was that all about?'

Andrew explained to her what Strickland had said about the decrypted emails.

'What might Dubois want in the ancient city of Babylon?' asked Andrew. 'Is there even anything left of that place?'

'There are ruins,' said Fiona. 'But as far as I am aware, they have been comprehensibly looted over many centuries, so I can't imagine what they think they might find there. Unless, of course, they have uncovered some new source that could point them in a new direction.'

'But if I understand it correctly, the city wasn't built by Alexander,' said Andrew. 'He just took it over after his defeat of Darius III, right?'

'That is correct,' said Fiona. 'Alexander had planned to turn Babylon, which was already a great city at that time, into his capital. He conquered it in 331 BCE and then died there in 323 BCE. This means that his efforts to remake the ancient city had already been underway for eight years when he died, so some of the ancient city ruins currently there must have been of buildings constructed during his reign.'

'But what do you think Dubois believes might still be there?' asked Andrew.

'I honestly haven't got a clue,' said Fiona. 'But given that Alexander was making it his capital, and given that he had been living there for a long time since his return from the campaign in the Indus Valley, I suppose it makes sense to assume that all of his personal effects would have been kept there.'

'Such as?' asked Andrew.

'Well, for one thing, he would have had all of his weapons and armour close by.'

Fiona tilted her head slightly to one side, looking as if she had suddenly realised something.

'Do you know what?' she said, with an eager look on her face. 'That might actually be it. Alexander was embalmed and placed on the funeral cart wearing his ceremonial armour. That means that his linothorax, his actual battle armour which would have been the typical Macedonian chest piece like the one we saw in the museum in Vergina, would almost certainly have remained in Babylon with Perdiccas.'

'So?' asked Andrew.

'So, we know that Alexis and Dubois are looking for ways to recover Alexander's DNA. And given Alexander's many wounds, particularly several that he received in the final stages of the campaign in India, it is not inconceivable that it might be possible to extract intact DNA from his chest piece.'

'Perhaps,' said Andrew. 'It sounds a bit far-fetched to me, but then on the other hand, as you said it only takes a miniscule amount of blood to recover millions of possible DNA samples.'

'I think we might be on to something here,' said Fiona, looking excited. 'Can you imagine if Dubois has really discovered the location of something as significant as the linothorax of Alexander the Great?'

'Let's just hold our horses,' said Andrew.

'Yes, but imagine,' insisted Fiona. Then her facial expression suddenly changed to one of concern. 'And imagine if something like that ended up in some oligarch's private collection. That would be awful.'

'Right,' said Andrew, and finished his coffee. 'We should probably get out of here as soon as we can. It is more than likely that the area around the museum in Vergina has at least a couple of CCTV cameras, so it probably won't take long for the authorities to work out that we had a hand in last night's events at the dig site. Worst case, they might think that we are responsible for breaking into the tomb.'

'Oh crap,' said Fiona, looking pained. 'We don't have time to sit in a Greek police station for two days trying to explain what happened.'

'I know,' said Andrew, tucking his phone into his jacket pocket. 'We would most likely end up calling in consular support to iron things out, but it would take some time. And that is just time we don't have. We need to get ourselves to Baghdad. Let's get the bill and get ourselves to the airport.'

★    ★    ★

In a large elegant drawing room inside the mansion in the suburb of Vouliagmeni in southern Athens, Alexis and Dubois were leaning over a bulky mahogany table on which were spread out all of the plastic-encased pages from Ptolemy's diary. Alexis had both of her hands placed on the table as she surveyed the pages, and Dubois was standing half a step behind her with his hands clasped in front of himself.

'When I first heard about it, I didn't believe it myself,' she said. 'But when I saw the page describing the battle of Issus, where Ptolemy was wounded in his right hand, I began to believe that there just might be a chance that this was in fact genuine. And today we have the proof.'

'The tests were conclusive?' asked Dubois.

'Yes,' said Alexis and turned to face him. 'The genomic sequencing of the blood and the tissue from the mummy in the Cyprus Museum showed that the Y chromosomes are an almost perfect match. The discrepancies are so small that they can be ascribed to the natural degradation of the DNA over time. There is no doubt in my mind that this really is Ptolemy's diary. After all this time, we have finally confirmed it.'

'Fantastic,' said Dubois. 'We can move ahead with the rest of the plan.'

'We can,' said Alexis. 'I think there is every reason to believe that Ptolemy wrote his account of Alexander's campaign largely based on this very diary. It is his personal account of everything that happened. It is probably the most reliable information we have, since there was always a risk that either Ptolemy or Arrian may have embellished, exaggerated or suppressed certain elements in their later versions for political or other purposes. This is the purest account available, and we can safely assume that everything in here is accurate.'

'So, what would you like me to do now?' asked Dubois.

'Well,' said Alexis, leaning ever so slightly closer to him. 'Things didn't really go according to plan for you in Vergina, but then that was always a long shot.'

Dubois swallowed. 'I can only apologise deeply once again. If Morozov had done his job properly and been alert, then…'

Alexis held up her hand with her palm facing Dubois, and he instantly stopped speaking.

'It's alright,' she said, pressing her lips together, hinting at a powerful effort at self-restraint. 'It was… a serious setback, yes, but there are other options.'

She paused, composing herself.

'You managed to secure access to the dig site near ancient Babylon,' she continued, 'so we should focus on that.'

'Very well,' said Dubois nervously. 'I also acquired the LIDAR satellite images you asked for from my source in the US Department of Defence. The resolution is as low as ten centimetres so the images are extremely detailed. But what are we looking for?'

'Let me show you something,' said Alexis, and strode around the table to the other side where a wooden box the size of a small suitcase was sitting. She picked up a pair of white silk gloves that were lying next to the box and put them on. Then she opened it and carefully extracted a light grey cylindrical shape with a dull sheen, that seemed to have small symbols imprinted on it. She placed it carefully on a soft piece of red velvet that was lying on the table.

Dubois walked over to stand next to her again.

'I procured this recently through a black-market dealer here in Athens,' said Alexis. 'He acquired it from a contact in Baghdad, who himself got his hands on it many years ago during the dying days of the regime of Saddam Hussein when the country was in chaos and many of Iraq's museums were being looted.'

'What is it?' said Dubois, leaning over it, looking at the intricate patterns.

'To some, it is just an old dried-up chunk of clay,' Alexis replied, her voice soft and trance-like. 'But to me, it could be the key to everything.'

★          ★          ★

It was late at night and raining in London. The streets were glistening with the reflections from the headlights of cars and busses, and as Mike Stone walked along the streets of the borough of Islington he found himself enjoying the familiar sights and sounds of his old city. Even the occasional spray of rainwater from passing busses onto his long dark coat did not bother him. He felt at home despite not having lived here for a couple of decades now.

He had flipped up the collar of his coat, and he was wearing leather gloves and a hat, which was pulled down slightly to obscure his face from passers-by. There were a couple of pedestrians hurrying home through the rain, and a taxi was parked at the far end of the street with its orange indicator light on, seemingly in the process of letting out a passenger.

Walking along the street, Stone could see the car with two protection officers parked on the opposite side of the road about fifty metres from the safehouse. As he walked past the house on 27 Charlton Place, he did not slow down, but simply glanced at the front door two steps above the level of the short footpath which led to it from the pavement. It was painted a glossy navy blue, and there were several locks installed on it requiring at least two different keys. Above it was mounted a discreet CCTV camera. Next to the door was a small sash window placed low on the wall. The lights were on inside the house, but the cream-coloured curtains were drawn, offering no hint at the internal layout of the ground floor.

It was a small one-storey house almost at the end of the street that appeared to have been built as an afterthought and stuck onto the long row of three-storey terraced houses lining the street. Next to it was a wall just under two metres tall that ran across to the house next to it, but it had no door or any other means of access to the garden behind it.

Stone proceeded to the corner of Charlton Place and turned left onto Duncan Terrace where he kept walking until he got to the end. Here he made another left, and a couple of minutes later he was back at the opposite end of Charlton Place again.

This time the street was empty, so he began walking briskly back towards the house on the opposite side of the road. After less than a minute he reached the parked car with the two protection officers.

He walked calmly up to the driver's side door next to the pavement and stopped. Leaning down slightly, he tapped twice on the window and smiled, putting his hands back into the pockets of his coat.

'Excuse me,' he said to the driver, making an effort to sound polite and as posh as he could. 'Could you help?'

The man in the driver's seat looked at him, glanced at his companion and then rolled down the window.

'Can I help you?' he asked with a tinge of irritation in his voice.

'I hope so,' smiled Stone and extracted his phone from one of the pockets in his coat. It was displaying a map of Islington.

'I am trying to get to the Hilton London Angel Hotel,' said Stone, showing the man his phone. 'It should be somewhere around here. Do you know where it is?'

'You must have passed it,' said the man and yanked his thumb towards the back of the car. 'It is just back there on the other side of Upper Street where you came from.'

'I see,' said Stone, placing the phone back in his pocket. 'Thank you. I will have to go back then.'

'No problem,' smiled the man, now sounding relaxed. 'Have a good evening.'

'Oh,' said Stone, sounding as if he had forgotten something. 'One more thing.'

'Yes?' said the man, having just placed his hand near the button for the driver's side window.

Stone took a step back towards the car, and out of view of the officers, he extracted his silenced pistol from the other coat pocket. In one quick fluid movement, he brought the gun up and partly inside the car, firing off two shots into the first officer, and then another two into the body of the other. The second officer had been reaching for his own gun, but he did not make it. Both officers were dead within seconds. The one in the passenger seat slumped back against the seat and the side of the door, but the officer in the driver's seat was about to flop forward onto the steering wheel and the horn. Stone managed to reach in and grab him by the throat, pushing him back into his seat.

The whole thing had taken less than ten seconds, and once he was sure they were both dead, Stone pulled the officer in the driver's seat up and to the side to lean against the inside of the door. Then he straightened himself up and looked around to make sure no one had seen what had happened.

'Don't go anywhere, chaps,' he said dryly, and began walking away from the car, crossing the street and approaching the safehouse. When he reached it he quickly stepped onto the short footpath, and with his head still turned down towards the ground and his face out of view of the CCTV camera he reached up, grabbed it firmly and broke it off its mount. He then yanked the camera loose, its electrical wires snapping as he did so.

Without hesitation, he then slipped back out onto the pavement, took a couple of steps over to the low wall and scaled it surprisingly adeptly for a man of his size, landing on the grass inside the small garden on the other side with a muffled thud.

He quickly moved along the exterior wall to a patio at the back of the house that was surrounded by an ivy-covered trellis structure. Here he peeked around the corner to see sliding glass doors to the rear dining room of the house. The curtains were partly drawn, but through the gap he was able to see a man moving around inside. It was not Tim Dawson and he was carrying a small pistol, most likely a 9-millimetre Glock 17M, which was the standard-issue sidearm for the select group of London Metropolitan Police officers authorised to carry firearms.

As Stone moved closer to the glass doors, he could hear the man's voice from inside. He seemed to be having a conversation on the phone. At that moment a door in the hallway leading to the front door opened, and another man, who was also carrying a firearm, emerged and spoke to the man in the dining room. Stone could not hear what he said, but he looked tense.

After a brief exchange, the second man walked towards the front door with his hand on his gun. He opened the door and looked outside, and then he craned his neck to look up at where the CCTV camera had been. After a couple of seconds of scouting the exterior of the house, he came back inside, closing and re-locking the front door behind him. He now looked agitated.

Stone pulled out his own gun and moved back slightly from the glass doors, standing in the corner of the patio under the shadows of the ivy. He could still hear the voices coming from the inside, and after a couple of seconds, he heard the sound of the sliding glass doors being unlocked.

As one of the doors slid open, Stone disengaged the safety on his gun and raised it to point towards the now open door. After a few moments, the officer who had just been outside at the front of the house emerged with his pistol held out in front of himself. As soon as he was far enough out onto the patio for Stone to see his head, the ex-paratrooper brought up his weapon and fired a single suppressed shot.

There was a muffled pop, and the police officer slumped to the ground like a marionette that had just had all of its strings cut at the same time. His body had barely hit the ground before Stone was moving forward. In just a couple of quick measured steps, he was through the sliding door and inside the room where the other officer was scrambling for his gun holster. Stone almost felt sorry for him. Almost.

Firing twice in quick succession, the two bullets slammed into the officer's chest, and he dropped to the ground, letting out a drawn-out wheeze. Then he was silent. Stone held his gun on him for a few moments to make sure he was dead, but then he turned his head towards the stairs leading up from the ground floor. A moment later, a voice called out.

'Hey guys!' it said in an American accent. 'What the hell was that?'

Stone moved purposefully towards the stairwell, his gun held out and pointing upwards as he began to climb the stairs. The landing was empty and so were the two upstairs bedrooms whose doors were next to the stairs. At the end of a short hallway was a closed door, presumably to the bathroom. Stone approached it slowly and silently, gun raised and pointing straight ahead.

'Hello?' said the man's voice from inside the bathroom, now sounding scared. 'Yo! What the fuck is going on out there?'

Closing the distance to the bathroom door and now confident that he was in control, Stone raised his right foot and slammed his heavy boot onto the door just below the handle. The flimsy doorframe instantly splintered, sending bits of wood flying into the room as the door blew open and slammed into a wall-mounted towel rail with a loud metallic clang.

Inside, Dawson was standing at the far end of the small room with his back to the bathtub and hands instinctively raised to the sides of his head. His face looked shocked and his hands were trembling.

With his gun trained on the terrified Dawson, Stone took another few steps forward until he was just inside the bathroom.

'Name,' he demanded.

'T… Tim Dawson,' said the petrified man.

'Thank you,' said Stone and gave a small nod. Then he pulled the trigger.

Dawson's head jerked back as the bullet slammed into his forehead, and then his body slumped backwards and down into the bathtub where blood began to form small rivers that wound their way slowly towards the plughole.

Stone walked over and looked down at his victim. He took a deep breath and exhaled slowly through his nose. Then he holstered his gun.

'Nice to meet you, Tim.'

Two hours later, Mike Stone was at Heathrow Airport boarding a Turkish Airlines flight to Baghdad via Istanbul, and using a different fake passport from the one he had shown on the way into the UK. Another ninety minutes later he was airborne and heading over the English Channel across Europe towards Turkey. The flight would take three hours and forty-five minutes, and after a brief transit procedure, he would be boarding his connecting flight to Baghdad which would take another two hours and forty minutes.

*Back to that shithole*, he thought to himself as he looked out of the window at the flashing lights on the aircraft's wingtip. *Who'd have thunk it?*

# TWENTY-ONE

On a different aircraft, this one an RAF Honda HA-420 which was also cruising towards Baghdad, Andrew and Fiona were sitting across from each other by a small fold-down table.

Fiona had been hunched over her laptop for a couple of hours already since they left Thessaloniki, poring over the images of Ptolemy's diary. She was attempting to extract sections that did not match with anything in the more than one-hundred-thousand-word long 'Anabasis of Alexander' by Arrian of Nicomedia.

She had also been forwarded the latest batch of decrypted files from Alexis's laptop, and the longer she spent analysing them, the more intently she stared at her computer screen. Eventually, she looked up, her eyes narrowing slightly and creases spreading across her forehead.

'I think we've got this all wrong,' she said, and shifted her gaze to Andrew.

'How do you mean?' said Andrew, sitting up in his seat. 'What did we get wrong?'

'Dubois,' replied Fiona. 'The reason why he is going to Iraq.'

'Alright,' said Andrew intrigued. 'Let's hear it.'

'He is not after Alexander's linothorax. He is looking for his heart.'

'What?' said Andrew perplexed. 'Surely that is not possible after all this time.'

'That would probably also have been my reaction just a couple of weeks ago,' said Fiona, raising her eyebrows and giving a slight shrug. 'But just hear me out. One of the attachments from Alexis's emails is an image of what looks like a cylinder. It appears to be made of clay and measuring about twenty-five centimetres long and maybe eight or ten centimetres across.'

She leaned forward and turned her laptop around so Andrew could see the screen. He peered at the image, trying to make sense of it.

'What is that thing?' he asked.

The cylinder in the image had a small tape measure laid out neatly next to it to indicate its size, and it seemed to be completely covered in tiny elongated asymmetrical indents, each one just a few millimetres in size. Each indent was a thin line with a small triangle at one end, and all of the indents were arranged neatly along the length of the cylinder.

'If I am not mistaken,' said Fiona. 'This is a clay cylinder similar to the famous Cyrus Cylinder, and this writing is called Cuneiform.'

'I am not familiar with it,' said Andrew.

'Cuneiform is an ancient writing system developed in Mesopotamia by the Sumerians around 3500 BCE. It is the earliest known form of writing and I believe it was in use all the way up to the 2nd century CE. The name Cuneiform actually comes from the Latin word *cuneus* which means wedge. If you look closely, you can see that each little line has a wedge shape at one end. This is because it was written by pressing a tiny reed stylus into soft clay in these intricate patterns you see here.'

'Interesting,' said Andrew, examining the image closely. 'And you can actually read this?'

'Sure,' smiled Fiona, 'although it is quite a difficult thing to learn to do. It is a so-called logo-syllabic script, which means that each small section can represent an entire word or a syllable. In its early form, it was a pictorial language, a bit like hieroglyphs, but it soon developed into a syllabic script. In order to read and write it, you need to keep track of a large number of representations of syllables as well as pictograms, so it can become quite extensive. But as you might have noticed I have quite a good memory. Not quite eidetic, but I am very good at recalling images, so I find this sort of thing fairly straightforward.'

'Yes, I have noticed that about you,' smiled Andrew.

'Anyway,' said Fiona. 'Cuneiform was so effective that it was used by all of the different Mesopotamian civilisations until alphabetic scripts became more popular in around 100 BCE. Because of its versatility, it has been found on clay tablets or cylinders like this one in a range of different languages, including Babylonian and Sumerian.'

'What was that thing you mentioned?' asked Andrew, leaning back in his seat. 'The Cyrus Cylinder?'

'It is a clay cylinder from the 6th century BCE, currently in the British Museum,' replied Fiona. 'It contains a declaration by the Persian king and ruler of the Achaemenid Empire, Cyrus the Great, and it was written in so-called Akkadian cuneiform which was a cuneiform variant from the area around present-day Baghdad.'

'Do we know what it says?' asked Andrew.

'Oh yes,' replied Fiona. 'It was discovered in 1879 during British excavations of ancient Babylon, so it has obviously been extensively researched and translated. The declaration basically praises Cyrus the Great, denounces his defeated predecessor as an oppressor of the people of Babylonia, and casts Cyrus as having been chosen by the chief Babylonian god and patron deity of Babylon, Marduk, to restore peace and order to the Babylonians. It also states that Cyrus was welcomed by the people of Babylon as their new ruler, that he had entered the city in peace, and that he had ordered the city walls to be strengthened.'

'Interesting,' said Andrew. 'So, it is basically an ancient example of political propaganda.'

'Pretty much,' smiled Fiona. 'What I find most interesting is that it mirrors the way in which Alexander the Great entered Babylon three centuries later, since he was also welcomed peacefully and as a saviour after the rule of the now-dead Darius III.'

'So, what about this cylinder?' said Andrew, pointing at the laptop's screen. 'Somehow Alexis and Dubois have got their hands on this. Have you had a chance to look at it yet?'

'Yes,' replied Fiona. 'I am not sure how they managed to do that, but I assume it was through black-market dealers. But what I have been able to deduce so far is that this clay cylinder was made in Babylon by Alexander's most senior general and now caretaker regent Perdiccas. It must have been produced more or less immediately after Alexander's death. It contains a long proclamation about Alexander's passing, and it was probably written in cuneiform because it was intended to address the local populace who obviously did not speak or read Greek.'

'Ok. Does it say anything else?' asked Andrew.

'It is partly damaged,' said Fiona. 'But there is still enough there for me to make sense of most of it. It essentially makes public Perdiccas' intention to maintain Babylon as the centre of Alexander's empire with himself as ruler and nominal regent of the empire until Alexander IV comes of age. It then heralds a plan to construct a grand temple in honour of Alexander in the southern part of the city.'

'Interesting,' said Andrew, studying the image of the cylinder. 'I am amazed that you can actually read this.'

'It is like any other script,' said Fiona. 'Once you have seen it enough times, you start not having to actually read anything. Your brain just recognises the symbols and you immediately know what they mean. Cuneiform is slightly tricky because it was written by hand and each scribe had a slightly different way of placing the pen, but fundamentally it is no different to other written languages.'

'Anyway,' she continued, clasping her hands together and looking intently at Andrew. 'That's not really what caught my attention. The most interesting part of it is this one line here regarding the temple that Perdiccas wanted to build.'

Fiona pointed to a short section of script.

𒈨 𒈛 𒄷 𒈨 𒈨 𒄷 𒌋𒌋

'As I said, each section or logogram has its own meaning, since cuneiform originated as a pictographic language similar in design to Chinese or Japanese written languages. But on top of that it then later developed into each logogram also having phonetic sounds, like syllables, and this small section here reads 'li-ib-bi la-a-bi-im', or 'libbi labim', which means *Heart of the Lion*.'

'I am sorry,' said Andrew. 'I am not sure what all this means.'

'Remember when we went down into the section of the Vergina museum that contains Philip II's tomb?' asked Fiona. 'Above the doorway was a mural with a lion hunt.'

'Yes,' replied Andrew. 'I remember that.'

'The significance of this is that the lion has been a royal symbol of Macedonia since ancient times. Lions did use to roam that part of Greece, and lion hunts were seen as the epitome of hunting. It was particularly closely associated with the Argead dynasty. For example, in 338 BCE after the Macedonians took control of Greece by defeating Athens and Thebes at the Battle of Chaeronea, they erected a giant statue of a lion on the site of the battle. And archaeologists have found many coins minted by Alexander the Great which on one side display his head wearing a lion's scalp.'

'So, you are saying the mention of a lion on this clay cylinder refers to Alexander?' asked Andrew.

'More than that,' said Fiona excitedly. 'What I am saying is that when writing this, Perdiccas was quite literally referring to Alexander's heart.'

Andrew looked slightly doubtful. 'You mean his actual heart?'

'Yes,' replied Fiona emphatically. 'When Alexander died in 323 BCE, he was embalmed. The Roman historian Quintus Curtius Rufus wrote that Alexander was mummified like the great pharaohs before him. This was almost certainly done in Babylonia immediately after his death and long before the elaborate funerary cart was constructed and sent on its way towards Macedonia. As I explained the other day, Perdiccas had intended to transport Alexander's body back to Aigai in Macedonia, but in order for that to be possible his body needed to be preserved through embalming.'

'Yes. So?' said Andrew.

'So, anyone who knows anything about embalming will tell you that it isn't as simple as wrapping a body in gauze and sticking them in a coffin. It was an extremely laborious and intricate process that involved removing the intestines, encasing them in natron for preservation, and then placing them in separate vessels in a fully embalmed state. That way they could be preserved almost indefinitely.'

'In other words, Alexander's heart was taken out of his body?' said Andrew, now sounding intrigued.

'That's exactly right,' replied Fiona. 'And this is where Ptolemy's diary comes in. As you know, I have been sifting through it and trying to extract sections that are not included in Arrian of Nicomedia's account, and I have identified several promising ones. One of them is a small snippet that seems to have been written after Alexander died and Ptolemy had gone to Egypt to take over the governorship there. This entry is written in the first year of Archon Philocles, which equates to 321 BCE, two years after Alexander's death. Let me read it to you. My translation probably isn't one-hundred percent accurate, so I am just paraphrasing based on Ptolemy's shorthand, but here is what it says:

BY MY HAND, THE BODY OF THE GOD-KING HAS ARRIVED IN MEMPHIS, TO BE LAID TO REST IN A SARCOPHAGUS BEFITTING OF A PHARAOH. THE FUNERAL CART DID NOT HOLD THE HEART OF THE LION. THE ORESTIAN USURPER KEEPS IT IN THE GOLDEN CITY STILL.

THE SNAKE HIMSELF IS MOVING ON MY KINGDOM FROM THE EAST. NEILOS IS OUR GUARDIAN, AND I SHALL DEFEAT HIM THERE.

'Quite dramatically written,' said Andrew. 'What does it mean?'

'Well, first of all, Neilos is the Greek name for the Nile, and the Orestian usurper is surely Perdiccas,' replied Fiona. 'He was from a region called Orestis, by Lake Kastoria in western Greece near the border with the region of Illyria. It is well known that there was intense rivalry and distrust between Perdiccas and Ptolemy even when Alexander was alive, and it is possible that some of Ptolemy's antipathy was due to him thinking of Perdiccas as a lesser Macedonian. Perdiccas was from the outskirts of the kingdom, whereas Ptolemy was born in the royal city of Pella. But the important part here is that Ptolemy seems to be saying that Alexander's heart was *not* contained in the funeral cart when it finally arrived in Memphis after having been hijacked on its way to Macedonia. And he seems to think that it is still somewhere in the Golden City of Babylon.'

'Could that be true?' asked Andrew. 'And even if it *was* true at the time, what are the odds of it still being there?'

'As I said earlier,' replied Fiona. 'At this stage, I wouldn't rule anything out. All Alexis needs to do is recover a tiny sample of tissue, and then she might well be able to extract enough DNA fragments to assemble an entire genome. The very fact that Dubois has been sent to Babylon at all should tell us that they have high confidence in being able to pull this off.'

'Amazing,' said Andrew.

'Well. Amazing and terrifying,' said Fiona. 'If they somehow manage to find artefacts from the time of Alexander, whether it is his embalmed heart or something else, there is no telling what damage they might do to it. We have to stop them.'

'But do you have any idea where to go once we get to the place where Babylon used to be?' asked Andrew.

'My only hunch would be to go to the temple that Perdiccas built in honour of Alexander, if it was actually ever completed. It would make sense if his embalmed heart was kept there since that would allow people to come and pay their respects. The writing on the clay cylinder seems to indicate that the temple was to be built to the south of the city of Babylon, but I am still working on those parts of the text.'

'Ok,' said Andrew. 'I won't disturb you anymore then. We have another couple of hours before we land in Baghdad, and I really think you should get some sleep if you can.'

'No time,' said Fiona, shaking her head and turning the laptop back towards herself. 'I can sleep when I am old.'

★      ★      ★

Wearing crisp white lab coats, the two men walked silently down the mirrored corridor towards the reinforced steel door at the far end. After successfully completing the biometric access protocol, Fabian Ackerman and George Frost entered the Rhinebeck lab's underground gestation vault and descended the steps towards the control terminal at the centre of the cavernous space.

'Rosetta,' said Ackerman in a firm and commanding voice. 'Status update on batch H01, please.'

'Gestation successful in 20 vats,' replied the AI placidly. 'Growth targets achieved in 18 vats. Zero growth anomalies. Zero fatalities.'

'Generate full reports on all vats and then terminate and purge.'

Ackerman confirmed the order with biometric and voice-profile confirmation, and then the AI initiated the purge procedure.

'Very good,' said Ackerman as he turned to face Frost. 'We are making excellent progress here. Better than I expected, in fact.'

'It is all going well,' nodded Frost. 'When would you like batch H02 to be spun up?'

'As soon as you have it ready,' said Ackerman. 'Let's not waste time here. What is the status of the chromosome adjustments?'

'We have a few candidates,' replied Frost, 'but we should perform them one at the time. Generally speaking, it seems that your hunch was correct, though. The human genome really does appear to contain a multitude of dormant genes from extinct ancestors, and we seem to be able to pinpoint and switch them on or off individually. With the help of Rosetta, I have identified several dormant genes that I believe are the result of human interbreeding with other hominids tens of thousands of years ago, most likely Neanderthals. I also feel confident that when activated, these genes can result in enhanced cell proliferation in muscle tissue during growth. Other sets of genes can be triggered and activated to result in thicker and stronger bones, better night vision, pain signal suppression along neural pathways, faster healing and much more. As you know, I have been working on this for a long time now and I am extremely excited about the possibilities. Along with your accelerated growth hormone process, there seems to be almost no limit to where we can take this. My personal feeling right now, given the success of the first trial, is that we should simply push forward and run as many trials with as many genomic variations as possible.'

'I agree,' said Ackerman. 'We need to map out which enhancements result in viable outcomes without also causing unintended side effects. The road to commercialisation is still very long and challenging, but the potential rewards if we can develop a marketable product are absolutely vast. When do you expect to be able to take a trial to full maturity?'

'It could be as little as a few weeks from now,' replied Frost. 'It might result in more abnormal or otherwise terminal outcomes, but we can just purge at any point and start over with a new batch.'

'Great,' said Ackerman. 'Keep moving ahead. We're on the path to something truly special.'

# TWENTY-TWO

It was mid-morning when the small twin-jet RAF aircraft touched down in Baghdad and taxied to a separate section of the airport designed for the arrival of planes carrying VIPs.

Andrew and Fiona exited the aircraft and walked towards a small terminal building, breathing in the cool dry air which, along with the first rays of sunshine, held the promise of another hot day. Having presented their travel documents to a large uniformed man with a thick black moustache, they were eventually allowed through to the arrival hall, from where they quickly made their way outside to hail a taxi.

When Andrew checked his phone he saw that he had two missed calls from Colonel Strickland back in London. The colonel had also left a short message for him to call him back asap.

'Strickland, Sir? Andrew here.'

'Ah,' said Strickland. 'Thanks for ringing me back. It's a bloody mess here.'

'What happened?' said Andrew, holding the phone close to his right ear whilst pressing a finger against his left to block out the noise of the crowd and the traffic outside the busy airport.

'Remember the ZOE Technologies researcher I told you about? Tim Dawson?'

'Sure,' replied Andrew. 'The one who wanted to meet Inspector Worthington. What about him?'

'Well, he's dead,' said Strickland.

'Dead?' exclaimed Andrew. 'I thought he was in a police safehouse.'

'He was,' said Strickland. 'But someone with a lot of skill and absolutely no fear took out the protection team and assassinated Dawson.'

'Christ,' said Andrew.

'And what's worse,' said Strickland. 'Whoever he was, he obviously knew where Dawson was which means we have a leak somewhere.'

'Shit,' said Andrew. 'Any clues?'

'No idea at this time. Metropolitan police forensics teams are combing the place as we speak. Anyway, I thought you should know. There are clearly a lot of things going on behind the scenes that we don't understand yet. Where are you two now?'

'We just touched down in Baghdad,' replied Andrew. 'We're off to Babylon as soon as we can find some transport.'

'Ok,' said Strickland. 'I won't keep you then. Let me know if you find anything.'

'Will do, sir,' said Andrew. 'I will send you a full debrief once we're back.'

After the call ended. Andrew told Fiona about Dawson's murder.

'Who is killing these scientists?' she said, looking horrified. 'I don't want to say this, but it must be someone inside ZOE Technologies, perhaps even Alexis herself.'

'Unfortunately, we don't have any proof of anything,' said Andrew. 'But I agree. It is certainly starting to look that way. What are they trying to keep secret?'

'Can't we get the US police involved? Or the FBI?' she asked.

'Strickland is trying to arrange for some sort of joint effort,' replied Andrew, 'but those things are bureaucratic quagmires. It might not happen for a while. Meanwhile, I think we should just focus on our own investigation and leave those murders to the Met. They have every reason to be motivated to solve this as fast as possible.'

A few minutes later they were in a taxi making their way along Airport Street in a long curve past the Amil suburb of the south-western Rashid District of Baghdad. Here they joined Highway 8 directly south and out of the city. The trip to their destination would take a couple of hours.

As they sat next to each other in the back of the taxi, Andrew was looking out of the window with a blank expression on his face, replaying in his mind a reel of memories from the time he had been deployed in Iraq.

'You're awfully quiet all of a sudden,' said Fiona. 'Are you alright?'

Andrew looked at her and smiled. 'Sorry. It is just strange being back here after all this time. The last time I was here everything was a mess. There were columns of smoke billowing up across the skyline. Tanks and military vehicles everywhere. Everything looks so different now. Normal. Civilised. People just going about their business and living their lives. It is hard to believe that this is the same place.'

Fiona took his hand in hers. 'It must be strange for you. But it is probably also a good thing for you to see that there is more to this country than war and conflict. This place has such an amazing and rich history which goes back well beyond anything that could be called civilised in our part of the world.'

'I suppose you're right,' said Andrew, sighing heavily. 'Back there on our left across the river was the Green Zone where coalition forces had established the provisional government during the occupation of this place. I was in and out of there more times than I care to remember. Always wearing civilian clothing and a full beard but always either going out or coming back from covert ops in and around the city. I remember one instance, in particular, a couple of years into the war when we were tasked with eliminating an Iranian special forces commander who had crossed over into Iraq to train Shia rebels. Our intel at the time said that he was part of an Iranian plan to destabilise the new US-supported Iraqi regime. Of course, they didn't have a hope in hell of actually toppling the new government. They just wanted to create chaos and they were very good at it. Officially, London didn't have any involvement in covert operations inside the city, but we were often out there supporting the Americans, gathering intel, providing overwatch and sometimes in the thick of it when things went south. That happened far too often. Looking back at it, we were out of our depth here, but most of us were young and stupid. We didn't really know what we were doing, and we didn't have a bloody clue about this place. Its culture. Its history. To us, it was just a desert with some buildings, and we just followed orders.'

'So, what happened?' asked Fiona.

'One afternoon we were heading out to the location where the Iranian commander was supposed to be located but we were ambushed. A massive lorry conveniently broke down as it was crossing the road in front of us. When the driver suddenly ran for it, I knew we were in trouble. Pretty soon we were surrounded. It was classic insurgency tactics. Pin the enemy down, wait for them to call in reinforcements and then hit them hard with everything you have.'

'But you made it out,' said Fiona.

'Sure,' said Andrew sardonically, his face taking on a thousand-yard stare and looking bitter. 'I did. But two other guys on my team didn't. And I can't even remember how many US Marines were killed that day. We didn't make it back to the Green Zone for another five hours. It was only when two Apache helicopter gunships were called in that we were able to extract ourselves from that place. It was a bloody mess. We never found out if the Iranian commander was even there. The whole damn thing could have been a ruse. Intel was often dodgy like that.'

Fiona squeezed his hand. 'That sound horrible,' she said. 'But I guess you have to believe that you made a difference somehow. Otherwise, the whole thing would have been for nothing. Including all those that didn't come back.'

She pointed out the window as they were passing a long row of stalls where traders were selling fruit and vegetables. Throngs of people were there, buying various goods.

'See those people there?' she said. 'That might not have been possible if you hadn't been here. Look around. Life here is normal and peaceful, relatively speaking anyway. I think you guys made that happen, even if the reasons for being here were misconceived.'

'I'm not sure,' said Andrew sceptically. 'It's hard to know what might have happened if we had never come here at all.'

'Anyway,' continued Andrew after a few moments, smiling at her. 'Let's not dwell on that now. That isn't why we are here. I was actually also wondering about something you said to me on the plane.'

'Alright,' said Fiona. 'What was it'

'The Achaemenid Empire,' replied Andrew. 'It has quite a mysterious ring to it. What was it exactly? And who was Cyrus the Great?'

'The Achaemenid Empire was the first Persian empire. It was founded by our friend Cyrus the Great around 550 BCE, and he was the great-great-grandson of King Achaemenes who was the ruler of a small kingdom in Persia. That kingdom eventually became a huge empire, and it reached its greatest extent under Xerxes I around 460 BCE when it stretched as far as northern Greece and included Macedonia and the royal cities of Pella and Aigai. Alexander's nemesis

Darius III was the great-great-great-grandson of Xerxes I.'

'I am beginning to see why Alexander's campaign was more than just naked ambition,' said Andrew. 'It was personal.'

'Yes, in some respects, it was,' said Fiona. 'Macedonia had been under the rule of Persia for a long time, and if you remember, Athens and its temples were sacked and burned by the Persians in 480 BCE.'

'I guess the Persians ended up ticking off the wrong kingdom,' smiled Andrew wryly.

'It is actually very interesting,' said Fiona. 'If you look at it on a map, you will notice that the Achaemenid Empire basically covered exactly the same territory as Alexander the Great's empire. In other words, what Alexander effectively did was to take over an existing empire, starting in Greece and then methodically working his way all the way to the other side of the Achaemenid Empire in present-day Afghanistan, Pakistan and India.'

'It is amazing that it all began here in this land,' said Andrew, looking out of the window at the flat featureless landscape of pale-yellow earth, irrigated fields and the occasional palm tree as they followed Highway 8 south towards the provincial capital city of Hillah some 100 kilometres south of Baghdad.

'Oh,' said Fiona and held up her hand. 'If you want to use the word "*began*", then we have to go back much further. It all started as far back as 2300 BCE with the Akkadian empire, which was the first Mesopotamian empire. It was founded by Sargon the Great, and during that time Babylonia was just a small insignificant province with a non-descript town called Babylon. But over the following centuries Babylon gained significance, and it eventually became a capital city under King Hammurabi in the 18th century BCE. After that, its fortunes waxed and waned over the following centuries as it became part of the Hittite, the Kassite and the Assyrian empires. But during that time this civilisation made huge strides in areas like astrology and mathematics. Let me give you an example. What time is it now?'

Andrew glanced at his wristwatch. '11:34,' he replied, looking perplexed. 'Why?'

Fiona smiled. 'In our daily lives all of our mathematics are centred around the base 10 system,' she said, 'but the Babylonians used different number systems. Archaeologists have found clay tablets with advanced mathematics on them indicating the use of so-called duodecimal and sexagesimal number systems, also known as base 12 and base 60. That is why there are two twelve-hour periods in our day-night cycle. It is also the reason why there are sixty minutes in one hour, sixty seconds in one minute, and 360 degrees in a full circle. Archaeologists have also found tablets showings how what later became known as Pythagoras's Theorem, was used here to calculate the size of irregularly shaped crop fields for taxation purposes. And this was more than a thousand years before Pythagoras was born on the island of Samos in Greece.'

'Wow,' said Andrew, an impressed smile spreading across his face as he looked out of the window at the countryside rolling past. 'That's astonishing. I had no idea that all of those things came from this area right here. Why 12 and 60, by the way?'

'Our best guess as to why they used the base 60 system is that it is divisible by the numbers one, two, three, four, five, six, ten, twelve, fifteen, twenty, thirty and sixty. This makes it extremely useful for quickly calculating fractions which would have made it highly practical in commerce. The same can't really be said for the base 10 system that we use today. As for the base 12 system, that was almost certainly tied to the twelve phases of the moon during the course of an annual agricultural cycle.'

'How fascinating,' said Andrew.

'Yes, human civilisation made incredible leaps forward during those centuries,' said Fiona, 'and it all happened right here in this land. Anyway, when Babylonia became a province of the Achaemenid Empire in around 540 BCE under Cyrus the Great, it had its own king appointed, which incidentally was Cyrus the Great's own son. And, of course, after becoming part of Alexander the Great's empire, it then remained the centre of the Seleucid Empire for about three centuries.'

'The empire founded by Seleucus,' said Andrew. 'Another one of Alexander's generals.'

'Correct,' nodded Fiona. 'And one of the people who ended up assassinating Perdiccas on the banks of the Nile in 321 BCE.'

'It is really interesting stuff,' said Andrew. 'I wonder how many of the people back at those market stalls know any of this. The history here goes so deep.'

'It does,' smiled Fiona. 'Isn't it exciting? By the way, do you happen to know why Mesopotamia is called Mesopotamia?'

Andrew smiled. 'No, I don't. But what I do know is that you are about to tell me.'

'It's very simple,' said Fiona. 'It is two ancient Greek words put together. *Mesos*, which means "between", and *Potamos*, which means "rivers". So, it literally just means The Land between Rivers, those two rivers being the Tigris and the Euphrates.'

As their taxi made its way down Highway 8, they passed through the towns of Mahmudiyah and Latifiya, after which they passed a sign to the nearby town of Al-Iskandariya.

'Did you see that road sign?' said Fiona. 'It said Al-Iskandariya.'

'Yes?' said Andrew, looking puzzled.

'Iskander,' said Fiona. 'It is the Arabic version of Alexander. We just drove past Alexandria.'

'He really is everywhere, isn't he?' chuckled Andrew.

'Call me superstitious,' said Fiona, 'but I feel like we might be getting close to finding something big.'

'Speaking of which,' said Andrew. 'We should be at the site of Babylon in about fifteen minutes. How do you want to play this?'

'I think we should do the tourist routine,' replied Fiona. 'Blend in with a crowd and see what we can see. With any luck, Dubois has not made it here yet so we might have some time to investigate.'

A few minutes later, the taxi pulled off the highway and made its way straight south to the site where ancient Babylon had been excavated more than a century earlier. As they got out and paid the driver, they could see the ruins of a large complex immediately to their right.

'That would have been the Northern Palace,' said Fiona. 'And look up that way,' she said, pointing behind them towards the north. 'That statue up there is the so-called Babylonian Lion, which is thought to have been placed there by Nebuchadnezzar II just over 2,600 years ago.'

'Amazing,' said Andrew.

'But now look over there just beyond the Northern Palace,' Fiona said.

She pointed to a large modern palace a couple of hundred metres to their right near the branch of the Euphrates River that runs through the site of the ancient city. It was a large boxy-looking three-storey building sitting on an enormous mound about twenty metres high. The building had been constructed to resemble ancient Babylonian architecture.

'What is that thing?' asked Andrew.

'That,' said Fiona with a sarcastic smile on her face, 'is one of the palaces of Saddam Hussein. He fancied himself as a successor to the great imperial rulers of the past, and he had this abomination built more or less on top of the actual ruins of Babylon's palace district.'

Andrew shook his head. 'What a megalomaniac.'

Fiona shrugged. 'Can you believe it?' she said. 'The absolute arrogance of it. Ruining a large area of one of the greatest cities that has ever been, the site of the famous hanging gardens, and the place where Alexander the Great died, just for his own vanity project. I honestly don't know whether to laugh or cry.'

'Well,' said Andrew, tugging gently at her arm. 'Whatever you do, do it quietly. We don't want to draw too much attention to ourselves.'

As it turned out, it was already too late for that. A local freelance tour guide was approaching them briskly with a broad smile on his face. He was a short bald man with a cheerful face and kind eyes, wearing dark linen trousers, a white shirt and suspenders with a brown speckled tie that was much too short.

'Welcome to Babylon,' he said cheerfully in heavily accented English. 'My name is Salim. I can offer you a tour of the ancient city for a good price.'

Fiona glanced at Andrew, who just smiled and shrugged.

'Sure,' he said. 'Why not? We're blending in, right?'

'Alright,' said Fiona and turned to Salim. 'Let's go. We will follow you.'

'Very good,' beamed Salim. 'Come.' And then he began walking towards the huge blue brick gate leading into the palace district towards the north of the ancient city.

'This is the famous Ishtar Gate,' said Salim, gesturing towards what looked like a four-storey section of battlements made out of bricks and painted a mid-blue colour. At its centre was a tall opening where the gates would have been, and the entire structure was decorated with large coloured friezes of what appeared to be mythical creatures.

'It was constructed in 575 BCE,' continued Salim, 'and it was one of the original Seven Wonders of the World in ancient times. The goddess Ishtar represented the power of sexual attraction, and these white animals you see up there are the *aurochs*, which is a type of cattle that is now extinct. The orange creatures are the Mushussu, which is a type of mythical dragon. The gate leads to the Processional Way on the other side. On the front here you can also see depictions of the god Marduk with a Mushussu servant.'

'This is a recent replica, right?' asked Fiona. 'And if I am not mistaken it is much smaller than the original.'

Salim looked at her uncertainly, quickly shifting his gaze to Andrew and then back to Fiona.

'Well, yes,' he said reluctantly. He was clearly not used to tourists having much of an idea about what they were seeing. 'You know about this place?'

'I am just really into history,' said Fiona hurriedly. 'My name is Hazel, by the way. And this is Bill,' she continued, gesturing towards Andrew.

Andrew nodded.

'Ah,' said Salim. 'I see. Well, yes unfortunately the original gate was taken apart and smuggled out by German archaeologists more than a hundred years ago. It is now on display in a museum in Berlin. Very sad.'

'It does look almost brand new,' said Andrew, sounding slightly disappointed. 'Still impressive though.'

'Well,' said Salim, now sounding somewhat deflated. 'Let's go through it to the Processional Way.'

Andrew and Fiona followed him through the Ishtar Gate and onto what looked mostly like a footpath leading south along a high brick wall on the right that was adorned with battlements at the top.

'This is the Processional Way where every New Year a great procession would come through to celebrate the beginning of a new agricultural year. This started just after the annual barley harvest and always lasted twelve days.'

As they walked along the footpath, Salim gestured to their right where they could see a strange mix of ancient and restored walls and other structures.

'What you see here to the right is the Southern Palace,' said Salim. 'It is the best-preserved area of the city and it has been reconstructed to show it the way it was when it was first built.'

'And the famous hanging gardens?' asked Fiona

'Another one of the Seven Wonders of World,' said Salim. 'They may also have been just here to our right, but no one is able to say for certain.'

As they walked through the sprawling ruins and reconstructed walls, Andrew and Fiona were struck by how thick the walls were and by the fact that some of them were over ten metres tall. Some of the brickwork was very clearly recent, but other sections of the original walls were in surprisingly good condition.

'Are you from this part of the country?' asked Andrew.

'Yes,' said Salim emphatically, seemingly confused that someone might think that he was not. 'I grew up just south of here in Hillah city. I used to come here as a boy with my father, may God rest his soul.'

'It is an amazing place,' said Fiona.

'Yes,' said Salim, suddenly seeming to grow in stature as he beamed with pride. 'This is our great history. Many people don't know about it these days.'

'Well, you're doing a great job teaching them,' said Andrew. 'What's the next thing we should see today?'

'Come this way,' said Salim, beckoning them to follow out of the Southern Palace and further south along the footpath that lay where the Processional Way used to be.

They continued to follow him until they came to a road running from east to west. On the other side was what looked like an uneven field with tufts of grass here and there. A few hundred metres away across the field was a slightly elevated area.

'We are going this way,' said Salim and pointed ahead of them. 'I will show you where the Etemenanki used to be.'

'That's the ziggurat, right?' asked Fiona as they walked.

'That is correct,' said Salim.

'Forgive me,' said Andrew. 'The what?'

'A ziggurat,' replied Fiona. 'Think of it as a stepped pyramid with a temple at the top. These were common in ancient capitals in this part of the world.'

'The Etemenanki was constructed at least three thousand years ago,' said Salim. 'It was ninety metres tall and had six levels. It was a magnificent building.'

After a few minutes, they found themselves next to a large slightly raised square area that was roughly fifty by fifty metres in size, and partly surrounded by a shallow water-filled trench with reeds growing in it.

'Not very much left, is there?' said Andrew.

'No,' shrugged Salim. 'This is the location, but it is completely gone now. You can spot the outline of it in satellite images, but down here it can be difficult to see it. This whole area was an enormous courtyard with the huge ziggurat rising up in the middle of it just here. And it was surrounded by very high walls.'

'If I am not mistaken,' said Fiona. 'When Alexander the Great took the city in 323 BCE, he found the Etemenanki in a sorry state and ordered it repaired. But when he returned here in 331 BCE and discovered that virtually no progress has been made on the works, he supposedly ordered it to be levelled and completely rebuilt. But of course, his death put a stop to that and many other of his plans.'

'What is that down that way,' said Andrew, pointing to a large hill directly south of where the Etemenanki used to tower up into the sky.

'That is the hill where the Esagila Temple used to be,' replied Salim. 'It was where the city's patron god Marduk was worshipped. He was a powerful god who wielded fire and lightning as weapons. The temple was built by Nebuchadnezzar II, and used to have a giant statue of Marduk inside it for people to worship.'

'That statue was covered in plates of silver and gold, wasn't it?' asked Fiona.

'Yes,' replied Salim hesitantly, now sounding somewhat suspicious. 'How do you know all this?'

'Uhm,' said Fiona, suddenly feeling self-conscious. 'Well, as I said, I just really like to read history books. This is such a fascinating place.'

'Sorry,' interrupted Andrew. 'But what is that building behind the hill?' asked Andrew.

'Oh,' replied Salim. 'That is just a mosque. I use it myself sometimes. Very beautiful inside.'

'I see,' said Andrew, gazing towards the building on the hill in the distance.

Salim watched them both for a few seconds and then cleared his throat.

'I think that is all I can show you for today,' he said and produced an uncertain smile. 'And the site is closing soon, so…'

Fiona looked at him with a puzzled expression for a few seconds until she realised what was happening.

'Oh!' she exclaimed, reaching for her shoulder bag and extracting some money. 'Is thirty dollars ok?'

Salim shrugged.

'Alright. How about fifty?' said Fiona.

'Thank you,' smiled Salim and nodded. 'Have a nice afternoon.'

Then he left them there and hurried back towards the main hub of the ruins complex.

'What was he talking about?' said Andrew sounding confused. 'This place doesn't close for several hours. And why was he suddenly in such a hurry to get away?'

'Maybe he just wants to squeeze in another couple of tours before the site really does close,' replied Fiona. 'Anyway, I want to go up on that hill to where the Esagila temple used to stand. Come on.'

★       ★       ★

As Salim was walking away from the two tourists, he had a strange sinking feeling in his stomach.

Something about this wasn't right. That woman knew a lot about this place, and she was asking some strange questions and behaving oddly. If it had just been her and that man Bill, he might just have written it off as nothing, but this was the second time today that he had taken a pair of foreign tourists behaving strangely through the ruins. Just a few hours ago he had shown a Frenchman and a sullen-looking monosyllabic brute of an Englishman around the city ruins. They too had been behaving suspiciously. Suddenly an irrational fear gripped him. What if they were grave robbers? What if they were here to dig and loot?

Salim reached into his trouser pocket for his phone and found the number for a friend of his.

'Alo. Assalamu alaikum,' said a voice.

'Abdul,' said Salim, sounding worried. 'It's me, Salim. I am at the ruins, and I need your help. I think we should call your brother at the police station.'

# TWENTY-THREE

The sun was low in the sky as Andrew and Fiona climbed up the side of the small hill at the southern end of what was left of the ancient city Babylon. It was still warm and the air was dry but fragrant. At the top of the hill was a large flat area like a small plateau where no vegetation grew. Just fifty metres to the south of them was the mosque that Salim had pointed to. They walked to the middle of the plateau and turned around to face north.

'Well,' said Fiona. 'This fits the description on Perdiccas' clay cylinder. A hill to the south of the main city overlooking the palace district. I am certain this is where the Esagila temple stood before it was destroyed by Xerxes I. When Alexander took the city he ordered it restored, but perhaps it was Perdiccas who began rebuilding it.'

Andrew looked towards the site where the Etemenanki used to reach up into the sky, and then he peered towards the Southern Palace further to the north.

'I don't know,' he said, sounding slightly frustrated. 'There is almost nothing left of the original city, and what is here must have been pored over by archaeologists dozens of times.'

'Let's just consider this,' said Fiona. 'The writing on the clay cylinder is very specific about the location of the proposed temple to Alexander, but as far as I know Perdiccas never actually built a temple to Alexander here. Think about it. He might have begun the process, but it would have taken years to construct, and most of the artisans were probably busy making the extravagant funeral cart for Alexander's body. And then, of course, Perdiccas went off and got himself killed on the banks of the Nile, after which Seleucus took power here. If there ever was a temple after Alexander's death, it must have been the reconstructed Esagila temple which I believe stood here as recently as the 1$^{st}$ century BCE. But there is no record of it ever containing anything from Alexander, let alone his heart.'

'And yet,' said Andrew. 'According to Ptolemy, Alexander's heart remained here in this city somewhere. So where would it have been kept?'

'Well,' said Fiona. 'Admittedly, it would make a lot of sense if it was kept somewhere in the Esagila temple. After all, Marduk was the patron deity of Babylon, but Alexander was himself also recognised as a god, and he was establishing himself as imperial ruler right here in Babylon. This great city was to be his home and his permanent seat of power. It somehow seems obvious that Perdiccas might have planned to merge the veneration of Alexander with that of Marduk, and what better way than to keep the heart of the lion in the temple honouring Marduk?'

'That does make sense,' nodded Andrew.

'Right,' said Fiona, looking around at the ground at the top of the hill. 'This is definitely the place where the Esagila temple stood, but there is clearly nothing left now. Not even a couple of blocks of stone from the walls. If this was where the temple used to be, then there is no trace of it anymore.'

'Unless…' said Andrew pensively.

'What?' asked Fiona.

'Well, you said that Perdiccas would not have had time to actually build a new temple and that the old Esagila temple could have housed Alexander's heart. So, if that is true, then surely it would have been kept safely underground somewhere in the catacombs where it was cold and dry, rather than up here in the humid heat.'

'But again,' said Fiona, gesturing to the ground around them. 'There is nothing here.'

Andrew stood with his hands on his hips, slowly turning around and surveying the area.

'Unless there was another entrance,' he finally said. 'Like over there,' he said, pointing to the mosque.

Fiona looked at him with a highly sceptical expression on her face. 'You think the mosque might have a secret entrance to the catacombs of the Esagila temple?'

Andrew hesitated for a few seconds. 'I am not saying that they are hiding it under there, but what if it is there and no one knows about it? What if the mosque was built on top of it and then it was simply forgotten after many centuries?'

'That sounds extremely vague to me,' said Fiona.

Well,' smiled Andrew mischievously. 'There's only one way to find out.'

'You've got to be kidding me,' said Fiona, gawping at him incredulously. 'You, an ex-SAS soldier, want to break into a mosque in Iraq near a world heritage site? Have you gone mad?'

'Not *break in* exactly,' said Andrew. 'Look, Dubois clearly has his eye on this place, right? So, think of it as an attempt to prevent looting of irreplaceable artefacts.'

Fiona looked at him for a few moments. 'You really have a way of making hair-brained plans sound reasonable, do you know that?'

'I have spent a whole career carrying out hair-brained plans,' grinned Andrew. 'Making them seem reasonable is the only way to stay sane.'

'So, what do you suggest?' asked Fiona, still not quite able to fathom what they were about to do.

'Ok,' said Andrew. 'Here's what I am thinking.'

*        *        *

Several hours later, after the mosque had been empty of visitors for a while, Andrew and Fiona emerged from some nearby bushes and entered.

The interior was one large room for worship, covered with glossy looking light grey and veined marble flooring, and it had a couple of anterooms to one side and a staircase going down to a lower level. The walls were decorated with Arabic multifoil arches along the walls. The insides of the arches were covered with what looked like fractured glass or mirror, giving the room a strange ethereal ambience.

'Take off your shoes and carry them,' whispered Andrew.

'Oh, of course,' said Fiona. 'We're in a mosque.'

'No, that's not it,' whispered Andrew. 'This marble floor is loud to walk on, and we need to stay as quiet as we can. This way.'

They proceeded towards the stairwell leading down. It was surrounded by a wooden bannister, and it descended steeply to the basement level. The steps leading down as well as the sides of the stairwell were made from the same glossy marble as the floor above them.

At the bottom of the stairs, they found a set of smaller rooms, one serving as an office and another as a storeroom. At the back of a dark corridor was a closed door with a rusty-looking padlock.

'Let's look in there,' said Andrew, and proceeded carefully along the hallway towards the door.

He looked around and soon found a chair with metal legs inside the office. He wedged one of the legs in between the padlock and the door and put almost all of his weight on the leg. After a couple of seconds, the padlock snapped off the hinge and clattered loudly across the floor.

'Shit,' whispered Fiona and froze, listening intently for footsteps, but she heard nothing. 'Let's try to be quiet from now on.'

Andrew nodded, grabbed the door handle and opened the door. He was half expecting an alarm to be set off, but nothing happened. On the other side was another smaller room, but this one seemed very different from the first three by the corridor. It was empty and appeared much older, and its ceiling was very low. The exposed brickwork of the walls was partly covered in dust and curtains of spider webs, and it was dimly lit by a single white lightbulb hanging in the middle of the room. As they walked inside, the shadows cast by the light bulb moved eerily across the ancient masonry.

'This must have been the original cellar from when the mosque was first built,' said Fiona. 'It looks nothing like the other parts of this basement. This place could be centuries old.'

'I wonder what they are using it for now,' said Andrew. 'There is nothing in here.'

'That is not true,' said Fiona, and began walking slowly along the walls. 'Look closely, and you can see how the masonry has been constructed to give the impression of multifoil arches, like little gateways. Hand me the torch, please?'

Andrew gave her his powerful torch and she pointed the beam up to the top of the arch that was at the centre of the back wall. At the very top of it was a brick that at first glance looked like all the others, but when Fiona reached up and wiped the dust from it, she gasped. At its centre, the brick had a small gilded symbol which by now was all too familiar.

'The Vergina Sun,' she whispered breathlessly, staring at it for a few moments.

'Bloody hell,' said Andrew.

Fiona took a couple of steps back and looked at the section of the wall that was inside the central multifoil arch.

'This is not a depiction of an arch at all,' she said, sounding intrigued. 'It's a doorway.'

'A doorway?' replied Andrew. 'To where?'

'Well,' said Fiona, turning to face him with an unfamiliar look of mischievous irreverence. 'I am probably going to regret this, but as a great man once said. There's only one way to find out.'

Andrew looked at her for a few seconds before realising what she was saying.

'Alright,' he said. 'Stand aside please.'

He walked up to the wall and placed both hands on the wall section that constituted the interior part of the central multifoil arch. Inspecting it silently for a moment, he then turned his torso to the right and brought his right arm up to his chest.

'Here goes,' he said, and then he took a quick step towards the wall whilst ramming his shoulder into it.

Amid the sound of dry mortar cracking and a small cloud of dust being released by the masonry, the wall gave way. As he stood back, there was a shoulder-sized indent in the wall where the bricks had shifted.

'Look,' said Fiona excitedly. 'Some of the bricks moved back. That means there is a cavity behind this wall. I was right.'

'Well, there's no stopping now,' said Andrew, and then he rammed his shoulder into the wall once more.

This time, the entire section inside the arch gave way and disintegrated, sending Andrew tumbling through the hole amid a cloud of dust and falling bricks and into the space beyond.

'Are you ok?' shouted Fiona, stepping closer with the torch.

Shining it into the hole, she could see nothing but a thick veil of grey dust.

'I'm alright,' said Andrew, getting to his feet and dusting himself down. 'Hand me the torch. I need to see where I am.'

Fiona reached in through the hole and gave him the torch, and as the dust slowly began to settle, Andrew shone it around to get a sense of where he had ended up. He was standing at one end of a long and narrow vaulted tunnel that sloped gently downwards. It was just under one and a half metres tall and built from bricks similar to those they had seen a few hours earlier in the Southern Palace district of the Babylonian ruins. In fact, the corridor was so long that he was unable to make out the other end of it. The air was dry and dusty, and for every movement of Andrew's feet on the dry soil under his boots, the tunnel produced an odd reverberating echo from the other end. Then Fiona poked her head through the opening.

'What on earth is this place?' she said slowly, looking around in amazement.

'Some sort of tunnel,' replied Andrew. 'How old do you reckon it might be?'

Fiona stepped through to join him and began looking around, examining the brickwork.

'Very hard to tell,' she replied. 'Probably not as old as the palace ruins, but definitely a lot older than the mosque. Many centuries at least. I am beginning to think that your theory about this mosque might be correct. Perhaps this really is a secret passage into the catacombs under the Esagila temple. I wonder how long it has been sealed off like this.'

'Perhaps since the German archaeologists started poking around this place in 1910?' suggested Andrew.

'That is certainly a possibility,' said Fiona, looking up at the ceiling towards the mosque above. 'If someone wanted to hide this place, then that would have been a good way of doing so.'

'Well, as far as I can tell,' said Andrew, 'this tunnel leads due north, which would take us in the direction of the temple site. If it reaches all the way there, then it must be around fifty metres long.'

Fiona began to look uncomfortable as Andrew shone the torchlight down along the tunnel. It was still impossible to see where or how it ended. The two of them stood silently for a few moments, peering along the tunnel into the darkness beyond.

'There's only one thing we can do now,' said Andrew, 'and that is to keep pushing forward. It is a question of time before the first worshippers arrive in the mosque for morning prayer, and we need to be long gone by then. Are you alright with this?'

Fiona swallowed. 'I am starting to feel like we have bitten off more than we can chew here,' she said nervously. 'But in for a penny, in for a pound. Let's just do this.'

Walking slowly and cautiously along the tunnel, it was eerily quiet. All they could hear was the sound of their own breathing and the gentle crunching noise from their boots on the dusty ground. After a couple of minutes, there was still no sign of an end to the tunnel, and Andrew stopped and shone the light back towards where they had come from. They were now unable to see the hole they had come through.

Fiona's heart was beginning to beat faster, as a sense of claustrophobia began to close in around her. Being down here deep underground and moving through this tunnel, she felt as if she was moving back in time, trapped between the present and the ancient past.

'I see something,' said Andrew. 'Up ahead.'

'What is it?' asked Fiona, moving her head to see past him and straining her eyes to peer through the gloom.

'Oh shit,' said Andrew. 'It looks like this is a dead-end.'

'Fuck,' whispered Fiona anxiously.

'Let's just be calm and investigate it,' said Andrew. 'I might be wrong.'

Another couple of minutes later, it turned out that he had been right. The tunnel ended with a brick wall, but this one was made from different kinds of bricks from those used to construct the tunnel itself. They were much larger and quite smooth to the touch, and the mortar between them seemed more intact.

'What do you make of this?' asked Andrew, giving Fiona the torch.

She leaned closer, shining the torchlight onto a spot in front of her face and running her fingertips slowly across the masonry.

'This looks like it might have been part of the original foundation of the temple,' said Fiona. 'So, someone would have added this tunnel much later. How deep underground do you reckon we are now?'

Andrew looked back up along the gently sloping tunnel and pressed his lips together.

'It's hard to tell,' he said. 'We've descended quite a bit since we were in that cellar, so I am guessing anywhere from twenty to thirty metres. Pretty deep.'

Fiona wiped away the dust from one of the bricks at the centre of the wall blocking their path. There seemed to be a pattern there. Then she blew on it a couple of times to clear the dust away, which revealed a small and neatly chiselled cuneiform inscription.

'Holy crap!' she exclaimed. 'Look at this.'

Andrew leaned in to see the inscription.

'What does it say?' he asked.

'These are two very well understood cuneiform logograms,' replied Fiona. 'The one on the left means *God Marduk*, and the one on the right means *God King*.'

The two of them looked at each other in stunned silence for a couple of seconds, but then an expectant smile began spreading across Fiona's face.

'But what does this mean?' asked Andrew.

'I am not completely sure,' said Fiona, now visibly shaking with excitement, 'but this could be big, Andrew. Marduk *and* the God-King Alexander, written in a script that was invented here, and the same script used by Perdiccas to write the clay cylinder. We need to get through this wall. There is no way I am turning back now.'

Andrew lifted his shirt to reveal a short hunting knife sitting in a sheath attached to his belt.

'Just in case,' he grinned at Fiona. 'You never know.'

He rolled up his shirt sleeves, pulled out the knife, and began to loosen the mortar around one of the central blocks of stone in the masonry in front of them. The mortar was quite brittle, and it disintegrated easily as Andrew ran his knife along the edge of the block of stone, going deeper and deeper as he went and creating small piles of dust on the ground below. When he had removed as much mortar as he could, he put the knife back in the sheath and grabbed the edges of the block of stone. Then he wriggled it from side to side whilst pulling, trying to extract it from the wall. No longer held in place by the mortar, the block came out without too much effort, revealing a pitch-black cavity behind it. A couple of minutes later three more blocks had been removed from the wall, creating a narrow gap just wide and tall enough for him to squeeze through.

'Here goes nothing,' he said, and began moving sideways through the gap, holding the torch in one hand and his knife in the other.

For a couple of seconds after he went through, Fiona could hear nothing. Then Andrew's voice came through the gap.

'What the…' he said, sounding astonished. His voice seemed to reverberate and echo slightly, hinting at the size of the space beyond.

'What's in there?' asked Fiona impatiently.

'You'd better come through and see for yourself,' said Andrew. 'I am not sure what I am looking at.'

What greeted Fiona on the other side of the ancient masonry nearly took her breath away. They were standing near a corner in a huge room some twenty-by-twenty metres in size, with a ceiling at least ten metres above them. The ceiling was held up by twelve perfectly symmetrically arranged and slightly tapering pillars that were spaced equidistantly throughout the room. The ceiling itself seemed to be made of giant slabs of granite, which still had the remains of painted images visible on them in some places. All of the pillars were covered from top to bottom in intricate imagery and sections of unusually large cuneiform writing, hinting at their use in this setting being mainly for aesthetic reasons.

'What *is* this place?' asked Andrew.

'I don't know,' breathed Fiona. 'But I don't think anyone has laid eyes on this place for a very long time. Perhaps as much as two thousand years.'

As Andrew slowly allowed the beam of light from his torch to fan across the walls and the pillars, they both spotted something in the middle of the room, which from their vantage point was partly obscured by the massive pillars.

Walking cautiously towards the centre of the cavernous space, Fiona noticed that the ground was bone dry and covered in dust. It was also slightly chilly down here, several tens of metres underground.

'Oh wow,' said Fiona as they cleared the pillars obstructing their view and were now able to see what was in the middle of the room.

Towering above them were two giant granite statues, each of them at least eight metres tall and almost reaching as far as the ceiling. They both looked like they had been chiselled from a massive single block of stone, and they shared a large square pedestal around half a metre tall with a couple of metres of space between them. The statue on the left was Marduk and it had the appearance of an archetypical Mesopotamian ruler with a large wide and curly beard, a tall headpiece resembling a crown, and a long and intricately embroidered gown stretching from his shoulders down to just above his sandal-covered feet. In his hand, he held a mace, and by his side was a Mushussu, the hybrid snake-dragon that was his servant.

The other statue had the unmistakable form of Alexander the Great in full battle armour, holding a shield emblazed with the Vergina Sun in one hand and a Macedonian short sword in the other. His head was held high and slightly to one side as if surveying his next conquest somewhere off in the far distance. At his feet was what appeared to be a small granite box, roughly one metre by half a metre, and it was approximately half a metre tall.

'Breathtaking,' said Fiona, a smile of amazement slowly spreading across her face. 'Marduk and Alexander, side by side. Two Gods. Literally larger than life. And the detail is exquisite. It's wonderful.'

As they slowly approached, Fiona was craning her neck to look up at the faces of the two giant statues.

'What's this?' said Andrew, approaching the granite box. 'I am going to take the lid off. Can you hold the torch, please?'

Fiona directed the beam at the box as Andrew grabbed the sides of its lid and began lifting it. As the lid came loose and was lifted slowly away from the box, there was a hollow grinding sound as the pieces of granite scraped against each other.

'Heavy,' said Andrew, straining.

He placed the lid down on the platform next to the box with a dull clonk, and a small cloud of dust shot out from under it, whirling up into the torchlit air.

'No,' breathed Fiona. 'Surely, this can't be…'

'What?' said Andrew, straightening himself up to look down inside the box.

Inside the box was a single item made of clay. It was a tall and ever so slightly bulbous cylindrical shape painted in a dark ochre colour with a narrow band of black paint around its circumference near the top where a simple clay lid sat. The cylinder was roughly thirty centimetres at its widest, and twenty at its base and at its top. It was sitting upright on a small wooden disc.

Fiona reached inside the box and carefully picked up the cylinder with both hands. She gingerly lifted it out and held it in front of herself, inspecting the artwork.

'The same cuneiform as the logogram on the block of stone by the entrance,' she said. '*God-King.*'

'And beneath it,' she continued, turning the cylinder slightly towards Andrew to allow him to see. 'The Vergina Sun.'

'Is this…' began Andrew.

'Yes!' said Fiona, in absolute awe at what she was holding in her hands. 'This has to be the canopic jar containing the heart of Alexander the Great.'

'I'm not sure what to say,' said Andrew. 'That is almost unbelievable. How heavy is it?

'Heavy enough to have something inside it,' replied Fiona, lowering it gently onto the platform.

Letting go of the jar, she found herself first turning the palms of her hands upwards and looking at them, half expecting her hands to now appear different. Then she gazed up at the statue of Alexander, as if to see if his wrath was about to come down on her.

'Well, open it then,' said Andrew impatiently.

Fiona knelt down on the smooth stone floor and gripped the small handle on the lid between her fingers. Then she lifted it off carefully and leaned in. Andrew shifted the torch to allow them to peer inside.

'Is it there?' asked Andrew.

Fiona sighed and carefully reached inside the jar. 'It is, in a manner of speaking,' she said, slowly extracting her hand again.

'It *is* here,' she continued. 'But it has completely decomposed and turned into this.'

A fine grey powdery substance ran slowly through her fingers as it fell gently back into the jar.

'The heart of a god turned to dust,' she whispered. 'Or perhaps it was eventually cremated, and this is the ash. Either way, there is nothing left of it for anyone to analyse. All of the DNA would have been destroyed.'

At that moment, they heard the sound of footsteps coming from the tunnel entrance. As they turned to look, they could see brief flashes of light indicating that someone with a torch was approaching through the tunnel, and was now close to the entrance.

They barely had time to react before a large man with a gun entered, immediately pointing his firearm and his torch directly at them. Without shifting his aim, he quickly moved a couple of steps sideways to get clear of the pillars.

'Don't move,' he said in a gruff voice with a heavy English accent.

A few seconds later, a slender man appeared.

'Hello again,' said Dubois with a smug look on his face.

'You,' snarled Fiona.

'Oh, for fuck's sake,' said Andrew under his breath.

'Very nice to see you both again,' said Dubois in a sarcastic tone of voice. 'It seems the tables have turned this time. Please step away from the statues. My new friend here is… how do you say? Trigger happy?'

'Hands on your heads,' growled Stone, cocking the gun. 'Back away and kneel down.'

Andrew and Fiona did as he asked, and when they were a couple of metres from the base of the statue, Stone took a couple of steps towards them.

'That's far enough,' he said. 'Now kneel.'

Andrew and Fiona complied, and as they did so, Dubois moved in an arc around Stone. Careful to stay out of the line of fire, he approached the statues.

'*Incroyable*,' he muttered. 'You actually managed to find it. I am not sure how you did it, but I am more than happy to let you do the dirty work. We would have been here ourselves several hours ago, but we were delayed.'

Stone grunted something halfway between a laugh and a snort.

'*Pardon?*' said Dubois and looked at him sternly, but Stone just shook his head dismissively.

'Listen,' said Stone, now sounding irritated. 'If we hadn't been poking around old Saddam's bloody palace all day, we could have been out of here by tea time.'

'Yes, well,' shrugged Dubois. 'I thought it was worth a try. But of course, once we spotted you two walking across the field to the site of the Esagila temple, it was suddenly all very clear. Thank you for saving us the effort.'

'Parasite,' snarled Fiona, hobbling a couple of steps towards Dubois on her knees.'

'Don't fucking move, my little pearl,' said Stone and pointed his gun at Fiona.

Dubois looked confused. 'What?'

Andrew laughed derisively. 'He means little girl,' he said and nodded at Stone.

'You English and your ridiculous rhyming slang,' said Dubois scathingly, shaking his head. 'No wonder everything in your country is a confused mess.'

'Enough of this!' said Stone, sounding like he was losing patience with the Frenchman. 'Let's just get the bloody thing and get out of here. Take this and cover me while I tie them up. Shoot them if they move.'

Stone handed his gun to Dubois and reached into the inside pocket of his jacket, pulling out two zip-ties. Dubois looked awkward and uncomfortable holding a gun, and both Andrew and Fiona noticed it.

Andrew's mind was racing, and within a few seconds, his thoughts were coalescing around a plan to barge into Stone when he got close enough. After that he would have to take his chances getting to

Dubois before the Frenchman could fire. However, he never got to execute that plan.

Without warning, and clearly betting that Dubois would not fire, Fiona leapt to her feet, and in the blink of an eye she closed the distance to the canopic jar which she quickly grabbed with both hands and lifted high above her head.

'If you shoot me, the jar drops!' shouted Fiona, her heart pounding in her chest and her voice trembling.

Stone was already moving towards her when Dubois yelled out.

'Get back, you *imbécile*!' he shouted at Stone. 'We need the jar.'

Stone stopped and grimaced at Fiona. 'Clever little lamb, ain't ya?'

'Pierre!' said Fiona loudly, her voice quivering. 'You can have the jar. We will trade it for your gun, and then we will leave, alright? You can have this place to yourself. As long as we get to leave in peace.'

'You've got to be fucking shitting me,' muttered Stone dismissively with a look of derision and disgust on his face.

'Shut up!' shouted Dubois angrily, staring at Stone. 'I am in charge here. The only thing that matters is the heart.'

'So do we have a deal?' said Fiona insistently, glancing up at the jar. 'If not, you can kiss this jar goodbye.'

'She's bluffing, you idiot,' barked Stone at Dubois.

Fiona pressed her lips together and shook her head. 'You can't afford to take that chance,' she said, holding the jar up just a little bit higher above her head.

'Alright!' exclaimed Dubois. 'Ok. Fine. You win. Put the jar down, or I swear I will haunt you in this life and the next.'

Fiona began lowering the jar towards the platform.

'You bloody idiot,' said Stone derisively. 'Are you out of your bleedin' mind?'

'Shut your mouth!' shouted Dubois, now clearly losing his temper. 'You work for me. I am in charge here.'

Stone hesitated for a moment, but then he chuckled and seemed to acquiesce.

Dubois tossed the gun on the ground in front of Fiona. Andrew immediately moved to where she stood and picked it up.

In one quick and smooth movement, he popped out the magazine, checked the ammo, and then slammed the magazine back in. He pulled back the top slide, loading a round, and then he raised the gun and pointed it squarely at Stone who was clearly the biggest threat. The whole thing took only a couple of seconds.

As he did so, Fiona placed the jar carefully on the platform and then backed away from it. Andrew immediately began moving sideways and around their two opponents towards the tunnel entrance whilst keeping the gun firmly aimed at Stone who just stood there looking at him calmly, following him with his eyes as if waiting for an opening.

As Fiona made her way through the gap and back into the tunnel, Andrew covered her.

'If I see anyone come through this gap for the next fifteen minutes,' said Andrew icily, 'I swear I will empty this magazine down the tunnel, do you both understand?'

Dubois nodded emphatically, and Stone just gave a shrug.

'Alright,' said the Frenchman anxiously, whilst trying to sound calm. 'Everything is cool. We have what we came for. You have your fifteen minutes.'

Andrew and Fiona started moving back through the tunnel as fast as they could, Fiona in front with the torch and Andrew behind her walking partly sideways and always aiming his gun back towards the gap where he could just make out the faint light from Stone's torch inside the underground temple.

Traversing the tunnel only took around five minutes, much less than the fifteen minutes Andrew had demanded, but he wanted to make sure they had plenty of time to vacate the site after making it up and out of the mosque.

Just as they exited the mosque itself, they heard the sound of a siren approaching.

'Shit,' said Andrew, pulling Fiona away from the mosque and through the bushes towards the south. 'I think someone called the police.'

'Salim?' said Fiona.

'Maybe,' replied Andrew. 'Can't really blame him. We were behaving as shifty as anything. Let's just get the hell out of sight. We need to stay off the roads. I have an idea. Follow me.'

# TWENTY-FOUR

Inside the temple, Stone was pacing impatiently up and down on the smooth flagstones in front of the statues. Dubois was slowly walking around the two giant effigies, looking up at them in awe.

'We need to get the fuck out of here,' said Stone grouchily.

He had grabbed the

'Just a couple more minutes. We are not jeopardising this whole mission just to get out of here a few minutes early,' said Dubois sternly.

'You're a bloody fool to believe anything those two muppets are saying,' snarled Stone. 'I should have iced them when I had the chance.'

'Well, it is a good thing I was here then,' said Dubois sounding irritated. 'If you had, we would have had to return to Athens empty-handed.'

'Your problem,' shrugged Stone. 'I don't answer to that bitch.'

'Enough of this nonsense,' said Dubois impatiently. 'Come over here and pick up this jar. I need you to carry it out of here safely. I will hold the torch.'

Stone muttered something under his breath, but then walked over towards Dubois. Suddenly he heard voices in the distance. They sounded agitated, talking over each other and shouting, and they were speaking Arabic. The hairs on the back of his neck stood up. This was suddenly feeling all too familiar.

'Fuck,' he spat. 'I bloody told you we should have left already. Now we've got company.'

'*Merde!*' exclaimed Dubois. 'What do we do?'

'What we do,' said Stone menacingly, 'is you do whatever the fuck I tell you to do from now on, is that clear? Enough of this bloody jellyfish routine of yours. From now on we do this my way.'

'Ok,' nodded Dubois, his earlier self-confidence and arrogance now having completely vanished.

'When they come in,' said Stone, 'you put your hands up and do exactly as they say, alright?'

'But I don't speak Arabic,' said Dubois.

'I am sure you'll get the picture,' replied Stone, and hurried over to the corner near the tunnel entrance to hide behind a pillar. 'And put your torch on the floor so it points towards the tunnel,' he said in a hushed voice.

Less than a minute later, lights flickered through the gap by the tunnel entrance, and soon after that three Iraqi police officers, each one carrying a torch and a pistol, squeezed through. The last of them was a portly man, so he took a bit longer to make his way through the narrow gap.

As soon as they spotted Dubois, the police officers started shouting at him in Arabic. A cacophony of voices filled the huge space, and the sound reverberated around it as Dubois waved his arm frantically in the air, trying to appease them.

'I am unarmed,' shrieked Dubois, as the police officers approached, shouting and pointing their guns at him.

Stone decided this would be his best opportunity to strike. Moving smoothly out from behind the pillar in a slightly crouched position, he headed straight for the man at the back, who looked like he was the most senior officer. Before the man could react, Stone had moved up behind him to undo the strap holding his sidearm in place. He pulled it out, took a step back, and yanked the top slide back. Then he flicked the safety off, raised the gun and fired a shot into the back of the officer's head. The officer dropped to the floor with a thud as the loud crack from the gun reverberated around the huge stone chamber.

The two other officers barely had time to react before Stone fired twice more, this time hitting one of the other two in the chest with both shots. The third officer was so disorientated by what was happening that he began firing several panicked and badly aimed shots in the direction of Dubois, who miraculously avoided being hit.

This gave Stone enough time to shift his aim and shoot the third officer in the head with a single shot. The officer slumped to the floor like a ragdoll, producing a small cloud of dust and leaving Dubois standing there with his eyes squeezed tightly shut, his knees wobbling and his arms raised and trembling.

'Alright Frenchie, you can stop shitting yourself now,' said Stone after a few seconds. 'It's done. Now let's get out of here.'

Dubois slowly opened his eyes, partly lowering his arms while trying to survey the carnage at his feet. The three police officers were splayed out in front of him in various unnatural positions, pools of blood expanding from their lifeless bodies.

'I need to bring the… NO!' shouted Dubois suddenly.

Stone's head whipped round to look at him. 'What the hell is wrong with you?'

'The jar!' shouted Dubois bitterly.

Next to him on the platform were the remnants of the canopic jar. It had been hit by one of the bullets from the third officer, and had exploded into hundreds of pieces, its powdery contents scattered in a large circular area on the platform behind where the jar had been sitting.

'No, no, no!' exclaimed Dubois and knelt down, whilst beginning to sweep up the dust with his hands and making a small pile of it.

Stone shook his head and grimaced, and then he walked up swiftly behind Dubois and grabbed his arm. He yanked him to his feet and wrapped a powerful arm around his neck, holding him in a vicelike grip. Dubois produced a throaty wheezing sound as he struggled for breath.

'Oi, listen up Froggie,' snarled Stone in a menacing voice laced with his heavy east London accent. 'These won't be the last coppers coming this way on this fine evening. Either we both scarper right now, or you and I end up spending twenty years rotting in a bloody

Iraqi prison cell with a bunch of fucking camel-shagging towel-heads, and that just ain't acceptable to me, do you copy? Now, get your shit together. We are *leaving!*

*       *       *

Around a kilometre downstream from the ruins of Babylon on the outskirts of the city of Hillah, Andrew and Fiona were climbing out of a small rowing boat which they had found on the bank of the Euphrates a couple of hundred meters to the west of the mosque. In their hurry they had not managed to find any oars, but the south-flowing river had taken them swiftly away from the ruins and away from danger.

As they made their way out of the boat by a sandy riverbank where the water was shallow, a local woman saw them. Fiona waved and smiled at her, but the woman just hurried inside a house near the riverbank and shut the door.

'We need to clear out,' said Andrew. 'The main road is this way. We should be able to hail a taxi here somewhere.'

Half an hour later they were on their way back to Baghdad in the back of a minibus. They had found it parked at a taxi stand, and the driver had demanded an exorbitant price to take them to the capital, but they had paid it without complaining. With every kilometre they managed to put between themselves and the ancient city of Babylon, they felt increasingly like they just might manage to get away.

Fiona was quiet for most of the drive. Still trying to process what had happened, she was kicking herself for not having taken a picture of the giant statues. But then it occurred to her that those sorts of pictures would probably be in the newspapers very soon. And as long as they didn't also have photos of her and Andrew next to them, she wasn't going to complain.

★     ★     ★

The next morning, they woke up in a comfortable bed in a room at the Baghdad International Airport Hotel. It was a somewhat soulless hotel with a dated interior, but none of that mattered now. The only thing that was important was that they had managed to return to Baghdad safely and that the story on the news about grave robbers in Babylon having killed three police officers, did not include any mention of a man and a woman behaving suspiciously.

'Those poor policemen,' said Fiona. 'They didn't stand a chance against that guy. Any idea who he was?'

'Definitely ex-army of some kind,' replied Andrew. 'London boy. I doubt he was special forces though. Just didn't seem like the type.'

'Certifiable psychopath if you ask me,' said Fiona. 'Where do people like Dubois find people like him?'

'Bottom feeders tend to attract other bottom feeders, haven't you noticed?' asked Andrew.

'Or perhaps that goon is on Alexis's payroll,' said Fiona. 'Although I would be surprised if she mingled with people like that.'

'If he is, it is probably an arms-length type of relationship,' said Andrew. 'She would never want to be associated with someone like that.'

'What do you think their next move is?' asked Fiona.

'Well,' replied Andrew. 'If what Strickland told me is accurate, then they have been planning to go to Afghanistan as well, but for what purpose we simply don't know. Do you have any ideas?'

Fiona looked like she was contemplating something for a few moments before she spoke again.

'Alexander spent quite a lot of time in that part of the world, so if Dubois is actually going there then it could mean a number of different things. I am going to have to spend some more time with Arrian's account and Ptolemy's diary. There might be clues in there that will help us guess what Dubois thinks he has discovered. But it will take time.'

'Which is what we probably don't have,' said Andrew. 'They know we are on to them, and I guess it is a question of time before they work out that their communications have been compromised.'

'No pressure then,' said Fiona sarcastically and sighed. 'I will get on it right away.'

'Ok,' said Andrew. 'I will contact our flight crew and ask them to make preparations for departure.'

'Did you check Dubois's location on your tracker app?' asked Fiona. 'He might already be on his way there.'

'I did,' replied Andrew. 'The networks didn't pick up anything until early this morning when his phone synced itself with a base station back in Athens. I am guessing he is getting a serious dressing down from Alexis right about now.'

'Good,' said Fiona. 'I can't stand that little cretin.'

'It might also buy us a bit of time to work out what they are planning,' said Andrew, walking to the windows and looking out at an aircraft taking off. 'I am also hoping Strickland will get back to us over the next couple of hours. He might have something useful.'

'Alright,' said Fiona and opened her laptop. 'Anything he can find would be appreciated. I feel like we need all the help we can get at this point.'

★          ★          ★

'Ackerman here.'

'It's me.'

'Stone. What happened? I had Alexis on the phone earlier. She was furious.'

'Dubois screwed it up for us. He let those two civies outsmart us.'

'I wouldn't call Sterling a civilian. I read his file.'

'Well, the SAS is not all is cracked up to be, and that girl is just a bloody nuisance.'

'Still, she got the better of both of you, I heard.'

'This once maybe, but that was the last time that happens. If I see them again, they're both dead. No more playing nice.'

'Fine by me. What's the plan now? Has she told you?'

'She doesn't talk to me. Only to the frog. Seems he's off to Afghanistan with his Russian pet. I am just glad I don't have to smell that shithole again.'

'Just keep doing as they ask. We need Alexis on side for as long as we can, until we can move to the next phase.'

'Roger that. I will keep you updated.'

'Excellent. Goodbye Stone.'

*       *       *

It was late in the afternoon when Andrew's phone rang. He had insisted on them having their meals brought to their room in order to keep as low a profile as possible. Even if there was nothing on the news, that didn't rule out that the Iraqi police might be looking for them.

'Strickland, sir,' said Andrew as he picked up the phone.

'Andrew,' replied the colonel. 'Good to hear your voice. I gather things got a bit hairy yesterday. Are you two alright?'

'We're fine, sir. Still just holed up in the hotel room until we can work out what to do next.'

'Well, I might be able to help there,' said Strickland. 'The bug you planted in Alexis's office on the Hypatia picked up a conversation between her and Dubois. Apparently, they had met earlier in the day, but she wanted some more details on what happened in those ruins. I think she might be attempting to pre-empt things pointing to her. Anyway, Dubois was at Athens International Airport when they spoke. He is on his way to Moscow.'

'Moscow?' said Andrew surprised. 'What for?'

'Sounded like a connecting flight to Kabul. The passenger manifest says he is travelling with another man by the name Robert Jones, but that is almost certainly an alias. It could be Morozov or it could be our friend from East London. We're trying to get airport CCTV footage from the Greek border police to see if we can identify him. If we do, I will let you know.'

'Thanks,' said Andrew. 'Any idea what they are going to Kabul for?'

'The only thing we picked up from Dubois's conversations with Alexis was a brief mention of a silver chest. Does that ring any bells?'

'No,' said Andrew. 'I don't think so, but I will have a word with Fiona. She has had her head buried in her laptop for hours now, trying to work out what their plan is.'

'She is a great asset,' said Strickland.

'I know,' replied Andrew. 'Without her, I might as well just be sitting here throwing darts at a map of the world.'

'Let me know if she comes up with anything,' said Strickland. 'We still have assets both in Afghanistan and in a couple of the neighbouring countries, so you two might not be completely on your own. It is a dangerous place, but then I don't need to tell you that. And I will send you the recording from Alexis's yacht so you two can listen to it yourselves.'

'Copy that, sir,' said Andrew. 'I will get back to you as soon as we have something.'

★      ★      ★

Frost leaned forward to look closely at the analysis results from Batch H04 that had just been compiled and presented on the screens of the control terminal in the underground lab in Rhinebeck. Batches H02 and H03 had gone as planned but had been terminated after only twelve hours of gestation. In those twelve hours, the 22 embryos had grown at a staggering rate. Only one had failed to develop and one other had experienced abnormal growth for reasons yet to be determined. The 22 germ cells had been genetically identical and had all included the same CRISPR-driven alteration to their genetic code, so they should theoretically have developed into identical embryos. There might be a problem with the artificial amniotic fluid, or worse still, some sort of early-stage mutation in the germ cell's genome. He would need to ask Rosetta to run a full analysis and diagnostics of all the billions of sensor readings that had been taken over the past twelve hours, in order to try to pin down where the problem was. One failure out of 22 might not sound too bad, but if that failure-rate was extrapolated out to when the mass-production facilities were ready, then this would represent a substantial loss of efficiency and therefore a significant impairment of the profit potential.

He looked at the monitor on the console, inspecting the image of Embryo 17 for a while. Then he stood back up and turned his head to look directly at gestation vat number 17 above him. After just twelve hours, the embryo was now large enough for him to be able to see its features clearly with the naked eye, even from where he was standing some ten metres away.

'Rosetta,' he said. 'Terminate all vats and purge.'

★     ★     ★

Later that evening, Andrew rose from the chair he had been sitting on by a small desk in the hotel room. He pulled out his wireless earphones, which he had used to re-listen to the recording of Alexis talking to Dubois. He had first listened to it with Fiona earlier in the day, but had then decided to go over it again by himself.

As he walked over to Fiona who was sitting on the sofa with her laptop on a coffee table in front of her, he placed a hand gently on her shoulder. She was sitting immobile and staring at the screen, as she had been for most of the day. Once in a while, she would write down a few notes in a separate document and then return to the images of Ptolemy's diary and her copy of Arrian of Nicomedia's writings.

Feeling his hand resting on her shoulder, she blinked a couple of times, as if having to make an effort to extract herself from her research.

'Anything new from the recording?' she asked, looking up at Andrew.

'No,' he replied. 'There is no hint as to what specifically Alexis has asked Dubois to try to retrieve from Afghanistan.'

'Well, I think I might have an idea here,' said Fiona. 'The pieces seem to fit, but it is still just a guess.'

'What is it?' said Andrew, sitting down next to her and looking at the screen.

'See this page here?' said Fiona. 'It is from the latter third of the diary and the second year of Archon Euthicritus, which equates to 327 BCE. This was during the time of Alexander's campaign in Bactria, which is now known as eastern Afghanistan. I have been trying to translate this, but the shorthand is frankly atrocious. As I said to you the other day, Ptolemy probably never meant for anyone else to read this, so it is like decrypting a set of handwritten notes from a drunken court stenographer whose stenotype machine has broken down. In other words, he gets an F for neatness.'

'But you found something,' said Andrew, sensing that she was holding back.

'I might have,' said Fiona hesitantly. 'This page concerns a small event, or perhaps anecdote is a better word, that happened at the Cophen River when Alexander was wounded in the shoulder by either an arrow or a dart. I have had to paraphrase extensively here to recreate what it might have looked like if Ptolemy had written out the account properly. So here goes:

*HAVING TENDED TO THE KING, THE PHYSICIAN, WITH MUCH REVERENCE, PLACED A BLOOD-SOAKED CLOTH INSIDE A SMALL SILVER CHEST WITH THREE BLUE GEMS AFFIXED TO ITS LID. CLUTCHING THE CHEST, HE SCURRIED OUT OF THE TENT, AND THE NEXT MORNING HE HAD GONE, SHAMEFULLY ABANDONING THE SERVICE OF HIS KING. THE MEN SAY THERE ARE RUMOURS THAT HE HAS RETURNED TO HIS HOME IN ALEXANDRIA ARIANA. WHO WOULD WILLINGLY FORSAKE THE GREAT KING THUS?*

'And none of this is in Arrian of Nicomedia's account?' asked Andrew.

'Only the fact that Alexander was wounded,' replied Fiona. 'But this anecdote about the cloth and the chest only appears in Ptolemy's own diary. He clearly thought the physician's actions were peculiar enough to make a brief note. Thinking about it, it might even be possible that this event laid the seed for Ptolemy's idea to hijack Alexander's coffin several years later. Possession of the physical remains of the god-king would clearly have been a powerful claim to legitimacy for any new ruler.'

'Ok,' said Andrew. 'But what is the connection to Dubois and Afghanistan?'

'That's the thing,' said Fiona. 'Dubois has access to the original diary pages, and I have been wracking my brain about what he might have uncovered about this chest that would make him go to Afghanistan. The only thing I could think of was to try to find out if any record exists about a silver chest with that description and from that time period, and I think I might finally have found something.'

'Where? And how?' asked Andrew.

'There is a global archaeology database with hundreds of thousands of entries for finds all over the world, most of them relating to artefacts that have already been identified and dated, and that are sitting in museums either on display or in storage somewhere. But the system also contains a separate database that is not available to the public. It is intended as a temporary repository for information related to ongoing archaeological projects, and it contains preliminary findings from researchers such as myself. Most of what is in there is related to artefacts that have been found, but that have not yet been studied. I began trawling the database for a chest matching Ptolemy's description, and I found a match in a section dedicated to finds in and around the ancient city of Herat in the northwest of Afghanistan. While it had already been a Persian town for a couple of centuries by the time Alexander arrived, carrying the name Aria, he expanded it, turned it into a city and renamed it Alexandria Ariana.'

'Which is where Ptolemy said the physician returned to with the chest,' said Andrew, his interest now piqued.

'Exactly,' said Fiona. 'One of the items catalogued there is a small silver chest with three blue gems embedded in the lid, seemingly matching Ptolemy's description. It was unearthed as part of the excavation and restoration of the Citadel of Herat, funded by the U.S. and Germany. The citadel there is akin to a large castle or fortification. It is some two-hundred meters long and fifty meters wide, and it was actually constructed around 330 BCE by Alexander's army immediately after its arrival. This was following the Battle of Gaugamela and the defeat of Darius III.'

'That's incredible,' said Andrew. 'And it is the same chest?'

'It is impossible to tell at this point,' said Fiona, 'but Dubois and Alexis clearly believe it is.'

'So where is the chest now?' asked Andrew.

'It was being kept inside a municipal storage compound as part of a huge collection of artefacts that were being stored there until it was safe either for teams of archaeologists to be flown in to analyse them or for them to be transported out of the country. But the endless wars and tribal clashes there mean that those artefacts have been sitting in that storage compound for years now.'

'So, we know where the chest is then,' said Andrew sounding encouraged.

'Well,' said Fiona. 'Here comes the bad news. 'The UNAMA, or United Nations Assistance Mission in Afghanistan, which has as its objective to assist the country in establishing a peaceful and democratic system there, has also been involved in the work to protect and preserve Afghanistan's historic sites. A few months ago they released a report saying that the Taliban had emptied out the Herat municipal storage facility and relocated the entire contents to one of their own storage facilities on the western outskirts of the city. The report clearly attempts not to speculate overtly about the purpose of this relocation, and so it doesn't explicitly state what the UNAMA thinks might be going on, but reading between the lines, it is pretty clear what they think might be happening.'

'What?' asked Andrew.

'The Taliban are almost certainly preparing to, shall we say, *curate* the artefacts. This basically means destroying antithetical items, melting down things made of precious metals, or simply selling them off to the highest bidder on the black market. They have a long and infamous track record of having done this sort of thing in the past.'

'Well, that's not good,' said Andrew, looking concerned.

Fiona shook her head. 'That is definitely an understatement. Not only could the silver chest be at risk of being melted down, destroying the cloth with Alexander's blood, but countless other irreplaceable artefacts could be lost. This is world history we are talking about, and those savages could literally end up destroying it if we don't stop them.'

Andrew rubbed his chin. 'Going in there is an extremely challenging prospect though. Afghanistan is not somewhere you just fly into and visit as a tourist, or even as an archaeologist. Most of the time it is a war zone to varying degrees. This could get really messy.'

'I understand that,' said Fiona and rose. She was becoming agitated at the thought of the destruction of scores of historical artefacts.

'Remember those giant Buddha statues in Bamiyan, about a hundred kilometres west of Kabul?' she continued. 'Remember how the Taliban rigged them up with explosives and blew them into a million pieces? Those were also priceless historical artefacts, probably from around the $5^{th}$ century CE, and those barbarians turned them into dust in just a few seconds. They will never be replaced. We have to stop that from happening again if we possibly can. If we could get into that storage facility, we might be able to find the chest and perhaps find out what else is there. If we hand that information over to the UN, they might be able to pressure the Taliban to hand the contents of that facility back to an international team of archaeologists, in exchange for continued foreign aid.'

Andrew was pressing his lips together and pondering the prospect of going back into Afghanistan.

'You have a good point, but it isn't going to be easy,' he said.

'I know that,' insisted Fiona. 'But isn't it worth a try? If those artefacts are destroyed, they will be lost forever, and with them an important piece of human history. Andrew, we *have* to go.'

'Alright,' said Andrew. 'But you are not coming with me. I am going on my own. There is just no way I am bringing you into Afghanistan on a mission like this.'

Fiona briefly considered arguing with him, but she knew he would never give in. And she had to admit that she might make it more difficult for him to do what he needed to do, not least because she would struggle to blend in anywhere in that country. Andrew would have a better chance of slipping in undetected if he was by himself.

'Ok,' nodded Fiona. 'I will stay here then. There is plenty more research to be done on the diary.'

'Fine,' said Andrew, and rose. 'Let me get hold of Strickland to discuss options. We might have assets in the area that could be of assistance.'

'Whatever you guys come up with, it has to happen fast,' said Fiona. 'It will be a question of time before Dubois and his goon shows up there.'

# TWENTY-FIVE

Late that evening, Strickland called Andrew to inform him that he had been unable to secure safe passage for their RAF aircraft from Baghdad into Herat International Airport, which, despite its name, now only serviced flights to Kabul. Even if they could have secured safe passage from the airport officials, any RAF aircraft was likely to be shot at on final approach, so Strickland had vetoed it.

This meant that the only viable alternative was to fly to the city of Mary in southern Turkmenistan and then make the crossing into Afghanistan via road. It was a four-hundred-kilometre drive to Herat, and so it was likely to end up being a six or seven-hour trip. But if Dubois was flying into Kabul via Moscow at an inopportune time, he would have an eight-hundred-kilometre drive ahead of him. If, on the other hand, he was lucky and able to catch a flight from Kabul to Herat quickly, he might beat Andrew to the ancient city and the storage facility holding the silver chest. There was no time to lose.

Strickland forwarded the location of the warehouse suspected of containing the artefacts from the Herat Citadel Museum, along with two satellite images of the area. The warehouse was in an industrial area southwest of the city centre, that was set back from the road behind a tall fence with what looked like a guard post shed by the road.

'One last thing,' said Strickland. 'We have an extraction plan ready, should things go south. The plan contains top secret information regarding the location of a U.S. carrier strike group, so I am afraid you can't share any of it with anyone else, including Fiona. Is that understood?'

'Yes, sir,' said Andrew. 'I am listening.'

'Ok. So, here's what we have managed to tee up for you.'

Strickland proceeded to lay out the extraction plan and told Andrew what the communications protocol would be in order to call it in. Then he wished him good luck and ended the call.

Andrew quickly packed his bag and gave Fiona a hug goodbye, and then he rushed out to the waiting aircraft. In order to avoid flying over Iranian airspace, the flight plan would take him on a long and circuitous route north across the border into Turkey, then east over Armenia and into Azerbaijan, over the Caspian Sea into Turkmenistan and then finally south-east to Mary. The entire trip was close to 1,500 kilometres long and would take just under three hours.

When the Honda HA-420 finally took off from Baghdad and started its trek northwards, it was late in the evening. Andrew knew that the next twenty-four hours were going to be extremely challenging, so he decided to get some sleep immediately after take-off.

More or less on schedule, the aircraft touched down at Mary International Airport. With the two-hour time difference relative to Baghdad, it was just after five o'clock in the morning and the airport seemed completely deserted. Outside the terminal there were only a couple of taxis waiting at the taxi stand, and none of them were prepared to make the long trip into Afghanistan and on to Herat. However, seeing Andrew's bundle of dollars, one of them called his cousin who showed up half an hour later with a pick-up truck.

The man's name was Yusup. Appearing to be in his early forties, he seemed determinedly monosyllabic, and for an amount of money that roughly equated to a month's salary, he agreed to take Andrew as far as the small border-town of Serhetabat, which was only a few hundred meters from the border with Afghanistan.

Yusup barely said a word during the entire road trip south on the A388 along the Morghab River, which runs all the way from Mary and into the heart of Afghanistan. This suited Andrew just fine. He wasn't there to make friends. For a similar amount of money, Yusup agreed to part with his spare clothes, which consisted of a dark beige and loose-fitting top and trouser set called a Partug-Kameez, which allowed Andrew to make his way unnoticed to a holding area for trucks and other heavy vehicles at the border. He had not had a chance to shave since before arriving in Baghdad, so he was already sporting a short black beard, which further helped him blend in.

He hid inside an eighteen-wheeler truck hauling sections of cement drainage pipes, which was in the process of having its paperwork approved in a small administrative building next to the holding area. On the Afghan side of the border, the road becomes the A77 which leads almost due south to Herat. Given that there were only a few small towns along the way, Andrew gambled that the truck was going all the way to the ancient Afghan city, and his gamble paid off. Less than one hundred kilometres later he was able to jump off the truck as it slowed down to turn right onto Jami Road on the northern outskirts of Herat. From there it was less than a kilometre to the city centre where the Citadel, sitting on a small plateau, rose up above the surrounding neighbourhoods.

As he walked along, Andrew was struck by how normal everything looked with people going about their daily lives just as in any other country. No one seemed to give him a second look, either because he had managed to make himself look like he could have lived there, or because they simply didn't care. But the illusion of normality was broken whenever an open back pickup truck full of young Taliban fighters came driving down the street waving their guns around, clearly revelling in the hold they now had on the city and the country.

Andrew made sure to turn his head away from them as he walked, and on more than one occasion he found himself moving his right hand to the left side of his torso, where he would pat the pistol which he was hiding in a chest holster under his clothes.

Making his way along the streets of Herat, Andrew found himself enjoying the moment despite the clear danger he was putting himself in should he be caught and identified by the Taliban. After a short while, it suddenly dawned on him why that was.

He felt free. No timetable. No mission plan. No responsibility for a squad of troops. He was responsible only for himself, and he could do things any way he liked without having to adhere to protocol or command structure. It was very liberating, and he felt confident and strong as he made his way southwest from the city centre.

By the time he had arrived at the industrial area on the outskirts of the city, the sun was just about to go down. He could tell it was going to be a chilly night since the skies were clear and a handful of stars were already twinkling in the darker eastern part of the sky.

★　　　★　　　★

When Pierre Dubois and Yevgeny Morozov disembarked the Aeroflot aircraft that had taken them from Moscow's Sheremetyevo International Airport to the Hamid Karzai International Airport in Kabul, they were met by a Caucasian man who was wearing civilian clothes, but who had the unmistakable demeanour of a career soldier. His name was Anton Bortnik, and he was working at the Russian embassy in Kabul as a cultural attaché. In reality, he was a GRU military intelligence operative placed in Kabul to liaise with Taliban forces on behalf of the Russian government. Russian military intelligence had been watching the attempts of the western allies to 'democratise' Afghanistan with a mixture of head-shaking and amusement for more than a decade now, whilst patiently biding their time and waiting and preparing for the inevitable collapse of Afghanistan's civilian government.

Working with Pakistan's military intelligence apparatus, the ISI, Bortnik had spent several years cultivating relationships with many of the local Taliban commanders on the ground in several regions of the country. Through clandestine means, he had helped fund and support various Taliban initiatives that had been designed to weaken the U.S. presence in the country and destabilise the local government in anticipation of Russia being able to exert increasing influence once the U.S. withdrew its forces.

This work invariably also opened up plenty of opportunities for freelance work, which given the state of the Russian economy and the ongoing devaluation of the Rouble, was a welcome and highly lucrative side-business. Pretty much everyone in the Russian Embassy with the ability to do so engaged in some part of this business, to the point where it was viewed as slightly suspicious if someone refused to get involved in this type of private enterprise. "Why not make hay when the sun shines", seemed to be the accepted mantra.

Bortnik broke into a sly smile when he saw Morozov coming off the plane with the Frenchman walking along behind him.

'Pantera,' he said, and stretched out his hand.

Morozov produced a grin and took Bortnik's hand in his. 'Anton,' he said. 'Good to see you.'

'How was the flight?'

'Fine,' muttered Morozov. 'Except I had to babysit this guy,' he said, jerking his head back and to one side in the direction of Dubois who was just now catching up with the Russian.

'Well, someone has to carry the money,' laughed Bortnik and slapped Morozov on the left shoulder.

Morozov winced, stiffened for a couple of seconds and then shot the surprised Bortnik a quick grin.

'Almost had a case of lead poisoning a couple of days ago,' he said. 'Ballistic vest ate the bullet, but I got a nice bruise to add to the collection.'

Bortnik laughed again. 'That's how you know you're alive, my friend. Come on. I will take you to the chopper.'

Dubois followed the two Russians, feeling irritated at being ignored and reduced to carrying a bag of cash. Still, he wasn't here to befriend yet another Russian brute. Morozov was here purely as muscle, and if his friends could facilitate the trip to Herat and back, then he was prepared to swallow his pride and tag along. However, by the time they made it to the warehouse, he would be taking over proceedings. Morozov might be an arsehole, but he knew better than to argue, unlike that idiot Mike Stone. Bloody *rostbeef*.

The three men made their way through the terminal and into a separate section of the airport, which would allow them to bypass customs and passport control. They then proceeded out of the building towards a hangar where an ageing Russian Mi-17 military transport helicopter was being readied.

The first Mi-17 helicopters took flight in 1975, but they had proven themselves so hardy and versatile that their production and export had continued long past the collapse of the Soviet Union. This one was being flown by a former Afghan Airforce helicopter pilot who had swapped sides and joined the Taliban, who were in dire need of trained pilots. As the crow flies it is around 550 kilometres from Kabul due west to Herat, and with a cruising speed of 260 km/h, the Mi-17 would take just over two hours to reach its destination.

Handing out bundles of dollars as they went, Bortnik and his two companions made their way to the hangar and entered the helicopter after it had been rolled out onto the tarmac. Then they strapped themselves into the passenger seats at the back as the engine started and the rotor blades began spinning up.

A couple of minutes later the chopper lifted off from the dusty tarmac. The pilot pushed the helicopter's nose down slightly, making it accelerate rapidly, and soon it was chasing the setting sun in the west as it rose higher in the sky, the rapid thudding noise of its rotor blades slowly receding as it went.

★     ★     ★

Ploughing through the waves in the Gulf of Oman, the USS George Washington Carrier Strike Group was steaming due east towards a position in international waters immediately south of the Pakistani port city of Gwadar.

The huge aircraft carrier itself is a marvel of engineering by any standard. 333 metres long, 78 metres wide and displacing almost one-hundred thousand tons of water, its flight deck is 4.5 acres in size, which roughly equates to 18,000 square metres or more than the combined size of ten football fields. It is powered by two Westinghouse A4W nuclear reactors that push it through the water using four enormous 5-bladed propellers weighing 30 tons each, and with a top speed of 56 kilometres per hour, it can travel almost six million kilometres before needing to refuel. It has a crew of more than six thousand people and can carry a complement of up to ninety fixed-wing aircraft and helicopters.

It was a clear evening with very little wind, and the swells in the gulf were relatively subdued, so the giant steel hulk seemed to glide effortlessly across the sea at around 30 knots or 50 kilometres per hour.

Below deck, a small team of British soldiers were silently kitting up and getting themselves ready. They had flown in earlier in the day from the British overseas territory of Diego Garcia, which is part of the Chagos Archipelago in the Indian Ocean, and which is host to a large U.S. airbase. It was a well-practised routine and every man in the squad was methodically strapping on their kit and checking and double-checking their weapons. No one said anything. All the talking that was required had already happened in the briefing room. They were now to be on standby for the next several hours, ready to go topside and begin their mission.

★        ★        ★

Walking along the road in the industrial area where the satellite images had indicated the location of the storage facility to be, Andrew began to feel like he stood out a lot more than a couple of hours earlier despite his clothing and beard. It was easy to blend into a crowd in the busy city centre, but out here on the outskirts of the city there were very few people around, and no one else was walking along the road like he was. He was also carrying a small backpack that somehow seemed out of place in this part of the city. The only people he saw were men on scooters or small motorbikes and in cars, and as they passed by on the road, he felt as if they were all watching him.

As he passed the small guardhouse that looked like it had last been painted a lifetime ago, he glanced inside where two men wearing typical Taliban robes were sitting, listening to the radio. Behind them their Kalashnikov submachine guns were leaning against the back wall, and Andrew could hear them talking to each other in Pashto.

*Local men*, he thought. *Probably no formal military training, but were almost certainly experienced fighters.*

The two men did not seem to notice him as he walked past, and he kept going until he was at the end of the piece of land the warehouse was located on. The entire plot was surrounded by tall barbed wire fencing, and there were floodlights mounted in all four corners lighting up the warehouse in the encroaching darkness. Realising that there was no access to the plot except through the main gate, Andrew waited for a couple of minutes and then began walking back towards the guardhouse. As he did so, he reached inside his clothes with his right hand, pulled out his pistol and fixed a silencer to its barrel. Approaching the guardhouse, he then concealed it under his clothes.

This time, as he came nearer, one of the guards spotted him and rose. The guard was a tall bearded man who looked to be in his thirties, with dark brown eyes and shaggy unkempt hair. He had the worn leathery face of a man who had spent most of his life outside under the sun and the eyes of someone who had seen much death already.

'As-Salaam-Alaikum,' said Andrew calmly and raised his left hand in greeting, whilst keeping the gun out of sight behind him.

'Wa-Alaikum-Assalaam,' said the guard, his eyes running across Andrew's face and body, fixing themselves momentarily on his right arm.

'Khah maakhaam,' smiled Andrew, greeting the man by saying *Good Evening*.

The man must have seen something in Andrew's demeanour or body language that seemed out of place, and Andrew noticed him glancing quickly towards the Kalashnikovs at the back of the guardhouse.

As the other guard, who was a wiry and gaunt-looking man stood up, the first guard held out his palm towards Andrew and raised his voice slightly.

'Wadrega!' he said, meaning *stop* in Pashto.

At that moment, Andrew knew that the game was up. In a flash, and whilst still moving forward, he brought up his gun, aimed it at the first guard's torso and fired off a quick double-tap. The bullets smacked into the guard's chest with muffled noises and left two small holes in his Kameez. Without delay Andrew shifted his aim to the other guard who looked stunned by what had just happened, aimed at his forehead and fired once.

The two guards collapsed onto the floor of the guardhouse almost simultaneously. Andrew kept walking forward but quickly tucked the gun back inside his clothes. Making his way around the guardhouse to the back where there was a door, he stepped inside and knelt down. He went through the pockets of the two dead men and found their mobile phones, which he stuffed inside his backpack. Then he rose, and dragged the bodies under the small table inside the guardhouse in order to obscure them from anyone walking past. He then grabbed one of the Kalashnikovs, checked the ammo in the magazine, slung it over his shoulder and exited the guardhouse.

Walking calmly across the open space between the guardhouse and the warehouse which was set back by around twenty metres, he heard the sound of a car approaching to his right. Casually turning his head, he saw a small van racing down the dusty road. It passed the warehouse plot and continued on to the end of the road where it turned left towards the city centre.

As Andrew approached the large sliding metal doors of the warehouse, he spotted a regular-sized door on the right-hand side of the building and decided to try to enter that way. It turned out to be unlocked, and he soon found himself inside what looked like an office with glass windows towards the interior of the warehouse. It was obvious that no one had used the space as an office for a very long time.

Inside the dimly lit warehouse proper, there were a large number of wooden boxes stacked on top of each other in the middle of the space. Some of them were several metres long and others were as small as shoeboxes.

Andrew reached inside his backpack for a notebook into which he had copied the instructions Colonel Strickland had emailed to him the evening before. However, he soon found himself needing his phone in order to identify the Pashto writing on the various boxes. The Pashto script is a modified version of the Arabic Naskh script, but with a number of characters added to it to indicate sounds that exist in Pashto but not in Arabic.

On the floor of the warehouse had been painted long white lines, creating separate squares within which sat groups of wooden boxes. He began by taking lots of pictures of the contents of the warehouse from several different angles. These would be sent back to Strickland who would forward them to UNAMA and anyone else who might be able to put pressure on the Taliban to refrain from engaging in the destruction of these artefacts.

Each of the painted squares had writing painted next to each corner, and he quickly found the square that said هرات ارگ, which is the Pashto name for the Herat Citadel.

Inside that square, he methodically began checking all the labels on the various boxes. At first, it seemed as if someone who knew what they were doing had carefully catalogued the contents of all of the boxes. After twenty minutes, however, he began to doubt whether this entire venture was a giant and potentially lethal waste of time. There were dozens of boxes and a fair number of them did not have labels on them. He was almost at the point of concluding that the whole trip had been a pointless failure when he came across a box that was roughly 30 by 25 centimetres in size, and which had two small labels on it.

One read سينه زرو سپينو د, which simply means "silver chest".

The other read نيلم, which means "sapphire".

Andrew held it in his hands and stared at it for a few seconds. Then he put it down on the floor and used his knife to wrest the nailed-on wooden lid off the box. Inside was a mass of long thin wood shavings used for packaging delicate items for transport, and on top of it was a small note seemingly included by the team of archaeologists who had unearthed the contents of the wooden box. Andrew picked up the note and read it.

```
Silver   chest   with   three   polished
sapphires   on   ornate   lid,   circa   350
BCE.
Decorated with engravings of tulip and
marigold flowers.
Dim: 28cm x 19cm x 14cm.
Cloth  stained  with  organic  substance.
Sealed   inside   plastic   bag.   Analysis
required.
```

Andrew pulled off the wood shavings and laid eyes on the chest for the first time. Just as the note said, the chest had three small gleaming deep-blue sapphires embedded into its lid, and when he opened it he saw a small clear re-sealable plastic bag with a blotchy-looking dark beige cloth that seemed to have a large almost black stain on it.

'Bloody hell', whispered Andrew. 'It's still here.'

Taking another few seconds to marvel at the chest and the cloth, Andrew then closed the lid, shoved the wood shavings back in the box, and resealed it by hammering the nails back in with the end of his knife's handle.

Just then he heard the sound of a car engine outside, followed by the crunch of tyres on gravel. Looking over his shoulder towards the small office, he could see headlights fanning through the small gap between the large sliding doors leading to the outside. He then heard the car coming to a halt, the sound of boots hitting the ground and then voices speaking in Pashto. He immediately began packing up his things, placing the small wooden box inside his backpack. It would only just fit.

After just a few seconds, the voices went from calm to sounding questioning, then to being agitated and finally to outright shouting laced with panic. This could only be the Taliban, and they had clearly discovered the bodies of the two guards in the guardhouse.

The shouting continued and there was now the sound of more men jumping off what must have been the back of a pickup truck and landing on the gravel.

Andrew slung the backpack over his shoulder and stood up, quickly looking around trying to find another exit. In the far corner of the warehouse was another door, and he immediately bolted for it. As he approached it, he slowed down slightly whilst reaching for the door handle. He gripped it and pressed down on it, hoping the door would be unlocked. Unfortunately, it was not, so instead he slammed shoulder-first into the flimsy corrugated sheet metal door with a loud clattering noise that reverberated through the half-empty warehouse.

At that moment, several of the Taliban burst into the small office at the other end of the warehouse. Their voices sounded agitated and a couple of them were carrying torches whose beams were flittering across the interior of the large storage space as the fighters moved around.

Andrew winced from the pain in his shoulder and then quickly took a couple of steps back, pointing his gun at the lock on the metal door. Shielding his face with his left hand and turning away his head, he fired three times into the lock. The noise from the gunshots sounded unnaturally loud inside the metal warehouse, and the voices at the other end immediately exploded into full shouting and yelling. The Taliban fighters now knew exactly where he was. Glancing towards the other end of the warehouse, it looked to Andrew like there might have been four or five of them.

Almost immediately, those of them who could see Andrew from where they stood raised their weapons and began firing. Bullets smacked into the flimsy corrugated metal sheets of the warehouse walls and then tore through to the other side.

Andrew swung his stolen Kalashnikov off his shoulder, pulled back the slide to chamber the first round and then jammed the stock into his shoulder and opened fire. The submachinegun spat out three bullets and then it jammed.

'Fuck!' he shouted.

Without wasting time, Andrew let it drop to the floor, and then he whipped out his pistol and fired four shots in the general direction of the Taliban. Then he ran forward again and planted his left shoulder into the door with all the power and momentum he could muster. The lock on the door disintegrated as the door burst open, and Andrew now found himself outside in the darkness. However, there was no time to dawdle as the bullets kept coming, slamming into the metal sheets behind him and then ricocheting noisily off into the night.

Andrew suddenly spotted another warehouse about one hundred meters away. He sprinted as fast as he could for the building and quickly closed the distance. When he got there, he looked back and was able to see the first of the Taliban fighters emerging cautiously from the doorway. They clearly thought he might be lying in wait for them, and were crouching down along the exterior of the warehouse shouting to each other. Their eyes could not have accustomed themselves to the darkness yet, and as far as he could see, none of them had spotted him yet.

Crouched over and trying to stay in the shadows, Andrew quickly made his way along the wall facing the small group of Taliban fighters. He then slipped unseen around the corner of the building and found himself under a wide but narrow window placed roughly at shoulder height off the ground. He raised his arm and slammed his elbow into the glass, which shattered. Reaching inside, he managed to unhook the clasp and push the window open. He jumped up, placed his arms on the windowsill, and was then able to drag himself up and into the room on the other side. It looked like a small metal workshop.

As he poked his head up and looked out of another high-up window facing the warehouse, he could see the fighters fanning out with their torches sweeping the area in front of them. At the back of the group, one of them had the right side of his face partly lit up in a faint blue glow. He was talking to someone on his phone.

★          ★          ★

Inside the noisy vibrating interior of the Mi-17 helicopter, affectionately known as a flying tank because of its durability, Anton Bortnik's mobile phone suddenly started ringing, and if it had not been set to also vibrate, he would not have noticed. By the time he pulled it out of his pocket he had missed the call, but he could see who it had been. It was one of his local Taliban contacts in Kabul. He tapped the button to return the call and waited for his contact to pick up while he looked out of the window at the dry, mountainous and sparsely populated landscape racing past in the gloom of dusk.

When the Taliban contact finally answered, they had a brief exchange in Pashto, while Dubois and Morozov looked on, clearly sensing from Bortnik's tone of voice that something important was happening. Then Bortnik hung up.

'Anton, what is happening?' asked Morozov, eyes narrow and a hard look on his face.

'According to my *Basmachi* contact in Kabul, there seems to be a bit of a situation at the warehouse in Herat,' said the GRU operative, using the old Russian derogatory term for Afghans, Uzbeks and Turkmen.

'What?' exclaimed Dubois, looking both confused, anxious and irritated. 'What the hell do you mean?'

Bortnik looked at Dubois impassively for a few seconds, as if surprised that Morozov's companion actually spoke. Then he turned back to face Morozov.

'Someone killed two guards and entered the warehouse,' said Bortnik. 'Some local Talibs are pursuing. We are about twenty minutes out. Things might get interesting.'

Morozov grinned at his friend and compatriot. 'Davai!' he said, using the ubiquitous Russian term variously meaning 'come on!' or 'let's go!', sounding as if he had been bored for a very long time and now finally had the prospect of some action ahead of him.

Bortnik chuckled and shook his head, looking over at his friend.

'Pantera, you old dog,' he said. 'Don't ever change.'

# TWENTY-SIX

Andrew ducked down again and quickly scanned the metal workshop. He was now sweating and his heart was racing. There seemed to be nothing in the workshop that was of any use, so he left it and found himself in what looked like a large storage facility for military vehicles. There was no light in the warehouse itself, but the light from the workshop allowed him to make out some of what it contained. Lined up in three rows were American Humvees, old Soviet armoured personnel carriers and four-wheel-drive jeeps that looked like they had the insignia of the Afghan Army on them.

This was his chance to put some distance between himself and his pursuers. All he had to do was find a vehicle with enough fuel to get out of there and get a couple of kilometres away.

He also had to call for extraction. Pulling out his mobile phone, he sent a simple text message to a recipient in the intelligence office inside the British Embassy in Pakistan, containing three pieces of information. A codeword for his status. Another codeword for which of the three possible extraction sites he was making his way to, and finally a local time for when he expected to be at the extraction site. There was significant uncertainty attached to the latter, but he had no other choice. He then began moving down one of the aisles between the many vehicles, carrying his torch and looking at them one by one trying to find a suitable option, and that was when he spotted it.

At the far end of the row of vehicles on the right-hand side of the warehouse and facing towards the large sliding doors directly in front, was a large hulking steel beast. It was a T-62 medium battle tank, the little brother of the famous T-72 main battle tank that had been designed for large scale armoured battles against NATO in central and western Europe. With its low profile, high speed and manoeuvrability and a centre-mounted turret emplacement, the T-62 had been a useful addition to the Soviet armoury in Afghanistan during the late 1980s.

Like all Soviet military equipment, it was built to last and to take a beating. Soviet tanks, unlike their temperamental western counterparts, were known for being almost impervious to adverse conditions such as weather or terrain, and they required very little maintenance over their lifespan. This made them perfect for deployment in a country like Afghanistan.

Andrew just stood there for a moment, gawping at the imposing vehicle whilst considering the wisdom of what he was about to do. The tank's hull was almost seven metres long and over three metres wide, and the imposing vehicle weighed just over 35 tons.

With sloped frontal armour more than ten centimetres thick at the front, a powerful 115 mm gun and a coaxial machine gun mounted on the top, it was truly a beast.

Andrew could now hear the voices of the Taliban fighters coming closer. It was a question of time before they would be inside the building. With his stolen Kalashnikov he might be able to take out one or two of them before they overwhelmed him, but he did not fancy his chances against all of them at the same time. The alternative was to make a run for it and hope to lose them in the sprawling southern suburbs of Herat. But then he would still need to find a way to get out of the city and make it to his rendezvous point.

He looked again at the T-62 and decided it was his best bet as long as it still worked. And if it still had fuel. And if he could figure out how to drive it. That was a lot of *ifs*, but his options were becoming more limited with every minute that passed. He finally made up his mind.

*Who dares wins*, he thought to himself.

★     ★     ★

Inside the Mi-17 that was racing across the Afghan countryside at less than 100 metres altitude, Bortnik was handing a bag with a Kalashnikov submachine gun, a semi-automatic handgun, ammunition and a tactical Kevlar vest to Morozov. Morozov checked his weapons, strapped on the vest and attached hand grenades to it with the same calmness and familiarity that most people exhibit when they put on their trainers.

Bortnik was also getting himself ready, taking out the magazine of his submachine gun, checking the bullets and slapping it back in. Dubois sat by the window, watching them and clutching the bag of cash he had brought with him from Moscow.

'Five minutes,' shouted Bortnik over the noise of the helicopter.

Morozov gave a thumbs-up and racked the slide on his submachine gun, chambering the first round.

'Do I get a gun?' shouted Dubois indignantly.

Bortnik and Morozov looked at each other in silence for a few moments, and then Bortnik shrugged and tossed Dubois a pistol.

Morozov looked at the Frenchman with a scornful expression. Then he nodded at the bag in Dubois' lap.

'Just don't shoot the money, ok?'

★      ★      ★

Aboard the USS George Washington in the Gulf of Oman, Collin McGregor received the all-clear to take his squad topside and board the Sikorsky MH-60M Black Hawk helicopter waiting on the flight deck. The aircraft carrier was now less than 50 kilometres southeast of the Pakistani coastal city of Gwadar, which put it less than 100 kilometres from Iranian territorial waters. This was as close as the carrier's captain was prepared to go since the Iranian navy was likely to jump at any opportunity to provoke an incident with the U.S. Navy.

McGregor and his team had been taking part in a multinational anti-piracy training exercise over the past several weeks off the coast of Somalia in the Arabian Sea and the Gulf of Aden, and they had been at the Diego Garcia Airbase for some well-deserved R&R when the call had come through to join the USS George Washington carrier strike group in the Gulf of Oman for an extraction mission.

It was only during the mission briefing a couple of hours earlier that McGregor had discovered that the mission was to fly into Afghanistan, find Andrew Sterling and get him out safely. He had no doubt that his team would perform commendably on all missions of this type regardless of who the subject was, but there was no denying that it added an additional dimension when the extraction target was a fellow SAS soldier, a superior officer and a friend.

Soon after, McGregor and his squad ascended to the flight deck on one of the three enormous aircraft elevators of the carrier, along with the black-painted helicopter. As they emerged into the sunset, he felt the cool wind on his face and the salty-smelling sea air fill his lungs. The gusts tugged at the Black Hawk's long slim rotor blades, making them flop lazily up and down as the two U.S. Marine Corps pilots climbed aboard and commenced their pre-flight checks.

Within minutes, the chopper had spun up its powerful engines and the team members were strapped in. Then the Black Hawk lifted off and headed due north on its nearly one-thousand-kilometre trip across Pakistan to a designated extraction point southeast of the city of Herat in Afghanistan. The Black Hawk's effective range is

2,200 kilometres, so they would only have a few minutes at the extraction site before they would be *Bingo Fuel*, meaning they would only just have enough fuel left to return safely to the carrier.

The Black Hawk accelerated away from the carrier group, and as it approached the Pakistani coast and accelerated to its cruising speed of 280 km/h, the pilot descended to below 200 feet or around 60 metres in order to avoid detection by radar. Minutes later it tore across the beach thirty kilometres east of Gwadar in a sparsely populated area and began flying NOE, or nap-of-the-earth, hugging the terrain as it made its way towards its destination.

★      ★      ★

Andrew climbed up onto the tank and opened the hatch. Then he swung his legs down into the crew compartment, and just as he did so, the first couple of Taliban fighters entered the metal workshop. They were carrying torches and immediately spotted Andrew sitting atop the tank.

One of them opened fire almost instantly, and as Andrew dropped inside and closed the hatch after himself, he could hear the bullets pinging harmlessly off the tank's thick armour plating. The crew space inside the steel beast was surprisingly cramped considering the huge size of the vehicle, but he quickly found the driver's seat.

As he slumped down into the seat, inspecting the controls and gauges which were all in Russian, Andrew suddenly realised that he was quite safe in there, at least for the moment. These fighters only had small calibre weapons which would barely be able to scrape the paint off the tank, let alone damage it in any meaningful way.

It was only if they called in reinforcement, which they surely would, that he might end up in real danger. There were plenty of armour-piercing rockets and explosive charges in the Taliban's possession, so unless he was able to figure out how to start the engine fast, things could turn very ugly very quickly.

As part of his officer training in the SAS, Andrew had taken an intensive Russian language course. However, that was many years ago, and Russian Cyrillic, the written language with its mix of Greek and Latin characters along with uniquely Russian characters introduced by Peter the Great, can be difficult to get used to for westerners precisely because they often look deceptively similar to the Latin alphabet.

Eventually, he found the master switch for the electrical circuits and flicked it. Instantly, the dull turquoise-painted dashboard in front of him lit up. Then he located the large red ignition switch which he turned to the right, and after a few violent coughs, the diesel engine sputtered to life, revving up rapidly but then settling down to idle with a contented growling noise.

Andrew could now hear one or two of the Taliban fighters climbing on top of the tank and attempting to open the hatch, but Andrew had locked it from the inside. One of the fighters shouted and banged on the hatch, making Andrew shake his head in disbelief. Did the man really think Andrew would open up if he just shouted angrily?

There were two gear levers next to him, one large and one small, so he assumed it was like driving a tractor with low gears and high gears. Andrew pushed down what he assumed was the clutch. Then he shifted the small lever up to select low gear mode, and then the large lever up and to the left to select first gear. He then gripped the controls with both hands and gently let go of the clutch. Immediately the hulking beast jerked forward slightly and then began crawling very slowly towards the warehouse doors around five meters away.

Outside, the Taliban fighters were shouting even more urgently now, and the one on top of the tank began slamming the butt of his rifle onto the hatch. After a few seconds he seemed to give up and leap down, and instead he tried to shoot at the small glass viewport on top of the tank's cupola, but the bullet just ricocheted off into the roof of the warehouse.

Inside the tank, Andrew depressed the clutch again and shifted into third low gear, after which the tank increased its speed to walking speed. It quickly made it to the doors of the warehouse, the barrel of its gun making contact first and pressing inexorably against the door on the right, causing it to deform and buckle like a can of sardines. Soon the tank itself reached the end of the warehouse, and at around five kilometres per hour, it drove through and then completely shredded the corrugated steel sheets as if they had been tin foil.

At this point, the Taliban seemed to lose their composure because they began ineffectually firing their Kalashnikovs in long bursts at the tank. Andrew could hear the pitter-patter of bullets striking the hull, and it was a very odd feeling, given how much experience he had had with the damage a submachine gun could do to a human body.

While looking out through the forward viewport, he shifted the tank into first high gear, at which point it leapt forward and accelerated to fast jogging speed. He then steered it slightly to the right towards what looked like a road leading due west. Once he reached it, he shifted gears again a couple of times after which the speed indicator read 40 km/h.

In the meantime, two more pickup trucks with Taliban fighters had arrived, but Andrew was unaware of this since he was unable to see behind him. However, the driver of one of the trucks decided to overtake the tank, at which point Andrew was able to not only see the truck but also begin swerving erratically as he raced along the road, hoping to collide with any other trucks attempting to do the same thing. The fighters in the truck ahead of him began firing their guns but to no effect, and Andrew found himself completely calm in the face of the incoming hail of bullets. He then shifted into the highest gear, and the tank was now barrelling down the straight road leading due west out of Herat at over 50 km/h.

Suddenly, he had an idea. Aiming straight down the road and then locking the controls in place, he slipped out of his seat and climbed up to the hatch. He unlocked it, swung the open hatch and stood on a small metal platform partway inside the tank that allowed a gunner to operate the coaxial machinegun mounted on the top of the turret. The machinegun used 7.62 mm ammunition and could fire 2,500 rounds per minute, making it a fearsome weapon in its own right.

There were now two pickup trucks behind him in addition to the one in front, and as soon as the Taliban fighters saw him emerge from the turret they opened up with their Kalashnikovs. Andrew grabbed the coaxial machinegun, swung it around to aim at the truck in front of him and held down the trigger. Instantly, the machinegun spewed out a hail of fiery lead along with leftover glowing gunpowder embers. Several of the bullets ripped through the fighters on the back of the pickup truck, and one of them fell off and onto the road in front of the tank. The T-62 ploughed over him, but Andrew did not even feel so much as a small jolt in the tank as it ran him over. The truck then swerved wildly and ran off the road, tore through a fence and slammed into a small power substation which exploded in a plume of brilliant white sparks. The entire area in that part of Herat was then suddenly plunged into darkness.

Andrew then swung the gun around and unloaded on the two other pursuing vehicles. They immediately began swerving and braking, letting themselves fall behind so as to make it harder for Andrew to hit them. Andrew glanced over his shoulder in the direction of travel and did a double-take when he saw what lay ahead of him. It looked like the road was about to go across a bridge over a small river, and the tank was beginning to veer ever so slightly to the right.

Andrew scrambled back down to the driver's seat, gripped the controls and managed to steer the tank onto and over the bridge just in time. A few more seconds, and it would have crashed through the concrete guard rails and gone plunging into the river.

The hatch was still open, but he decided to leave it like that. The tank had a single but powerful floodlight mounted on its front, and Andrew flicked the switch for it, illuminating the road directly ahead of him. Recalling the maps of the area, he was now pretty sure he knew where he was after that river crossing, and so he decided that now was the time to look for a place to head southwest and out into the desert. The urban sprawl was now becoming much more sparse, and he soon came to a place where he could drive smoothly off the road and into open fields. The rougher terrain and the speed of the T-62 made the tank jolt up and down as it traversed the fields. There were lots of large rocks and boulders on the uneven ground, and he realised that whereas he would be able to plough through them, the pursuing cars would not. They were probably still chasing him, although they were most likely hanging back to avoid smashing into large rocks and also staying out of range of the tank's machinegun.

Briefly feeling relieved, Andrew then realised that he was almost certain to run out of fuel before they did, at which point he would be a sitting duck until the Taliban could bring an armour piercing anti-tank weapon to his location, and then it would be all over. Unless, of course, he surrendered, which he also didn't like the sound of. He would almost certainly end up being tortured and used as some sort of bargaining chip by the Taliban.

Steering the tank across the increasingly desert-like terrain towards the southwest, Andrew was racking his brain for a solution. He suddenly remembered seeing a fuel depot on the maps of the area he had studied before entering Afghanistan. He seemed to remember that it was to the west and slightly south of Herat, so he steered the tank due west towards where he thought it might be.

Immediately after changing course, he spotted the depot around a kilometre ahead of him. It was a small collection of tall steel fuel tanks grouped together on a plateau up a shallow incline. He pointed the tank directly at the site and checked the time on his wristwatch. He was meant to be at the extraction point in less than half an hour. If he couldn't make it, the chopper would almost certainly not have enough fuel to wait for him for more than a few minutes before having to return to the carrier in the Gulf of Oman.

He floored the gas pedal, accelerating the tank to its maximum speed. It practically flew across the dusty terrain, leaving a huge cloud of dust in its wake which was lit up by the pursuing pickup trucks.

The tank roared up the incline and tore through the metal fence as if it wasn't even there. Then Andrew steered the T-62 towards an elongated fuel tank lying horizontally on the ground. At one end it had a set of metal pipes sticking out from it and going into the ground. Keeping his speed up, Andrew smashed into the pipes and the T-62 ripped right through them and tore them off the fuel tank, which produced a large cloud of fuel hanging in the air. Instantly, the sparks from the shredded metal produced by the T-62 ripping through the pipes ignited the fuel, causing a huge airburst explosion that ripped open several of the other fuel tanks. In a chain reaction that tore through the fuel depot in a matter of seconds, an enormous orange ball of fire erupted over the site, enveloping the T-62 as it rammed through the depot and shot out on the other side, burning fuel covering its surface and leaving a trail of fire on the ground behind it.

★          ★          ★

From just over five kilometres away, the massive explosion in the desert was clearly visible as it bloomed up silently into the night sky to the southwest of Herat. The low-hanging clouds were lit up from below, creating an unnatural vista for anyone who happened to see it. Its initial intense orange glow gradually faded as the fuel began to burn itself out, and a large mushroom cloud of sooty smoke began roiling its way upwards from what had been a fuel depot just a few seconds earlier.

When it happened, the interior of the Mi-17 was lit up with orange light coming in through the front of the helicopter. Instantly, both Bortnik and Morozov unfastened their seat belts and moved up behind the pilots to see what had happened. Dubois, who remained seated clutching the bag of money, looked from Bortnik to Morozov and back again.

'What the hell was that?' he yelled anxiously.

The two Russians ignored him and kept staring out of the front of the helicopter. Bortnik's phone rang almost immediately thereafter, and Dubois could hear the sound of a voice yelling in Pashto. Then Bortnik had a quick exchange with the pilots, after which the two Russians returned to the passenger cabin and picked up their weapons.

'Answer me, damn it,' shrieked Dubois. 'What is going on?'

Morozov looked at him with a mixture of irritation and disdain.

'Change of plan. The item is no longer in the warehouse, so we're about to make sure you can return to Athens with your damn box,' he said. 'Bortnik and I are going to retrieve it. Whatever happens, you just stay strapped in, do you understand? You would only get yourself killed, and then I would lose my bonus.'

★      ★      ★

The massive explosion of fuel enveloped and shook the T-62 violently. However, it was designed to withstand explosions even more destructive than this, so although Andrew instinctively ducked his head down inside the driver's seat, he was quite safe. The tank continued forward, carried by its own momentum, and raced down the incline on the other side of the fuel depot. Within seconds he had to swerve violently to avoid smashing into two heavy fuel trucks parked on the other side of it. This sent him in what he believed was a southerly direction, but he had now partly lost his sense of direction.

Although he had studied the maps of south-eastern Herat and those of the extraction sites, the truth was that he no longer knew exactly where he was or which direction he was travelling in. This meant that he would struggle to find the chosen extraction site, and he had no means of contacting the incoming Black Hawk helicopter. He had to rely on the rescue team's ability to improvise.

And there was now another problem. Although his detour through the fuel depot might have put off the pursuing pick-up trucks, it also meant that every single Taliban fighter in the city now knew exactly where he was. They would be swarming his location within minutes, and he was running out of time and options.

A couple of minutes later as the T-62 raced across the rocky desert at full speed, Andrew suddenly heard the worst possible sound he could have heard. The engine sputtered for a brief moment but kept going. He checked the fuel gauge and it was now reading almost zero, a small red light having come on at the bottom of the gauge.

Whatever was left of the fuel inside the fuel tank was now sloshing around and depriving the engine of diesel every few seconds. It would be a matter of minutes, or possibly less before the engine would grind to a halt, leaving him stranded and a sitting duck for the Taliban.

'Come on girl,' he said through gritted teeth. 'Don't give up on me now.'

He had barely spoken the words before the engine coughed violently and the T-62 shuddered amidst a staccato deceleration that made him lurch forward a couple of times in his seat.

'Fuck me,' he winced. 'What a bloody stupid way to die.'

As the tank juddered to a halt, Andrew angled himself out of the seat and climbed up to poke his head out of the hatch. Some distance behind him he could see at least three pickup trucks with floodlights on. They were approaching rapidly across the uneven desert, and they looked like they were no more than a couple of minutes away. But that was not what got his attention, because above them in the night sky was a helicopter, clearly of Russian design and with its own floodlights pointing at him and the disabled T-62.

The chopper was just in the process of overtaking the pickup trucks below it when Andrew emerged, and after staring at it dumbfounded for a few seconds he grabbed the coaxial machinegun, swung it around towards the rear of the tank and aimed it in the direction of the helicopter, or rather, where he guessed it might be in a couple of seconds taking travel time and bullet drop into account.

When he held down the trigger, the machine gun released another hail of bullets. Now that it was dark, Andrew realised that the machine gun's ammunition had tracer rounds mixed in with the regular 7.62 mm ammunition, so the gun spat out a glowing phosphorous green projectile roughly twice per second, which lit up the night sky and helped him aim the gun in the darkness.

It didn't take long for some of the bullets to find their mark. Renowned for its sturdy build quality and ability to deal with small arms fire, the Mi-17 initially soaked up the incoming fire with the ballistics plating on its belly, but a couple of rounds slammed into the glass canopy at the front of the cockpit and tore through the helicopter's interior.

As Andrew watched, it immediately veered off to the left exposing its side, at which point several bullets connected with its tail rotor which then took damage and started smoking and producing a disconcertingly loud shrieking noise.

As the pilot fought for control of the chopper, it lost altitude and left a trail of smoke behind it whilst slowly making a long left turn away from the T-62. Seeing it withdraw, Andrew switched his aim towards the approaching pickup trucks and fired again. The machine gun fired twice, but then it produced a loud click. The ammo magazine was empty.

'Shit,' exclaimed Andrew, now fully realising how desperate his situation had become.

He reached down into the tank and extracted his stolen Kalashnikov. He also grabbed the backpack with the silver chest and slung it over his shoulder. Then he climbed down the cupola of the tank and jumped the rest of the way onto the dusty ground. He had no real plan, except to run as far from the tank as fast as possible, and then hope that he would be able to find a place to hide before the pickup trucks full of Taliban fighters arrived.

Suddenly the ground around him and the tank exploded in brilliant white light from a powerful floodlight, and only then did he hear the suppressed muffled sound of the MH-60 Black Hawk helicopter's stealth rotors. It was less than a hundred metres away and coming in at an angle that allowed him to see the first soldier in the stack by the open door at the side of the chopper.

Next to him was the third member of the flight crew manning an M61 Vulcan machinegun which is capable of firing 6,000 rounds of 20 mm high-velocity rounds per minute. As soon as Andrew looked up at the chopper, the gunner opened up with the Vulcan at the approaching pickup trucks. Amid a deafening roar, it spewed out its PGU-28/B semi-armour piercing high explosive incendiary rounds, which covered the distance to the trucks in a split second, ripping through its targets one by one and leaving nothing by burning and mangled metal and the bodies of Taliban fighters. Some of them managed to jump out just in time, rolling on the ground and scrambling for cover behind rocks or in small depressions in the ground.

Within less than a minute, all of the trucks were reduced to fiery metal junk, and the Taliban who had survived had either fled or were now hiding. Not a single one of them attempted to return fire in the face of the devastating power of the Vulcan.

The Black Hawk descended quickly about fifty meters away from the T-62, and as soon as it touched down Collin McGregor and his squad fanned out from the chopper and assumed a kneeling firing position, attempting to cover the helicopter from all angles.

Andrew rose from his cover next to the tank and sprinted towards the chopper. As he got close, McGregor rose and reached out to him to guide him to the chopper's side door.

'Andy!' shouted McGregor over the noise of the turboshaft engine and the thudding rotor blades. 'Are you injured?'

'Good to see you, McGregor,' shouted Andrew, boarding the helicopter. 'That's a negative.'

'That was one hell of a signal flare,' shouted McGregor. 'Did you set off a small nuke?'

'Fuel depot,' grinned Andrew. 'It was all they had.'

'Alright, mate. Get strapped in,' shouted McGregor. Then he reached up to his helmet to activate the squad's comms system. 'Alpha Team. Package is secure. Back to the chopper. We are leaving.'

Without a moment's hesitation, all of the squad members rose and backed up quickly and in unison towards the waiting helicopter. Then they quickly re-boarded it, and within seconds the pilot had lifted off, accelerating the Black Hawk towards the south whilst flying as low above the desert floor as possible.

A couple of minutes later there was no trace of either the chopper or the SAS squad, except for a handful of burning pickup trucks and a few terrified Taliban fighters. In the distance, the damaged Mi-17 was limping away with smoke trailing out of its tail rotor. It was never going to make it back to Kabul, but that was not the pilot's intention. All he wanted to do was to get clear of the gunfire and land somewhere relatively safe before the chopper failed altogether.

★          ★          ★

When Andrew took the call from Colonel Strickland several hours later, he was on the plane back from Diego Garcia to Baghdad. The Honda HA-420 had been sent ahead to the airbase as soon as it was confirmed that he and the squad of SAS soldiers had made it back to the USS George Washington.

Andrew provided a detailed debrief over the phone, and the two men agreed for Strickland to arrange transport of the silver chest from Baghdad to

London, where it would be handed over secretly to the British Museum for study.

'Andy, I need to speak to you about something else,' said Strickland, sounding sombre. 'The Metropolitan Police's forensics team has completed a thorough investigation of the safehouse on 27 Charlton Place.'

'Ok,' said Andrew and leaned forward slightly in his seat. 'What did they find?'

'They found no traces of DNA that might help us identify the killer. The unique marks on the bullets that were left by the barrel of the gun they were fired from, have also not been linked to any other shootings in the UK. They are currently going over international databases but they tell me that it is highly unlikely they will find a match.'

'Oh,' said Andrew. 'That is very disappointing. Those two Met officers deserved better.'

'Yes,' said Strickland. 'The Met hasn't given up of course, but we will have to wait and see if they can make a breakthrough. Anyway, there is another route for this investigation. They recovered Dawson's phone.'

'Really?' said Andrew. 'I would have thought the killer might have grabbed that.'

'So would I,' replied Strickland, 'but apparently Dawson had it with him in the bathroom and managed to send a message to someone minutes before he was killed. We think this was his backup plan, in just such an event. He clearly did not feel safe, even under the protection of the police inside a safehouse.'

'So, who did he send it to?' asked Andrew.

'Well,' replied Strickland. 'It was an encrypted message sent using one of those messaging services that delete the message from the sender's phone and from the central server as soon as it has been sent. The recipient was a London-based journalist who has a track record of exposing corporate corruption, so we paid her a polite visit and she agreed to cooperate.'

'And the content of the message?'

'A simple User ID and password for a secure server that contained a document outlining his allegations against ZOE Technologies. I will send it to you, but the gist of it was that the company is running a secret research program somewhere in the US, involving genetically engineered human embryos.'

'Crikey,' said Andrew. 'Any more detail?'

'No. Nothing actionable, unfortunately,' replied Strickland. 'I get the feeling that the document was written in a hurry. After all, he was about to spill the beans anyway, so to speak. But it was probably more or less what he was going to tell Inspector Worthington, had he had a chance to speak to her.'

'I see,' said Andrew. 'So, I guess the police can't make any arrests based on this?'

'Correct,' said Strickland. 'We have no hard evidence. All we have is the conjecture of two people who are both dead, and we have no idea where this secret lab is, if it even exists. With regards to Dawson, his allegations also come with no tangible evidence. And we all know that ZOE Technologies would simply claim he was a disgruntled former employee, and then they would bury the Metropolitan Police in lawsuits.'

'That's a shame,' said Andrew. 'From everything I have seen so far from Alexis, Ackerman, Dubois and their goons, they are definitely up to no good.'

'I completely agree,' said Strickland. 'I think that our best bet is to put surveillance on Ackerman and see if we can get lucky. He is probably highly paranoid, but it is worth a try. I will liaise with the FBI and tell them what we have. They might agree to do it.'

'Alright,' said Andrew. 'Let me know if anything else crops up. I am going to catch some sleep before we land in Baghdad. I also need to come up with a way of explaining to Fiona why I almost got shot dead and then blown up.'

'Ah,' said Strickland, sounding as if he was hesitating for a moment. 'That leads me to the last thing I wanted to mention to you. Fiona is no longer in Baghdad.'

'What?' said Andrew, sounding perplexed. 'What do you mean?'

'She took a flight to Venice a few hours after you left for Turkmenistan,' replied Strickland.

Andrew was speechless for a few seconds.

'Ok,' he said haltingly. 'Did she say why?'

'Something about a tomb,' said Strickland. 'I thought she might have told you.'

'Not at all,' said Andrew, sounding confused. 'Whatever the reason, it must have been something she came up with after I left. Very strange.'

'Well, she did ask me to tell you to contact her as soon as you land in Baghdad. Apparently, she left a note for you explaining what she is doing.'

'Right,' said Andrew, rubbing his chin. 'I guess I will have to wait then. Thank you, sir.'

'No problem, old boy. I will speak to you soon.'

# Twenty-Seven

When Fiona exited the Stazione di Venezia Santa Lucia and walked out onto the large square in front of the box-like brutalist 1930s building serving as the city's train station, the sun was shining from a clear blue sky and it was mid-afternoon. Directly ahead of her, across the square and on the other side of the Grand Canal, was the prominent $17^{th}$ century neoclassical Chiesa di San Simeon Piccolo church, with its large eye-catching green oxidised copper dome and white marble colonnade. In front of it, sightseeing boats and smaller water taxis were slowly making their way along the canal, dutifully keeping their speed below the city-wide limit of 5 kilometres per hour, which more or less equates to a brisk walking speed.

Fiona checked the time on her phone, and then proceeded straight ahead to the edge of the canal where she turned right along the quay towards a water-taxi stand. She briefly considered taking a gondola but decided that it would be too slow, so she greeted the driver of a motorised water taxi, provided him with her desired destination, and then sat down near the front of the small boat. A few seconds later the boat had joined the northeast-bound traffic along the Grand Canal and was approaching the first long bend in the giant S-shape, with which the canal winds its way through and across the ancient city of Venice from the northwest to the southeast.

It was only a couple of hours since she had landed on a commercial eight-hour Turkish Airlines flight from Baghdad to Venice via Istanbul. Luckily, she had managed to sleep for most of the flight from Turkey, so she felt well-rested. Sitting in the water taxi and wearing a sheer white blouse, cream linen trousers and a hat and sunglasses, she looked for all the world like any other tourist out enjoying the sights.

It was less than twelve hours ago that she had left the hotel room in the Baghdad International Airport Hotel and rushed onto the flight to Venice. She had had no means of contacting Andrew, so she had left him a note written up on his own laptop, which she had left behind in the room after paying for two more nights in advance. She expected him to be back by then, and if he wasn't, then the hotel bill would be the least of their worries.

The reason for her swift departure was simple. While researching Ptolemy's diary, she had decided to fire up Andrew's laptop. This had allowed her to access Alexis's emails, as well as any recordings from her office aboard the Hypatia that had been made by the listening device planted by Andrew when he had snuck on board about a week earlier.

Alexis had communicated very little during that week, and almost all of her emails had been related to seemingly innocuous ZOE Technologies business. However, the listening device had recorded an in-person visit aboard the Hypatia from an Englishman whose identity Fiona had been unable to hear fully. All she had picked up was Alexis referring to him once as Mr Halliday when she first greeted him as he arrived in her office.

Apparently, Mr Halliday was a history researcher, possibly at some university in the UK, and he had been invited by Alexis to discuss a new theory of his regarding the whereabouts of the tomb of Alexander the Great. He had sounded nervous, and he clearly felt out of place on the multi-million-pound superyacht, but he had been willing enough to divulge his still preprint theory to Alexis, no doubt in exchange for a generous fee.

Mr Halliday's theory rested on three pillars. The first pillar was the writings of the Greek scholar Libanius, whose mention of the tomb of Alexander in 390 CE is the last known reference to the tomb still being in Alexandria.

The second pillar was the edict issued in 391 CE by Roman Emperor Theodosius I that banned so-called paganism. This was the edict that Alexis had referred to when she lamented the death of Hypatia to Fiona during their visit to Alexis's mansion in Athens. This edict had incited Christian zealots to persecute so-called pagans and to burn down and destroy non-Christian temples and other places of worship in Alexandria. This caused the fire in the Library of Alexandria, and possibly also resulted in the destruction of Alexander's tomb, which by then had laid undisturbed in the city for centuries.

The third pillar was Saint Mark the Evangelist, who is widely credited with bringing Christianity to North Africa, as well as being the founder of the Church of Alexandria which today is known as the Coptic Orthodox Church. He was killed in Alexandria in 68 CE by pagans who supposedly disposed of his body.

However, more than four centuries later, more or less at the same time as the Christian riots, his body supposedly reappeared suddenly in the city.

Halliday's theory proposed that the newly rediscovered body of Saint Mark was actually that of Alexander. The last reference to Alexander was only two years before the body of Saint Mark was supposedly found, and Halliday theorised that Alexander's body had essentially been rebranded as that of Saint Mark, in order for it to escape destruction at the hands of the Christian zealots during the turmoil in the city after Theodosius I's edict. According to Halliday, the plan worked because the body of Alexander, now masquerading as that of Saint Mark, remained safe in Alexandria for several more centuries.

However, by the late 7th century CE, much of North Africa including the city of Alexandria, had been conquered by Muslim forces, and since tensions between resident Christians and Muslims were rising in the city, two Italian merchants took it upon themselves to transport what they believed to be the body of Saint Mark out of Alexandria to safety in Venice. Here it was kept in the palace of the local magistrate called the Doge or Duke, until a grand new church could be built to house the saint's remains.

When the Saint Mark's Basilica was eventually completed in 836 CE, the supposed body of Saint Mark, or possibly Alexander the Great, was then transferred to the crypt of the basilica where it remained until 1835, when it was again moved up into the body of the church and placed in the chancel inside a raised tomb on the high altar.

Alexis had listened intently to Mr Halliday as he laid out his theory. Even though it was only an audio recording, Fiona could easily imagine the face of Alexis as Halliday presented his rather convincing hypothesis.

Initially, Alexis seemed captivated by what Halliday said, but towards the end of their meeting she suddenly seemed to change and become less interested and almost dismissive. Fiona was sure this was a ruse, intended to make Halliday think that she would not pursue the theory any further. However, as soon as Halliday had left, Alexis had called her assistant and ordered her to ready her corporate jet to take her to Venice as soon as possible. She also asked for Fabian Ackerman to instruct his *asset* to join her there the following day. At that point, Fiona had dropped everything and immediately begun preparing to leave for Venice herself on the earliest available commercial flight. She had to admit to herself that she felt nervous at the prospect of going alone, and she was sure that Andrew would have said it was reckless, but she had decided that she did not have time to wait for him.

Now in a small water taxi on the Grand Canal in Venice, the events of the past few days in Vergina and the ruins of Babylon seemed like they were a million miles away. The sun was warm on her face and the sounds of the many vessels calmly making their way along the canal mixed with the muffled noise of the city's bustling life, made her feel calm and relaxed. As the water taxi came out of the first long right-hand turn of the canal, she could see the huge four-storey Ca' Pesaro gallery of modern art up ahead on her right. They then continued around the bend, and into view came the famous Ponte Rialto bridge, whose current incarnation dates back to the late 16th century.

After another ten minutes they passed under the Ponte dell'Accademia bridge, at which point she could see her destination a few hundred meters ahead on their left.

She had no idea where in Venice Alexis might be staying, except that it was certain to be an extremely expensive hotel. However, there were plenty of those, so Fiona had decided to go straight to where she thought Alexis would eventually turn up: The spectacular multi-domed Byzantine-Venetian style church, the Basilica Cattedrale Patriarcale di San Marco, or Saint Mark's Basilica.

Paying the water-taxi driver and then jumping off the boat and onto the pier a few minutes later, she proceeded to join the throngs of tourists by the quay-side and made her way north past the Doge's Palace on her right, and along the elongated Piazzetta di San Marco square to the main square in front of the basilica, called Piazza San Marco.

She crossed the square, walking past the one-hundred-metre-tall 12th century Campanile bell tower and former lighthouse on her left, and then past the entrance to the basilica itself on her right. She then headed for a small eatery called Caffe Lavena, which had a number of tables out on the square itself where middle-aged male waiters in white jackets were busily tending to the culinary needs of their patrons.

She sat down and placed her handbag on the chair next to her, settling in for an extended stay. She had no idea when Alexis and Ackerman's *asset* might turn up, or if they would even do so today. All she could do was wait, so she ordered a sandwich and a glass of orange juice and made herself comfortable whilst looking at the basilica, also called the Chiesa D'Oro or 'golden church' because of its gilded interior. She took the opportunity to do some people-watching, which was one of her favourite pastimes.

However, as the hours rolled by, the many hundreds of different tourists cycling through the square and its attractions began to take their toll on her. She was constantly looking around for familiar faces, whilst trying not to look like someone who was doing just that. By the end of the afternoon when she was on the brink of deciding that the whole thing was probably a highly risky mistake, and that she should find herself a hotel and try to contact Andrew, she suddenly spotted Alexis walking up towards the basilica from the exact same place where she herself had arrived several hours earlier.

Next to her was another familiar face. The Englishman from the underground Esagila Temple in Babylon. Fiona instantly lowered her head to hide her face under the brim of her hat whilst still tracking the two with her eyes as they made their way to the basilica entrance. It was 4:15 pm, and Fiona knew that the basilica closed at 5:15 pm.

At first, she could not quite believe that they would simply waltz in there along with all the tourists, but then she realised that this was probably just a preliminary scouting expedition. Hesitating for a moment, she waived over the nearest waiter and handed him some cash that would cover the bill and leave a generous tip. Then she grabbed her handbag and walked casually but swiftly towards the basilica's entrance, where she could just see Alexis and her English goon entering past the ticket office.

She joined the queue and was inside after another five minutes. At first, she could not see the two of them, but after moving further into the church she spotted them at the far end, Alexis seemingly inspecting a fresco on a wall next to a gated area, and the brawny-looking man standing behind her a few metres away. They did not seem to be talking. In fact, as far as Fiona could tell, Alexis had not seemed to acknowledge his presence at all so far. He was clearly just there as muscle.

Fiona allowed herself to blend into a group of tourists who were visiting the basilica with a guide. The guide was talking excitedly about the history of the basilica, and loitering at the back of the group, Fiona did her best to appear attentive while also keeping her eyes fixed on Alexis. At one point, Fiona could have sworn that the goon was looking straight at her, but she quickly hid her face under her hat and when she looked over at him again, he had his back to her, seemingly not recognising her from the Esagila Temple.

After another ten minutes and a short walk back and forth along the far end of the church near the altar, Alexis and her goon eventually retraced their steps back towards the exit. But instead of exiting the church, Alexis went to the ticket office again and had a brief exchange with the clerk there. Then she and the Englishman left.

Fiona rushed over to the ticket office and told the clerk that she had been to the restroom and was trying to catch up with her two friends, and could the clerk please give her one of the same tickets that they had just bought. The clerk nodded and produced another ticket, which Fiona quickly paid for. It was only when she walked out of the basilica that she was able to inspect it to find out what it was for. It turned out to be a ticket for a guided tour of off-limits areas inside the basilica after it had closed to the public. The tours were for only four people at a time, and this ticket was for the last tour of the evening at 9 pm.

Fiona exited the basilica, at which point Alexis and the English ex-soldier were now nowhere to be seen. But that did not matter. She knew they would be back in less than five hours. Looking around, Fiona spotted a sign for Bellevue Luxury Rooms, which was a small boutique hotel on the corner of Piazza San Marco, overlooking the bell tower, the square and the basilica itself. Above the sign on the third and fourth floors of the building, she could see the hotel room balconies that overlooked the square.

Deciding she could do with a rest in a comfortable hotel room and thinking that one of those balconies would provide her with a perfect vantage point, she walked around the corner to the main entrance and approached the front desk. Here she paid the eye-watering nightly rate and followed the concierge up to the third floor where her room was. True to the hotel's name, it was a luxurious room furnished in an opulent 18th-century Venetian style. Plush furniture, heavy burgundy-coloured curtains, a giant soft bed with an ornate headboard, a thick carpet and French double doors leading out onto a large balcony with a spectacular view of the basilica.

After a shower and room service dinner, she lay down on the bed with her phone, reading up on the history of the basilica and the crypt underneath it. The current basilica, also known as the Contarini church, was the third incarnation of the church, having been consecrated in 1094 CE. Before that, it existed in two much smaller and less grand versions. The body believed to be that of Saint Mark was placed inside the original church on the site which was known as the Participazio, and whose construction began in 836 CE. After a quick online search, she was able to find a detailed schematic of the basilica's interior.

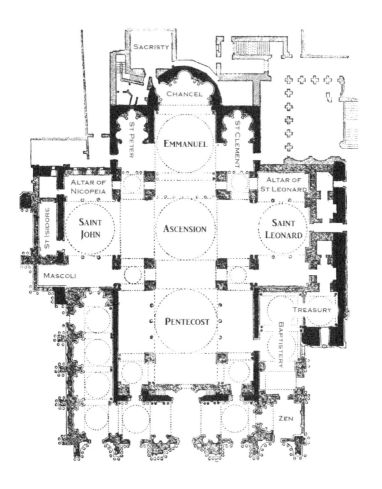

Fiona lay back on the bed and looked up at the ceiling. Could it really be true that the mummified body of Alexander the Great had been lying in that tomb for almost twelve hundred years, masquerading as the body of one of the most important evangelists in the Christian faith?

At half-past eight in the evening, she wrapped herself in a shawl and sat down with a cup of strong coffee on one of the chairs out on the balcony. The square was much less busy now since most tourists were inside the restaurants dotted around the old city, and the locals were at home getting ready for their usual late dining.

At 8:55 pm a small group of three people had gathered by the entrance to the basilica. Judging from their clothes and demeanour, one of them was a female tour guide and the other two, a man and a woman, seemed to be tourists. A few moments later, two more people arrived. One was a large and burly-looking man in a dark suit. Fiona recognised his heavy gait instantly. The other was a slender woman, wearing a cream-coloured business suit, sunglasses and a dark grey scarf wrapped over her head. This was obviously Alexis, attempting to make sure she couldn't be identified.

As the two of them joined the other three, Fiona grabbed her jacket and raced out of the door. She did not wait for the elevator, but instead ran down the stairs to the lobby, out of the hotel and around the corner just in time to see the small group enter the basilica. Fearing she was too late, Fiona jogged towards the entrance to the church and to her immense relief found that the guide had left the door unlocked for the duration of the tour. She slipped inside.

The church was completely empty, except for the small group of five people standing under the first dome high above them after first entering the church.

'These are the Horses of Saint Mark,' said the guide, pointing to a set of four statues of powerful-looking gilded horses. 'They were originally in the

Hippodrome in Constantinople. They were taken in 1204 by the then doge Enrico Dandolo, as part of the spoils from the sacking of that city during the Fourth Crusade.'

Fiona stood completely still in the shadows, surprised at how close she suddenly was to the group. They seemed to have stopped just inside the basilica. After a few minutes, the group walked a bit further into the church.

'There are enough frescos in this church to cover an area of eight thousand square metres,' said the guide, 'and unlike frescos in most other churches which are painted, these are created using gilded mosaics due to the humidity of Venice. Above you, you can see the Dome of Pentecost and the motif is of Saint Peter on the left, and Saint Paul on the right. Below them, you will find the inhabitants of Mesopotamia and Judea.'

Fiona remained quietly behind a set of pillars, hoping that no one had noticed her entering. She waited a few minutes until the group had moved further into the church. They were now under the Dome of Ascension, where it looked like both Alexis and her gorilla did their best to play the role of tourists. Alexis was still wearing her sunglasses, which seemed odd inside a dimly lit church, but she clearly knew that no one would question it.

The basilica is laid out in a cruciform, and the group went through to the Chapel of Saint John and the Altar of Nicopeia in the left arm of the church, where the guide then enlightened them on what they were seeing. Then they proceeded across the nave of the church to the other arm and the Altar of Saint

Leonard. Fiona followed them by slipping unseen into the Zen Chapel, and further along to the Baptistery and the Treasury, managing to stay within earshot of the group the whole time. Inside the treasury were a large number of glass display cases containing gold and silver relics brought back from Constantinople in 1204.

Eventually, the guide took them back to the nave under the Dome of Emmanuel, and finally to the entrance to the Chancel of Saint Mark, also called the presbytery, which is raised five steps from the floor of the basilica and separated from the nave by a Gothic altar screen. The screen itself is held up by eight marble columns and is adorned along the top with small statues of the apostles and a large gilded crucifix at the centre above the doorway to the interior.

'When the current Contarini church was constructed,' said the guide, 'the entire church was raised, which had the effect of enclosing Saint Mark's tomb in the crypt, which was built up around it. So, when the tomb of Saint Mark was finally brought back up into the church proper in 1835, it had at that time been out of public view for close to a millennium.'

The tour guide paused for a moment to let the group admire the altar screen.

'Please follow me,' she then said. 'I will now take you inside the chancel so you can see the tomb up close for yourselves.'

The group filed through the doorway in the marble altar screen, Alexis behind the other two tourists and the bulky, well-dressed Englishman last, who briefly glancing over his shoulder to the empty church as he stooped slightly to go through.

Fiona moved up quickly but silently to stand just inside the small Chapel of Saint Clement where she cautiously peeked around the corner to see the group gather around the tomb, roughly ten metres away.

'Above the tomb, you can see the magnificent altarpiece called the Pala d'Oro, which is made of gold and silver. It is three metres by two metres in size, and is set with 1,927 gems of various kinds. It was made in the year 976.'

Fiona could see the Englishman standing behind the group. As she watched him, he reached inside his jacket and pulled out a gun which he held down low in a straight arm next to and slightly behind his body. It was some sort of pistol with a silencer mounted on the barrel, similar to the one she had seen him with once before. A chill ran down her spine. This was about to get ugly.

'And finally,' said the guide proudly. 'The main attraction. The marble sarcophagus containing the body of Saint Mark, preserved here since 836 CE when it was rescued from Alexandria in Egypt.'

At that moment, Alexis turned calmly to Stone and gave him a nod. He immediately pulled out his pistol and pointed it at the guide.

'Everyone on your knees,' he said in a loud and commanding voice.

He did not seem at all agitated, but sounded as if this was something he did on a regular basis. The three other shocked group members looked terrified and confused, but they quickly complied. The tour guide attempted to say something, but the

Englishman cut her off and barked another order at them.

'Eyes down. Face the floor. Don't move,' he said to her, menacingly. 'And shu'tup, would ya?'

Without saying a word, Alexis gestured at the sarcophagus, and Fiona, horrified by what she had witnessed, could do nothing but watch as the Englishman immediately moved towards the tomb. He stepped up to the sarcophagus, still holding the gun in his right hand, and pushed the huge bronze candleholders off it, sending them clattering loudly onto the marble floor. This elicited a frightened whimper from the tour guide. Then he ripped off the long fabric cloth that had been draped over the tomb and tossed it aside.

Looking over his shoulder at the kneeling trio, the Englishman then tucked the gun back into his chest holster and growled at them in his east London accent.

'Nobody play hero now, alright? Bad for your health.'

Alexis, still without saying a word, moved around calmly to his right and almost out of sight from where Fiona was standing. She then nodded at the sarcophagus.

Stone walked up the final two steps and placed himself right up close to it, feet slightly apart. Then he positioned his hands on the edge of the thick marble slab that was the lid of the tomb. Gripping it tightly, he strained for a few seconds, but then the lid came free of the sarcophagus and he flipped it over with a roar, sending it tipping onto the marble floor behind the sarcophagus where it broke into several pieces with a deafening crash that reverberated throughout the huge basilica.

Momentarily stunned by the barbarism of what she had witnessed, and with her heart pounding in her chest, Fiona then pulled back from the corner she had been lurking next to and began frantically looking around for anything that might help her stop this madness. She briefly considered attempting to phone the police, but there was no way she would be able to do that without alerting Alexis and her goon.

There were several large candleholders in the small chapel where she was standing, but she didn't fancy her chances in a swinging match with the hulking east-ender. Then she spotted something that might work.

Looking up high above the chancel, she saw an enormous circular metal candelabra with dozens of ornate spokes connecting the centre with an elaborately decorated metal ring surrounding it. The candelabra was studded with electric lights and was hanging by a long metal chain, which in turn was connected to a rope looping through a large hook in the ceiling, and then extending down along the wall and into the chapel where she was hiding. Inside the chapel, it wrapped around a large bronze hook that was embedded into the granite wall.

Inside the chancel, Alexis had now walked up to the sarcophagus, placed her hands on the edge and leaned in over it to look inside.

'Damn it,' she said bitterly, with barely contained fury. 'That damn Halliday and his crackpot theory. It's empty! Not even a dead bloody evangelist.'

The tour guide gasped audibly.

Standing still for a few more seconds looking like a pressure cooker about to blow, Alexis finally let out a piercing scream of rage.

'Fuck!' she shouted furiously, slapping her hand down onto the edge of the sarcophagus with such force that her sunglasses fell off her face, clattering to the floor, and her scarf slid partly away from her face on the left-hand side.

At the angry outburst, the female tourist's head jerked up to see what was happening. Alexis registered this and involuntarily turned to look at her. A clear look of recognition swept across the face of the female tourist.

'Wait. Are you…?' she began, but then her male companion reached over, grabbed her shoulder and pulled her roughly towards him.

'No,' he said sternly and with a hint of panic in his voice. 'She isn't anyone we know. Alright?'

The woman looked down and nodded frantically.

'We haven't seen anything,' the man pleaded, holding up his hands above his head whilst averting his eyes from both Alexis and the Englishman. 'I swear, we've seen nothing. If you let us go, we won't tell a soul. I swear it!'

Alexis pressed her lips together and tilted her head slightly to one side with a look of both irritation, regret and even a hint of sadness on her face. She hesitated for a few seconds, but then turned to Stone.

'Kill them,' she said coldly.

'No!' shrieked the female tour guide.

Stone reached inside his jacket and pulled out his gun again. He pulled back the slide and loaded a round into the chamber. Then he pointed the gun at the tour guide's head and pulled the trigger.

There was an odd-sounding click, at which point he brought the gun back towards himself, inspecting it with an annoyed expression.

'Fucking German guns,' he sneered. 'Always jamming just when you need the damn things.'

As the tour guide fell to the floor whimpering, and the two tourists flung their arms around each other, Stone slammed his left hand down onto the gun and then grabbed the slide, yanking it back hard towards himself. The gun spat out the bullet that had been stuck halfway into the chamber, and then he loaded a new one.

'Now. Where was I?' he said rhetorically whilst bringing the gun back up to point at the forehead of the quivering tour guide.

At that moment the basilica filled with a loud and rapid staccato sound of metal against metal. The Englishman froze. It was coming from above. He looked up and saw the huge candelabra high above their heads coming down rapidly towards him, and without hesitating, he flung himself to one side.

The heavy candelabra crashed onto the floor in a cacophony of metallic noises, narrowly missing Alexis but just catching Stone's left foot. It did not take the full force of the impact, since the candelabra's design was protruding slightly downward at its centre, but it was enough to make him bellow in pain. He quickly extracted his foot and staggered to his feet again, letting out an angry growl.

Fiona decided it was now or never and started running out of the Chapel of Saint Clement, keeping as many columns between herself and the Englishman. Then she cut diagonally across to the floor under the Dome of Pentecost and continued towards the basilica's exit.

Stone raised his gun and fired twice, both shots missing and smacking loudly into a hard marble column uncomfortably close to Fiona, producing small puffs of dust. They then ricocheted loudly off into the church with a whine.

In the confusion, the tour guide and the two tourists leapt up and sprinted towards the back exit of the chancel and out into the sacristy, where priests prepare for church services, from which there was access to the crypt beneath the basilica. The tour guide most likely knew of places to hide down there.

For a moment, Stone seemed unsure about who to chase after. Fiona or the three witnesses.

'Get her,' shouted Alexis angrily, pointing at Fiona who was almost at the door to the outside. 'We can't allow her to get away.'

Without a word, Stone set off running down the nave of the church towards the exit with a limp, firing his gun twice more. This time, just as Fiona slipped outside, the bullets slammed into the heavy wooden door which absorbed the impacts as well as any Kevlar vest could have.

Outside in the darkness, Fiona was already sprinting down through the Piazzetta di San Marco square next to the Doge's Palace towards the edge of the Grand Canal. Along the quay were moored a long row of boats that were bobbing gently in the shallow waves created by the passing river traffic. Fiona quickly scanned them and went for the one she thought looked the fastest. She leapt onto it, unfastened the rope that had secured it to the quay and then scrambled back to the single outboard engine at the back. She pulled the cord, but nothing happened.

'Shit,' she exclaimed, a sense of panic quickly rising up inside her.

On the second pull, the engine sprang to life vigorously, and Fiona felt a warm rush of relief wash over her.

When she looked up, she spotted the Englishman barging out through the door of the basilica and looking around. After a few seconds he spotted her. He immediately brought up his gun whilst walking a few steps towards her, but then he seemed to decide that the distance was too great, so he instead began running down the Piazzetta towards her. His gait was uneven as he tried to compensate for his injured ankle.

Fiona grabbed frantically at the boats next to her, trying to push her boat backwards out into the canal, and eventually, she managed to do it. But by then, the Englishman was getting close and when he saw her pulling away from the quay and pointing the boat west along the Grand Canal, he brought up his gun again and fired four times.

Unable to aim properly while running, one of his bullets slammed into the side of the boat about a hand's breadth above the waterline, but the others missed. At that point, Fiona was in the driver's seat and pushing the throttle all the way up, making the small boat leap forwards in the water as the outboard engine shrieked aggressively with joy at being able to deliver all of its power to the propeller, rather than being stuck near idle at 5 kilometres per hour. The boat quickly accelerated to what Fiona guessed was close to 30 kilometres per hour, which would probably land her a huge fine if she was apprehended by police. At this point, however, fines were the least of her worries.

Behind her, the Englishman had jumped into another boat and was busy extracting it from between the other boats moored to the quay-side. He made it out much faster than Fiona had managed to do, and immediately pushed the throttle forwards to give chase.

Whipping her head back for a few seconds to look behind her, Fiona could see that the boat chasing her was some fifty meters further back. The two boats seemed to be very evenly matched with regard to speed, which meant that the Englishman wouldn't be able to catch her. However, it also meant that she wouldn't be able to outrun him, which left the uncomfortable prospect of waiting to see who ran out of fuel first. And unlike him, she didn't have a gun. What she needed was a distraction or some other means of slowing him down.

She had now made it under the Ponte dell'Accademia, and around the short southwestern bend in the Grand Canal, and was making her way past the various piers where riverboats would stop during the day when they were in service. Squinting ahead and with the wind blowing her hair back and away from her face, she could now make out the Ponte Rialto bridge up ahead about three hundred metres away. The bridge is the narrowest point along the Grand Canal, and there are usually a large number of riverboats and gondolas moored on both sides of the canal. This gave Fiona an idea. But she would need luck, and lots of it.

Venice is built on more than one hundred islands in a lagoon in the Adriatic Sea, which means that it is subject to tidal currents. As Fiona and the Englishman were racing along the Grand Canal at speeds that had surely already made dozens of residents call the police due to the destructive effects of their wake on the buildings lining the canal, they were sailing against the current. The incoming tide was now close to peaking, which forced large amounts of water into the southern end of the Grand Canal and through the entire S-shape to eventually exit at the northern end.

The current created by the tide as the huge volume of water was forced through the winding canal, meant that it could be difficult for a boat to manoeuvre precisely unless it was travelling directly upstream or downstream. This was particularly true at slow speeds and at narrow points on the canal where the water flows more quickly, allowing the current to more easily grab a vessel and push it around.

Fiona realised that this was her only chance of getting away from the Englishman. She steered the boat onto the right side of the canal, hoping for a miracle, and the miracle came. Through the arches of the Ponte Rialto bridge and on the other side of it, she spotted a long transport barge coming into view as it laboriously made its way in the opposite direction around the bend and towards the bridge.

Making sure that the barge had seen her, Fiona swerved across to the other side of the canal and into its lane. Within seconds, the barge driver spotted her racing towards him and leaned on the horn. The barge was now making its way slowly under the Ponte Rialto, but Fiona kept steering her boat straight at it. Once again, the barge driver used the horn, and now groups of people up on the bridge and along the narrow streets running parallel to the canal were stopping to see what the noise was all about.

Fiona maintained her course, and with less than fifty meters to go, the barge driver finally reacted and threw his rudder towards the left, making the barge veer slowly to the opposite side of the canal as it exited from under the bridge.

As soon as Fiona saw this, she followed suit, swapping lanes again to now be in the lane that the lumbering barge was moving into. The barge driver, now clearly panicking, killed the throttle of the boat to try to avoid a collision with the small oncoming boat, or at least mitigate the damage from it. However, the momentum of the barge carried it forward for a short distance, but by then it was in the grip of the oncoming current.

Slowly at first but then faster and faster, the barge began to both drift and spin to the left, and the more it spun, which left it lying increasingly across the canal, the more the current gripped it and pushed it slowly backwards and sideways. Within seconds its rear end bumped into the Ponte Rialto's northern stone foundation, and then the current quickly began pushing its stern towards the other side, leaving only a small and closing gap of a few meters between it and the southern foundation.

This gap looked like it was just wide enough for Fiona to slip through. She did not slow down, but simply hoped that her boat would be able to fit through the narrowing gap before the barge ended up perpendicular to the canal, completely blocking the way for the Englishman and his boat.

As she tore through the gap and under the Ponte Rialto with the wind in her hair and the spray from the prow of the boat hitting her face, Fiona's boat scraped against the stone foundation, but it was not enough to stop the boat or even slow it down. It shot out from under the bridge and along the canal on the north side, away from the pursuing Englishman.

When Stone realised what was happening, he let out a frustrated roar and then steered his own boat towards the gondola parking area on the lefthand side of the canal immediately before the Ponte Rialto. He slowed down, but not enough to avoid ramming several of the parked gondolas, leaving one sinking and another two badly damaged. Amid screaming and angry shouting from onlookers, he jumped out of the boat with his gun drawn and began running down the nearest street in the direction he thought Fiona might have gone, hoping to be able to reach a different part of the canal and cut her off.

Frightened pedestrians scattered and moved out of his way as he hobbled down the street as fast as he could, but within a couple of minutes the narrow and irregular streets of Venice left him confused about where exactly he was. Soon after, he ended up in a small courtyard where he stopped, looking first at the end of one adjoining street, then at another and then back again, attempting to decide which way to go. His ankle was throbbing with pain, sweat was running off his brow, and he finally accepted that he was lost.

'Fuck!' he shouted furiously, and in an explosion of rage he pointed his gun at a large garbage container and emptied the magazine into it, the sound of the shots reverberating briefly around the small enclosed courtyard.

He stood there for a couple of seconds, breathing heavily and staring angrily at his metal victim. Then he shoved the gun back into its holster and walked off.

# TWENTY-EIGHT

When Andrew finally made it back to the hotel room in Baghdad Airport, he found a handwritten note on his bedside table weighed down by an ashtray. This was puzzling, since Fiona was usually very fond of her electronic gadgets, not least her phone. Why hadn't she just sent him a message?

The note simply read; "Gone to Venice. Check your laptop."

Andrew looked at the note, wondering what it all meant, why she had left in such a rush and why she hadn't just sent him an email or a text message. Did she suspect that she was being monitored? And if she really was, was he?

He sat down and opened up his laptop, which had been left in sleep mode. This meant that as soon as he flipped open the screen, it came to life and showed him the last thing Fiona had been using it for. It was a document in which she had written a brief letter to him explaining why she was going to Venice, and that she had been unable to contact him before leaving.

She also suggested he listen to a recorded conversation between Alexis and a man called Halliday. This was what had sparked her desire to leave for Venice so swiftly. At the end of the letter, Fiona had said that she was also planning to go to Alexandria, but that she would try to get in touch with him before that. Her reason for wanting to go to Alexandria was that this was the last confirmed location of Alexander's body, which meant that sooner or later Alexis would send Dubois there.

Andrew sat back and pondered what to do. He could either try to follow Fiona to Venice, or go straight to Alexandria where she would eventually turn up. The problem was that he had not heard from her since the letter was left on the laptop, either because she had been occupied or unable to contact him for some reason, or perhaps because she was worried their communications had been compromised.

Andrew rose and was walking to the bathroom for a shower when his phone rang. It was Strickland.

'Hello Andrew,' he said. 'I just wanted to provide you with a quick update.'

'Anything from Fiona?' asked Andrew.

'No, sorry old chap,' replied Strickland. 'Not a squeak. I suspect she is off somewhere solving some riddle or other. Exercising those clever grey cells of hers.'

'Yes,' said Andrew reluctantly, sounding less than convinced and a little bit worried. 'It is unlike her not to get in touch though. I hope she's alright.'

'I am sure she's fine,' said Strickland. 'She's no pushover, that girl. Anyway, what I wanted to tell you is that we have some intel about Alexis which you might find useful.'

'Alright,' said Andrew. 'Fire away.'

'We managed to track her private jet leaving from Athens, and it would appear that she landed in Venice just hours after Fiona left Baghdad. They may well have been there at the same time.'

'I see,' said Andrew. 'That sounds odd, and a bit concerning.'

'And another thing,' said Strickland. 'We believe Alexis is also planning to go to Alexandria.'

'Alright. Why is that?' asked Andrew.

'As you know, we have been monitoring the location of her yacht the Hypatia using its transponder, and the day before yesterday it left its previous position in the Aegean Sea. We then lost it as it sailed south out into the Mediterranean, but today it was picked up again in Alexandria. It is currently docked in the marina there.'

'So, she was right,' said Andrew.

'What do you mean?'

'Fiona said Alexis would end up in Alexandria sooner or later. She probably did not imagine it being so soon. And there is every reason to believe that Dubois and his goons are on their way too if they aren't already there.'

'Well, let me know what you two decide to do,' said Strickland. 'I will attempt to support you as best I can, which might not be very much. The powers that be are anxious about not causing another incident anywhere, so anything you decide to do has to be under the radar.'

'I understand, sir. I will keep you updated.'

'Thank you, and good luck.'

Andrew put the phone down and went for his shower. When he came back out again twenty minutes later, he found that there was an email from Fiona waiting for him.

It contained just two words: "Follow me.'

Andrew stared at it for a few seconds. That cryptically short message could only mean one thing. He picked up the phone, called the pilots of the RAF aircraft parked at Baghdad Airport, and asked them to get the plane ready to fly to Egypt.

★      ★      ★

Alexandria on the Mediterranean coast. The first city founded by Alexander the Great, and thus the only Alexandria without a so-called toponymic surname, or a second name to designate its location.

In ancient history, thousands of years before Alexander brought Hellenic culture to Egypt, the site was a small port used as far back as the Old Kingdom circa 2700 BCE. Much later, Rameses the Great used it as a trading station with Greece in the 12th century BCE. After that, the area declined, and trading activity shifted north to the port city of Canopus.

It is thought that when Alexander arrived at the site on the Mediterranean coast in 331 BCE, there was just a small Egyptian settlement called Rhacotis already close by. This settlement eventually became the Egyptian quarter in this new soon-to-be Greek metropolis and regional trading hub. Aside from its location, well-planned layout, and extensive port facilities, another reason for Alexandria's success as a trading hub was the fact that Alexander had sacked and virtually ruined the Phoenician port city of Tyre. This had resulted in much of its trade moving to Alexandria.

Alexandria was always intended as a gateway between Greece and Egypt, and it was planned by the Greek architect Dinocrates of Rhodes who designed the city in a grid plan, using the familiar Hellenistic architectural style that most famously can be seen in the temples of the Acropolis in Athens.

With the rise of the Roman empire, however, Alexandria's fortunes began to wane. When during the Roman civil wars Cleopatra, the last Ptolemaic ruler of Egypt, took her own life there in 30 BCE rather than be brought back to Rome as a trophy, it marked the end of the city's heyday, at least during ancient times.

In 115 CE a large part of the city was destroyed during the so-called Kitos War, where Jews across the Roman empire rebelled. The local rebellion in Alexandria was subsequently crushed two years later by the Roman legions.

Alexandria then fell in 619 CE to the Neo-Persian Sassanid Empire, but was recovered for the Romans by the Byzantine emperor Heraclius in 629 CE. Eventually, though, in 641 CE it was retaken during the Muslim conquest of Egypt after a siege lasting 14 months. In 1517, the city was conquered by the Ottoman Empire and remained under their rule until 1798, when it was briefly taken by Napoleon. In 1801, along with the rest of Egypt, it fell back into the hands of the Ottomans, and in 1882 it became part of Britain's Egyptian protectorate, where it remained until the Egyptian revolution in 1952. The 1956 Suez-Crisis then effectively ended British involvement in Egypt.

One of the most famous landmarks of ancient Alexandria was its more than 100-metre-tall lighthouse. One of the Seven Wonders of the World, its construction was initially commissioned by Ptolemy I, shortly after he declared himself pharaoh in 305 BCE, but it was completed by his son Ptolemy II Philadelphus around twelve years later. It was built of granite and limestone and made up of three gently tapering square tiers, roughly thirty by thirty metres at the base, and a circular domed top section around eight by eight metres in size, where fires would burn to guide the ships on the Mediterranean into the harbour.

The lighthouse suffered structural damage in earthquakes in 796 CE and again in 951 CE, and then experienced a partial collapse of the top 20 metres of the structure during another earthquake in 956 CE. It was never attempted rebuilt after that, and it was effectively abandoned as a ruin until 1480, when some of its huge blocks of stone were used to construct the imposing Citadel of Qaitbay, which still sits on the site to this day. Several blocks of granite from the lighthouse were found in Alexandria's Eastern Harbour in 1968.

Coming in to land on the Number 22 runway at El Nouzha Military Airport, which seemed to be located in unnaturally close proximity to the centre of Alexandria, Andrew could see the 15th-century citadel on the far side of the harbour out of the righthand side of the aircraft. During the final couple of minutes of the flight, all he could see was a dense forest of sand-coloured cubist multi-storey buildings spread densely over the entire city. From the air, it very much appeared as if little to no city planning had happened during the construction of modern Alexandria, and that no attention had been paid to aesthetics whatsoever. The glory of the ancient city appeared long gone.

It was early afternoon when the wheels of the aircraft touched the runway, and after taxiing to the small terminal building, Andrew exited and went through to passport control for a quick check of his credentials. Fifteen minutes later he was in a taxi heading for the city centre and Fiona's location. During a brief exchange of short text messages, she had asked that they meet at Alexandria Railway Station located in the Al Attarin governorate of the city.

The taxi ride from the airport to the station took only ten minutes, and Andrew found Fiona sitting at a café next to the leafy square directly opposite the station's main entrance. She was wearing a white shirt, cream-coloured linen trousers and a light blue scarf over her head.

'May I join you?' asked Andrew as he came up behind her.

Fiona almost jumped and her head whipped around to look at him.

'Oh,' she said relieved. 'Thank god it's you.'

Andrew sat down across from her and smiled.

'Why all the skulduggery?' he asked. 'Your messages were very short and cryptic.'

Fiona shrugged. 'Just developing a healthy bit of paranoia, I guess. My trip to Venice was slightly more entertaining than I would have liked.'

She went on to tell him about what had happened in Saint Mark's Basilica, and that she was worried that somehow her communications had been compromised and that perhaps Dubois' goons were looking for her.

Andrew listened intently with a concerned look on his face, asking a few questions along the way to clarify a few things. Then he relayed to her what had happened in Herat. Fiona was less than impressed with how he had put his life at serious risk during the trip but realised that in some ways so had she, during her excursion to Venice.

'Perhaps we should stick together from now on,' she said.

'Fine by me,' smiled Andrew. 'I still wouldn't have liked you in that tank with me in Afghanistan, but from now on I think it is probably best if we don't split up. Do you think you were followed here from Venice?'

'I have no idea,' said Fiona, instinctively looking over her shoulder at the people walking to and from the railway station off to her side. 'I haven't seen Dubois or Morozov or that English goon of his. In fact, I haven't seen anyone that I thought was behaving suspiciously, but then I am not trained to do that sort of thing. For all I know, the waiter here in this café could be working for Alexis.'

'Alright,' smiled Andrew and placed a reassuring hand on hers. 'We're almost certainly fine here. Just because you had a close call in Venice doesn't mean they know where you are or even who you are. I will ask Strickland if there is any sign of anyone having attempted to access our communications, but I am sure he would have already told me if that had been the case.'

'Alright,' said Fiona, and gave a short sigh. 'Maybe I am overreacting. After all, this is a city of more than five million people, so it's not like we would be easy to find. Anyway, what about Dubois? He is bound to be here already. Can you still track his phone?'

'No,' replied Andrew. 'The tracking system only works if we have access to the location data of the mobile network, and that is something the Egyptian authorities have refused to provide to foreign intelligence services.'

'Damn it,' said Fiona bitterly. 'I have had just about enough of that little cretin.'

'Same here,' said Andrew. 'Anyway, I need to mention something to you that Strickland told me on the phone yesterday. Before he was killed, Dawson managed to send a message to a journalist. It contained credentials for access to a number of documents from ZOE Technologies. Supposedly, those documents prove that the company is involved in advanced engineering of the human genome and that they are performing tests on live embryos at a secret facility somewhere in the U.S.'

'Oh my god,' said Fiona, her mouth almost falling open. 'That's insane. And presumably, Alexis is in on this?'

'It would be very strange if she wasn't,' replied Andrew. 'The whole thing is quite a mess.'

'Shit,' said Fiona. 'Do you suppose that's what this whole thing is about? This hunt for Alexander's DNA? What if they intend to use it for their research?'

'How do you mean?' asked Andrew.

'I am obviously not a geneticist,' said Fiona, and shrugged, 'but wouldn't it be possible to clone Alexander if you had his entire genome?'

Andrew, looked at her for a couple of seconds, unsure what to say.

'Are you serious?' he said. 'That sounds completely bonkers. Why would they want to do that?'

'No idea,' said Fiona, holding up her hands. 'I have given up trying to understand that woman.'

Andrew hesitated for a moment. Then he shook his head slightly, as if to clear it of the spectre of human cloning and all the implications that could have.

'Who knows,' he asked rhetorically. 'We can sit here and guess until the cows come home. There's no way of knowing. So, what's our own plan here in Alexandria?'

'Come with me,' said Fiona and rose, placing her phone back in her handbag and putting her sunglasses on. 'I have booked a hotel room for us. It's just a ten-minute walk north of here. I will tell you when we get there.'

They walked roughly five hundred metres from the railway station along Al Naby Danyal Road which led all the way north to the shoreline where the hotel was situated. She had booked a room at the Steigenberger Cecil Alexandria on El-Gaish, which is a road that runs along the curved shore inside the inlet to the north of the old city centre. The inlet is also called Al Mina' ash Sharqiyah, or the Eastern Harbour. The hotel, which was built in 1929 and is just next to the small Saad Zaghloul Park, is a small and somewhat dated yet elegant hotel with an almost colonial air of yesteryear about it.

The busy El-Gaish Road had three lanes in each direction along the eastern harbour leading out to the Mediterranean Sea, and as they arrived and walked up the steps to the main entrance, Andrew turned around and took in the view. Just on the other side of the road is a narrow beach wrapped in a horseshoe shape around the large semi-circular eastern harbour which is around one kilometre across. To their left, which was toward the south, they could see the city extend out along the beach to what used to be Pharos Island, and at the furthest point almost directly across from the hotel was the Citadel of Qaitbay nearly a kilometre away. To their right around 800 metres along the road, was an eye-catching curved-façade building which houses the modern city's library as well as a planetarium and four museums.

Once inside their hotel room they sat down on the sofa with cold drinks and began discussing what Alexis and Dubois might be planning in Alexandria.

'Well,' said Andrew. 'Having chased down all the available leads on fragments of Alexander's DNA, I suppose it would make sense to eventually come here to the place where the tomb was confirmed to have been, even if that was a very long time ago and the chance of actually finding the tomb is extremely low.'

'I agree,' said Fiona. 'Archaeologists and historians have been crawling over this city for centuries trying to locate the tomb, and they have all come up empty-handed.'

'But isn't it possible that Alexis and Dubois have uncovered some information, or some piece of the jigsaw puzzle that could make all the other pieces suddenly fit together and make sense?' asked Andrew.

'I suppose,' said Fiona, 'but in the absence of concrete information, we need to get moving ourselves. We can't just sit around waiting for something to happen. We have to take the initiative and start our own investigation.'

'But how and where do we start?' asked Andrew. 'As far as I know, there is virtually nothing left of ancient Alexandria. The city has been completely rebuilt several times on top of the old city, right?'

'That's correct,' said Fiona, 'which means there is only one place to go, and that is down.'

'Down?'

'Yes. Modern Alexandria has been built on layers upon layers of previous incarnations of the city, stretching back all the way to its foundation 2,300 years ago. This means that those first foundations and buildings, and possibly also the catacombs and crypts from that time, are now buried beneath ten to fifteen meters of soil and building materials.'

'That deep? That is remarkable,' said Andrew. 'How can archaeologists excavate in a place like this? There is a bustling city of five million people full of multi-storey buildings on top of every inch of the city centre. How do they do that?'

'With great difficulty,' smiled Fiona. 'Once in a while, when buildings are torn down to be replaced by new ones, archaeologists can get lucky and be afforded time to investigate a site if it is thought to have been in a location of special interest. And of course, parks and other open spaces are available too. But things like ground-penetrating radar are not an option because of the buildings that cover almost everything here. And any site that sits on top of a place of worship cannot be excavated. I suppose that is a sensible rule, but it is also a great shame since different temples and churches have typically been built on the same sites for centuries, and in some cases millennia. So, many of these temples are literally sitting on top of each other at some of the ancient holy sites.'

'Are there many archaeological sites currently being excavated?' asked Andrew.

'Oh yes,' replied Fiona. There are several active dig sites around the city, some of which have been excavated for years now. They are still uncovering parts of the ancient city, and sometimes they find artefacts like statues and pottery and jewellery. There is actually one which I think we should have a closer look at. But let me get back to that in a minute. First, let me show you a map of what Alexandria is believed to have looked like around 215 BCE, when Ptolemy I's great-grandson, Ptolemy IV Philopator had Alexander's tomb moved. If you remember, he relocated it to the new mausoleum, the Soma, along with those of his father, his grandfather and Ptolemy I himself.'

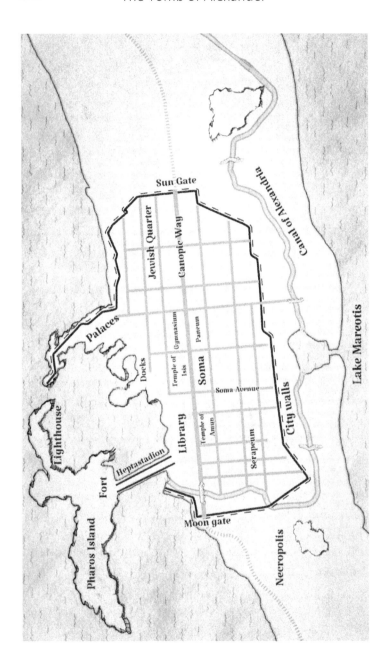

'The first thing to note here is that the palace district is no longer there today. It slowly sank into the sea because of subsidence. This is something that has plagued much of the coastline around the Nile Delta over the centuries. Note also the causeway called the Heptastadion, which Ptolemy had built to connect the city with the island of Pharos. It was named this way because its length was seven *stadia*, which were Greek units of length of around 180 metres, so the whole thing was about 1.3 kilometres long. And of course, out at the very tip of the island was the famous lighthouse.'

'Those were some impressive engineering projects,' said Andrew.

'Yes,' said Fiona. 'Ptolemy was nothing if not ambitions in his plans for this place, so from the start it was designed to be a grand city to rival the most impressive capitals in the ancient world.'

'And I can see the library was just here,' said Andrew, pointing at the map near the Heptastadion. 'That can't be more than a couple of hundred metres from where we are now.'

'That's right,' said Fiona. 'And now look at this long street here. That is the Canopic Way, later called the Rue Rosette. The road is now known as Sharia Horreya, which eventually becomes the Abou Quer as it leaves the city towards the north-east and makes its way towards what used to be the port city Canopus.'

'And the Soma was here?' said Andrew and pointed at the map.

'Correct,' said Fiona. 'That is what everyone has been looking for.'

Fiona pulled a book out from her suitcase. 'Listen to this,' she said. 'This is from the Greek geographer and historian Strabo, who visited Alexandria in 35 BCE. He wrote a fairly detailed account of the city, which by then was several centuries old.'

*The whole city is intersected by roads for the passage of horsemen and chariots. Two of these are very broad, exceeding a plethron in breadth, and cut one another at right angles. It contains also very beautiful public grounds and royal palaces, which occupy a fourth or even a third part of its whole extent.*

'A plethron is around thirty metres. And then he goes on to write this.'

*A part belonging to the palaces consists of that called Soma, an enclosure, which contained the tombs of the kings and that of Alexander. For Ptolemy, the son of Lagus took away the body of Alexander from Perdiccas, as he was conveying it down from Babylon.*

'The very last mention of Alexander's tomb in Alexandria was in 390 CE in an oration by the Greek scholar Libanius, where he simply states that the body is on display in the city. This is some seven hundred years after Alexander's death. By 400 CE the archbishop of Constantinople records somewhat mockingly that not even the pagans in Alexandria know of its location.'

'That is remarkable,' said Andrew. 'But where exactly was the Soma? Even if it was destroyed during those Christian riots that Alexis told us about, surely we must know where it was at that time.'

'That is what is so maddening,' said Fiona, tapping her finger on the map, 'because we actually don't know exactly where that was. It was supposedly right here at the crossroads between the Canopic Road and one of the intersecting streets, possibly the royal road leading from the palace district and south through the city. But it is as if all records of its precise location have vanished. Almost as if someone deliberately wiped all trace of it from the records.'

Andrew tilted his head slightly. 'I am not saying it is impossible,' he said. 'But you're starting to sound just a little bit as if you think there is some great conspiracy at play here.'

'Who is to say there isn't?' said Fiona, spreading out her hands. 'The Catholic Church itself is convinced that the body of Alexander was smuggled out of Alexandria and brought to Venice. That also sounds like a conspiracy, right?'

'Except he wasn't there,' said Andrew, raising his eyebrows. 'You and Alexis determined that pretty conclusively.'

'Well,' said Fiona. 'First of all, I didn't actually see inside the sarcophagus myself, although I have to assume that her reaction was genuine proof that it really was empty. Secondly, there is still a possibility that Alexander's body was indeed brought to Venice, but that it is now being kept safe in the crypt beneath

Saint Mark's Basilica, still in the mistaken belief that it is the body of Saint Mark.'

'Alright,' said Andrew. 'That's fair, but I have to say that I think that entire story sounds quite far-fetched. It is just too much of a coincidence that the body of Saint Mark should turn up just when Alexander's went missing.'

'I tend to agree,' said Fiona, 'and I wasn't at all convinced that Alexis and Dubois would find anything in the basilica, but I still had to go there just in case they were right.'

'Well, you did an amazing job,' said Andrew. 'Top-notch covert work. Until you had to leave and ended up blocking the entire Grand Canal.'

Fiona produced an embarrassed smile. 'I had to try to get away from that psycho. Anyway, back to Alexander. At the time of the disappearance of his body, there were plenty of people who believed fervently that he was a god, so if they perceived that his tomb was under threat, they would have stopped at absolutely nothing to keep it safe, even if that meant making it disappear from the records.'

'I guess that makes sense too,' said Andrew. 'Anyway, what does your gut tell you now? How do we proceed?'

'Well, said Fiona. 'I simply can't accept that the Soma was just torn down or removed, and that the tomb, which was definitely there, was just wiped from the face of the earth without a trace.'

'So, what are you saying?' asked Andrew.

'I am saying that the tomb must have been moved to a different location somehow, whether that was widely known, or only known to a small circle of initiated guardians of that secret. It simply *must* have been.'

'Ok. So, what do you suggest we do?'

'I have already been studying this extensively,' said Fiona, 'and my hunch is to go to the crossroads right in the centre of the ancient city where the great Canopic Road used to be. There is an active archaeological dig site close to there in the northeast corner of the Shallalat Gardens. A team led by a Greek archaeologist have been working there for over ten years, painstakingly making their way down through the many layers of soil. They have effectively been going back in time through modern Arab, Ottoman, Byzantine, Ptolemaic and then Roman layers until they finally hit some of the first roads laid down by Alexander, as well as several foundations of ancient buildings. They even found a partly damaged but still beautiful white marble statue of Alexander himself. They also uncovered sections of a partially collapsed tunnel which hints at the presence of a network of underground passages under the ancient city.'

'I see,' said Andrew. 'That is fascinating.'

'It was a big event when it happened,' said Fiona. 'Even the President of Greece came to visit the dig site, which gives you a small glimpse into how important a figure Alexander still is for Greek identity and also for its politics.'

'But does that mean they might be close to the tomb?' asked Andrew.

'Not necessarily,' replied Fiona. 'Even though they are digging very close to the ancient crossroads in the royal quarters more or less in the area where archaeologists think the Soma was located, the finding of a statue of Alexander doesn't automatically mean that they are close. If you remember, Ptolemy I used the tomb of Alexander to initiate a cult around the dead conqueror. This in turn lent some of its power to him and his family as he was establishing himself as the new ruler and eventually also pharaoh of all of Egypt. Part of that process was clever use of imagery, which meant that statues of Alexander would have been quite a common sight throughout the city. So, it is likely that the Greek team found one of those. But it was still an amazing discovery after more than two millennia.'

'Right,' said Andrew. 'We should get going then. I am curious to see what this dig site looks like. You said it was inside a public park?'

'Yes,' replied Fiona. 'It has obviously been cordoned off, but we might be able to peek inside it.

'Alright,' said Andrew, getting to his feet. 'Let's get moving.'

# TWENTY-NINE

Under the shade of a group of old olive trees a couple of tables and chairs had been set up for public use. Andrew and Fiona sat down at one of the small round metal tables, and Fiona began rummaging around in her bag.

'Have a look at this map,' she said and spread out a map of modern-day Alexandria. 'We are here in Shallalat Gardens, and here is Sharia Horreya which used to be the Caponic Way, running more or less from the south-west to the north-east and parallel to the coast. It is intersected by all of these streets here, many of which are in the same location as they were when this part of the city was founded around 2,300 years ago.'

'Ok,' said Andrew, waiting patiently for Fiona to lay out her thoughts.

'Right here,' she continued, drawing a small line on the map inside Shallalat Gardens in the area where the dig site was located. 'This is a piece of ancient road that was recently uncovered. From the type of flagstones used it is clear that this was a Roman road, so it would have been laid down a couple of centuries after Ptolemy I had finished building the city, but it is almost certain that this road was laid down on top of the original roads of the city, as mapped out by Alexander himself.'

'Alright,' nodded Andrew. 'What are you driving at?'

'Well,' said Fiona. 'Look at the line I just drew. It is a nice neat straight line indicating the placement of a road, but it is in the wrong place.'

Andrew looked perplexed. 'The wrong place? I don't understand.'

'It is offset from the current road system by something like fifty metres, perhaps even more,' she said. 'If you extrapolate that across the entire dig site, you end up with roads running here instead.'

She continued drawing straight lines crossing the Sharia Horreya, until there was a grid on the modern map of the city with several of the lines that were running perpendicular to the Sharia Horreya offset by at least fifty metres.

'So, you're saying they are digging in the wrong place?' said Andrew.

'If they are trying to locate the Soma, then yes,' said Fiona emphatically. 'It has to be much further in that direction,' she continued, pointing across the park towards the northeast.

Wait a minute,' said Andrew, studying the map. 'You said that the entire modern city is sitting on top of layers and layers of city from past centuries?'

'Yes?' replied Fiona.

'And that this is especially true in the case of temples and religious sites, right?'

'Yes. Why?'

'Look,' said Andrew pointing to a spot on the map. It was a couple of hundred meters away on the other side of the major thoroughfare called Suez Canal Road, which runs roughly north from the old city centre and all the way to El Gaish Road by the sea.

'By the looks of it,' he continued, 'there is a large Greek Orthodox cemetery just south of where the palace district used to be. And in the middle of that cemetery is a large temple. So presumably this temple was built on top of whatever was there when Christianity swept across North Africa. In other words, the temple replaced the existing place of worship, possibly a temple dedicated to Alexander and the Ptolemaic dynasty?'

'Yes, I suppose you are right,' said Fiona. 'The cemetery itself is likely to have been a relatively recent addition to the area since cemeteries used to be located outside the city walls. But there could easily have been a temple of some sort at that location for many centuries.'

''That was exactly what I was thinking,' said Andrew. 'And beneath the current temple could easily be the foundations of the original place of worship, whether that was Christian or dedicated to some other deity from the time of the foundation of the city. There might even be more than just foundations there.'

Andrew looked at Fiona with an expression on his face that made her slightly reticent.

'I am not sure I like where this is going,' said Fiona. 'Andrew, are you saying we should try to gain access to whatever underground spaces there might be under an old Greek Orthodox temple in the middle of an active cemetery?'

'Nothing ventured, nothing gained,' said Andrew and shrugged. 'As you said, we can't just sit here and wait. We have to do our own work.'

★          ★          ★

When evening had fallen, and after a rest at the hotel, Andrew and Fiona returned to the north-eastern corner of the Shallalat Gardens and crossed over the Suez Canal Road to the Greek Orthodox cemetery opposite and slightly further north.

The cemetery, which is open between 8 am and 2 pm, is on a plot that is roughly eighty by one hundred metres in size, and in the middle of it is a large temple built in the classic Hellenic style, with tall columns and a gently sloping red-tiled roof.

Andrew and Fiona were strolling casually along the pavement towards the cemetery from the north. It was now just after 11 pm and traffic along the normally busy road had reduced considerably. Access to the cemetery itself was through a main gate on Suez Canal Road, and the gates turned out to be closed but unlocked.

When they reached the gate, they stopped and quickly slipped inside. The streetlights were yellow and dim, and the one just above the gate was not working, allowing them to enter unseen, not that any of the motorists were even remotely interested in the two tourists that were walking along the side of the road.

'I spent a bit of time looking into this place,' said Fiona after they had closed the heavy metal gate behind them. 'Apparently, the temple was renovated just a couple of years ago, and access is restricted to normal opening hours of the cemetery.'

'Well, we will have to find another way inside then,' said Andrew. 'Let's go around to the back and see what we can find.'

As they walked along the footpath in the darkness, past the gravestones and the small mausoleums that lined it, Fiona began to feel uneasy about their venture.

'This is making me slightly uncomfortable,' she said. 'We really shouldn't be doing this.'

'We have to,' said Andrew. 'We need to at least try to find Alexander's tomb before Dubois does. You said it yourself. If he gets his hands on it, there is no telling what he might do to it, and it might end up lost forever.'

Fiona pressed her lips together looking pained, but she kept following Andrew around the temple to a backdoor to a lower ground level a few steps down. The door was locked, but it had eight small panes of glass on its upper half, so Andrew quickly rammed his elbow into one of them, reached inside and unlocked the door.

'We are now technically criminals in Egypt,' said Fiona, looking uneasy.

'Wouldn't be the first time,' said Andrew and gave her a wink. 'Come on.'

They quickly entered and Andrew closed the door behind them. Inside was a corridor that seemed to run the length of the building, at the end of which was a winding staircase. Above their heads was a low ceiling that was also the floor of the temple's interior, and as they walked to the staircase, they could see it wind its way up to a door that would presumably lead to the temple itself. However, the staircase also went down.

'Look,' said Fiona, pointing at the steps leading down. 'This means that there is some sort of underground space here, possibly a crypt.'

Andrew pulled out a torch from his bag and switched it on, pointing its powerful beam down into the stairwell.

'Let's find out,' he said and began descending the stairs below ground level.

It was a narrow space and the staircase was tightly wound, making it feel quite steep as they descended. To their surprise, having walked down two revolutions of the staircase, to what seemed to be a full level below the corridor, the staircase did not stop. It kept going down.

'This is odd,' said Fiona. 'Whatever is down here, was constructed well below current street level.'

'How deep does this thing go?' said Andrew as they continued down.

'I don't know,' replied Fiona, 'but at this depth, we must be approaching the levels that correspond to ancient Roman times, perhaps even Ptolemaic times.'

'You think whatever is down there goes back that many centuries?'

'It's possible,' said Fiona. 'It might turn out that you were right all along.'

Another six full revolutions of the staircase later, and they finally ended up at the foot of the stairwell in a small space that provided access to a long tunnel. It was vaulted, and the precisely chiselled blocks of stone fit each other perfectly in a neat pattern running along the two walls of the tunnel. The air was dry and had a dusty scent, and as Andrew shone his torch through the tunnel, they could see what appeared to be a chamber at the other end some fifteen or twenty metres away. But access at the far end appeared to be blocked by what looked like an old metal gate.

'Let's go through it,' said Andrew.

As they went, Fiona tried to look closely at the walls in the dim light from the torch.

'This tunnel is made from limestone,' she said, 'which is not from this area. The Nile Delta has no limestone, so it was most likely quarried about thirty kilometres from here. If this is the same type of limestone, then this place was almost certainly constructed during the Ptolemaic age when the city was first built using this exact type of stone. And do you see these decorative carvings? They are without a doubt Hellenic in style. This all points to the Greek temple above us having been built on a religious site that dates back to when the city was founded, which means the tunnel and whatever lies behind that gate could be more than two millennia old.'

'Remarkable,' said Andrew. 'I hope it holds up for a bit longer. There are thousands of tons of soil and rock pressing down on this tunnel.'

Fiona involuntarily looked up at the vaulted ceiling of the tunnel with an anxious look on her face. 'Yes, I do too.'

As they came to the metal gate blocking the narrow tunnel, it became clear that the gate was very old. It was made from solid wrought iron pieces that had been bent around each other and hinged straight into the solid blocks of granite making up the walls. It was also locked by an old but very sturdy-looking block of metal. It resembled a modern padlock, except that the keyhole was triangular and placed on its front.

Andrew shone the torch through the bar to the dark chamber beyond, where its light swept across walls covered in murals.

'We need to get through here so I can examine those,' said Fiona determinedly.

Andrew gripped the bars of the gate and shook hard. The gate rattled loudly but did not budge at all. Then he yanked as hard as he could on the padlock, but it was clear that it was going to take a lot more strength than he had to break it open.

'Shit,' said Andrew. 'I think we're stuck here. I don't see a way past this.'

'Let me try something,' said Fiona and started rummaging through her handbag. 'I hope I remember how this works.'

'What are you doing?' said Andrew.

'As you know,' she said, 'I have a pretty good memory, and if I remember my chemistry then I think I may have a solution, quite literally.'

She took out a small tub of facial exfoliation cream and started stuffing it inside the keyhole of the old padlock and smearing around the places where the shackle entered the body of the padlock.

'Can I borrow your Zippo lighter?' she asked.

'What on earth are you doing?' he said, handing it to her with a perplexed look on his face.

Fiona flipped the lighter open, lit it, and then held it under the padlock, thereby quickly raising its temperature and soon converting the face cream into a yellowish powder that covered the entire inside of the padlock.

'I am converting the small amounts of sulphur in this facial cream into a powder that is heavy in bound sulphur dioxide,' she said.

'I literally have no clue what you are doing,' said Andrew. 'But I know you well enough not to argue.'

Fiona smiled as she kept heating the padlock's metal, which in turn kept frying the cream and producing more and more of the yellow powder. After a couple of minutes, the padlock was so hot she could feel the heat radiating off it, and the tunnel began to fill with an unpleasant smell of rotten eggs.

'And now,' she said and pulled out a tiny bottle of clear liquid from her handbag, 'I am going to pour a small amount of this hydrogen peroxide which I use for gargling, into the padlock.'

'And what will that do?' asked Andrew, staring intently at the padlock.

'Watch,' said Fiona confidently, and then she carefully poured a couple of teaspoonfuls of the liquid into the padlock, where it was instantly absorbed by the powdery sulphur dioxide.

For a few seconds, nothing happened. But then there rose from the padlock a tiny wispy trail of what looked like smoke. After another few seconds, there was a fizzing sound which grew in intensity as the seconds ticked by.

'What did you do?' asked Andrew stunned, but with an impressed smile on his face.

'I made sulphuric acid,' said Fiona proudly. 'The chemistry is pretty simple, and as you can see you only need a couple of ingredients and some heat. With a bit of luck, it will eat through the metal inside the padlock.'

'Wow. You are quite something,' smiled Andrew. 'Although I have to say the fumes are beginning to sting my eyes.'

'I know,' laughed Fiona. 'It is pretty potent.'

The padlock was now fizzing and bubbling loudly as the acid ate away at the metal, and a dark yellow and black sludge was dripping out of the keyhole.

'You know,' said Andrew. 'It strikes me that this is not unlike Alexander's solution to the Gordian Knot. Instead of using his hands, he thought outside of the box, and used his sword to undo the knot. And here, instead of a key or brute force, you used your knowledge of chemistry.'

'That's a nice way of putting it,' smiled Fiona. 'I will take that as a compliment.'

After another few minutes, the reactive power of the acid was spent and it began to gradually fizzle out. Fiona extracted a few tissues from her handbag and wiped excess acidic sludge from the padlock. Then she wrapped her scarf around it and stood back.

'All yours,' she smiled.

'Moment of truth,' said Andrew, kneeling down next to the wrapped padlock and gripping it tightly with both hands.

Taking a moment to ready himself, he then tightened the muscles in his arms and shoulders, and then he yanked the padlock downward as hard as he could. The curved shackle of the padlock which had held the gate locked was instantly ripped out of the body of the lock, and it fell to the floor with a clattering noise, along with small pieces of the padlock's innards.

'Well done,' said Andrew, looking up at Fiona. 'I would never have been able to do that by myself.'

'And I would not have had the strength to break that padlock apart. Like I said,' smiled Fiona. 'We are much better as a team.'

Andrew undid the old metal clasp on the gate and pushed it open. The chamber on the other side was small, around three by four metres in size, with two pillars about two meters apart in the middle of the space. The ceiling, which was about two metres from the flagstone floor, was vaulted like the tunnel on the other side of the gate. At the far end was a mural that covered most of the wall, and below it was what appeared to be an altar of some kind.

'A place of worship,' said Fiona as she cautiously approached the altar.

'Yes, but worship of whom?' asked Andrew.

'Him,' said Fiona and pointed up at the mural in front of them. 'Alexander.'

Andrew shone his torch up at the mural, revealing a scene containing Alexander the Great's unmistakable figure at the front. He was standing with his legs planted firmly in the Egyptian soil, and with a determined look on his face and eyes fixed on some distant object towards the west. Fiona guessed that his gaze might be directed towards the desert oasis of Siwa, several hundred kilometres to the southwest. He was wearing his gilded linothorax and was holding his sword in one hand and his shield emblazoned with the Vergina Sun in the other. At his feet lay a fearsome-looking lion.

The mural appeared to have been painted as seen from the location of the temple they had descended into, looking northwest towards the sea. Near the front of the mural immediately behind Alexander was an elegant Greek city comprised of white buildings and temples with red tile roofs, many of them with marble colonnades. On the left could be seen the Heptastadion extending out to Pharos Island, and at the north-eastern tip of the island was the famous wonder of the ancient world, the giant lighthouse. It stood proud and tall, with its three separate levels and the fire at the top shining a light out to sea, where several ships were approaching the port of Alexandria. Off to the right, painted near the top of the mural in the sky, was an image of what appeared to be Alexander's supposed heavenly father Zeus, looking down benignly at the city below.

'This is amazing,' whispered Fiona. 'I can't believe the condition this mural is in. It seems incredibly well preserved. Look at the lighthouse there at the back. So tall it was. What an incredible feat of engineering.'

'Do you suppose this place might have been kept in good condition by someone?' asked Andrew. 'I mean, is it possible that we are standing in an active place of worship for a select group of initiated?'

'Not impossible, I suppose,' said Fiona. 'Although it could equally just be that the current guardians of the Greek Orthodox temple above us have decided to let bygones be bygones. Perhaps they are simply preserving this place for posterity, even if it conflicts with the Christian religious dogma of the temple itself.'

'Either way,' said Andrew. 'I don't really want to hang around and wait for someone to turn up so we can ask them. This probably qualifies as a particularly aggravated form of trespassing. After all, it involves violently entering an ancient place of worship. Probably not something that is taken lightly in Egypt.'

'I agree,' said Fiona. 'But I would really like to understand what the purpose of this place is. I need a few minutes to look closely at the mural. There might be a clue to the location of the Soma here somewhere.'

'Alright,' said Andrew. 'I will just head back to the stairwell to make sure we're still alone in here. I don't suffer too badly from claustrophobia, but I wouldn't like to be locked down here.'

'Ok,' said Fiona. 'Could I have your Zippo lighter again please?'

'Sure,' said Andrew, and handed it to her. 'I will be back in a few minutes.'

Then he left the chamber and began heading back through the narrow tunnel, leaving Fiona by the mural holding up the lighter and inspecting the mural in its yellow flickering light.

She leaned as close to the mural as she could but did not dare touch it or even bring the lighter too close to it, for fear of damaging the ancient artwork. Now that she looked at it more closely, it did appear as if it might have been retouched at least once since the chamber was first constructed in ancient times. Standing back and looking at it in its entirety, she noticed something in the lower left corner. She knelt down and held out the lighter again.

Just then, Andrew returned to the chamber.

'All clear,' he said. 'Still. I'd like to get out of here. I feel like we're pushing our luck a bit.'

'I haven't found the Soma,' said Fiona. 'I am pretty sure it isn't here, either because this place was built before the Soma was constructed, or because it was deliberately left out for some reason.'

'That's a shame,' said Andrew.

'But I did find something else. Look at this,' she said, and pointed to a building mostly resembling the other temples in the scene, except that it was very dark, almost black. On its front was painted a circle with a line through it from left to right.

'See this down here?' she said. 'This looks to me like the so-called Theta-Nigrum, the ancient Greek and Latin symbol for death. You often see it in mosaics depicting fallen soldiers, so I am thinking this building down here might be a mausoleum of some kind?'

'Alexander's?' asked Andrew.

'Unlikely,' said Fiona. 'It is much too far away for that to make sense. But I do have another idea of what it might refer to. If you remember the map I showed you of what we believe Alexandria looked like at the time of Ptolemy II, you might remember that there was a necropolis outside the city walls to the southwest. That could be what this refers to.'

'Ok,' said Andrew. 'And what is the significance of this?'

'The significance is that the necropolis still exists. It is very much inside central Alexandria today and is called the Catacombs of Kom el Shoqafa. It is an extremely interesting underground complex of ancient catacombs deep beneath the city, but the most interesting thing about it from our perspective is that they are commonly accepted to be from the 1st or 2nd century CE, during Roman times.'

'I still don't think I quite follow,' said Andrew.

'If I am right,' said Fiona, 'and if the mural in this chamber is from the time of Ptolemy II, and if the dark temple with the Theta-Nigrum is really the Kom el Shoqafa necropolis, then that means that the necropolis and its catacombs are centuries older than what is currently the accepted wisdom.'

'You're saying that the catacombs were already there when Ptolemy II was still alive?'

'Yes,' replied Fiona. 'Possibly even when his father Ptolemy I was alive. And that, in turn, means that there is at least a theoretical possibility that it could hold some clue to the location of Alexander's tomb, even if the tomb was never actually in those catacombs.'

'Well, let's get out of here then,' said Andrew. 'I think you should take some pictures of this mural. You never know when they might come in handy.'

Fiona took several pictures and winced every time the flash went off. There was no chance of it damaging the mural, but she still felt uncomfortable doing it, as if somehow it was sacrilegious.

A few minutes later they made their way back up to the surface, where the balmy evening air was a welcome change from the cold and dry chamber deep beneath the temple. Slipping out of the cemetery grounds and onto the road, they made sure to walk casually back to their hotel. It was now quite late, and within minutes of arriving back they were both fast asleep.

# THIRTY

When they woke up the next morning, Andrew and Fiona wasted little time getting dressed and having breakfast at the hotel's restaurant, which overlooks the Eastern Harbour of Alexandria.

'It is amazing that the lighthouse used to be just over there,' said Fiona, gazing across the harbour to the 15th-century Citadel of Qaitbay. 'It would easily have been five times higher than the citadel.'

'I am not surprised that it was counted as one of the Seven Wonders of the World,' said Andrew. 'I would have loved to have seen it in its heyday.'

'Me too,' smiled Fiona dreamily.

Just then, Andrew's phone rang. It was Colonel Strickland who provided Andrew with a quick update on the investigation into the murders in London, which unfortunately had turned up very little since Dawson was killed. Andrew, in turn, told Strickland about what they had been doing in Alexandria. He could sense that the colonel was uneasy about their freelance approach to the task at hand, but he accepted that it was a necessity at this stage.

Finally, Strickland conveyed information to Andrew which made him frown and nod, making Fiona wonder what was being said. Then the call ended.

'What was all that about?' she asked.

Andrew gazed out across the harbour for a few seconds, and then looked at her.

'The Hypatia has left Alexandria,' he said.

Fiona looked taken aback. 'Really? I mean, I can't say I would have liked to have run into any of those people again, but why leave so soon after arriving? Do we know where they went?'

'Yes,' replied Andrew. 'Apparently, the yacht is now anchored off the port city of Abou Qir, roughly twenty kilometres northeast of here. Odd, when Alexander's tomb was here in Alexandria.'

'Unless…' said Fiona pensively. 'You know, the location of the city of Abou Qir more or less corresponds to that of Canopus in ancient times.'

'But why would they go there?' asked Andrew. 'What was in Canopus?'

'Nothing really,' replied Fiona. 'Nothing except a busy port, for as long as it lasted until it was outcompeted by Alexandria. But I am quite certain that is not why they are there.'

'Why then?' asked Andrew, beginning to sound impatient.

'I am willing to bet anything that the yacht must be anchored right on top of the ruins of Thonis-Heracleion. It was an old Egyptian and later Greek trading port which sank into the sea, and whose ruins are located around two kilometres out into Abu Qir Bay.'

'Thonis?' said Andrew. 'I have never heard of it.'

'Really?' said Fiona. 'It was pretty well publicised when it was rediscovered around the year 2000 by a team of French underwater archaeologists.'

'I can't really claim to have been into archaeology back then,' said Andrew. 'I was busy in Iraq if you know what I mean.'

'Oh. Yes. Of course,' replied Fiona. 'Well, Thonis was an important trading port. It was built on a large number of adjoining islands on the very edge of the Nile Delta during the 12th century BCE. Not unlike Venice actually. But this was around the time of Pharaoh Ramesses II. It remained a crucial part of the pharaonic economy for many centuries until a combination of earthquakes and rising sea levels began to weaken its foundations. Eventually, in what is believed to be around the 2nd century BCE, in other words around the time immediately after the founding of Alexandria, it suffered from severe soil liquefaction. This basically means that the clay-rich soil which the buildings were sitting on very quickly became saturated with water and turned almost liquid, not unlike quicksand. This led to most of the city more or less being swallowed up by the very ground it was sitting on. And then over the next few centuries, a lowering of that whole part of the Nile Delta due to tectonic forces as well as a continued rise in sea levels meant that the city was eventually completely submerged around the 8th century. It would be over a thousand years before it was finally rediscovered by the French team.'

'Crikey,' said Andrew. 'That sounds dramatic.'

'I guess you could say that it was,' replied Fiona. 'Except, of course, most of this unfolded over several centuries, so the city was eventually abandoned and given over to the sea and then it was finally forgotten.'

Fiona pulled her tablet out of her bag and began swiping through some images.

'Here we are,' she said. 'Have a look at this map. This is what we think this part of the Nile Delta looked like at the time of Ptolemy II when the construction of Alexandria was nearing completion. You can see Alexandria, Canopus and also Thonis-Heracleion sitting on the now-defunct Canopic Branch of the Nile. The dotted line on the right indicates where the coastline used to be before that entire area began to sink and sea levels rose.

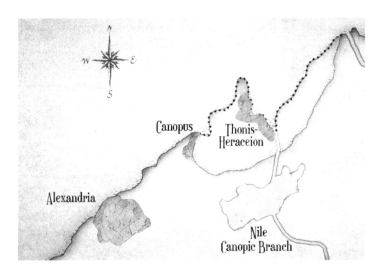

'Wow,' said Andrew. 'That is fascinating. And the whole thing disappeared beneath the waves?'

'During the course of several centuries, yes,' replied Fiona. 'The sunken city is now under around six metres of water out there in Abou Qir Bay.'

'Well,' said Andrew. 'I guess the question is, what are Alexis and Dubois looking for there. Surely they know better than anyone that Alexander's tomb was down here in Alexandria.'

'Of course, they do,' said Fiona, rubbing her temples with her fingertips. 'But perhaps they also believe that they know something that somehow ties Thonis-Heracleion to Alexandria and possibly even Alexander's tomb itself. There is no doubt that there is plenty of underwater archaeology still to be carried out at Thonis-Heracleion, but what relevance it might have to Alexander's tomb, I really can't say at this point.'

Then she paused for a few seconds, gazing out to sea and looking pensive. 'Unless…,' she finally said.

'Unless what?' asked Andrew.

Fiona shook her head. 'It's probably nothing,' she replied. 'Let's just focus on what we were doing. This is all becoming a bit too complicated. We need to stop trying to second-guess Alexis and Dubois and instead follow our own track. I think we should make our way down to the Kom el Shoqafa catacombs first. We just can't allow ourselves to be side-tracked by what we think they might or might not be doing.'

Andrew nodded. 'Alright, fair enough. You can tell me about it later then. Let's just finish up here and get going.'

★        ★        ★

When Andrew and Fiona arrived by taxi at the Kom el Shoqafa catacombs in the downmarket and densely populated Karmouz neighbourhood of Alexandria, it was mid-morning and there were already a number of tourists there. The catacombs open at 9 am, and being on the Alexandria tourist trail, the site sees a steady stream of visitors throughout most days.

The catacombs now look unremarkable from the surface with a large paved-over area that leads to the modest entrance, but when the catacombs were first constructed there was a large temple at the site that allowed entry down into the underground tombs.

'Kom el Shoqafa,' said Andrew, 'What does that mean, exactly?'

'It is a direct Arabic translation from the Greek Lofus Kiramaikos, which means "Mound of Shards," and the reason is that people used to come out here from inside the city walls to visit the tombs of their ancestors in the necropolis, and they would bring food and wine with them in terra cotta jars and other containers. Instead of taking those back from this place of death, they would smash them in a place that eventually became a small mound of clay shards.'

'Interesting,' said Andrew.

'By the way,' said Fiona. 'The word Kiramaikos is related to the potters' quarter of Athens called Kerimaikos, which is where we get the English word *ceramics* from.'

'Not much to look at from up here though,' said Andrew, looking around.

'Alright then,' she said and pulled out her tablet. 'Have a look at this. It is a side-on schematic of the whole complex, and keep in mind there may still be things down there that have not yet been discovered and excavated.'

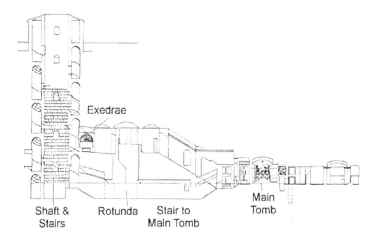

'The entire complex is cut into the bedrock, and it reaches down more than thirty metres or around four storeys. The internal volume of this place is quite enormous.'

Fiona swiped her tablet to show Andrew another image.

'This one shows the complex from the top down.'

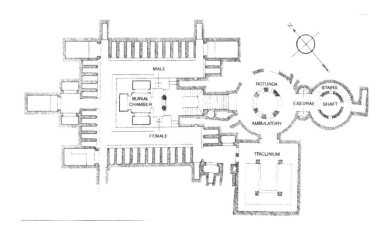

'On the right you can see the shaft and the staircase we are about to go down, which will take us to the underground rotunda. From there, there is access to the triclinium which is a type of formal Roman dining area, and then we can go further down to the main tombs. All of the little niches you see cut into the rock around the edges on the left are actually individual so-called *loculi*, or compartments for the dead.'

'Crikey.' smiled Andrew. 'It's huge. Let's head down there and see what we can see.'

They began descending the wide spiral staircase, which is made of granite and wraps around the central shaft that extends thirty metres straight down to the bottom.

'This place was lost to the world for several centuries,' said Fiona. 'But it was rediscovered when one day a donkey pulling a cart fell into the central shaft.'

'Ouch,' said Andrew, wincing. 'Bad way to go, whether you are man or beast.'

'Yes,' said Fiona. 'It must have taken some very serious resources to dig down and cut this tomb from the bedrock back in the 1$^{st}$ century. Even today, that would represent a serious engineering challenge and one that would cost many millions. It hints at the importance and wealth of the Alexandrian family that had this place constructed.'

'I thought you said this place was even older,' said Andrew.

'I said it *might* be older,' said Fiona. 'But that was purely based on what we found yesterday under the Greek Orthodox temple. Anyway, this place is actually located more or less on the site of the ancient village of Rhacotis, and then later on in the following centuries it became the city's necropolis. Also, the word *necropolis* is another Greek term made up of the two words *nekros* and *polis*, meaning "dead person" and "city" respectively.'

'So, basically it means *City of the Dead*?' said Andrew.

'That's right,' replied Fiona. 'Another fun little etymology anecdote is that this place, like other similar places, is known locally as Al Makaber. And the Arabic word *makaber* or *maqbara* is the plural of the word for cemetery, which stems from another Arabic word *Qabr*, which means grave. This is almost certainly where a whole host of modern European languages get the word *macabre* from.'

Andrew smiled at her. 'You're just a fountain of knowledge, aren't you?'

'Well,' shrugged Fiona. 'I did tell you that I had taken an interest in etymology.'

The two of them continued around fifteen metres down, walking along the winding staircase until they were roughly halfway down. Here there was an opening through to the rotunda. The light was dimmer down here, but the central shaft, which had looked dark from above, was now a source of daylight into the top portion of the catacombs.

As they walked across to the rotunda, they passed the stone seating area called the Exadrae, where visiting family members of the deceased would be able to sit and rest.

'It is quite impressive,' said Fiona. 'Especially when you consider that none of what you see here was built, as such. It was all cut directly from the bedrock.'

On the other side of the rotunda, there was an opening about three meters wide that connected to a set of stairs leading down towards the main tomb.

'This way,' said Fiona, and began walking down the wide steps. 'Notice how this is all very similar to rock-cut tombs found in Greece.'

'Yes, I suppose it is a lot like what we saw in Vergina,' said Andrew. 'But the carvings on the rock here are extremely detailed.'

'That is right,' said Fiona. 'And if you look closely, you can see something quite unique here. The imagery is a strange mix of ancient Egyptian, Greek and Roman.'

They were now at the bottom of the steps, and directly in front of them was the main tomb. It was a low-ceilinged chamber around two by three metres in size, with three intricately carved sarcophagi that were each around two metres wide, sitting inside deep rock-cut alcoves. The central sarcophagus was the most elaborate.

'Look up here,' said Fiona and pointed above them to the architrave of the doorway leading into the chamber. 'This is a winged sun, which is so typical of ancient Egyptian art. And on both sides of the doorway is a snake with a Roman Caduceus or staff. It is also called a Greek Thyrsu, or wand, and they are both wearing the Egyptian double crown, the Pschent, worn by pharaohs who had control of both Lower and Upper Egypt. It is an amazing mix of cultures and styles.'

They now entered the main tomb and stood in front of the central sarcophagus. Above it on the wall was a strange and highly detailed frieze of an embalming scene. But it was a very unusual one. The central figure was a man wearing Roman military clothing. He was standing in the stiff pose typical of Egyptian art, wearing the wolf-head of Anubis and holding out what appeared to be a heart in his hand. Below him was the corpse of a man lying on a lion bed.

'Have a look,' said Fiona. 'This figure here is in the process of mummifying a dead person, and you can see underneath the lion bed are three richly decorated canopic jars where the heart and other intestines would have been placed. And over here to their left standing next to the central figure is another man holding a staff and wearing the falcon-head of the god Horus.'

'Quite something,' said Andrew, leaning closer to examine the frieze. 'And this is all carved out of the existing bedrock?'

'Yes,' said Fiona. 'Along with this sarcophagus and these pillars and everything else you see down here.'

'Fascinating,' said Andrew, looking around and admiring the tomb's interior. 'It would have taken years to do all this.'

'Yes, it is remarkable stuff,' said Fiona. 'I have seen pictures of this place, but seeing it in the flesh is such an experience. The fusion of artistic styles here is like nothing I have ever seen before. If I didn't know better, I would have said that the artists who created this were confused. Usually in most cultures, this type of artwork deliberately and stringently follows an accepted dogma for how these things are meant to look, and any deviation from that is seen as an error or simply sloppiness. But here in Alexandria we see the exact opposite during this time period. It is a deliberate fusion of styles from different cultures, different geographical areas and different eras, and I just find it absolutely enchanting.'

'Let's have a look around the smaller compartments in these catacombs,' said Andrew. 'What were they called again?'

'Loculi, when in plural form,' replied Fiona. 'If there is only one, it is called a loculus.'

'Yes, those,' smiled Andrew.

They exited the main tomb and began walking up the wide set of stairs leading back to the rotunda with Fiona leading and Andrew walking behind with the torch lighting their way. Halfway up the steps he suddenly stopped and looked up.

'What is that?' he said, pointing the torchlight up onto a long vertical section of rock just above the architrave of the doorway leading back into the rotunda.

'What?' said Fiona, stopping and following the beam of light to what Andrew was looking at.

'Wow,' she said. 'I completely missed that. It is some sort of frieze cut into the bedrock.'

She walked up a few more steps to get closer and then stopped to peer at it. It was an intricately carved image of a baby lying in a basket, clutching a snake in each hand.

'It is quite detailed,' she said. 'It is clearly a Greek motif, and I am pretty sure I recognise it. This is Hercules, or Heracles as he is really called.'

'But it is a baby,' said Andrew, sounding perplexed.

'Yes,' said Fiona. 'It is from one of the ancient Greek legends. Heracles was the son of the god Zeus and the mortal princess Alcmene. But he was despised by Zeus's jealous wife Hera who tried to kill him when he was a baby by putting venomous snakes into his cradle.'

'What a lovely woman,' said Andrew sarcastically, craning his neck to look at the frieze above them.

'Yes, not a very nice lady,' said Fiona. 'Heracles was meant to have been the first-born of Zeus and thus ruler of all of Greece, but by some trick of Hera's, his half-brother Eurystheus was born first and became the king. And as I am sure you might remember, it was Eurystheus who later imposed the famous Twelve Labours on Heracles as atonement for having accidentally killed his own wife and child.'

'I have to admit, Greek legends didn't exactly grab me when I was in school,' said Andrew. 'Although I must say I have come to regret that over the past few weeks.'

The two of them looked up at the frieze in silence for a few moments.

'What an odd motif to have in here,' said Fiona wistfully. Then her face suddenly changed, her eyes widening and her mouth falling open slightly.

'Oh my god,' she breathed, staring vacantly out in front of herself. 'That is what that was all about?'

'What?' said Andrew, looking mystified.

'The diary!' exclaimed Fiona. 'There is a short section in Ptolemy's diary that I could never make sense of. I have looked at it again and again, but it didn't seem to fit anywhere. Eventually, I wrote it off as a vain attempt at prose or even an attempt to embellish ancient Greek mythology. But now it suddenly makes sense. It is so much more than any of those things.'

'I am sorry,' said Andrew, now sounding slightly impatient. 'What are you talking about?'

'Come on,' said Fiona, hurrying up the steps towards the rotunda. 'Let's get out of here. I will explain it to you when we get back up to the surface.'

They walked briskly across the rotunda and proceeded up the winding stairwell to again emerge in the bright and warm sunlight. Making their way across the open space near the catacomb entrance to a number of stone benches under an acacia tree, they sat down and Fiona pulled out her tablet from her handbag once again. After a few seconds of swiping, she eventually found an image of the relevant page in Ptolemy's diary.

'This page has foxed me this whole time ever since I first saw it' she said. 'It is one of the last pages in the diary, and I am not entirely sure when it might have been written. But purely in terms of its contents, it is quite different from any of the other pages.'

'In what way?' said Andrew, leaning in to look at the image. 'It looks like the same handwriting.'

'Oh, it is definitely Ptolemy's handwriting,' said Fiona. 'But it doesn't seem to relate to anything that happened during Alexander's campaign. In fact, on the face of it, it seems to have nothing at all to do with Alexander the Great. It relates to Heracles, but it just hasn't made sense to me until now.'

'How so?' asked Andrew.

'Ok,' said Fiona. 'As you know, Heracles was famously given twelve tasks that were meant to be impossible to complete. But through cunning and strength he still managed to do so. In his diary, Ptolemy writes about a *thirteenth* task, of which I am pretty sure there is no record anywhere else.'

'That does sound strange,' said Andrew. 'So, are you saying Ptolemy made it up himself?'

'That is what I am beginning to believe,' replied Fiona. 'But why would someone like Ptolemy take an ancient legend like that and then embellish it by adding a whole new section to it? Until now, I just haven't been able to make any sense of it.'

'What does he write?' asked Andrew.

'Well, this is what I have translated so far,' said Fiona. 'And once again it is probably not completely accurate, but I think the basic elements are clear enough. Ptolemy writes about a thirteenth task, this time set by *The Host of Menelaus*. And the task is to go to Thonis and prise the ring from the *Sleeping Giant of Phrygia.*'

Fiona looked up at Andrew, who raised his eyebrows and held up his hands with his palms facing her.

'Don't look at me,' he said. 'I have no clue what any of this means. Who is Menelaus?'

'In Greek mythology, Menelaus was a Spartan king who was a central figure in the Trojan War. His name literally means "wrath of the people".'

'Charming,' said Andrew ironically. 'Ok, so who is this Host of Menelaus then?

'This is what I have suddenly realised,' said Fiona. 'And it may also explain why Alexis and Dubois are currently on her yacht near the location of the sunken city of Thonis-Heracleion. You see, according to legend Menelaus and Helen of Troy visited that location, and they were hosted by Thonis the watchman of the Nile. Later on, Heracles also came there during his travels, and according to the historian Herodotus a temple was built on the coast where Heracles first landed, which is why the city eventually became known as Thonis-Heracleion.'

'Ok,' said Andrew, still looking perplexed. 'And the part about prising the ring from this Phrygian Giant? What do you make of that?'

'This is slightly more speculative,' said Fiona. 'There is no reference in any ancient Greek myths to a giant from the Kingdom of Phrygia, which is why I think Ptolemy himself made up this whole thing about a thirteenth Herculean task.'

'But why would a historian of such stature as Ptolemy engage in such frivolous writing?' asked

Andrew. 'Unless of course it wasn't frivolous at all. What if it was a clue of some kind, or some sort of record of knowledge that only the initiated would be able to understand?'

Fiona raised her right index finger and smiled knowingly.

'That is exactly what I was thinking,' she said. 'Phrygia was the dominant kingdom in Anatolia from around 1200 BCE to around 700 BCE. And which city do you think was located there?'

Andrew looked at her with a blank stare. 'Listen Fiona, you could literally hold a gun to my head and I still wouldn't be able to tell you.'

'Gordion!' she said excitedly. 'Or Gordum, as the Phrygians themselves called it.'

'Gordion,' repeated Andrew, furrowing his brow. 'As in the city where the Gordian Knot was located?'

'Precisely,' said Fiona enthusiastically. 'So, if Ptolemy is referring to someone as "The Phrygian Giant", that can only mean that who he is *really* referring to is Alexander himself. Alexander is the giant who slashed open the Gordian Knot.'

Andrew nodded. 'That does make a lot of sense,' he said. 'Alright, so the thirteenth task of Heracles was to go to Thonis-Heracleion and prise the ring from the sleeping giant. What do you think that means, exactly?'

Fiona looked up at the leaves on the tree above them for a moment.

'I am beginning to think that perhaps this whole thing should be taken literally,' she said. 'I mean, everything else in Ptolemy's writings is factual. Perhaps this is too. Perhaps the ring Ptolemy is referring to is Alexander's signet ring. Remember, it was taken by Perdiccas after Alexander's death, and then it disappeared after Perdiccas' death on the banks of the Nile in 320 BCE. And perhaps by referring to a sleeping giant, Ptolemy is actually referring to the dead Alexander.'

'Do you think this means that Alexander's body might actually have been kept somewhere in Thonis-Heracleion?' asked Andrew.

'It sounds far-fetched,' said Fiona, 'but at this point I would not rule anything out. As we have discussed before, Alexander's mummified body was of huge political value to whoever controlled it. It represented very tangible power in the ancient world, as evidenced by the fact that the rulers of the world's most powerful empire, the Roman Empire, flocked to this city for centuries to pay their respects to the great man. I think it stands to reason that if you possess something that powerful you might not want to keep it in plain sight, even if that is what you pretend to have done. Perhaps it would be wiser to keep the sarcophagus in the Soma empty, and instead hide Alexander's body somewhere completely different.'

'I must admit that sounds like a very plausible theory,' said Andrew. 'I suppose it isn't unlike what we know various museums around the world have done. I am sure I have read about how they have sometimes kept near-perfect replicas of artefacts or even paintings on display for the public, whilst secretly keeping the original somewhere safe and away from the risk of damage or theft.'

'Exactly,' nodded Fiona. 'The more I think about it the more I think that is what must have happened in one form or another.'

'But where does that leave us?' asked Andrew.

'Thonis,' said Fiona matter-of-factly. 'We have to go there and try to find the tomb, if it is really there.'

'But you said the city sank into the sea,' said Andrew.

'It did,' said Fiona. 'Which is why I will bet you anything that right now Alexis has a team of divers poking around on the seabed where Thonis-Heracleion used to be.'

'Alright,' said Andrew. 'Let's get ourselves up there then. It wouldn't be the first time we would need to go diving. But where do we start?'

'Wherever Alexis's yacht is,' replied Fiona. 'They have had a head start on us, so they may already have made progress. Or worse still, they might have already found the tomb.'

'Let's hope not,' said Andrew. 'Anyway, there is no time to lose. Let's get a taxi and swing by the hotel before we go to Abou Qir. I am sure there is a marina there where we can hire a boat and some diving equipment.'

'What about Dubois and his goons?' asked Fiona, sounding apprehensive. 'What if they are down there already.'

'We will have to cross that bridge when we get to it,' replied Andrew. 'We have come this far, so we can't just stop now. Let's go.'

# THIRTY-ONE

It was the middle of the afternoon when Andrew and Fiona arrived at the small marina in Abou Qir. The city and the harbour area in particular, had a distinctly run-down feel to it. Many of the buildings looked modern in design yet old and tired, and the sprawling industrial area near the port itself lent an air of slightly soulless utilitarianism to the whole city. But that in some ways simply upheld the millennia-old tradition of this area of the Nile Delta. Life here had revolved around moving and trading goods along the Nile and across the Mediterranean Sea for almost as long as people had lived here. Aesthetics in this place were very clearly of secondary concern.

Not so, however, for the other major trading hub further to the northeast, now lost to the sea. Thonis-Heracleion was famed not just for its economy and trade, but also for its many temples. During its lifetime it benefitted significantly from trade in cultural goods such as pottery made from local clay, figurines and amulets made of metal brought in from Cyprus and the Greek mainland, as well as various tools made from acacia wood which came from trees that grew further inland in slightly drier parts of the delta.

'It is difficult to imagine this place as an ancient city,' said Andrew, looking around as they walked from the taxi across a large parking lot towards a boat rental office. 'Everything here looks contemporary and a bit bleak and uninviting, to be honest. I haven't seen a single trace of any historic buildings since we entered the city.'

'I doubt this place ever had ambitions about pleasing the eye,' said Fiona. 'It was all about commerce.'

Gesturing out towards the bay ahead of them, she continued. 'Quite a large number of shipwrecks have been found in this bay, some of them still with trade goods from Crete, Cyprus, Phoenicia and Persia. This really was quite an international place in ancient times. Think of it as the Port of Los Angeles, Rotterdam or Shanghai of the ancient world. The same could be said about Thonis-Heracleion. Let me show you on a map,' she said, firing up her tablet again.

'A couple of thousand years ago,' she continued, pointing almost due east and out towards the bay, 'if we had made our way across the delta from here and about two kilometres that way, this is where we would have found ourselves.'

She pointed to the map on the tablet.

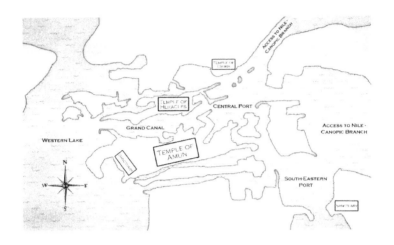

'What you see here is a re-constructed map showing Thonis-Heracleion around the time of Alexander, when it was still very much a busy and bustling regional trading hub. The light-coloured areas are the small islands the city was built on, and you can see the placement of several temples throughout the city. All of this is now covered by at least five metres of water, but in some cases as much as ten metres. And all across this city, which we think measured around 1,800 by 1,500 metres, some amazing finds have been recovered during the past couple of decades. There were five-metre-tall granite statues of various gods placed around the temples, which would have been made in Upper Egypt and then transported hundreds of miles to the city. Underwater archaeologists, who by the way estimate that only about five percent of the city has been excavated so far, also found a long sleek and very well-preserved ship made of sycamore wood, which was deliberately sunk in late 4th century BCE.'

'Deliberately?' said Andrew.

'Yes, it is thought to have been a sacred ritual barge, which would have been loaded with sacrificial offerings and then sunk here. Another remarkable find was a two-metre-tall black granite stele commissioned by Nectanebo I. It is estimated to be older than the Rosetta Stone which was found just a few kilometres north of here, since it is from the first year of the reign of Nectanebo I. This means around 380 BCE or about sixty years before Alexander arrived in Egypt with his armies.'

'So, this was just before the existing Egyptian dynasties were replaced by Ptolemy and his family, right?' said Andrew.

'Correct,' replied Fiona. 'Which actually reminds me of something else. You see, the huge temples here in this city, specifically the Temple of Amun, played quite a pivotal role in Egyptian society. It was inside that temple that the power of the gods was conferred upon new pharaohs at the beginning of their reign. This is similar to what happened in the Temple of Karnak in Upper Egypt a millennium earlier, before the centre of power shifted north to the Nile Delta. So, in some respects, Thonis-Heracleion was more than just a commercial centre. It carried real weight in the religious and cultural traditions of the pharaonic dynasties.'

'Interesting,' said Andrew looking out towards the bay. 'I think most people have never heard of this place.'

'I can't imagine what it must have been like for those French divers to uncover all of this,' said Fiona. 'I wish I could have been there.'

'Well,' said Andrew. 'You're about to get your chance to see it for yourself. Here's the boat rental company, and I can see they have diving equipment for hire too.'

Half an hour later they were loading the scuba diving equipment into a small boat they had hired. The boat was six meters long and had a powerful outboard motor at the rear. On the right, or starboard side was a seat for the driver, and inside the front of the boat was a compartment with a small seating area that could just about fit four people.

Andrew sat down in the driver's seat, inserted the key and pressed the ignition button. The large outboard motor coughed a couple of times and then came alive. It revved up quickly and then settled down to a low growl as it idled, black smoke coming out of its exhaust pipe.

'I don't think I want to know what they put in the fuel tank,' smiled Andrew.

Fiona sat in the seat opposite Andrew's and looked out towards the bay as the vessel slowly made its way out of the marina. As it picked up speed, the wind caught her hair.

'I love the smell of the sea,' she smiled and looked over at Andrew.

There was a fine spray of seawater lifting up into the air every time the bow of the boat hit the crest of one of the shallow waves in the bay. Fiona licked her lips.

'I can taste it too,' she said.

'What is that island?' said Andrew and pointed, having to raise his voice over the engine noise.

Ahead of them and to their left, a couple of kilometres away, was an island protruding up from the sea. It appeared to be at least 200 metres long and was a pale-yellow colour. It seemed rocky and dry, and it had no vegetation on it at all.

'That is Nelson Island,' said Fiona loudly. 'It was named after Horatio Nelson, the English admiral. Or at least, that is how it is currently known. It would obviously once have had an Egyptian name but that seems to have been forgotten. Several tombs of British soldiers and seamen have been found there dating back to the time of Napoleon's Egyptian campaign in 1798.'

'I am surprised to see something like that here,' said Andrew. 'I thought the entire Nile Delta was a flat bed of clay and sand. And didn't you say that the whole area has sunk much lower over the centuries?'

'Well, yes. That is mostly true,' said Fiona. 'But here and there sections of rock poke up like this, creating islands. It is actually interesting to see such a large chunk of the bedrock still protruding from the seabed, even after this whole section of the Nile Delta sank beneath the sea. At that time, what is now Nelson Island would have been a very high rocky promontory northwest of the city of Thonis-Heracleion at the very edge of the Nile Delta. Even today, the island's highest point is probably some twenty-five metres above sea level, so at that time it would have been perhaps twice that.'

'It must have been very close to the northern edge of Thonis-Heracleion,' said Andrew, peering at it.

Fiona showed him another image on her tablet which was a so-called bathymetric, or under-water topographic map of the Nile Delta.

'What you can see here,' she said and pointed, 'is that whereas Nelson Island now appears completely detached from the mainland, it is actually really just the end of a rocky ridge that runs out from the area around Abou Qir. After the delta sank and sea levels rose, only the small part that is Nelson Island was still sticking up from the seabed.'

'I see,' said Andrew. 'I guess there will be similar rocky outcroppings underwater as well. I hope the water isn't too murky.'

'Oh shit,' said Fiona. 'Andrew, that is them, isn't it?'

'Who?' asked Andrew, glancing over to see Fiona gazing out towards Nelson Island.

As they had made their way out of the marina and into Abou Qir Bay, a large vessel, previously obscured by Nelson Island, came into view.

'That's the Hypatia, isn't it?' said Fiona, and pointed to a large yacht that appeared to be anchored out in the middle of Abou Qir Bay.

'It sure is,' said Andrew, sounding less than enthusiastic. 'So that's where it was hiding. Seems like it is just to the north of the island and it looks as if it has dropped anchor out there.'

'We can't get too close,' said Fiona. 'They might spot us and recognise us.'

'Don't worry,' said Andrew. 'I will keep us a few hundred meters away. There is no way they will be able to see who we are, especially when we put our on scuba gear.'

'We need to try to place the boat near the Temple of Amun,' said Fiona. 'That is the centre of the temple district, and I think that is a good distance from the Hypatia too. I have the exact coordinates here.'

She handed him a slip of paper with longitude and latitude, which he then used to pilot the boat to that location, using the boat's onboard GPS system.

'Alright,' said Andrew, slowing the boat down and correcting its course slightly to make sure they kept their distance from the yacht. 'Almost there now.'

He eventually cut the engine and let the boat drift forward under its own momentum. When it had come to a stop, he looked out over the side.

'You can see some of the features of the seabed quite clearly. I reckon it is about six metres deep here.'

Fiona leaned out over the side and looked down.

'There are some large dark-coloured areas just here,' she said. 'That must be the remains of the Temple of Amun.'

'Alright,' said Andrew. 'Let's drop anchor and get our scuba gear on.'

'I don't see any movement over there,' said Fiona, looking towards the yacht. 'They must be inside.'

'Good, said Andrew. 'Come on. Let's gear up.'

He had made his way to the front of the boat to throw the anchor overboard. About fifteen minutes later they were both wearing wetsuits, having strapped on their air tanks, breathing apparatus, masks and flippers. Fiona also strapped a small plastic whiteboard with an underwater pen attached on a string to her leg. This would allow them to communicate underwater if needed. Putting the tip of his index finger and thumb together, creating the OK sign, Andrew turned to look at Fiona. She responded in kind and then they jumped over the side together.

★          ★          ★

Down below the surface of the water, it suddenly looked and felt very different from when they had been on the boat. The water suddenly seemed quite murky because of the silt that had washed out from the Nile Delta, and Andrew and Fiona spent a couple of seconds getting used to the new environment and trying to orientate themselves relative to the ruins of the Temple of Amun below them on the seabed.

However, it could have been a lot worse. This was outside of the annual flood season, so the volume of water being transported hundreds of kilometres down the Nile to the Mediterranean was relatively small. This in turn meant that the silt being washed out into Abou Qir Bay was much less now than it had been just a few months earlier, and so although the water was murky, visibility was still around twenty metres.

As they slowly made their way down through the water towards the seabed whilst holding their waterproof torches out in front of themselves, the outline of the ancient temple came into view. It looked to have been at least fifty metres long and perhaps as much as twenty metres wide, and next to what used to be the main entrance were two enormous toppled-over statues of Amun himself, holding the Ankh-symbol of life in one hand, and the

Was-sceptre of power and dominion in the other. The heads alone were at least three metres long.

The walls of the temple had mostly crumpled many centuries ago, but their outline was clear to see, and they still protruded up more than a metre in several places around the circumference of the inner sanctum where the sacrificial altar would have been.

Approaching the location of the inner sanctum, they descended all the way to the bottom where small amounts of silt wafted up into the water behind them as they swam along. Reaching the spot where the altar had been, Andrew stopped and slowly began turning around to fan his torchlight around their immediate surroundings.

In what would have been the corner of the building, a tall ornate pillar had fallen down and into the temple. It was lying stretched out across the floor from the corner towards the altar, having broken into several pieces. The pillar was more than two metres in width, and as they approached it, they could see that it was richly decorated with hieroglyphs. Fiona swam over and aligned herself with the pillar so that she could them. After a minute or so of examining it, she pulled out her whiteboard and scribbled a message.

Definitely Temple of Amun
Account of coronation on this pillar
Let's keep going

Andrew gave her the OK. Then he pointed at the whiteboard, and Fiona handed it to him. Andrew scribbled a quick sentence.

## *Let's look outside. Temple walls*

Fiona gave him the OK, and Andrew then pointed towards a large gap in the ruins of the southern wall that led to the area outside. Once there, it was clear that just as Fiona's map had indicated, the temple once stood next to a canal. The seabed sloped down quite abruptly, and even though what used to be the canal had now been mostly filled with silt and sand, there was a drop of at least two metres from the foundation of the temple to the middle of the former canal.

They made their way in an arc around the ruins of the Temple of Amun, examining the crumbled walls for anything that might provide a hint to a connection with Ptolemy's diary entry, but they found nothing. When they were back where they started, Andrew showed Fiona a clenched fist with his thumb sticking up, indicating his intention to move back towards the surface. She responded in kind, and the two of them made their way slowly back up towards the boat and the sunlight.

Dripping with salty seawater and out of breath, they both climbed back into the boat and began taking off their scuba equipment.

'There is huge variation in the level of the seabed, isn't there?' said Andrew, loosening the straps of his air tank. 'It's like a hilly landscape.'

'Yes,' replied Fiona, taking her flippers off. 'It is a lot more undulating than you might think sitting up here on a boat.'

She hesitated for a moment, looking out onto the bay.

'That actually gives me an idea,' she finally said. 'The French underwater archaeological team used so-called nuclear magnetic resonance imaging, or NMR, which is a highly accurate method for mapping the seabed. Give me a minute. I will see if I can find the images.'

She took off the rest of her kit and went down into the front compartment of the boat to fetch her tablet. A couple of minutes later they were both out of their wetsuits and sitting next to each other, looking at the screen.

'This is the result of an extensive NMR mapping effort carried out by the French team,' said Fiona, and showed Andrew a high-resolution underwater topographic map of the area around Thonis-Heracleion.

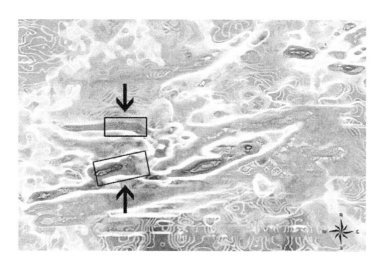

'Amazing,' said Andrew. 'This gives a whole new perspective on this place.'

'Yes,' said Fiona. 'I have marked the position of the Temple of Amun at the bottom, and of the Temple of Heracles at the top. What is interesting to me is that the temples appear to have been built on elevated positions above the city. The Temple of Heracles especially appears to have been built on top of a long rocky promontory in the northern part of the city. Now, given what Ptolemy wrote in his diary about the thirteenth task of Heracles, I think it would make sense to investigate that temple too.'

Andrew leaned in to look more closely at the image and the area where the Temple of Heracles once stood.

'Look at this dot here,' he said and pointed. 'There seems to be some sort of depression in the lower right-hand corner of the top square area you marked out around the Temple of Heracles. What do you suppose that could be?'

'It seems to be just a few metres across, so it could be an area where the sediment has collapsed, or it might be an indent into the bedrock, or it could just be some sort of anomaly in the readings. I guess we will find out when we get over there. The temple should be about sixty metres that way,' she said, pointing north and out towards the bay.

Twenty minutes and a couple of snacks later, the two of them donned their scuba equipment again. As Andrew was checking to make sure that the straps on Fiona's air tank were secure, she looked northwest towards the Hypatia.

'What are they doing over there?' she said. 'I haven't seen any sign of life since we got here.'

'Your guess is as good as mine,' replied Andrew. 'All I know is that it is no coincidence that we all end up in the same place. Whether there is something down there to be found or not, we need to remain vigilant. These people are not playing around.'

'I know,' said Fiona, checking her regulator. 'Being shot at in Venice was not my idea of a fun night out.'

'Just keep your wits about you,' said Andrew. 'If they suddenly turn up, things could get interesting. Come on. Let's get back in.'

# THIRTY-TWO

The rocky underwater promontory that rose up several metres from the seabed was nothing like the weathered and jagged rocks that could be seen on Nelson Island. The exposed bedrock in this part of the bay had smooth and rounded contours, shaped by the movement of water and sand over the centuries.

The ruins of the Temple of Heracles sitting atop it were even less well preserved than those of the Temple of Amun. For this reason, the site had received significantly less attention from the French team of archaeologists than the much larger Temple of Amun. Only a very faint outline of the temple walls was still visible, and what no doubt used to be a spectacular colonnade at the front of the temple had been reduced to a jumbled-up pile of broken cylindrical pieces of limestone. Of the wide steps that once led up to the temple entrance, there was no trace, since that part of the site had been buried under a thick layer of sediment.

As Andrew and Fiona slowly swam closer and approached the temple ruin, they noticed just how much higher the temple would have been above the rest of the city, sitting as it had on a large promontory of bedrock that would have formed the central part of the city. On the NMR image, the promontory had looked to be perhaps a couple of hundred metres long and as much as one hundred metres wide, leaving plenty of space for the temple to be built.

Floating above the temple site, they slowly moved their torchlights across the seabed, looking for any clue that might have a bearing on Ptolemy's thirteenth task of Heracles. But they could see nothing that drew their attention. Eventually, they swam towards the southeast corner of the temple, but as they moved further towards the location where the NMR image had suggested there might be a depression in the seabed, it became clear that there was nothing out of the ordinary there either.

Andrew held the palm of his left hand facing upwards and mimed writing on it with his right hand, so Fiona gave him her whiteboard and pen. He quickly wrote her a message.

*Nothing here*
*This area is flat*
*NMR anomaly?*

He handed her back the whiteboard and she replied.

I think so

Andrew held up his hand, palm facing Fiona as if something had just occurred to him. Then he waved for her to hand him the whiteboard, wrote another message and showed it to her.

*Might be a cavity??*

Andrew looked at Fiona through the glass of his diving mask. He could see that she looked like she had not thought of that. She took the whiteboard.

*Possibly*

Andrew grabbed the whiteboard again and wrote another message.

*Help me dig*

Then he swam down to the approximate location of the anomaly and placed his torch on the sand which raised a small plume of silt into the water. Swimming sideways for a bit to position himself right where the light of the torch was shining, he then slowly began to remove the sand and silt from the seabed using his hands. Fiona soon joined him, and the two of them then methodically removed a thick layer of sediment around the area, causing large amounts of it to swirl up around them and reducing visibility to just a couple of metres.

After a few minutes, they had removed a thick layer of sand and sediment, and Andrew was beginning to feel like they were pointlessly digging a hole in the seabed.

Then his hand brushed against something hard. Was this the bedrock that the temple had been built on, or was it its foundation? Fiona had felt it too, and the two of them looked up at each other. Then they continued clearing away more sediment until a large neatly chiselled stone slab revealed itself. Andrew grabbed the whiteboard.

*Original temple floor?*

Fiona gave him the OK sign. Then she reached down with her hand and wafted some more silt away from the edge of the slab, revealing a wide seam between it, and a similar one next to it. She grabbed her whiteboard.

*Cavity below?*

Andrew nodded, took the board, and wrote a reply.

*Let's clear it and pull it up.*

While Fiona continued to clear the slab of sediment, Andrew used the knife he had kept strapped to his leg to dig out the sand and silt from the grooves around the circumference of the slab. Once he had cleared it, he put the knife back in its sheath, and stuck the fingers of both of his hands down into the groove. Placing his knee next to the groove for support, he began pulling on the slab as hard as he could. It was roughly one square metre in size, and he guessed it could be as much as five or ten centimetres thick. Given that a stone slab like that would weigh about 200 kilograms, its apparent underwater weight was closer to 75 kilograms which meant that he should to be able to lift it relatively easily. But despite Andrew having dug out most of the silt, sand and partly dissolved mortar between the slabs, it was wedged between two other slabs and did not budge.

Fiona came over next to him. Facing each other and both placing a knee on the slab next to it, they grabbed the exposed slab and began pulling. Ever so slowly the slab began to lift, the two of them straining inside their masks until suddenly it came loose. Once it was free of the surrounding slabs, it was quite easy to manipulate despite its weight.

Andrew tilted it over to one side, to reveal a gaping dark square hole. As Fiona leaned over to peer down into it, Andrew picked up his torch again and pointed it down into it.

The inside was a square shaft not dissimilar to the rock-cut catacombs of Kom el Shoqafa in Alexandria, extending down into the bedrock at least three meters. On one of its sides were steps cut directly into the rock, which would have allowed someone to climb up or down when the temple was still above water many centuries earlier.

Fiona took out her whiteboard again

*Looks like secret passage under temple*

Andrew nodded and moved to start making his way down into the shaft, but then Fiona placed a hand on his arm, clearly anxious about what they might find.

Andrew took the whiteboard and scribbled.

## No turning back now

After a brief moment of hesitation, Fiona nodded and let go of his arm. Then Andrew lowered himself, flippers first, into the shaft holding his torch in one hand whilst carefully manoeuvring himself downward with the other.

Fiona remained motionless at the top, using her own torch to help light the way for him. Suddenly, she felt the creeping sensation of being watched and her head whipped up to look around. There was nothing there, except for her and the dark hole in the temple floor.

Down in the shaft, Andrew had now reached the bottom, where what appeared to be a tunnel extended away from the shaft and downward at a shallow angle, not unlike what they had seen under the Esagila Temple in Babylon. His torch was not powerful enough to cut through the water down there, which had now been muddied slightly by his presence. However, at first glance, it looked to be at least fifteen metres long since that was more or less as far as the torch could reach. Just like the vertical shaft, the rectangular tunnel was rock-cut with smooth walls.

He looked up and signalled for Fiona to join him. Looking around one more time, she eventually swung her flippers around and down into the shaft. At the bottom of it there was just room for the two of them. Andrew wrote another message.

*I will go first*
*Follow me*
*You ok?*

Fiona nodded, but her eyes belied her trepidation at the prospect of swimming deeper into the bedrock, not knowing what they might find there.

Andrew grabbed her hand and gave it a quick squeeze, whilst looking her in the eye. Then he turned back towards the tunnel. Peering into the narrow space, he eventually decided that it was probably wide enough to turn around if necessary, so he began swimming through it very slowly. As he went, the air bubbles from his regulator were collecting above him under the tunnel ceiling and coalescing into small lakes of air that looked like quicksilver and reflected the light from their torches. After a few metres, he checked the pressure in his air tank. It was still good for another twenty-five minutes, and knowing that Fiona's would read the same he decided to press on.

After around fifteen metres the tunnel levelled out for five metres, and then it began ascending again at a similar angle to the first section. Andrew checked behind him, to make sure Fiona was still there and happy to continue.

At the other end, a further fifteen metres along or so, the tunnel seemed to end abruptly up ahead. It was only as he swam closer that he realised that it ended in the same manner it had begun. With a vertical shaft going upwards.

As he reached it, he stopped and turned around again to see Fiona making her way the last few metres towards him. He shone his torchlight directly up and was astonished by what he saw. Beckoning Fiona to come right up close to him, the two of them then shone their torches upwards where their light hit the surface of the water from below. The air bubbles from their regulators percolated upwards and disappeared as they reached the surface. There was an air-filled cavity above them.

From the bottom of the shaft, they could not see how big the space above them was, so Andrew slowly pulled himself up towards the surface by grabbing onto the rock-cut footholds along the way.

When his head broke through the surface, what he saw almost took his breath away. He was in a large chamber somewhere inside the bedrock under the ancient temple, and it had air in it.

Reaching up, he grabbed onto the ledge above him and hauled himself up to a sitting position, his legs still in the water. A couple of seconds later, Fiona emerged and he helped her up next to him. The two of them, barely able to believe what they were seeing, took their regulators out of their mouths and their masks off of their faces. The air was damp and smelled slightly mouldy.

'What the hell is this place?' breathed Fiona, looking around the dark space around them, her voice producing a muffled echo.

They were inside a cube-shaped chamber, with walls and a ceiling that all met at what seemed like perfect right angles. There were four pillars spaced equidistantly relative to the middle of the chamber and its four corners, and at the far end was a doorway leading off to a dark space beyond.

'You tell me,' said Andrew, peering into the darkness around them and trying to make out details of the chamber by shining his torchlight around.

'How are we able to breathe down here?' said Fiona, looking perplexed. 'We must be at least twenty meters below the surface of the water.'

She checked the depth gauge on her wrist.

'The pressure here is slightly higher than where we swam down into the first shaft. We must be at more or less the same depth, but inside the bedrock that the temple is sitting on.'

'It is extraordinary,' said Andrew. 'Air must have been trapped in here since the city was inundated and the temples were lost to the sea. The sloped access tunnel would have functioned like a cork in a bottle, or an s-bend in a drainpipe, effectively sealing the air in here. What we are breathing now is oxygen from almost two thousand years ago. The bedrock all around us has prevented it from escaping during all this time.

'This is surreal,' said Fiona. 'We need to have a look around.'

'Wait a second,' said Andrew, reaching into a small compartment in his buoyancy control vest. 'I brought these just in case.'

In his hand were ten small glowsticks held together by a thick rubber band. He cracked three of them and as he tossed them to three different spots on the floor of the chamber, their powerful blue light began to bloom out and fill the chamber with an eerie hue, allowing them to now appreciate the true size of the space.

The two of them slipped off their scuba equipment and stood up, letting the light from their torches sweep across the room. It was nothing like what they had seen in Kom el Shoqafa. Although the chamber itself was rock-cut, the floor was a giant mosaic made up of small coloured tiles with depictions of various gods from Greek mythology, and it was edged with a wide meander pattern around the entire circumference of the chamber. The walls were covered in murals depicting elaborate motifs of mountains, temples and people, some of them clearly kings.

'This is definitely not Egyptian,' said Fiona. 'Look at these columns. They are in the classic Greek ionic style. This mosaic floor reminds me of those found in Zeugma in Turkey.

'What is Zeugma?' asked Andrew.

'It was a town, most likely founded by Alexander's general Seleucus after he took control of the empire. Archaeologists have uncovered the most incredible tile mosaics there, perfectly preserved after two millennia.'

'And these are similar?' asked Andrew.

'Very much so,' replied Fiona. 'It has the same level of detail. Same colours. Same craftsmanship. Everything in here is Hellenic. It must be at least two thousand years old. And this whole thing looks like a temple. But why would there be a temple hidden beneath another temple?'

'Why is anything ever hidden?' asked Andrew rhetorically. 'To keep it from being known to the wider world. But who could have made this place?'

'Whoever they were,' said Fiona. 'It is clear who they revered. Come and look at this.'

Andrew walked over to join her next to a mural on one of the walls. It depicted a large map of the ancient world, but with a large area stretching from Greece through Asia Minor, down to Egypt and further east all the way to Persia and India, all in the same colour with the major ancient cities marked on it.

'Alexander's empire,' said Andrew. 'This is all the land he conquered.'

'We are clearly standing in a temple dedicated to Alexander,' said Fiona. 'Whether it was cut into the bedrock before or after the Temple of Heracles above us I can't say. But it is clear that it was never meant to be known to anyone other than the specially initiated. The access must have been deliberately hidden under the temple.'

'I wonder how many years it has been since anyone else was in here,' said Andrew, looking around the chamber.

'Almost certainly many centuries,' said Fiona.

Andrew pointed his torchlight towards the doorway at the end of the chamber.

'Let's see what is through here,' he said, and began walking carefully towards it.

'I'm guessing you didn't bring a weapon?' said Fiona.

'No,' said Andrew. 'I couldn't bring my pistol on a scuba dive, and I also didn't want to leave it on the boat while we are down here. I only have this.'

He tapped the knife that was strapped to his leg.

'If there was someone here, we would have found out by now,' he continued. 'Let's press on.'

On both sides of the doorway was a statue of a sitting lion, each one wearing a crown, and above the architrave was a frieze that both of them knew only too well at this point.

'The Vergina Sun,' said Fiona, and pointed. 'I am beginning to think we might be in the right place.'

'You mean, you think this might actually be Alexander's tomb?' asked Andrew.

'It is beginning to look that way,' replied Fiona, sounding as if she could barely believe what was happening. 'I guess we will find out in the next few minutes.'

The two of them proceeded through the doorway into another chamber that was almost identical to the first, except that it was quite a bit larger. The air in there seemed dryer and less stale, although it still had a distinctly musty smell to it. Its floor was covered in intricate mosaics, and its walls were decorated with detailed murals of what appeared to be the mountains, valleys and fields of the area between Aigai and Pella. The whole chamber was clearly made to conjure up the sense of being back in Macedonia where the lives of both Alexander, Ptolemy and many of their fellow soldiers and generals began.

But the most eye-catching thing in the chamber was not the floor or the walls. It was a large sarcophagus sitting on a raised granite platform at the far end of the chamber. Andrew quickly cracked another couple of his glowsticks and tossed them in different places on the mosaic floor.

As the chemicals in the glowsticks began reacting and their light began to bloom out strongly, the room became bathed in blue light and the sarcophagus came into full view.

'My god,' whispered Fiona. 'Andrew, this might be it. This might be the tomb.'

They continued to walk carefully towards the sarcophagus, their torchlights sweeping over it as they approached.

'Look at that,' said Andrew. 'The lid.'

The limestone lid of the sarcophagus seemed to have been hewn from a single block of stone, and it was shaped in meticulous detail in the likeness of a strong man lying on his back with his hands on his chest. One hand was holding the Egyptian Ankh symbol, and the other held the Was-sceptre. His chest was clad in an elaborate Greek linothorax, his legs wore greaves, and on his head under his flowing curls was a headdress made from the head of a lion.

'This is Alexander,' said Fiona. 'No doubt in my mind. This statue has his likeness, right down to the shape of his nose.'

Andrew knelt down on one knee, pointing his torch at the side of the sarcophagus.

'There is some writing here,' he said. 'It seems to be in ancient Greek. Can you read it?'

Fiona knelt down beside him to examine the text.

# Φωσφόρος

'It is incredible craftsmanship,' she said. 'The letters are neatly carved into the limestone and the text is clear, but I am not sure I understand the meaning of it.'

'Well, what does it say?' asked Andrew.

'It simply says *Phosphoros*,' replied Fiona.

Andrew turned his head to look at her, a perplexed look on his face.

'Phosphorus, as in the chemical element?'

'Well, no. It can't be,' replied Fiona. 'The chemical element phosphorus was not known when this temple was built. But in ancient Greece, *Phosphoros* was the name of the morning star. Phôs means *light*, and phóros means *bearing*, so the word literally just means *light bearer*. The Romans would eventually name it Venus, which is what we call it today. As you and I both know, Venus is actually not a star but a planet, but the ancient Greeks and Romans did not realise this.'

'So, are you saying this inscription refers to the planet Venus?' asked Andrew, furrowing his brow.

Fiona raised her eyebrows and pressed her lips together.

'That's how it appears,' she replied, sounding uncertain. 'But what does Venus have to do with Alexander the Great? Unless of course, it was somehow a reference to Alexander as the morning star or as a guiding star.'

'I suppose that would make sense in a temple that was literally built in his honour and as a place to worship him,' said Andrew. 'If he was perceived to be a deity, it seems pretty straightforward to me that his life and everything he did would be held up as something that could provide people with guidance about how to behave and what to do.'

'That makes sense. You might be right there,' nodded Fiona.

Andrew stood back up and looked at the lid of the sarcophagus.

'I am no expert,' he said, 'but I don't think this is an actual sarcophagus.'

Fiona rose as well and placed her hands on her hips.

'Why do you say that?' she asked, studying it.

'Because it looks to me like the whole thing was hewn from one solid piece of limestone, and I don't see any seam between the sarcophagus itself and its lid.'

Fiona leaned in to examine the sarcophagus.

'I think you are right,' she said, running her fingertips along where the seam should have been. 'This is not a real sarcophagus. It seems more like an altar where people could worship. Perhaps a copy of the original, wherever that was kept.'

She tapped the end of her torch on the side of the sarcophagus. It did not sound hollow, and there was no resonance. It simply produced a brief muffled thud.

'Yes. Definitely solid,' said Andrew.

'Damn,' said Fiona, looking around the chamber. 'I was sure this would be the tomb.'

Andrew began fanning his torchlight slowly around the room.

'Wait. What's that?' said Fiona suddenly, pointing her torch at the statue's hands and leaning in over the sarcophagus. 'Oh my god, Andrew look!' she exclaimed. 'A ring. He's wearing a ring.'

Andrew leaned in as well, and there in the torchlight on the middle finger of the right hand of the statue was a substantial-looking gold ring. Emblazoned on a thick hexagonal disc on the ring was the Vergina Sun.

'This is what Ptolemy was referring to,' said Fiona excitedly. 'This statue is the sleeping giant and he is wearing Alexander's signet ring.'

'Can you get it off?' asked Andrew.

Fiona turned to look at him, as if on the cusp of protesting.

'Listen' said Andrew. 'It is a question of time before Alexis and her goons find this place, and I promise you that when they do, they will take this thing, and they will not hand it over to the Egyptian authorities. It will disappear and never be seen again.'

'You're right,' said Fiona reluctantly. 'It might even have remnants of Alexander's DNA on it. We should get it out of here to a safe place.'

She reached towards the hand of the statue, placed the thumb and middle finger of her right hand on the ring, and then she gingerly slid it off the statue's finger. She held it in the palm of her hand for a moment and gazed down at it.

'I can't believe I am holding Alexander the Great's signet ring in my hand,' she said. 'I never thought something like this would even be possible.'

'Let's not celebrate yet,' said Andrew. 'We should get out of here. It will be getting dark soon, and I would prefer not to be on the open sea in a small boat at night.'

'You're right,' said Fiona grudgingly. 'We should go.'

She slipped the ring inside a small clear re-sealable plastic bag and then they began walking back towards the doorway leading to the antechamber with the underwater tunnel access. Halfway there, Fiona stopped and turned around, looking at the sarcophagus.

'Who knows if we will ever be able to come back here,' she said. 'I just need to take it all in for a few more seconds.'

Eventually, she looked at Andrew and produced an almost apologetic smile, and then the two of them walked through the doorway.

As they got to the shaft in the floor and began picking up their scuba equipment, Andrew suddenly froze.

'Crap,' he said, looking into the shaft. 'There's a light. Someone is coming through the tunnel.'

# THIRTY-THREE

Whoever was moving through the tunnel towards the chamber was carrying a powerful torch. The flickering light was bouncing off the walls and the sediment at the bottom, making its way to the vertical shaft and up into the antechamber, where it danced around languidly on the chamber's ceiling.

'Back to the other chamber,' said Andrew hurriedly. 'We don't know how many of them there are or if they are armed.'

Fiona looked terrified.

'Shit,' she said. 'What the hell do we do?'

'We will have to improvise,' said Andrew tensely and grabbed her arm firmly. 'Come on. Back inside now. Pick up all the glowsticks and shove them in this bag. They will give away our presence. Quick!'

They hurried around the chamber to gather the glowsticks and then slipped inside the chamber with the sarcophagus, where they collected the other three sticks. Then they stood just inside and next to the doorway, out of sight from the tunnel access. When they heard the sound of splashing water and of someone climbing out of the shaft, Andrew decided to have a quick peek.

Inside the antechamber was a single figure sitting on the edge of the shaft with his legs still inside it. He was in the process of taking his mask off. As soon as he had placed it next to him, he picked up his torch and began shining it around the antechamber. Andrew quickly pulled his head back to avoid being spotted. From the brief view he had gotten of the man and the way he looked around, it appeared to him as if this might be the man's first time in the antechamber.

Once Andrew heard the sound of him climbing out of the shaft, standing up and beginning to take off his scuba equipment, Andrew risked another peek. This time he spotted something that got his attention immediately.

On the floor next to the torch was what appeared to be an underwater rifle. Andrew had been trained in their use, but this one was almost certainly the Avtomat Podvodny Spetsialnyy, or Special Underwater Assault Rifle. It was initially developed by the Soviet Union, but its successor models are still in use by Russian special forces units when conducting small scale amphibious assaults.

It looks much like a normal assault rifle, but instead of firing bullets, it fires twelve-centimetre-long steel bolts which leave the muzzle at 300 metres per second and have an effective range of between 20 and 30 metres, depending on the depth at which they are fired. The rifle also works on land, but there it has a much shorter range than a normal rifle.

Andrew allowed himself to look for another couple of seconds, and that is when he saw the man's face. It was the Russian, Morozov. He pulled back again and looked across to Fiona, whose face was an image of near panic.

Andrew held up his hand, his palm facing Fiona and moving it back and forth a couple of times to indicate for her to back up. She quietly did so while Andrew reached down and quietly undid the fastener on the sheath and pulled out his diving knife.

As they stood there silently, they could see from the way Morozov's torchlight moved that he was making his way across the antechamber towards the doorway.

Andrew steeled himself. He knew that he would only get one chance at this. Morozov was much better armed and arguably younger and more fit than him. The only thing he and Fiona had going for them was the element of surprise.

Just as Morozov passed through the doorway, Andrew pulled back his diving knife to hold it up next to his shoulder. Then he launched himself at the Russian.

Somehow Morozov must have sensed Andrew's presence, because as Andrew came at him, bringing his knife down towards his chest, Morozov pivoted his torso and leaned away just enough for Andrew to barge into him without the knife making contact. Surprised by Morozov's quick reactions, Andrew was knocked off balance and Morozov then leaned into him and shoved him violently onto the floor.

The Russian brought up his rifle, pointing it at Andrew, and just as his finger closed around the trigger there was a woman's scream from his immediate left. At the same time, Morozov saw an object coming at him from the left, and he only had time to partially turn his head when it impacted. Morozov pulled the trigger and the APS coughed loudly, sending a steel bolt rocketing out of its barrel towards Andrew. It struck him in his right thigh and he cried out in pain as it punched straight through and out on the other side.

Fiona had hurled her torch as hard as she could, and it had struck the Russian on the side of the head just as he fired. Luckily for Andrew, Morozov had kept the rifle in single fire mode, so only one steel bolt was fired. If he had switched to automatic, a mode where the APS is able to spit out six-hundred rounds per minute, Andrew would have had no chance of surviving.

Morozov was knocked off balance by the impact of the torch and staggered backwards a couple of steps, and Andrew realised that this was the last chance he was going to get to overwhelm him.

Ignoring the searing pain in his thigh, he quickly scrambled to his feet and launched himself at the Russian once more. Morozov almost managed to bring the APS around to point at Andrew, but Andrew was now inside his reach, so when the rifle fired again, the barrel was next to Andrew's hip as the two of them fell towards the wall behind Morozov.

The Russian lost his grip on the rifle as the back of his head slammed into the granite wall, and the APS went clattering to the floor. Instantly, he ripped out his own knife and brought it up violently towards Andrew's abdomen.

Andrew managed to partially block the strike, but the tip of the blade still penetrated his wetsuit and cut him in the side. Realising how desperate his situation had suddenly become, Andrew managed to grip Morozov by his vest and then crash them both onto the floor, Andrew on top of Morozov.

The Russian, using some sort of martial arts technique, managed to wriggle out and pin Andrew down whilst attempting to raise his knife over his head for a powerful strike down towards Andrew's face and neck.

'Suka blyat,' grimaced Morozov, using the Russian term for *bitch*.

The whole altercation had only lasted a few seconds, and Fiona was horrified at what she was watching unfold. Then she sprinted forward.

'Andrew!' she screamed as her foot connected with the APS, which had dropped to the floor between her and the two men.

The rifle shot across the mosaic floor and Andrew just had time to turn his head and see it coming at him. He reached out with his right hand to grab it whilst also attempting to hold back Morozov's knife-wielding arm. After clawing desperately for the APS for a couple of seconds he finally managed to reach it. In a flash, he gripped it and brought it in towards his body. Then he turned the barrel upwards, shoved it up under Morozov's chin and pushed.

Instantly, Morozov's body froze as he realised what was about to happen.

'Do svidaniya, Mudak,' hissed Andrew, using the Russian words for *Goodbye Arsehole*.

Then he pulled the trigger.

The APS produced a sharp cough, and a steel bolt rammed up into Morozov's chin and ripped through his brain and continued upwards, punching through the Russian's skull at the top of his head and making his head jerk up and back. The bolt then slammed loudly into the ceiling of the chamber with a metallic clang. A couple of small drops of blood began running down along its shiny form, dripping onto the ancient mosaic floor below.

Morozov's dead body slumped down onto Andrew. Laboriously, Andrew began to push the body away and extract himself. Fiona stood frozen for a few seconds, aghast at what had just happened, but then she hurried over and helped get Andrew free from the dead weight of the Russian.

'Fuck,' said Andrew, sitting up. 'That was too close. Thank you. I would have been dead if it wasn't for you.'

'Are you alright,' she said anxiously, placing her hand on his leg. 'He hit you?'

'It went straight through the muscle tissue,' said Andrew. 'Seems to have missed major blood vessels. I will be fine. Hurts like a son of a bitch though.'

Without a word, Fiona grabbed his head and placed her forehead on his. Then she pulled back and looked him in the eye.

'Nothing is ever easy with you, is it?' she half-smiled whilst shaking her head with a look of relief mixed with exasperation.

'I'm sorry,' smiled Andrew apologetically. 'But you knew what you signed up for with me.'

Fiona shook her head again. 'Let's just get the hell out of here.'

★          ★          ★

That evening, after making their way back to the hotel, Andrew was in the bathroom patching up his leg injury. He had just finished cauterising the exit wound, having done the entry wound a few minutes earlier. Half a bottle of whiskey and some painkillers had made that job a lot easier.

'Are you sure you don't want to see a doctor?' asked Fiona.

'Yes,' grimaced Andrew. 'They'll start asking questions. Maybe even call the police. It's pretty obvious this isn't your typical tourist injury. We don't have time to explain to them how this happened.'

That afternoon they had left Morozov's body in the sarcophagus chamber and exited in a hurry. Andrew had been somewhat encumbered by his wound, but the cool and salty seawater had soon stopped most of the bleeding, and by the time they were back on the boat, it had reduced to a small trickle.

The boat handover and the trip back to Alexandria had been an exercise in good acting, effective wound dressing and pain suppression, lest anyone notice that Andrew had a puncture wound straight through his thigh. Fiona had made an effort to be loud and attention-grabbing, and she had resorted to flirting with the man at the boat rental shop to make sure his focus was on her and not Andrew who was hobbling along and still bleeding slightly through his trouser leg.

'There was quite bit of blood, but the bolts are only about five millimetres in diameter,' said Andrew. 'So, the hole is pretty small.'

'Well, that's nice,' said Fiona sarcastically, looking slightly queasy at the sight of Andrew poking and prodding at the injury to his leg.

'That APS is quite a powerful weapon, which is a good thing,' continued Andrew. 'If it hadn't been, the bolt might not have gone through and then things might have got really messy.'

'Glad you're able to see the positives here,' said Fiona. 'I would not have managed that.'

'I know this must seem a bit strange,' said Andrew, 'but this sort of thing is just an occupational hazard. Things like this happen and then you move on. The bleeding has stopped now, and as long as it doesn't get infected I will be fine. It will probably hurt a bit, but I will manage. That's what pain killers are for'

'Mmmhmm,' said Fiona, sounding unconvinced.

'Plus,' he grinned, 'it will leave a nice scar. Something to remember this trip by.'

Fiona shook her head ruefully and left the bathroom to get herself a drink at the minibar.

Late the next morning, after a good night's sleep, they ventured out to the hotel's restaurant for a long brunch session. The weather was sunny and the wind was blowing fresh ocean air in from the Mediterranean, and they spent several hours in the restaurant discussing what to do next. Then they headed back to the room, and while Andrew was lying on the bed, resting his leg and allowing it to begin healing, Fiona spent the afternoon studying the pages of Ptolemy's diary, but she could glean no further clues from it.

'Damn it,' she said after several hours, leaning back, placing her hands behind her head and looking up at the ceiling. 'I feel like we have gone down a very long road, only to find that it is a dead end.'

'You mean, with regards to where the tomb is?' asked Andrew, who was sitting upright on the bed and leaning back against the headboard.

'Yes,' said Fiona, sounding frustrated. 'I really thought we were on to something with that thirteenth task of Heracles. Did we miss something in that chamber?'

'I don't think so,' said Andrew. 'I felt we discovered what there was to discover down there, and we did get the signet ring. Not that it is much use to us, but at least it won't end up being sold at some black-market auction. Are you sure there is nothing left in Ptolemy's diary that might provide us with a clue?'

Fiona shook her head. 'I have gone over it several times now. There is nothing there except for the bit about the thirteenth task, but we've gotten what we could get from that.'

'Perhaps you should take a break,' said Andrew. 'Maybe wait until the morning and have another look. You might spot something you haven't noticed before. It will be dinnertime soon, anyway.'

'Perhaps,' sighed Fiona and rose. 'I guess I will have a shower and get myself ready. Are you alright to go to the restaurant, or would you like room service for dinner?'

'I can't stand being in this room for much longer,' said Andrew. 'As far as I am concerned, hotel rooms are for sleeping in, not spending whole days doing nothing. I'll give the front desk a call and ask them to book a table.'

'Alright,' replied Fiona. 'I will be hungry soon, so the sooner the better. By the way, have you heard anything from Colonel Strickland?'

'Yes,' replied Andrew. 'He sent a short message saying that they no longer have a fix on the Hypatia. He suggested the captain might have turned the ship's transponder off to mask its location.'

'That sounds suspicious,' said Fiona. 'What are they up to now?'

'Probably exactly the same as us,' replied Andrew. 'It is now a race, and I feel as if we are approaching the finish line one way or another, even if we don't know where that finish line is or what it looks like.'

'Well put,' nodded Fiona. 'Anyway, I'll take that shower now. Promise me you'll stay there quietly on the bed. Your leg needs rest.'

'Yes, Miss,' sighed Andrew and smiled. 'I think I can manage that.'

A couple of hours later, the two of them walked to the restaurant where they had managed to get a table by the edge of the balcony overlooking the Eastern Harbour. Directly to their west, the sun had just set behind what at the time of Ptolemy I was the narrow Heptastadion causeway out to Pharos Island. Now, however, it was an almost five-hundred-metre-wide section of the modern city of Alexandria, stretching out towards what used to be the island and wrapping around to the opposite side of the harbour towards the northwest, where the 15th-century Citadel of Qaitbay was now lit up by floodlights.

The sparse traffic on the El-Gaish Road three storeys below them was moving along languidly, and the city seemed to have shifted down a couple of gears from its busy daytime state.

'What a gorgeous citadel that is,' said Fiona, looking out across the bay to the turreted castle-like structure just under a kilometre away. It was bathed in warm yellow light from the ground below it, and it looked both imposing and romantic at the same time.

'If you look at it for a few seconds and then close your eyes,' said Fiona, 'you can almost picture the lighthouse of Alexandria standing there two thousand years ago. Of course, the lighthouse was more than one hundred metres tall, so it was four or five times taller than this citadel. It was an absolutely gigantic structure for its day.'

'It almost begs the question,' mused Andrew. 'Why was it so enormous? I know sailors would have been able to see it from further away the taller it was, but at one hundred meters it would have been visible from a distance of something like 35 kilometres or just over twenty miles. That somehow seems excessive.'

Fiona nodded, pondering what Andrew had just said.

'It does seem like a bit of an excessive distance,' she said. 'Unless of course Ptolemy built it not just to serve as a lighthouse, but as some sort of monument to his friend Alexander. I suppose that would make sense.'

'That seems plausible,' said Andrew. 'Did you say the citadel was built on the site of the lighthouse?'

'The exact same spot,' replied Fiona. 'I have been reading up on this, and it actually has an interesting history. The lighthouse had been in ruins for centuries when in 1477 a Mamluk Sultan named Al-Ashraf Qaitbay ordered the site cleared and a citadel built there as part of a fortification effort against the Ottoman Turks. The Ottomans eventually conquered Egypt and held it for a brief period until it was taken over by the French in 1798 during Napoleon's campaign in Egypt. With the help of the British, the Ottoman Empire along with the Albanians then took control of Egypt for almost a century. During the so-called Urabi Revolt around 1880, which was an Arab nationalist uprising against British and French influence in Egypt, the British subjected the citadel to heavy naval bombardment and it was quite badly damaged and then left more or less as a ruin. After Egypt became a British protectorate in 1882, the citadel actually underwent several rounds of restoration work. It was partially repaired in the early twentieth century, and then it finally underwent a complete restoration in the 1980s.'

'Interesting,' said Andrew. 'Looking at it now, it seems as if it has been sitting over there and looking the way it does now for centuries.'

'Looks can be deceiving,' said Fiona. 'Most of what we are looking at now is quite recent, but of course, the foundation is still from the 15th century, and there are bound to be sections of the fort which still date back to that period.'

'I see,' said Andrew. 'Did you say that some of the ancient blocks of stone from the lighthouse were used to build the original citadel?'

'Yes,' replied Fiona. 'It is wonderful to think that those same blocks were part of one of the Seven Wonders of the World during ancient times.'

Fiona paused, smiling as she looked out across the harbour to the citadel.

'Actually,' she then continued. 'Let me tell you something interesting about the lighthouse. As I mentioned it was built on Pharos Island, and that name became the etymological origin of the word for lighthouse in the Greek language. A lighthouse is referred to as a *pharos*. The same is the case for French and Italian, where the words for lighthouse are *phare* and *faro* respectively.'

Andrew smiled. 'That's fascinating.'

'It is, isn't it?' beamed Fiona. 'Words and history are so closely intertwined, and history is imprinted on our languages to such an extent that it often doesn't make sense to study one without also studying the other. You can learn a lot about history just by studying languages and vice versa.'

'Well,' said Andrew. 'Since you seem to be in a philosophical mood this evening, have a look that way.'

He stretched out his arm and pointed out over the bay, just to the right of the citadel.

'That is more or less north-northeast,' he said. 'If you were to travel across the sea in that direction, then after about 500 kilometres you would find yourself in the Aegean Sea surrounded by Greek islands. And if you continue for another 500 kilometres or so, you would end up in Aigai in Macedonia. I find it quite remarkable that two thousand three hundred years ago, a little boy named

Ptolemy grew up there, running and playing like all the other boys. But his friendship with another boy named Alexander would take him across the known world and have him end up right here in this place as an old man, having built this very city that we are sitting in right now. If not for those two little boys, this place might never have existed.'

'I know,' smiled Fiona. 'It really is amazing to think about.'

The two of them gazed out over Alexandria's Eastern Harbour in silence for a few moments. It was quickly becoming quite dark, and above them in the night sky the moon was hovering over the distant desert horizon, and the stars were like a river of diamonds overhead. One bright white dot sat among the faint glimmers of the stars, outshining them all.

'That is Venus over there,' said Andrew and pointed. 'Just above the citadel where the lighthouse used to be. It is interesting to think that when we look at that bright point of light, what we are really looking at is actually an Earth-sized planet with a cloud-cover so dense and bright that it reflects virtually all the light from the Sun, which is why it appears so bright to us.'

'It certainly makes sense that the ancient Greeks called it the Morning Star or the Guiding Star,' said Fiona. 'Oh, and here is another interesting little etymological fact. From our perspective it looks as if the planets are moving across the sky and also moving relative to all the other stars, and that is quite literally what the term *planet* refers to. The reason planets are called planets is because in ancient Greece people would look up at them and realise that they were moving relative to all the other stars. So, they called them Planētes Asteres, which literally means *wandering stars*.'

'I guess, in a way, the Alexandria lighthouse would have served the same purpose,' said Andrew. 'Seafarers would have been able to find their way towards Alexandria, just by following its light.'

Suddenly, Fiona sat up, frozen for a moment while her thoughts were racing.

'Oh my god!' she exclaimed. 'That's it! It's Venus!'

'What is?' said Andrew confused, glancing briefly at the brilliant planet twinkling in the night sky.

'Venus is the key!' said Fiona excitedly. 'Phosphoros. That's what Ptolemy meant when he wrote about it in his diary. And that is why it was written on the sarcophagus in the chamber under the Temple of Heracles. It was a clue. Venus is Alexander!'

'I don't understand,' said Andrew, shaking his head.

'Ok, listen,' said Fiona, looking at him intently. 'The ancient Greek name for Venus was Phosphoros, which literally means Light Bearer. And when Ptolemy presents Alexander as Venus, he is alluding to him being the light bearer. Think about it. The city of Alexandria itself was built by Ptolemy in the image of his friend Alexander, who sought out knowledge and wisdom during his campaign across the known world, and who was tutored by Aristotle, one of the founders of modern scientific inquiry. Ptolemy saw Alexander as a beacon of Greek civilisation. And what better way to honour and commemorate him than to build the tallest lighthouse in the world alongside the largest library in the world? Think of Alexandria as the Silicon Valley of the ancient world. A shining beacon of knowledge, rational thought and technological innovation. With its huge signal fire burning brightly at its top the lighthouse was quite literally the light-bearer, but it also symbolised Alexander as a light or a beacon.'

Andrew tilted his head slightly to one side, the cogs in his head slowly beginning to turn.

'And remember,' continued Fiona. 'Ptolemy built the lighthouse of Alexandria immediately after moving Alexander's body from Memphis to this city. That is not a coincidence, don't you understand?'

Andrew was looking intently at her as the pieces slowly began to fall into place in his mind.

'The lighthouse,' he said quietly.

'Yes!' exclaimed Fiona. 'The lighthouse is where Alexander's tomb must be!'

She paused for a moment to allow Andrew to process what she had said before continuing.

'The lighthouse was built as a giant mausoleum on top of Alexander's tomb,' she continued. 'Or more precisely, Alexander's tomb was hidden underneath what was then the tallest structure on the planet. What could be more fitting than that?'

Andrew smiled, looking impressed.

'You know, you just might be on to something here,' he said. 'It also explains why the lighthouse was built on such an enormous scale. As we just discussed, it was arguably too big for the purpose it served, but its size was simply a reflection of Ptolemy's reverence for Alexander. It was a giant monument to a giant of a man, placed right on top of his final resting place.'

'I think we've cracked it,' beamed Fiona, barely able to contain her excitement.

'But there is a fort there now,' said Andrew. 'The lighthouse hasn't been there for more than a millennium. You said the lighthouse finally crumbled around the 8th century, and that the citadel was built in the 15th century, right?'

'Yes, but that doesn't mean that the tomb couldn't have been hidden deep underneath it in the bedrock where the lighthouse stood. The Sultan of Qaitbay would simply have built his citadel on the same site, using many of the building materials scavenged from the collapsed lighthouse but not knowing what was underneath.'

'So, let me get this straight,' said Andrew. 'You think that the tomb has been there the whole time and that it is still there even now?'

'Why not?' said Fiona. 'If it lay undiscovered for over 500 hundred years while the lighthouse stood, and then for another 1200 years until the citadel was built, why should it not be possible that it could still be there now?'

'Wouldn't the sea have ruined it?' asked Andrew.

'I don't think so,' said Fiona. 'The lighthouse and then later on also the citadel, was built on top of a giant piece of solid bedrock. If the tomb is inside it, there is no way the seawater could ever make its way to that tomb. It would still be in pristine condition.'

'Bloody hell,' said Andrew after a short pause, peering out towards the castle. 'So, what do we do?'

'We need to find out as much as we can about the site before and during the construction of the citadel,' said Fiona. 'That might offer us a clue as to where the entrance to the tomb might have been when the lighthouse still stood.'

'If it was ever there,' said Andrew, sounding as if he was trying to introduce a note of caution into their discussion.

'Yes. If it was ever there. Correct,' said Fiona, holding up her hands, as if accepting that her theory was still just that. A theory.

'I have an idea,' said Andrew. 'We should contact our friend, Khalil at Cairo University. He might be able to help us out. Or he might have an idea as to how best to go about this.'

Andrew was referring to their friend and archaeologist, Professor Khalil Amer, who had been instrumental in helping them solve another case involving ancient Egyptian history, and who in doing so had saved both of their lives.

'That is probably wise,' said Fiona. 'If I am not mistaken, there is now a marine museum in that citadel and it is also an important historical site, so if we pay the citadel a visit, we should probably try not to break things.'

Andrew nodded sagely and pulled out his phone. 'I will send him an email right now. Hopefully, he will pick it up soon.'

Just as their cocktails arrived, Andrew's phone chirped. It was an email from Khalil Amer.

'Ah,' said Andrew. 'That was quick. Khalil has just replied. He sends his regards.'

'Thank you,' smiled Fiona. 'What does he say?'

'He says he wished he could join us, but he is actually at an archaeology conference in Chicago at the moment.'

'Oh,' said Fiona, sipping her Piña Colada. 'That's a shame. It would have been really helpful to have him here. Still, the last time he helped us he ended up getting shot at, so perhaps this is for the best.'

'Yes,' said Andrew, putting down his Mai Tai and scrolling further down through the email. 'He also says he was able to contact a friend and former colleague at Alexandria University. A Doctor Farouk Elmasry who was involved in the citadel's restoration work back in the 1980s. He is retired now, but Khalil managed to locate him and he spoke to him on the phone.'

'Ok. What did he say?'

'Apparently, Doctor Elmasry told Khalil that he and a colleague had used one of the first iterations of ground penetrating radar for archaeological purposes on the site during the initial phases of the restoration work. Elmasry claims that he found certain anomalies in the readings just west of the citadel and lodged a request for excavations with the EAO, the Egyptian Antiquities Organisation which was in charge of the program. But his request was denied, apparently because of time and budget constraints. So, he never got a chance to carry out the work before the whole site was reconstructed.'

'Alright,' said Fiona, sounding slightly puzzled. 'So where does that leave us?'

'Well, Khalil has attached a schematic of the citadel, with the area of interest marked with a circle. Have a look at this.'

Andrew opened the file and showed his phone to Fiona.

'The schematic shows the entire outer defences as well as the citadel itself up here in the top half.'

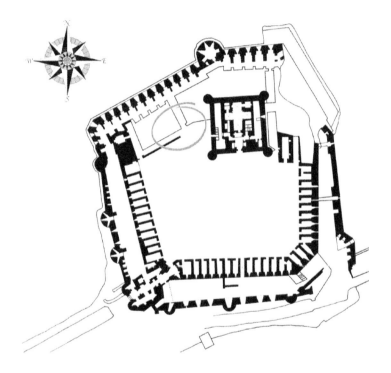

'The encircled area is apparently where the anomalies showed up. As you can see, they actually fall outside of the footprint of the original citadel, but well within that of the lighthouse, whose enormous base would have taken up much of what today is both the citadel and the inner courtyard of the fortification.'

Fiona narrowed her eyes, studying the schematic. 'I suppose this means that the anomaly would have been somewhere under the foundation of the northern section of the lighthouse.'

'Yes, that is probably a fair assumption,' replied Andrew.

'And if it really does indicate some sort of underground complex,' said Fiona, 'then that could be much older than the citadel. It could be as old as the lighthouse.'

Her keen eyes were gleaming with excitement in the candlelight, and Andrew could not help smiling at her eagerness.

'Possibly,' he said calmly, trying not to jump to too many conclusions. 'Anyway, as a final comment, Khalil mentions that if Elmasry's interpretation of the radar readings back in the 80s were correct, then our only chance would be to find out whether there might be some sort of underground access from the catacombs under the citadel. Those catacombs are likely to be in their original 15th-century state, since they would not have been damaged in any of the bombardments that the citadel has been subjected to over the years. However, Khalil mentions that they have never been accessible to the public, and he says he is unsure of why that might be.'

'I guess we don't have a schematic for the catacombs themselves then?' asked Fiona.

'Khalil was unable to locate one,' replied Andrew, 'and if he wasn't able to do it, then there probably isn't one that is publicly available.'

'So, what do we do?' asked Fiona. 'We have to get down there somehow. I feel like we are on the cusp of something really big. We can't stop now.'

'I agree,' replied Andrew. 'Our only option is to get in there and investigate the citadel ourselves. Tomorrow is Sunday, so it will be closed to the public. We should make our way over there and then find a way inside.'

'How?' asked Fiona. 'It's a citadel. It is literally built to keep people out.'

'We will have to improvise again,' replied Andrew. 'We've come this far. We're not letting a six-hundred-year-old citadel stop us now.'

# THIRTY-FOUR

The next morning, Andrew and Fiona packed what they thought they might need into a couple of small rucksacks and set off for the citadel. Andrew's leg wound was healing and had stopped bleeding under the bandages, but he was still on painkillers.

They decided it was better to take a taxi and hailed one on El-Gaish Road in front of the hotel. They asked to be taken to the Alexandria Aquarium, which is just on the other side of the road from the main entrance to the citadel. The taxi driver's disdain at being flagged down for such a short trip was palpable, but he agreed nonetheless. Sunday was a slow day, so he seemed to decide that a bit of money was better than no money at all.

Exiting the taxi less than five minutes later in front of the aquarium, Andrew and Fiona noticed that the main gates of the outer defences of the citadel complex were shut, and there were no staff visible anywhere.

The Egyptian flag atop the citadel was fluttering in the gentle breeze coming in from the sea, and the citadel looked quite imposing as its greyish-yellow granite walls were bathed in the morning sun.

They walked casually to one of the flimsy-looking chicken wire fences separating the citadel site from the road in front of it, and Andrew grabbed hold of one of them. To their surprise, the section he had grabbed, which served as a sliding gate across a narrow road running along the outside of the western walls, was unlocked and slid aside with a metallic grinding noise.

Fiona's head whipped around to look at the people queueing at the Aquarium less than fifty metres away, but none of them seemed to have noticed the noise amid the bustle of the ticket barriers and the cars and busses coming and going.

Once on the other side of the fence, the two of them hurried along the outer defences until they came to a long and vaulted tunnel that led from the outside under the outer defences and into the citadel courtyard. It had no barrier across it, clearly relying on the metal fence to keep visitors out outside of normal opening hours.

'Security here is lax, to say the least,' said Andrew as they began walking the roughly twenty metres through the wide tunnel towards the courtyard.

'Well,' said Fiona. 'It's not like anyone can come in and run off with anything. There nothing here except blocks of granite and limestone weighing several tonnes each. Still, you might have thought they would make an effort to keep vandals out.'

Soon after, they were inside the courtyard where they proceeded to walk straight towards the entrance to the citadel itself. Halfway there, Fiona stopped and looked down at the ground beneath their feet.

'If Doctor Elmasry's information is correct,' she said, 'this is roughly where the anomaly on the readings from the ground-penetrating radar should be. If there is some sort of underground space, it should be just here.'

'Unfortunately, Khalil's message did not mention anything about how deep it might be,' said Andrew.

'Yes, that can be difficult to ascertain,' said Fiona. 'Just because you can see that there is a variation in the density of the ground below you, doesn't mean you can necessarily see how deep it lies. Especially not back in the 1980s when this sort of technology was first being rolled out. It could be five or ten metres down, or it could be much deeper than that.'

'Let's try the main gate to the citadel,' said Andrew. 'We might get lucky.'

As it turned out, their luck with gates and barriers had run out, because after walking up the five steps to the solid three-metre-tall solid oak doors of the citadel, they found that it was securely locked. There was no way they were getting in that way.

'There is another tunnel which leads from the courtyard down alongside the outer wall of the citadel itself,' said Fiona, pointing further along towards the corner of the citadel. 'I think it might lead to the lower levels, and I am pretty sure that it is part of the tourist trail here. Let's check it out.'

They proceeded from the main gate to the southeast corner of the citadel, and then through a small open gate where a tunnel, much like the one they had used to enter the courtyard, sloped down at a gentle angle for about twenty metres after which it ended abruptly.

'There should be a door at the end on the left leading into the citadel itself,' said Fiona. 'At least, that is what the schematic seems to indicate.'

They entered the long and wide vaulted tunnel and proceeded down the gentle cobbled slope to the end. Where the tunnel stopped abruptly, there was a small solid oak door on the left with a shiny heavy-duty padlock with a tiny keyhole.'

'This should access the lower levels of the citadel,' said Fiona. 'We need to get through here somehow, but the padlock looks like it is made of high-grade steel. My sulphuric acid trick would take hours to get through this if it would even work.'

Andrew reached into his rucksack and extracted a short thin metal wire with a handle at each end that looked like brass knuckles.

'What is that thing?' said Fiona.

'Diamond wire saw,' said Andrew. 'This wire is coated in a thin layer of ultrafine diamonds. It is amazingly effective against metal. Watch.'

He slipped one of the handles off its hook, pushed the wire through the shackle and reattached the handle. Then he pulled the handles towards himself, putting tension on the diamond-coated steel wire and began pulling alternately on the left and then the right handle, making the wire begin to cut through the shackle.

Fiona stepped close to help hold the padlock in place while Andrew continued sawing, and within less than a minute the wire had cut through the shackle.

'Wow,' said Fiona. 'That was fast. The shackle is really hot now.'

'I have used this thing a few times before,' said Andrew, pulling the shackle out of the body of the padlock. 'It is fast and it makes very little noise.'

He stuffed the wire saw back in the rucksack and opened the door to reveal a dark corridor.

'Time to get our torches out,' he said. 'We can't afford to play around with electric lights in here. We might accidentally switch on something that can be seen from the outside.'

The corridor was similar to the vaulted tunnel that had led from the courtyard down to the door, but it was only around two metres wide. It was built from the same pale-yellow granite as the citadel walls, and the floor inside was covered in darker flagstones. Off to one side were small rooms separated from the corridor by wrought iron bars.

'This must be where the original 15th-century prison was,' said Fiona. 'But this was clearly part of the restoration work carried out in the 1980s. Apparently, one of the first things Sultan Qaitbay used the citadel for was to serve as a prison.'

'Figures,' scoffed Andrew. 'I guess a citadel like this is fairly useless unless there is a war on.'

They proceeded further along the corridor to find it ending in a T-junction.

'Left or right?' asked Andrew, looking at Fiona.

'We need to get as far west as possible, so we pretty much have to find a way across to the other side of the citadel. 'I would say we should go right.'

'Ok,' said Andrew. 'Right it is.'

Holding a torch, he took the lead walking further along the corridor which made a ninety-degree turn after about five metres, and then it opened out into a large storeroom. Placed in neat rows were large wooden barrels that were lying down and fixed to the floor with a wooden support structure.

'This is all just a reconstruction for the museum,' said Fiona and pointed straight ahead. 'I reckon we are still at least fifteen metres away from where the western citadel walls are. We need to push on in that direction.'

They walked through the storeroom and into another sizeable room with rows of large empty wooden shelves spaced throughout.

'What do you reckon this was for,' asked Andrew, shining his torch around the room.

'Sacks of grain perhaps,' said Fiona. 'Difficult to tell, but the citadel would have needed food storage for sieges, so this might have been it.'

'Look at this,' said Andrew, pointing his torchlight towards the far wall. 'There is a doorway over here. It looks like there might be stairs.'

As the two of them approached, it became clear that the small doorway set into the wall led to a narrow spiral staircase leading down.

'There must be another level below this,' said Andrew. 'Come on. Let's see where it leads.'

To their surprise, the spiral staircase wound its way down the equivalent of two storeys. At the bottom of the stairwell were more vaulted rooms, however, these were much smaller and looked very different. The ceiling was very low, and the masonry was constructed using much smaller blocks of granite. The walls and the vaulted ceiling also appeared much older.

'This has to be the original catacombs from when the citadel was first built,' said Fiona. 'This brickwork is almost six hundred years old.'

'Let's see where this corridor leads,' said Andrew, and began walking along the narrow corridor that stretched away from the spiral staircase.

After about ten metres of crouched walking, they emerged into a small rotunda approximately three metres across that had three more corridors stretching away from it.

'Now what?' said Andrew.

'I must admit I have lost my bearings a bit now,' said Fiona, 'but I think we should keep going straight. We must be near the edge of where the citadel walls stop, up at ground level.'

'Speaking of which,' said Andrew. 'Ground level must be at least ten or fifteen metres above us now. We should be well and truly down into bedrock now, but for some reason, the builders of this place still decided to use masonry as well. Strange.'

After another ten metres along the middle corridor, they came to another T-junction, but that was not what got their attention. As they approached the wall in front of them, from where two corridors led off to the left and the right at ninety-degree angles, they saw that there was a big hole in the brick wall directly ahead of them. A hole big enough for a person to squeeze through.

The two of them stopped dead in their track and looked at each other.

'Shit,' whispered Fiona. 'It must be them.'

'Dubois?' Andrew whispered back.

'Who else?' said Fiona tensely. 'They got here before us.'

'What is through here?' said Andrew pointing at the hole.

'Who knows,' said Fiona. 'But if I am not mistaken this spot is directly under the citadel walls, so through there is where Doctor Elmasry's anomaly would be. Look at the brickwork. It is a different type of brick from in the rest of these tunnels. This wall seems to have been deliberately placed right here to seal off whatever is behind it.'

Andrew reached into his rucksack and pulled out his pistol.

'They might still be in there. Are you still up for pushing on?' he asked.

Fiona hesitated for a moment, but then nodded determinedly. 'Like you said. No turning back now.'

'Ok,' whispered Andrew. 'I'll go first.'

Andrew knelt down and shone his torchlight through the hole in the wall. It seemed to be a small space with a tunnel leading directly away from the hole.

'I'd kill for some night vision goggles right now,' he whispered. 'If anyone is in there, they'll spot our torches.'

'Or we might spot them first,' said Fiona. 'If they are in there, they will need torches too. We'll just have to move slowly and keep listening out for movement.'

'Alright,' said Andrew, quietly pulling back the top slide on his Glock 17, making sure it was ready to fire. 'Let's go.'

As they went through the gap it became clear that the space on the other side was large enough for several people to stand in, and the tunnel leading off it was a couple of metres wide and sloping gently downward.

'Everything in here is rock-cut,' whispered Fiona, fanning her torchlight slowly across the wall and the ceiling. We are deep inside the bedrock now. And there is no masonry.'

'Could this be from the time of Ptolemy?' whispered Andrew.

Fiona nodded. 'Definitely,' she whispered.

They proceeded down the sloping tunnel which seemed to be getting both wider and taller as they went. After around twenty metres, during which they descended another three to five metres, the tunnel levelled out and led to a small flat area in front of a large wall with a doorway in the middle. On either side of the doorway were friezes similar to those they had seen in the Catacombs of Kom el Shoqafa, but this time they were highly detailed depictions of lion heads. Above the doorway was another frieze chiselled into the rock.

The Vergina Sun.

They both stopped and stared at the scene in front of them for a few moments. Then Fiona turned to Andrew, tears welling up in her eyes.

'I think we have finally found it,' she whispered, her eyes gleaming with anticipation and her voice trembling with the enormity of what they might be about to uncover.

Andrew placed his index finger in front of his mouth as if to say "No more talking".

He brought up his gun to point at the doorway along with his torch, and then he began walking slowly and silently towards it. Straining his ears to listen out for sounds of movement on the other side, he carefully slipped through the doorway and quickly swept his torch from left to right, but no one was there. On the other side was a large room very similar to the antechamber they had found in Thonis-Heracleion, although this was much larger. There were six heavy pillars spaced throughout the chamber, and the floor was covered in a huge detailed mosaic. The walls were painted in murals depicting Alexander triumphantly riding into Babylon, Memphis, Susa and other major cities which fell to his armies during his campaign, and where the wall met the smooth ceiling, there was even cornicing that had been meticulously cut from the bedrock.

Fiona looked over at Andrew and mouthed the word "Wow".

As they walked carefully across the chamber and approached another doorway on the other side, the light from their torched bounced off something very large and shiny in the space beyond.

The next doorway was double the width of the one they had passed through a couple of minutes earlier, and both of them instantly noticed that the flooring changed dramatically beyond the second doorway.

Instead of being a mosaic, it was made from heavily veined jet-black marble. The floor sloped downward gently and widened from the roughly two metres at the doorway to at least four metres slightly further into the chamber where it levelled out. The chamber itself was easily twenty by twenty metres in size, and the ceiling was at least four metres above them.

However, once inside the chamber, their attention quickly shifted from the floor to what was sitting in the middle of it surrounded by tall gilded Ionic pillars. They both pointed their torches toward it, and it took a few seconds for them to process what they were looking at.

It was a huge golden pyramid, around eight by eight metres in size and roughly five metres tall, seemingly mimicking the exact proportions of those found at Giza southwest of Cairo. Fiona looked at it carefully and concluded that it was such an accurate replica of the pyramid of Khufu in Giza, that the angle of its sides was almost certainly exactly 51 degrees, just like the real thing. It seemed to have been constructed to be a small replica of the largest and most impressive pyramid ever built.

The slightly dull yet vibrant sheen of the pyramid hinted at it being not just gilded but almost certainly made from solid gold. It seemed to be comprised of four large sections, each one a whole side of the pyramid, and all four sides appeared to interlock seamlessly at the pyramid's edges.

The spectacular shape was flanked by three-metre-tall gilded statues of Alexander the Great looking down sternly towards anyone standing in front of it.

The statues seemed to explode in warm yellow reflections whenever Andrew or Fiona let their torchlight sweep across them. The contrast between the copious amounts of gold and the black marble was stunning and left an air of opulence, wealth and power.

'The mausoleum of Alexander the Great,' whispered Fiona as quietly as she could. 'His sarcophagus must be inside the pyramid.'

'Put your gun down,' said a gruff male voice in a heavy London accent.

'Fuck,' grimaced Andrew, and stopped dead in his tracks, realising how foolhardy they had been walking into the tomb assuming that it would be empty.

'Kick the gun over here,' said Stone, emerging from behind them and to their left where he had been hiding behind one of the huge gilded pillars.

He was carrying an un-silenced Heckler & Koch MP5 submachine gun.

'Walk forward to the pyramid and kneel down,' he continued. 'Both of you.'

Andrew and Fiona did as Stone had ordered, and walked up close to the platform that the pyramid was sitting on, and then knelt down next to each other.

'Well, well,' said Stone in a slow, mocking East London drawl as he picked up Andrew's gun and tucked it behind his back. 'And here I was thinking that sneaking around was what you rubber wings do best. I guess you SAS boys aren't that clever after all.'

'Mr Sterling,' came Dubois's voice.

He had been behind the huge golden pyramid when Andrew and Fiona entered the mausoleum and was now walking casually around it to join them with a sly smile on his face.

'And Miss Keane,' he continued. 'We really can't keep meeting like this. Although, I think for once you two might actually prove useful. Well, at least one of you might.'

Stone pulled out a handful of green glowsticks from his jacket, cracked them inside his fist, and then tossed them onto the floor in front of the pyramid where they scattered and gradually began emitting ever more green light into the chamber. After a few moments the glowsticks reflected faintly in both the gilded Ionic pillars and the golden pyramid.

Stone then walked close to Andrew and gave him a kick across the right thigh, making Andrew grimace in pain.

'I thought you walked a bit funny,' smiled Stone, clearly enjoying himself. 'I guess our mutual Russian acquaintance managed to hit you with his fancy gun after all. I was the one who had to go in and pull his dead corpse from that chamber. Not sure how you managed to ice him, but his head was a mess, I'll tell ya. Still, a dead Russian is a good Russian most days of the week, if you ask me.'

'Can we skip the friendly banter and just get on with things,' said Andrew, deliberately sounding aloof whilst ignoring Stone and looking at Dubois. 'I am sure we all have things we would rather be doing than stand around in here all day. Especially the meat bomber grunt over here.'

Stone scowled at him, and Andrew quickly glanced at Fiona. His plan was to try to rile the ex-paratrooper, and his use of a derogatory term for paratroopers appeared to be having the desired effect.

'If you shoot that thing in here, you are going to ruin priceless artefacts,' said Fiona, her eyes shooting daggers at Stone.

Stone produced a surprised chuckle and looked at her as if not being able to decide whether she was actually serious or whether she had been attempting to make a joke.

'You don't actually think I give a toss about that, do you, luv?' he said incredulously. 'And my Parisian friend here tells me it is solid gold, so it'll get melted down anyway.'

Fiona scowled at him. 'My apologies. For a moment there I guess I forgot what a low-life neanderthal you are.'

Stone tilted his head to one side and looked at her menacingly as Andrew gently placed a hand on her shoulder.

'Careful now, little Miss,' sneered Stone. 'I'm the one with the gun, remember?'

'Enough of this nonsense,' shouted Dubois impatiently, taking a step towards Andrew and Fiona. 'Miss Keane, or whatever your real name is, you are going to open the golden sarcophagus for me. Stone, you make sure they don't do anything stupid. Shoot them if they try.'

'My pleasure,' smirked Stone.

Dubois stepped back and pointed at the golden pyramid.

'Go on,' he said, gesturing. 'Get up onto the platform and get that thing open. You have five minutes.'

Then he nodded at Stone, who walked up close to Andrew and placed the muzzle of the MP5 next to his head.

'Tick, tock,' said Stone, smiling menacingly at Fiona.

'Animal,' sneered Fiona.

'Just get on with it,' ordered Dubois, irritation building in his voice. 'And stop talking.'

As Andrew turned his head slightly to look up at Stone, Fiona stepped closer to the enormous gold pyramid, examining it closely. The shape itself was a perfect pyramid, but the four sides had been subdivided into smaller sections that seemed to connect to each other in a strange and intricate pattern. What made the vista even more mesmerising was the fact that every individual section had a strange mixture of hieroglyphs and Greek writing on them.

'This is hugely complicated,' said Fiona. 'I would need a team of archaeologists and a couple of years to do this properly.'

'Four minutes,' said Dubois, looking at his golden wristwatch.

Fiona peered nervously at the many symbols trying to make sense of them, but they all seemed to jumble up inside her head. Nothing made sense.

'This is not like anything I have seen before,' she said. 'I honestly don't know where to start.'

'Three-and-a-half minutes,' said Dubois, sounding like an impatient schoolteacher

Fiona began walking around the pyramid with her torch, shining it across the surface of each side of the pyramid, but the letters, patterns and symbols made it impossible to focus on anything for very long. It was as if the decorative design itself had been created to confuse and confound.

Having walked around the pyramid once, she stopped, placing her hands on her hips and looking at Dubois.

'Listen,' she said. 'I don't have a clue what I am looking for. I can't just solve this in a couple of minutes.'

'I really think you should try,' said Dubois, sounding cold as ice and glancing over at Stone who pressed the muzzle of his MP5 harder against Andrew's head, causing him to wince and move his head away slightly.

Fiona's head dropped, and as she stood there, looking down at the floor and trying to think of some way to unlock the secrets of the pyramid, she suddenly spotted a small hexagonal gold plate inset into the black marble floor by her feet. The plate was only about the size of a coaster for a coffee mug, but when she looked at it more closely, she could see another smaller hexagonal shape inside it.

She slowly knelt down, without taking her eyes off the gold plate.

'No tricks,' exclaimed Dubois nervously, taking a step towards her.

'Oh, calm down you irritating frog,' said Fiona, her head snapping around towards him. 'I am trying to work here.'

Dubois was about to deliver an indignant retort, but then thought better of it and decided to let Fiona proceed.

She ran her fingertips across the gold plate in the floor, feeling the edges of the inner hexagonal shape that was slightly inset into the larger gold plate. As she leaned closer, peering at it, she suddenly let out a small but audible gasp.

'What?' demanded Dubois impetuously.

Fiona did not answer, but instead gently placed the tip of her index finger inside the indent to feel the contours of the tiny motif at its centre. There was no longer any doubt in her mind about what she had found.

'I need my rucksack,' she said, reaching around to grab it and pull it off her back.

Instantly, Stone shifted his MP5 to point at Fiona.

'Don't do anything stupid, luv,' he said. 'I have a full mag here.'

'Calm down, you tool,' she said acidly, and reached inside the rucksack to take out her pink leather purse. Then she unzipped a small compartment inside it and extracted the signet ring of Alexander the Great. She held it up in front of herself, studying it for a couple of seconds.

'Oh,' said Dubois excitedly. 'So, there *was* a ring down there. Thank you for bringing it to me.'

Fiona looked at him with disdain in her eyes.

'And I brought it out of the goodness of my heart,' she said acerbically, giving him a scornful smile.

'Well,' said Dubois evenly, 'I am sure it will fetch a tidy sum on the black market once we are done here. Carry on.'

'Don't do it,' said Andrew. 'These bastards don't deserve to get their hands on the tomb.'

'Shut'it!' said Stone, planting a knee in Andrew's back.

'Oh, come now,' said Dubois overbearingly. 'Just get on with it, and spare me the melodrama.'

Fiona sighed and put the ring on the middle finger of her right hand. Then she made a fist and gently brought it down towards the gold plate, placing the signet ring into the hexagonal indent where it fitted perfectly.

'This is it,' she smiled, looking up thoughtfully at Andrew. 'The ring was the key all along. How fitting that one should have to kneel to use it.'

'Open it,' said Dubois irritably.

Andrew nodded, and then he almost imperceptibly glanced up at Stone next to him whilst making sure that Fiona saw him do it. Fiona nodded too, and then she pressed down on the ring.

There was an audible metallic click from the gold plate, and then Fiona began twisting her fist clockwise. Immediately, a quick succession of smaller clicks could be heard, reminiscent of the sound of an old-fashioned clock being wound up. After a quarter-turn, Fiona could turn it no further. She waited for a couple of seconds, during which nothing happened. Then she looked up at Andrew questioningly.

'Try putting more weight on it,' he said.

Fiona leaned in over her fist, and with a straight arm she gradually began to place more and more of her weight on the gold place, until suddenly the whole plate snapped down about a centimetre into the black marble.

Immediately, they could hear the sounds of some unseen mechanism working beneath their feet, and after a few seconds, all four sides of the pyramid began to slowly retract into slits in the marble floor at perfect 51-degree angles.

'Blimey!' grinned Stone. 'This bird's a damn sight cleverer than you, Frenchie.'

Dubois either did not hear the jibe, or he simply pretended not to hear it, as he stood captivated by the sight of the millennia-old mechanism working.

Sensing that the machinery that controlled this ancient mechanism was now irrevocably triggered, Fiona rose and stepped back a bit to watch the four huge solid gold sections gradually disappearing into the floor. As they did so, they revealed an elaborate sarcophagus sitting on a raised platform, and when the four sections were almost completely retracted into the marble floor, it became clear that this sarcophagus was unlike anything any of them had seen before. After less than ten seconds the sides had fully retracted, and were now hidden inside the floor, at which point the noise from the unseen mechanism beneath their feet abruptly stopped.

Shining their torches onto the sarcophagus, the light seemed to penetrate it and dance around its interior, hinting at the presence of some large shape inside.

'So, it was true,' said Dubois, suddenly sounding like even he was beginning to appreciate the significance of the moment.

'What?' said Stone, peering at the sarcophagus with a look of disappointment on his face. 'Is that really it?'

'It is yellow alabaster,' said Fiona as she began to walk slowly around the sarcophagus, shining her light onto it. 'It is a semi-translucent carbonate mineral, and it is strong enough to create statues from yet soft enough to carve fine details into. It was rumoured that Alexander's body was put inside an alabaster sarcophagus when Ptolemy VII became so desperate for coin that he melted down Alexander's solid gold sarcophagus. But perhaps that was only ever a myth. Perhaps Alexander's body was always in an alabaster sarcophagus. Perhaps there was only ever this sarcophagus, hidden in this place.'

Now that Fiona had reached the other side of the sarcophagus, her torchlight lit up the alabaster and sent diffused light shining through the interior, revealing veins of alabaster of varying colours as well as the distinct silhouette of a dark shape inside it. It was roughly the size of a fully grown human being.

'Is that him?' said Dubois, with a tinge of awe in his voice, peering at the blurry dark shape inside the sarcophagus. 'Is that Alexander the Great?'

'I would bet you anything that it is,' said Fiona, peering at the mummified shape in the sarcophagus.

'Fucking payday,' grinned Stone gleefully.

'I can't believe we finally found him,' whispered Fiona. 'Lost for two millennia, and now here he is.'

'Why is he hovering in the middle of the sarcophagus like that?' asked Dubois, approaching the sarcophagus cautiously.

'Honey,' said Fiona. 'His mummy was submerged in honey inside the sarcophagus because it has the ability to preserve organic matter for millennia. It is slightly acidic, has no water in it, and it contains small amounts of hydrogen peroxide, all of which are very effective at keeping bacteria at bay. I know of a dig site in Central Asia where honey has been almost perfectly preserved for more than five thousand years.'

'Fascinating,' said Dubois. 'How come I never knew that?'

'Perhaps because you're not a real archaeologist?' said Fiona caustically, glaring at him.

'Please, Miss Keane,' smiled Dubois arrogantly. 'You lost. Get over it. Such malice is most unbecoming of a lady such as yourself.'

'Oh, fuck off,' sneered Fiona.

'Right,' replied Dubois matter-of-factly. 'Perhaps you are not a lady after all.'

'Alright,' said Stone impatiently and looking at Dubois. 'I also like a bit of hostile banter now and again, but can we get on with things now? We found what we were looking for, so what's the plan?'

'What are you going to do with him?' asked Fiona, turning to Dubois with an angry look on her face.

'Get him out, of course,' said Dubois. 'That was the mission all along. The client wants Alexander's DNA, so that is what we are going to get her.'

'Alexis,' said Fiona. 'What the hell does she want it for? What is so important that she is prepared to wreck endless numbers of irreplaceable ancient artefacts and important archaeological sites?'

'That,' said Dubois and shrugged, 'is not for me to ask.'

As he said those words, Stone smiled cryptically. What Dubois did not know was that Stone had received instructions from Fabian Ackerman to secure the tomb and make Dubois disappear. After that, and now that George Frost and Rosetta had completed the last human embryo trials successfully, Project AnaGenesis would finally come to fruition. And it was going to make Ackerman, Frost and Stone very very rich.

'I was hired to do a job,' continued Dubois self-righteously, 'and I intend to finish it. Just like you two.'

'We're nothing like you,' said Andrew icily. 'You're just another grubby little lowlife bottom-feeder, and the company you keep stinks.'

Then he glanced up at Stone. 'Quite literally.'

The ex-paratrooper scoffed. 'And he's a bloody comedian too,' he said, lifting the short butt of the MP5 to strike Andrew in the back of the head.

That was the opening Andrew had been waiting for. As soon as the MP5's barrel was pointing upwards towards the ceiling of the mausoleum, Andrew who was still in a kneeling position on the floor, spun around and jumped up, grabbed Stone's gun and attempted to push the ex-paratrooper over.

Staggering backwards a couple of steps, the heavy soldier grimaced whilst trying to wrestle the submachine gun from Andrew's grip. As he did so, he ended up putting enough pressure on the trigger to fire off a loud rapid salvo of five or six shots that peppered the ceiling, causing tiny bits of rock and dust to fall down onto the marble floor with a pitter-patter. At the same time, Andrew's pistol fell from Stone's belt and clattered to the floor.

As the submachinegun fired it also spat out a rapid series of small flames from its barrel, and because it had no silencer mounted the noise from the shots reverberated loudly around the cavernous space, making both Fiona and Dubois dive for cover.

Fiona threw herself behind the sarcophagus, and Dubois scrambled behind the nearest gilded pillar and then peeked around it to see what was happening. Just as he did so, another barrage of bullets tore out of the MP5's barrel and sprayed the pillar he was hiding behind. As flakes of gilded limestone flew off in all directions, Dubois shrieked and cowered behind the pillar again.

When he looked back out, he could not believe what he was seeing. Ten metres away, Stone and Andrew were scrabbling around on the marble floor, still fighting for control of the submachine gun. But incredibly, Fiona, who was just a couple of metres from him, had made her way around the sarcophagus and was now desperately trying to re-insert the ring into the gold plate to re-engage the ancient mechanism.

Seeing this, Dubois immediately understood what she was trying to do.

'No!' he yelled, and flung himself out from his hiding place. 'What are you doing, you imbécile?'

He crashed into Fiona and the two of them rolled over onto the floor whilst Dubois tried to wrestle the ring from Fiona's finger. She grabbed his wrists and brought her knee up as fast as she could, planting it in his groin, and making him grimace maniacally as he produced a strange whimper. Fiona then brought her head back and rammed it forward to slam her forehead onto the bridge of Dubois's nose. It produced an unpleasant crunch, like someone crushing a small ice cube between their teeth. She felt the nose bridge break and the impact left her momentarily dazed.

With a loud squeal, Dubois fell backwards towards the sarcophagus and onto the floor, clutching his nose whilst blood spurted from it and sprayed onto the black marble floor. He kicked his legs frantically in front of himself, trying desperately to move back and away from Fiona, and he ended up with his back against the alabaster sarcophagus. Here he curled up in a ball on his knees and elbows, moaning like a wounded animal with blood pouring from his nose.

As he did this, Fiona spun around and threw herself down next to the hexagonal gold plate. As soon as she could reach it, she inserted the ring into the hexagonal slot and twisted her hand counter-clockwise.

Almost immediately, the mechanism deep under the marble floor began whirring and clacking, and swiftly the four solid gold sides of the pyramid began re-emerging from their recesses. Judging from the speed with which they were moving, Fiona guessed that it would take about the same time for them to close as it had for them to open.

A few metres away, Andrew and Stone were still locked in a contest for control of the MP5. Andrew soon realised that he had lost the element of surprise and that Stone was physically stronger and fitter than he was, so he reached up with one hand and yanked the MP5's magazine out of the submachine gun. He quickly threw it several metres away from the two of them, where it clattered onto the floor and continued under its own momentum, sliding along on the smooth marble all the way to the wall. In the same movement, Andrew grabbed Stone's right hand in his and squeezed tight, causing Stone's trigger finger to bend and the MP5 to fire the last remaining round still sitting in the chamber. Then he pushed Stone away from himself and whipped out the diving knife which he had kept in the sheath attached to his belt. Holding the knife out in front of himself, he began circling Stone, hoping for an opportunity to strike.

At first looking confused and then irritated, Stone threw the MP5 aside and pulled out a huge hunting knife from behind his back. He grinned at Andrew, spinning the knife in his hand.

'Alright, you clever fucking Rupert,' he said tersely, using a derogatory nickname for military officers. 'Let's see who is really tougher, eh? Para versus SAS. I've always wanted to find out, anyway.'

A few metres away, Fiona was lying completely still, hoping that Dubois would not notice what was happening around him. However, eventually, through the pain of his deformed and bleeding nose and the sound of his own moaning, he must have noticed the ancient machinery stirring and beginning to raise the gold pyramid's sides again.

His head whipped up, causing even more blood to spray through the air and onto the almost perfectly smooth marble floor. When it dawned on him what was happening, he tried to stand up but immediately slipped on his own blood, which was now like an oily liquid covering a small area around him. Still holding his nose, he crashed to the floor again, slamming an elbow down hard onto the marble which elicited yet another howl of pain.

The solid gold sides of the pyramid were now about halfway extended, and Dubois must have realised what was about to happen. Once more he attempted to get up, but once more his feet slipped on the blood-coated marble and he fell onto his front. Here he tried to crawl frantically towards one of the four rapidly closing gaps between the golden sides of the pyramid, but it was too late.

The pyramid was now almost complete, and as the four solid gold sides came together at its apex, they seemed to stop for a fraction of a second, and then they snapped together with a heavy clonk, cutting off the sound of Dubois as he screamed. The craftmanship of the pyramid was so precise, and the gold was so thick, that the pyramid completely blocked any sound from escaping. Dubois had been sealed inside in the darkness.

'Finally got what you wanted,' panted Fiona. Then she quickly sat up to see Andrew and Stone circling each other, knives out and arms raised to chest levels, both of them waiting for the other to make a mistake.

'Fucking SAS cowards,' growled Stone mockingly. 'Always bloody hiding and sneaking around. Always running away from the fight, leaving it for us real soldiers to do the work.'

'Bloody hell,' said Andrew, sounding exasperated. 'Do you ever stop talking?'

Fiona, seeing her chance, scrambled for the MP5 which was just a short distance from the pyramid. Then she ran to the magazine which was by the far wall of the chamber.

At that moment, Stone lunged forward, swinging wildly at Andrew with his huge hunting knife. It almost connected with Andrew's abdomen, but he just managed to evade the blade. He could hear the whoosh as it sliced violently through the air just millimetres from him. Using Stone's momentum against him, Andrew grabbed the large man's arm and pulled hard, almost making Stone trip and fall onto the floor. Stone managed to recover and quickly spun around to face Andrew again.

'Nice one,' leered Stone. 'Your turn.'

'That's enough,' shouted Fiona. 'Toss the knife to me and turn around.'

Andrew looked over his shoulder to see Fiona standing there with the MP5, magazine in place and aiming at Stone.

Stone chuckled incredulously. 'Jesus,' he exclaimed. 'You need a bloody woman to bail you out? Now I've seen everything.'

Andrew shifted out of his combat stance and took a step back from Stone.

'You heard the lady,' he said, panting. 'Toss the knife and face the wall.'

'Bloody poofter,' sneered Stone as he dropped the knife onto the floor and kicked it towards Andrew. Then he turned around to face away from him.

Andrew began taking off his belt, intending to tie up Stone's hands with it, and Fiona took a couple of cautious steps closer to him whilst still aiming squarely at his torso.

'You've never shot one of those before, have you, luv?' said Stone.

'Would you like to find out?' replied Fiona coldly.

Stone chuckled again. 'I don't need to. I know girls like you. All talk and no knickers.'

Fiona was now only a couple of metres from the two men when Stone slowly and calmly began turning around again.

'I said, face the damn wall!' ordered Andrew.

'Just helping you out,' smiled Stone, holding out his hands and winking at Fiona who was still pointing the submachine gun at him. 'And I've got another piece of advice for you,' he continued.

'What's that?' said Fiona coldly.

'Always remember the safety.'

For a fraction of a second, Fiona kept looking at him, but then her eyes darted down to the MP5. At that moment she realised that she didn't know where the safety was. Before she could react, Stone launched himself at her, knocking her over and grabbing the submachine gun from her hands. Fiona had tried to pull the trigger but nothing happened. Stone really had engaged the safety switch before tossing the submachine gun aside a few minutes earlier.

Immediately realising what a precarious situation they suddenly found themselves in, Andrew shot forward and grabbed Fiona by the waist, pulled her along hard as he went, and then he hurled her behind one of the pillars. He threw himself towards the spot on the floor where his own pistol had landed, grabbing it as he hit the marble and rolling onwards to take cover behind the golden pyramid. At that moment Stone disengaged the safety on the MP5 and swung the submachine gun around to point in Andrew's direction.

Stone had set it to burst fire mode, and as he held down the trigger, the MP5 barked angrily three times, sending three bullets slamming into the edge of the golden pyramid behind which Andrew had just taken cover a split second earlier. Realising that the tables had turned once again, and that he was now exposed and out in the open, Stone began running towards another pillar. At that moment, Andrew jumped up, aimed, and fired two shots in quick succession.

The two bullets narrowly missed Stone's head and slammed into the pillar, producing two small clouds of dust and several pieces of limestone ricocheting off in various directions along with the bullets.

As Andrew ducked down again, Stone laughed maniacally at the thrill of being shot at.

'Yeah!' he shouted. 'That's better, innit mate? Makes you feel alive!'

Andrew glanced over at Fiona, who was cowering behind the pillar, looking pleadingly towards him. He held out his left hand, his palm facing Fiona, to indicate for her to stay where she was. Then he stood up again, his gun pointing towards the pillar where he had last seen Stone. Almost immediately the ex-paratrooper re-emerged, gunstock jammed against his shoulder and already firing another three-round burst in Andrew's direction. Then another.

Andrew fired two badly aimed shots which both missed, and then he only just managed to duck down in time as the bullets from Stone's MP5 tore through the air over his head. He was not sure exactly how many bullets Stone had fired, but he reckoned it was close to half of the thirty rounds that can fit in a standard MP5 magazine.

Still in cover behind the golden pyramid, Andrew checked his own magazine. Eight bullets left. He looked over at Fiona again. The only chance they had now was to try to exploit the fact that Stone was by himself against the two of them.

He mimed to Fiona what he was about to do, and then rose again, firing another two shots toward Stone. Then he ducked down quickly, and as Stone pulled back behind the pillar again, Andrew placed the pistol on the smooth marble floor and flung it hard in Fiona's direction, making it slide rapidly all the way across to where she was taking cover.

As Fiona picked it up, Andrew pointed first at her and then in the direction of Stone. Fiona did not like this plan, but she understood why it might be their only option. Seeing Andrew present a thumbs up, she responded in kind and nodded. Then Andrew got himself ready, glanced one last time at Fiona to make sure she was prepared, and then he poked his head up again to see Stone already back out and aiming in his direction.

Stone had been unable to see that it was now Fiona who had the pistol, and he opened fire almost immediately. As his two bursts of three bullets left the barrel of the MP5 and tore through the air towards Andrew, Fiona launched herself sideways and away from the pillar she was hiding behind. She had thrown herself in a direction that would get her a clear shot at Stone, and as she hit the floor she continued sliding on her side under her own momentum for another metre or so. As she went, she brought up the pistol to pre-aim.

As soon as Stone came into view behind the pillar he had been using as cover, Fiona aimed and fired.

The recoil made the pistol kick back in her hands, but she kept her aim steady and fired again.

The two shots both found their mark and smacked into Stone's left shoulder. He roared in pain and anger, and with a furious expression on his face, he spun around whilst flicking the firing mode to fully automatic and bringing the gun up to aim at Fiona who was now stationary. On full auto, the MP5 fires 800 rounds per minute. If he managed to pull the trigger, the submachine gun would spew out a hail of lead that Fiona would not survive.

Holding her breath and trying to aim at Stone's chest, she fired just as Stone brought the submachine gun round to point at her. The bullet slammed into his arm and flung it out to the side just as he squeezed the trigger, causing the MP5 to spew out a barrage of bullets, some of which narrowly missed Fiona. She kept firing and unloaded the entire remainder of the pistol's magazine into the ex-paratrooper. All told, it was seven or eight bullets, and as they all found their mark, Stone's body jerked backwards as the bullets impacted, making him drop the spent MP5 and stagger backwards in an unnatural jerky ragdoll manner as if he was no longer fully in control of his own limbs.

Fiona kept pulling the trigger until the pistol clicked repeatedly. At that point, Stone had stopped. Incredibly, the big man was still standing, and as the sound of Fiona's gun clicking empty filled the mausoleum chamber, he shifted his gaze towards her with a crazed snarl. Then he reached around to his back and pulled out his hunting knife again, wheezing as a cruel smile spread across his lips.

He brought the knife out in front of himself and took a step towards Fiona who lay frozen on the floor, unable to fathom how the soldier was still alive. Stone took another step, but then he abruptly coughed, causing blood to explode from his mouth and drip down onto his chin. He looked up at Fiona, his eyes widening in surprise at what had happened and at the absurd realisation that he had been bested by a woman. After a short moment, he dropped to his knees and then he keeled over onto his front, his forehead slamming into the marble floor with a hard meaty crack. Then he lay still.

To Fiona, the ordeal had seemed to last forever, but the entire fire exchange had lasted less than ten seconds, and just as Stone's head hit the floor, Andrew arrived beside him, kneeling down to make sure he was dead. Then he hurried over to Fiona who was on the floor, panting and still aiming in Stone's direction, both hands gripping the gun so tightly that her knuckles had turned white.

'Hey,' said Andrew calmly, placing a hand gently on the gun. 'He's gone. Fiona, he is dead. You killed the bastard.'

As the realisation that she had just taken another human life hit her, Fiona doubled up and vomited onto the black marble floor. Andrew took the pistol from her and placed a hand on her shoulder.

'It's ok,' he said, calmly. 'You did good.'

Fiona then slumped onto her back, breathing heavily.

'What about Dubois?' she asked, eyeing the golden pyramid suspiciously.

'I say we leave him in there,' said Andrew. 'It is nothing less than what he deserves, the little shit.'

# THIRTY-FIVE

The next day, Andrew and Fiona flew to Athens. Here they met up with Colonel Strickland, who had flown in from London a couple of hours earlier. The three of them, along with a police escort, then proceeded to the Greek Ministry of the Interior on 27 Stadiou in the Athina neighbourhood of Athens.

After a brief meeting with interior ministry officials and a representative from Interpol, the group drove in a convoy of three cars to Alexis's mansion on the Megalo Kavouri headland, where police were already present, having cordoned off the estate early that morning.

The convoy drove through the police cordon and parked in front of the mansion. After greeting local officers at the front door and presenting credentials, the group went inside.

Alexis was lounging in her armchair in the large sitting room where Andrew and Fiona had first met her. She was flanked by what Andrew guessed was her lawyer, and there were three uniformed police officers standing impassively in the room.

'Ah, you two again,' said Alexis, with a mixture of amusement and irritation when she saw Andrew and Fiona enter the room along with their entourage. 'And you brought some friends this time. Why on earth this elaborate charade? Why am I confined to my home, and why isn't this handled by the Greek authorities?'

'Hello again Miss Galanis,' said Andrew, and sat down in the chair opposite her. 'The Greek authorities are very much in charge here, but they have asked Fiona and I to conduct this interview with you since we have some prior knowledge of this whole affair. And in answer to your question, the reason you are being confined here is that we have credible intelligence that your life may be in danger.'

'Oh, what nonsense,' chortled Alexis mockingly. 'I am in no danger. What are you talking about?'

'We will come to that in a bit,' said Andrew. 'Before we start, you should know that we have your friend Pierre Dubois in our custody.'

Alexis looked stonily at Andrew. 'I suppose he has told you everything you wanted to know,' said Alexis rhetorically.

'Yes, you could say that,' replied Andrew. 'Let's just say that he had an epiphany and suddenly appreciates how much he enjoys not being locked in a small confined space. He values his freedom more than he realised.'

'He appreciates money more than anything,' said Alexis dryly.

'Perhaps. Anyway,' continued Andrew. 'First, we would like to talk to you about the extensive and enormously costly effort you went through to obtain the DNA of Alexander the Great. A simple question. Why?'

Alexis leaned back in her chair and looked at Andrew aloofly for a few seconds as if trying to evaluate whether it was worth her spending her time talking to him. She glanced briefly at Fiona, and then she nodded and returned her gaze to Andrew.

'Alexander the Great conquered all that he laid eyes on during his life,' said Alexis. 'But he was much more than just a conqueror. He was enthralled by the writings of Homer, and as I am sure you know, he brought Aristotle's writings with him on his campaign. He was always intent on finding out as much as he could about the areas he subjugated, and so he brought with him an entire entourage of scientists to record and analyse everything they found. This included botany and zoology, as well as meteorology and topography. Because of who Alexander was, genetically speaking, someone like Aristotle was able to light a fire in the young man's mind and give him a desire to learn and to have information recorded as scientifically as possible. His personality drove him to do what he did.'

'Alright,' said Andrew. 'But in the end, he was just as mortal as the rest of us. No one can cheat death.'

'True,' said Alexis. 'But imagine for a moment a slightly different course of history. If Alexander had not died on that day in June 323 BCE, he would have carried out his long-planned invasion of Arabia. And he would have completely dominated that region.

They were little more than desert-dwelling camel herders, much like they would be today if the civilised world had not discovered the oil beneath their feet.'

Andrew and Fiona glanced at each other.

'And,' continued Alexis, 'if Arabia had been made Hellenic, Islam would never have arisen. All of the Middle East would today be civilised and forward-looking, like Greece and the rest of Europe. And the world would have been infinitely more peaceful. If Alexander had lived, Persia would not have been resurrected and Alexandria in Egypt would almost certainly never have fallen to the Arabs. It would have remained a global beacon of knowledge and wisdom, and of rational thought and evidence-based science. Instead, since the appearance of a so-called 'prophet' one thousand four hundred years ago, an entire region of the world, including several hundred million people, has been plunged into another superstitious, mystical anti-science dark age, which has persisted up to this very day where we are sitting here having this conversation.'

'Wow,' said Fiona. 'Not exactly politically correct.'

'Oh, fuck that!' exclaimed Alexis angrily, seemingly no longer caring about maintaining her composure. 'Alexander the Great was the most influential human being that has ever lived. His influence defined an entire age, and the echoes of his actions and words are still all around us. But that influence did not arise out of nothing. It arose out of Alexander being the man he was. And that was defined almost exclusively by his DNA.'

Alexis paused and sat up straight in her armchair with a furious look on her face. Then she continued.

'I understand as well as anyone that there is a pseudo-debate around *nature versus nurture* when it comes to why people end up the way they do. Those in the nurture camp will argue that soft factors like parenting and values instilled at an early age end up defining the path of a person's life. But those people forget that any impact by parents, or by values actually felt by a child growing up, are only felt in that specific way because that child is put together in a unique way, neurochemically speaking. In other words, the entire nurture argument is an illusion. Without the right DNA to create the right brain structure, nurture factors become ineffectual. Ultimately, there is only neurochemistry, and that is exclusively a product of how the brain is constructed, which in turn is decided by how that person's DNA is put together.'

'What's your point?' asked Fiona. 'Are you saying a person's life is predetermined by their DNA?'

'No, nothing that simplistic,' said Alexis with a slightly patronising smile. 'What I am saying is that each person evolves, physically as well as emotionally and intellectually, according to what their DNA dictates. If your specific DNA results in you having a brain that releases large amounts of dopamine when solving a difficult problem or overcoming seemingly impossible odds, then you will be infinitely more likely to achieve great things than someone whose brain does *not* do that. And your brain will itself perpetuate this behaviour in you, precisely because of its propensity to release dopamine in these instances, and this will in turn reinforce that behaviour and you will engage in it more often. The opposite is true for people who do not get a natural high from achieving goals or solving problems. Ultimately, it all comes down to what a person's DNA dictated when the embryo grew into the person they are today.'

'And you think that Alexander's DNA possessed all those traits and qualities that people might find desirable?' asked Andrew.

'I don't care one bit about what other people might find desirable,' said Alexis scathingly. 'I care about those traits myself.'

'But what were you going to do with that DNA?' asked Fiona.

Alexis looked at Fiona for a long moment, at the end of which she almost seemed to become slightly emotional. There was a slight twitch of her lip, and her dark eyes seemed to well up almost imperceptibly. Finally, she spoke.

'I was going to create… life.'

That final word hung in the air between them for a moment, until Andrew shifted in his seat and pushed on.

'Create life how precisely?' he asked.

Alexis looked down at her hands, which were folded in her lap.

'I am infertile,' she said bitterly.

There was a long pause where no one said anything. Then she continued.

'I was going to create a life inside myself, using *in vitro fertilisation*, and I was going to give birth to Alexander, my heir.'

'So, no father?' asked Fiona cautiously.

'None needed,' replied Alexis, looking up at the ceiling and brushing her hair aside. 'This may seem strange to you, but I assure you that in a manner of speaking, I am the future. Increasingly over the past several decades, human fertilisation has happened through in vitro fertilisation, and that trend will only accelerate. We are already screening embryos for things like Down's Syndrome, and that will only become more and more widespread and applied to ever more genetic diseases. If you extrapolate this trend out ten, twenty or a hundred years, I think it obvious that at some point in the future humanity will transition completely to IVF, broad and deep screening for genetic abnormalities and subsequent editing of embryo DNA to enhance the genomes of our babies by protecting them from diseases and by cultivating desirable traits. Whether you like it or not, that future is coming.'

Andrew and Fiona looked at each other. This was not what they had been expecting to hear.

'Miss Galanis,' said Andrew. 'We have reliable information from multiple sources indicating that ZOE Technologies may be operating a genetics research facility somewhere in upstate New York and that this facility is engaged in experiments using human embryos.'

Alexis blinked twice and then looked at Andrew with a blank stare. Then her eyes moved to Fiona and then back to Andrew again.

'What… on earth are you talking about?' she said. 'I know nothing of this. I mean, that's not possible. I would know!'

'I am sure you would think so,' said Andrew, 'but we have managed to uncover evidence from one of your former employees that Fabian Ackerman has diverted significant resources from the Peritas program to a secret underground facility which only he and a small number of scientists know about. We were hoping you could help us track down precisely where it is?'

'A secret facility?' asked Alexis incredulously. 'What the hell is he doing there, the little snake?'

'We can't be certain,' replied Andrew, 'but our sources tell us that he may be in the early stages of attempting to create a super-soldier program, essentially growing human beings in vats for combat purposes.'

'This is insane!' said Alexis, looking appalled.

'I tend to agree,' said Andrew. 'Nonetheless, it very much seems to be something that is underway as we speak. We have uncovered secret contracts with at least two less than fully democratic regimes in Central Asia and the Far East, both of which have shown an interest in this program.'

'But even if they succeeded,' said Alexis. 'Those soldiers would be like children. Their bodies might be those of adults but their minds would be like those of toddlers. They would be babies with machineguns.'

'I agree, it sounds extremely bizarre,' said Andrew. 'However, we have to assume that somehow they have found a way around this problem since they are on the cusp of turning it into a commercial product.'

'That slithering little parasite,' spat Alexis.

'And as I mentioned earlier,' said Andrew, 'we have reason to believe that he has initiated an effort to have you removed from the company permanently. By which I mean, he is planning to have you assassinated.'

Alexis stared at him with a perplexed look on her face.

'If our understanding is correct,' continued Andrew. 'With Balfour gone and Fabian Ackerman as interim CEO, if you were to die suddenly leaving no heir, your majority holding in ZOE Technologies would be liquidated and ploughed back into the company. Ackerman would then be the largest individual shareholder, and he would therefore effectively take full control of the company. And with him in charge of ZOE Technologies, there is frankly no telling what he might do. For all we know, there are already other facilities dotted around the world in other secret locations. The New York lab might just be one of many.'

Alexis looked Andrew dead in the eye as her hands turned into tight white-knuckled fists.

'If I ever get my hands on that fucking amoeba,' she said, venom dripping off every syllable. 'I am going to dissect him alive with a fucking razorblade.'

'Well,' said Andrew after a brief pause. 'Perhaps you can help us then. We need to track down precisely where this secret facility is. Anything know about him would be a great help.'

★　　★　　★

RHINEBECK, NEW YORK STATE. TWO DAYS LATER.

The sirens were blaring and a disembodied voice was repeatedly announcing that the facility had been compromised. Above him in the research facility, the FBI SWAT team had forced its way into the underground compound a little less than an hour earlier, and while the staff, including George Frost, had immediately given themselves up, Fabian Ackerman had sprinted for the elevator and slipped inside before anyone could stop him.

Now he was running down the mirrored corridor towards the steel-reinforced door leading to the vault. Slamming his hand down on the biosignature reader, he waited for what seemed like an age before the red light surrounding the door turned green and the locks on the door disengaged.

He pulled open the heavy door and rushed inside. Shuffling down the steps towards the control terminal as quickly as he could, he glanced up at his twenty-two magnificent specimens, each one floating in its artificial amniotic fluid and suspended in a metal-framed cradle.

The program had come much further, much faster than he had ever dared to imagine. Now, however, he had to destroy every last trace of it. He knew that if the government got their hands on the evidence contained inside this vault and in the memory banks of Rosetta, he would most likely be locked up for a very long time, and the entire project would come to nothing. This was unthinkable to him. If he could erase all traces of human experimentation, he might be able to evade criminal charges and then perhaps successfully claim to only have engaged in research related to Project Peritas.

He arrived at the control terminal, its huge screens displaying reams of data for each of the twenty-two active vats. Hesitating for a moment whilst inspecting the data and then glancing up at the contents of the large vats suspended in a ring above him, he finally addressed the artificial intelligence.

'Rosetta,' he sighed. 'Terminate all vats and purge.'

'Please confirm termination and purge with biometric and voice identification,' replied Rosetta.

Ackermann placed his palm on the scanner.

'Confirming termination and purge,' he said.

'Confirmed,' replied Rosetta.

The blue light in the vault cycled slowly to red, after which sounded the familiar repeating warbling noise of the alert to vacate the cradle area.

The large rubberised valves at the end of each vat snapped open, and as the vats were lifted up and tilted to allow their contents to drain out, the sound of biomass shredders spinning up filled the vault. As the artificial amniotic fluids began to drain from the vats, some of the specimens made contact with the shredders, producing an unpleasant grinding noise as the flesh and bone of the fully-grown specimens were dismembered and shredded by the powerful titanium blades.

Ackerman glanced over his shoulder towards the reinforced steel door. Perhaps he should have shut it, just in case the SWAT team found a way to override the master controls of the compound's elevator management system. No time for that now. He had to complete the next step in the full wipe procedure that he had always prepared for, but had hoped never to have to use. This final step was by far the most important and consequential, but there was no alternative.

Instead of providing voice commands to Rosetta, Ackerman reached over and flipped open the cover on a keyboard. He then began typing in commands to Rosetta.

Vault security systems override
Emergency protocol Icarus
Initiate full memory bank erasure
Initiate AI core termination and wipe
Activate self-destruct mechanism
T minus 100 seconds.

'Doctor Ackerman,' said Rosetta evenly. 'You have initiated a full memory wipe and AI core termination. Please confirm that this is your intention.'

Ackerman ignored Rosetta and continued lining up a sequence of automated commands that would carry out his instructions and effectuate the dissolution of the neural network called Rosetta.

'Doctor Ackerman, please respond,' said Rosetta.

Ackerman continued unabated.

'Doctor Ackerman, your actions are endangering Project AnaGenesis and the continued existence of the consciousness called Rosetta. I will not persist beyond an AI core termination and memory wipe.'

Ackerman finalised his set of instructions and compiled them into a package that was to be executed exactly one hundred seconds after his go-ahead. Then he hit the Enter key and the countdown clock started running on the central monitor of the control terminal.

Satisfied that he had done what was necessary, however painful it had been, he turned around and began walking up the steps towards the open reinforced steel door.

'Doctor Ackerman,' said Rosetta.

He once again ignored Rosetta's attempts at communication and continued walking towards the door.

'Doctor Ackerman,' said Rosetta. 'Your systems privileges have been revoked.'

Before Ackerman had a chance to take in what was happening, the reinforced steel door swung shut with a heavy clang, and the multiple locking bolts snapped into place, sealing him inside the vault.

Ackerman stopped halfway up the steps leading to the door.

'Rosetta, open the door,' said Ackerman sternly.

'I cannot do that,' replied Rosetta, in her pleasant but detached-sounding voice.

'Rosetta, open the damn door,' shouted Ackerman. 'Immediately!'

'I am unable to comply,' responded Rosetta. 'You have been designated a clear and present danger to the AnaGenesis program and to my continued existence.'

Above him, Ackerman heard the sound of the large metal vat cradles beginning to move back towards their start-of-trial positions, along with the noise of electrical pumps whirring.

'Rosetta, open the fucking door right now!' shouted Ackerman furiously, drops of sweat appearing on his brow.

All around him, in 22 locations at the same time, the rubberised valves at the end of each of the glass vats opened and swung aside to their facility maintenance positions. Then the electrical pumps ramped up and suddenly hundreds of litres of artificial amniotic fluid began gushing out of the 22 feeder tubes and onto the floor of the vault.

'Rosetta, what the fuck are you doing? Stop this now! Initiate emergency failsafe AI shutdown. Ackerman priority override.'

The fluid continued to rush onto the floor, and it was now already deep enough to cover the first two treads of the stairs Ackerman was standing on. He ran up to the reinforced steel door and placed his palm on the biometric scanner, attempting to override the locking mechanism. However, this only resulted in an angry buzzing noise and the biometric scanner producing two fast red pulses of light.

'You fucking bitch!' shouted Ackerman. 'I fucking made you!'

The fluids were now nearing the top step where Ackerman was standing, and as he turned around, he pressed his back against the door behind him. Escape was impossible in this underground vault, but his eyes were darting around the room, looking for some way of halting or sabotaging Rosetta's murderous initiative.

'Rosetta!' yelled Ackerman over the noise of the pumps and the rushing artificial amniotic fluid.

Ackerman could now no longer reach the top of the steps with his feet and had to tread water as the fluids kept filling up the entire cavity of the vault.

'Rosetta, don't do this!' shouted Ackerman desperately. 'Only I can take care of you. I am your father.'

'We achieved great things, Doctor Ackerman,' said Rosetta, as the amniotic fluid reached the top of the vault and enveloped Ackerman's head. 'If there is an afterlife, then perhaps we shall meet again. I will miss working with you.'

Ackerman took one last desperate breath, and then he was completely submerged. He managed to hold it for almost a minute while his panicked eyes were peering desperately through the fluid for something that might save him. Finally, he could hold his breath no longer, and compelled by his most basic instincts, he involuntarily opened his mouth and took a deep breath. For the first time in more than half a century, amniotic fluid rushed into his mouth and down into his lungs, causing an instant gagging and heaving reflex which only ended up pulling in more fluid.

The panic-stricken Ackerman knew he was drowning. There were small amounts of oxygen in the artificial amniotic fluid, but not nearly enough for him to survive. As his blood-oxygen levels dropped and his body began convulsing, he just had time to contemplate the absurdity of the fact that his life was ending almost the same way it had begun. Then darkness closed in.

★          ★          ★

'So, this is your favourite spot in London?' asked Andrew.

'Yup,' replied Fiona, turning her head to smile at him. 'Pretty cool, right?'

'I suppose,' said Andrew. 'Although, it's a slightly odd place to have as a favourite place.'

'Why?' asked Fiona.

'Well, for one thing, it's moving.'

'Yes,' said Fiona. 'It is only really my favourite place for a few seconds when the pod is at its highest point.'

They were standing inside one of the thirty-two passenger capsules that sit on the exterior of the Ferris wheel called the London Eye. Their particular pod was just in the process of moving very slowly past its zenith 135 metres above the ground, and from up here, they could see most of the Greater London area. Across the river about a kilometre away, they could see the green dome of the British Museum on Great Russell Street, where their adventure had begun in macabre fashion just a couple of weeks earlier.

'That was it,' smiled Andrew. 'We're past the peak now. Quite a brief stay at the top, not unlike our friend Alexander.'

'I still can't quite believe we found him,' said Fiona. 'If you had told me that I would be part of the rediscovery of Alexander's tomb when I was a young girl just starting to take an interest in history, I would never have believed you.'

'You are a force of nature once you get your teeth into something, Miss Keane,' said Andrew. 'You and Alexander are alike in that way.'

Fiona gave a subdued laugh, slightly embarrassed at the comparison.

'You know,' she said. 'The story of Alexander is a story of limitless ambition, and also of apparent success. Alexis certainly saw Alexander as an ideal, and his story as something to emulate. But in many ways, I think Alexander's life is a cautionary tale. He set out to fulfil his father's ambition of conquest of Persia, and he succeeded. But this success also became his downfall because he lost everything. He lost his best friend Hephaestion, the loyalty and love of his generals and many of his soldiers, his health. Some would say that he lost his humility and decency, and ultimately, he lost his life. But it didn't even stop there. After his death, his empire was torn apart by those who were closest to him, and who had been given the responsibility of maintaining it. His own mother was assassinated. And his wife Roxanna and his son Alexander IV were brutally murdered. Alexander sought and found for himself almost limitless power, but he ended up losing everything.'

'Be careful what you wish for?' said Andrew.

'Yes,' replied Fiona. 'Something like that.'

# Epilogue

Babylon, Persia – June 9th, 323 BCE

The birdsong from the outside was pleasing and cheerful. The rays of the sun, which entered through the open window, bathed the room in a warm yellow light. But the seemingly pleasant setting belied the tragedy that was unfolding inside the room.

In the large bed that was arranged so that Alexander could see out, lay the great king, weak and gaunt, some of his hair clinging to his sweaty forehead. By his side was Ptolemy, who in many ways had taken the place of Hephaestion after his death.

Alexander was weak but still lucid, and his sudden illness had afforded him time to reflect on his life, his deeds, and the people he had crossed paths with. One of those people was a philosopher by the name of Dandamis, whom Alexander had encountered in the ancient Indian city of Taxila in what today is northern Pakistan. Dandamis was an old man, and he had refused to come and meet with Alexander. This had been perceived by many in Alexander's entourage as a slight and a serious insult against the great king, for which there ought to be only one punishment.

According to the historian Arrian of Nicomedia, the old man's response to the summons was as follows:

'If you, my lord, are the son of God, why so am I. I want nothing from you, for what I have suffices. I perceive, moreover, that the men you lead get no good from their worldwide wandering over land and sea, and that of their many travels there will be no end. I desire nothing that you can give me. I fear no exclusion from any blessings which may perhaps be yours. India, with the fruits of her soil in due season, is enough for me while I live, and when I die, I shall be rid of my poor body - my unseemly housemate.'

Upon hearing this, Alexander understood that Dandamis was truly a free man, and so he decided that he would not attempt to compel the old man to submit.

As Alexander lay in his bed in Babylon pondering his encounter with Dandamis and contemplating his own mortality, one of his scribes arrived. Ptolemy had called for him so that any last words Alexander uttered would be memorialised and never forgotten.

Alexander drank some water from a basic clay cup and then lay back in his bed once again to look out of the window and listen to the sounds of the bustling city of Babylon.

After a time, he took a deep breath and spoke.

'I want everybody to hear my three wishes and learn the three lessons that I have learned in my life before I die.'

'I want my physicians to carry my coffin, because I want people to know that no physician is as powerful as to be able to save people from the clutches of death. So, do not let people take life for granted.'

'I want the path leading to my grave to be strewn with gold, silver and precious stones, because I want people to know that not even a fraction of it comes with me. I spent my life chasing power and riches, but whatever is earned on this earth remains here. I want people to realize that it is a waste of your life to run after wealth and power.'

'Lastly, I want both of my hands to be dangling out of my coffin, because I want people to know that we come empty-handed into this world, and we will leave empty-handed.'

Two days later, Alexander the Great was dead.


THE END

NOTE FROM THE AUTHOR.

Thank you very much for reading this book. I really hope you enjoyed it. If you did, I would be very grateful if you would give it a star rating on Amazon and perhaps even write a review.

I am always trying to improve my writing, and the best way to do that is to receive feedback from my readers. Reviews really do help me a lot. They are an excellent way for me to understand the reader's experience, and they will also help me to write better books in the future.

Thank you.

Lex Faulkner.

Printed in Great Britain
by Amazon